Once Upon a Crime

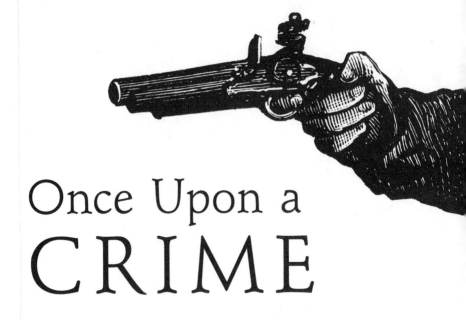

Once Upon a
CRIME

edited by Janet Hutchings

ST. MARTIN'S PRESS NEW YORK

ONCE UPON A CRIME: Historical Mysteries from *Ellery Queen's Mystery Magazine.* Copyright © 1994 by Bantam Doubleday Dell Magazines. All rights reserved. Printed in the United States of America. No part of this book may be used or reproduced in any manner whatsoever without written permission except in the case of brief quotations embodied in critical articles or reviews. For information, address St. Martin's Press, 175 Fifth Avenue, New York, N.Y. 10010.

Design by Sara Stemen

LIBRARY OF CONGRESS CATALOGING-IN-PUBLICATION DATA

Once upon a crime / Jane Hutchings, editor.
    p.   cm.
  ISBN 0-312-11032-4
  1. Detective and mystery stories, American.   2. Detective and mystery stories, English.   3. Historical fiction, American.
  4. Historical fiction, English.   I. Hutchings, Janet.
PS648.D405   1994
813'.08108—dc20   94-4328
                                                                  CIP

First Edition: June 1994

10 9 8 7 6 5 4 3 2 1

CONTENTS

ACKNOWLEDGMENTS

Special thanks are due to Steve Stillwell for letting us borrow the name of his bookstore Once Upon a Crime for the title of this collection, to Keith Kahla of St. Martin's Press for making this project possible, and to Tara Ann Cuddihy of *Ellery Queen's Mystery Magazine* for help in preparing the manuscript.

INTRODUCTION

Think of the most thrilling histories you have read, and chances are they record some sinister crime: the poison plots of the Borgias; the murder linked to Mary, Queen of Scots; the treachery of Rasputin . . . One wonders why crime writers did not begin to till the fertile soil provided by history when the detective story was in its infancy in the late nineteenth century. The historical crime story is not a new invention, of course: in 1945 Helen McCloy placed second in *Ellery Queen's Mystery Magazine*'s worldwide short story contest with her historical mystery "Chinoiserie," included here with one other notable historical tale from that golden decade of short mystery fiction. But such examples aside, the historical mystery only recently began to enjoy a true heyday, with series sleuths emerging all across the historical spectrum, from ancient Rome to old New York.

The rise in interest in historical settings for the mystery coincides with a resurgence in the popularity of the cozy mystery—the traditional whodunit—and it is easy to see why. For both writers and readers of the whodunit, history provides settings that may appear more congenial than those of the modern world. Today's reader, bombarded with media reports of random violence, madmen on the loose, and petty bureaucratic crime, may find it refreshing to step back into a time when rogues and villains behaved from motives common to everyman and understanding the logic of a crime was less likely to require a grasp of abnormal psychology. For writers more interested in constructing an enticing puzzle than exploring the psychological and sociological aspects of a crime, history provides clearcut notions of good and evil which need not be questioned as they would be in a contemporary setting and can therefore serve as part of a readymade backdrop for the mystery. Besides, placed in an era before modern forensics and other branches of technical knowledge assumed their crucial role in police work, the historical detective may ply his trade relying primarily on observation and his own wits, qualities cherished in the traditional detective. The reader, too, then has the pleasure of attacking the puzzle with a stock of common, unspecialized knowledge.

Historical material has another allure, not only for practitioners of the whodunit but for crime writers of all sorts. History itself being "little else," as Voltaire put it, "than a picture of human crimes and misfortunes," it provides a rich source of plot material. Indeed, some of the most teasing questions to consume the historical mind involve unsolved crimes and their ramifications: Was Richard III the murderer of the little princes? Was Lee Harvey Oswald the sole assassin of John F. Kennedy? Several of the stories in this volume tackle real historical mysteries which, like William Bankier's speculation about the stabbing death of the poet and playwright Marlowe, may be less notorious than the events surrounding Richard III, but are no less intriguing. As we read these meldings of fact and fiction, we cannot but wonder how history might have been different had the fatal blow not been struck, or had the murderer been brought to justice. And so the historical mystery, when centered around an actual crime, provides the imagination with an extra dimension in which to move. The large number of books and stories recently published in the genre allows those whose interest is piqued by such questions a large field in which to range.

No single period has dominated this flowering of the historical mystery, though some of the most notable series sleuths are clustered in the ancient Roman and medieval periods, and two of them, Ellis Peters's Brother Cadfael and Steven Saylor's Gordianus the Finder, are represented here. Locales have proved to be less varied, with Europe tending to dominate despite some ventures as far as the Orient; two of the stories contained in this collection revisit those crossroads of the East and West, nineteenth-century Russia and Old Pekin. Readers fearing a sameness in stories set in a common period and place may put their fears to rest, for the homogenization of society is more a product of our own time than of any era to which these stories will take us. Elizabethan England claims the space of three stories in this book, yet so different is the thriving metropolis of London in which one of them is set from the country estate on which the events of another unwind, that one might almost have traveled the breadth of a continent.

In pointing out how readily history lends itself to the crime story, one does not want to forget the difficulties that skillful writers of crime historicals must overcome. An accurate historical writer may find it difficult to satisfy the need to leave the reader with a sense that justice has prevailed, for the further we travel from our own society, the more likely we are to encounter values widely different from our own. The writer must walk a fine line, without, on the one hand, giving way to glaring anachronisms of speech or deed, or on the other forgetting that his primary job is to entertain, and that the entertainment will be complete for most crime readers only when the world has been brought back into a recognizable harmony.

The thirteen stories in this book are presented in chronological order in the hope that readers will experience a sense of movement through history. Our time machine touches down first in ancient Rome, and finishes up in early twentieth century America, so gather together your period garb, buckle up, and enjoy the trip. . . .

JANET HUTCHINGS

THE LEMURES

Steven Saylor

With its riches of political plots, assassinations, and intrigues, the decaying Roman Republic is a crime writer's gold mine. San Francisco writer Steven Saylor staked his claim to the first century B.C. in 1992 with a story that won the Robert L. Fish Award. The three novels and seven stories that have subsequently appeared in the series draw upon the author's extensive readings for a degree in history at the University of Texas at Austin, but they are inspired more than anything by his fascination with exotic and remote locales, and his belief that historical research is itself delightful detective work.

The slave pressed a scrap of parchment into my hand:

From Lucius Claudius to his friend Gordianus, greetings. If you will accompany this messenger on his return, I will be grateful. I am at the house of a friend on the Palatine Hill; there is a problem which requires your attention. Come alone—do not bring the boy—the circumstances might frighten him.

Lucius need not have warned me against bringing Eco, for at that moment the boy was busy with his tutor. From the garden, where they had found a patch of morning sunlight to ward off the October chill, I could hear the old man declaiming while Eco wrote the day's Latin lesson on his wax tablet.

"Bethesda!" I called out, but she was already behind me, holding open my woolen cloak. As she slipped it over my shoulders, she glanced down at the note in my hand. She wrinkled her nose. Unable to read, Bethesda regards the written word with suspicion and disdain.

"From Lucius Claudius?" she asked, raising an eyebrow.

"Why, yes, but how—?" Then I realized she must have recognized his messenger. Slaves often take more notice of one another than do their masters.

"I suppose he wants you to go gaming with him, or to taste the new vintage from one of his vineyards." She tossed back her mane of jet-black hair and pouted her luscious lips.

"I suppose not, he has work for me."

A smile flickered at the corner of her mouth.

"Not that it should be any concern of yours," I added quickly. Since I had taken Eco in from the streets and legally adopted him, Bethesda had begun to behave less and less like a concubine and more and more like a wife and mother. I wasn't sure I liked the change; I was even less sure I had any control over it.

"Frightening work," I added. "Probably dangerous." But she was already busy adding to the household accounts in her head. As I stepped out the door I heard her humming a happy Egyptian tune from her childhood.

The day was bright and crisp. Drifts of leaves lined either side of the narrow winding pathway that led from my house down the slope of the Esquiline Hill to the Subura below. The tang of smoke was on the air, rising from kitchens and braziers. The messenger drew his dark green cloak more tightly about his shoulders to ward off the chill.

"Neighbor! Citizen!" a voice hissed at me from the wall to my right. I looked up and saw two eyes peering down at me, surmounted by the dome of a bald, knobby head. "Neighbor—yes, you! Gordianus, they call you; am I right?"

I looked up at him warily. "Yes, Gordianus is my name."

"And Detectus, they call you—'the Finder,' yes?"

"Yes."

"You solve puzzles. Plumb mysteries. Answer riddles."

"Sometimes."

"Then you must help me!"

"Perhaps, Citizen. But not now. A friend summons me—"

"This will take only a moment."

"Even so, I grow cold standing here—"

"Then come inside! I'll open the little door in the wall and let you in."

"No—perhaps tomorrow."

"No! Now! They will come tonight, I know it—or even this afternoon, when the shadows lengthen. See, the clouds are coming up. If the sun grows dim, they may come out at midday beneath the dark, brooding sky."

"*They*? Whom do you mean, Citizen?"

His eyes grew large, yet his voice became quite tiny, like the voice of a mouse. "The lemures . . ." he squeaked.

The messenger clutched at his cloak. I felt the sudden chill myself, but it was only a cold, dry wind gusting down the pathway that made me shiver; or so I told myself.

"Lemures," the man repeated. "The unquiet dead."

Leaves scattered and danced about my feet. A thin finger of cloud obscured the sun, dimming its bright, cold light to a hazy grey.

"Vengeful," the man whispered. "Full of spite. Empty of all remorse. Human no longer, spirits sucked dry of warmth and pity, desiccated and brittle like shards of bone, with nothing left but wickedness. Dead, but not gone from this world as they should be. Revenge is their only food. The only gift they offer is madness."

I stared into the man's dark, sunken eyes for a long moment, then broke from his gaze. "A friend calls me," I said, nodding for the slave to go on.

"But neighbor, you can't abandon me. I was a soldier for Sulla! I fought in the civil war to save the Republic! I was wounded—if you'll step inside you'll see. My left leg is no good at all, I have to hobble and lean against a stick. While you, you're young and whole and healthy. A young Roman like you owes me some respect. Please—there's no one else to help me!"

"My business is with the living, not the dead," I said sternly.

"I can pay you, if that's what you mean. Sulla gave all his soldiers farms up in Etruria. I sold mine—I was never meant to be a farmer. I still have silver left. I can pay you a handsome fee, if you'll help me."

"And how can I help you? If you have a problem with lemures, consult a priest or an augur."

"I have, believe me! Every May, at the Lemuria, I take part in the procession to ward off evil spirits. I mutter the incantations, I cast the black beans over my shoulder. Perhaps it works; the lemures never come to me in spring, and they stay away all summer. But as surely as leaves wither and fall from the trees, they come to me every autumn. They come to drive me mad!"

"Citizen, I cannot—"

"They cast a spell inside my head."

"Citizen! I must go."

"Please," he whispered. "I was a soldier once, brave, afraid of nothing. I killed many men, fighting for Sulla, for Rome. I waded through rivers of blood and valleys of gore up to my hips and never quailed. I feared no one. And now . . ." He made a face of such self-loathing that I turned away. "Help me," he pleaded.

"Perhaps . . . when I return. . . ."

He smiled pitifully, like a doomed man given a reprieve. "Yes," he whispered, "when you return. . . ."

I hurried on.

The house on the Palatine, like its neighbors, presented a rather plain facade, despite its location in the city's most exclusive district. Except for two pillars in the form of dryads supporting the roof, the portico's only adornment was a funeral wreath of cypress and fir on the door.

The short hallway, flanked on either side by the wax masks of noble ancestors, led to a modest atrium. On an ivory bier, a body lay in state. I stepped forward and looked down at the corpse. I saw a young man, not yet thirty, unremarkable except for the grimace that contorted his features. Normally the anointers are able to remove signs of distress and suffering from the faces of the dead, to smooth wrinkled brows and unclench tightened jaws. But the face of this corpse had grown rigid beyond the power of the anointers to soften it. Its expression was not of pain or misery, but of fear.

"He fell," said a familiar voice behind me.

I turned to see my one-time client and since-then friend, Lucius Claudius. He was as portly as ever, and not even the gloomy light of the atrium could dim the cherry-red of his cheeks and nose.

We exchanged greetings, then turned our eyes to the corpse.

"Titus," explained Lucius, "the owner of this house. For the last two years, anyway."

"He died from a fall?"

"Yes. There's a gallery that runs along the west side of the house, with a long balcony that overlooks a steep hillside. Titus fell from the balcony three nights ago. He broke his back."

"And died at once?"

"No. He lingered through the night and lived until nightfall the next day. He told a curious tale before he died. Of course, he was feverish and in great pain, despite the draughts of nepenthes he was given. . . ." Lucius shifted his considerable bulk uneasily inside his vast black cloak and reached up nervously to scratch at his frazzled wreath of copper-colored hair. "Tell me, Gordianus, do you have any knowledge of lemures?"

A strange expression must have crossed my face, for Lucius frowned and wrinkled his brow. "Have I said something untoward, Gordianus?"

"Not at all. But this is the second time today that someone has spoken to me of lemures. On the way here, a soldier, a neighbor of mine—but I won't bore you with the tale. All Rome seems to be haunted by spirits today! It must be this oppressive weather . . . this gloomy time of year . . . or indigestion, as my father used to say—"

"It was not indigestion that killed my husband. Nor was it a cold wind, or a chilly drizzle, or a nervous imagination."

The speaker was a tall, thin woman. A stola of black wool covered her from neck to feet; about her shoulders was a wrap of dark blue. Her black hair was drawn back from her face and piled atop her head, held together by silver pins and combs. Her eyes were a glittering blue. Her face was young, but she was no longer a girl. She held herself as rigorously upright as a vestal, and spoke with the imperious tone of a patrician.

"This," said Lucius, "is Gordianus, the man I told you about." The woman acknowledged me with a slight nod. "And this," he continued, "is my dear young friend, Cornelia. From the Sullan branch of the Cornelius family."

I gave a slight start.

"Yes," she said, "blood relative to our recently departed and deeply missed dictator. Lucius Cornelius Sulla was my cousin. We were quite close, despite the difference in our ages. I was with dear Sulla just before he died, down at his villa in Neapolis. A great man. A generous man." Her imperious tone softened. She turned her gaze to the corpse on the bier. "Now Titus is dead, too. I am alone. Defenseless . . ."

"Perhaps we should withdraw to the library," suggested Lucius.

"Yes," said Cornelia, "it's cold here in the atrium."

She led us down a short hallway into a small room. My sometime client Cicero would not have called it much of a library—there was only a single cabinet piled with scrolls against one wall—but he would have approved of its austerity. The walls were stained a somber red and the chairs were backless. A slave tended to the brazier in the corner and departed.

"How much does Gordianus know?" said Cornelia, to Lucius.

"Very little. I only explained that Titus fell from the balcony."

She looked at me with an intensity that was almost frightening. "My husband was a haunted man."

"Haunted by whom, or what? Lucius spoke to me of lemures."

"Not plural, but singular," she said. "He was tormented by one lemur only."

"Was this spirit known to him?"

"Yes. An acquaintance from his youth; they studied law together in the Forum. The man who owned this house before us. His name was Furius."

"This lemur appeared to your husband more than once?"

"It began last summer. Titus would glimpse the thing for only a moment—beside the road on the way to our country villa, or across the Forum, or in a pool of shadow outside the house. At first he wasn't sure what it was; he would turn back and try to find it, only to discover it had vanished. Then he began to see it inside the house. That was when he realized who and what it was. He no longer tried to approach it; quite the opposite, he fled the thing, quaking with fear."

"Did you see it, as well?"

She stiffened. "Not at first . . ."

"Titus saw it the night he fell," whispered Lucius. He leaned forward and took Cornelia's hand, but she pulled it away.

"That night," she whispered, "Titus was brooding, pensive. He left me in my sitting room and stepped onto the balcony to pace and take a breath of cold air. Then he saw the thing—so he told the story later, in his delirium. It came toward him, beckoning. It spoke his name. Titus fled to the end of the balcony. The thing came closer. Titus grew mad with fear—somehow he fell."

"The thing pushed him?" I said.

She shrugged. "Whether he fell or was pushed, it was his fear of the thing that finally killed him. He survived the fall; he lingered through the night and the next day. Twilight came. Titus began to sweat and tremble. Even the least movement was agony to him, yet he thrashed and writhed on the bed, mad with panic. He said he could not bear to see the lemur again. At last he died. Do you understand? He chose to die rather than confront the lemur again. You saw his face. It was not pain that killed him. It was fear."

I pulled my cloak over my hands and curled my toes. It seemed to me that the brazier did nothing to banish the cold from the room. "This lemur," I said, "how did your husband describe it?"

"The thing was not hard to recognize. It was Furius, who owned this house before us. Its flesh was pocked and white, its teeth broken and yellow. Its hair was like bloody straw, and there was blood all around its neck. It gave off a foul odor . . . but it was most certainly Furius. Except . . ."

"Yes?"

"Except that it looked younger than Furius at the end of his life. It looked closer to the age when Furius and Titus knew one another in the Forum, in the days of their young manhood."

"When did you first see the lemur yourself?"

"Last night. I was on the balcony—thinking of Titus and his fall. I turned and saw the thing, but only for an instant. I fled into the house—and it spoke to me."

"What did it say?"

"Two words: *Now you.* Oh!" Cornelia drew in a quick, strangled breath. She clutched at her wrap and gazed at the fire.

I stepped closer to the brazier, spreading my fingers to catch the warmth. "What a strange day!" I muttered. "What can I say to you, Cornelia, except what I said to another who told me a tale of lemures earlier today: why do you consult me instead of an augur? These are mysteries about which I know very little. Tell me a tale of a purloined jewel or a stolen document; call on me with a case of parricide or show me a corpse with an unknown killer. With these I might help you; about such matters I know more than a little. But how to placate a lemur, I do not know. Of course, I will always come when my friend Lucius Claudius calls me; but I begin to wonder why I am here at all."

Cornelia studied the crackling embers and did not answer.

"Perhaps," I ventured, "you believe this lemur is not a lemur at all. If in fact it is a living man—"

"It doesn't matter what I believe or don't believe," she snapped. I saw in her eyes the same pleading and desperation I had seen in the soldier's eyes. "No priest can help me; there is no protection against a vengeful lemur. Yet, perhaps the thing is really human, after all. Such a pretense is possible, isn't it?"

"Possible? I suppose."

"Then you know of such cases, of a man masquerading as a lemur?"

"I have no personal experience—"

"That's why I asked Lucius to call you. If this creature is in fact human and alive, then you may be able to save me from it. If instead it is what it appears to be, a lemur, then—then nothing can save me. I am doomed." She gasped and bit her knuckles.

"But if it was your husband's death the thing desired—"

"Haven't you been listening? I told you what it said to me: *Now you.* Those were the words it spoke!" Cornelia sobbed. Lucius went to her side. Slowly she calmed herself.

"Very well, Cornelia. I will help you if I can. First, questions. From answers come answers. Can you speak?"

She bit her lips and nodded.

"You say the thing has the face of Furius. Did your husband think so?"

"My husband remarked on it, over and over. He saw the thing very close, more than once. On the night he fell, the creature came near enough for him to smell its fetid breath. He recognized it beyond a doubt."

"And you? You say you saw it for only an instant before you fled. Are you sure it was Furius you saw last night on the balcony?"

"Yes! An instant was all I needed. Horrible—discolored, distorted, wearing a hideous grin—but the face of Furius, I have no doubt."

"And yet younger than you remember."

"Yes. Somehow the cheeks, the mouth . . . what makes a face younger or older? I don't know, I can only say that in spite of its hideousness the thing looked as Furius looked when he was a younger man. Not the Furius who died two years ago, but Furius when he was a beardless youth, slender and strong and full of ambition."

"I see. In such a case, three possibilities occur to me. Could this indeed have been Furius—not his lemur, but the man himself? Are you certain that he's dead?"

"Oh, yes."

"There is no doubt?"

"No doubt at all . . ." She shivered and seemed to leave something unspoken. I looked at Lucius, who quickly looked away.

"Then perhaps this Furius had a brother?"

"A much older brother," she nodded.

"Not a twin?"

"No. Besides, his brother died in the civil war."

"Oh?"

"Fighting against Sulla."

"I see. Then perhaps Furius had a son, the very image of his father?"

Cornelia shook her head. "His only child was an infant daughter. His only other survivors were his wife and mother, and a sister, I think."

"And where are the survivors now?"

Cornelia averted her eyes. "I'm told they moved into his mother's house on the Caelian Hill."

"So. Furius is assuredly dead, he had no twin—no living brother at all—and he left no son. And yet the thing which haunted your husband, by his own account and yours, bore the face of Furius."

Cornelia sighed, exasperated. "Useless! I called on you only out of desperation." She pressed her hands to her eyes. "Oh, my head pounds like thunder. The night will come and how will I bear it? Go now, please. I want to be alone."

Lucius escorted me to the atrium. "What do you think?" he said.

"I think that Cornelia is a very frightened woman, and her husband was a frightened man. Why was he so fearful of this particular lemur? If the dead man had been his friend—"

"An acquaintance, Gordianus, not exactly a friend."

"Is there something more that I should know?"

He shifted uncomfortably. "You know how I detest gossip. And really, Cornelia is not nearly as venal as some people think. There is a good side of her that few people see."

"It would be best if you told me everything, Lucius. For Cornelia's sake."

He pursed his small mouth, furrowed his fleshy brow and scratched his bald pate. "Oh, very well," he muttered. "As I told you, Cornelia and her husband have lived in this house for two years. It has also been two years since Furius died."

"And this is no coincidence?"

"Furius was the original owner of this house. Titus and Cornelia acquired it when he was executed for his crimes against Sulla and the state."

"I begin to see . . ."

"Perhaps you do. Furius and his family were on the wrong side of the civil war, political enemies of Sulla's. When Sulla achieved absolute power and compelled the Senate to appoint him dictator, he purged the Republic of his foes. The proscriptions—"

"Names posted on lists in the Forum; yes, I remember only too well."

"Once a man was proscribed, anyone could hunt him down and bring his head to Sulla for a bounty. I don't have to remind you of the bloodbath, you were here; you saw the heads mounted on spikes outside the Senate."

"And Furius's head was among them?"

"Yes. He was proscribed, arrested, and beheaded. You ask if Cornelia is certain that Furius is dead? Yes, because she saw his head on a spike, with blood oozing from the neck. Meanwhile, his property was confiscated and put up for public auction—"

"But the auctions were not always public," I said. "Sulla's friends usually had first choice of the finest farms and villas."

"As did Sulla's relations," added Lucius, wincing. "Yes, I'm afraid that when Furius was caught and beheaded, Titus and Cornelia didn't hesitate to contact Sulla immediately and put their mark on this house. Cornelia had always coveted it; why pass up the opportunity to possess it, and for a song?" He lowered his voice. "The rumor is that they placed the only bid, for the unbelievable sum of a thousand sesterces!"

"The price of a mediocre Egyptian rug," I said. "Quite a bargain."

"If Cornelia has a flaw, it's her avarice. In that, she's hardly alone. Greed is the great vice of our age."

"But not the only vice."

"What do you mean?"

"Tell me, Lucius, was this Furius really such a great enemy of our late, lamented dictator? Was he such a terrible threat to the security of the state and to Sulla's personal safety that he truly belonged on the proscription lists?"

"I don't understand."

"There were those who ended up on the lists because they were too rich for their own good, because they possessed things that others coveted."

Lucius frowned. "Gordianus, what I've already told you is scandalous enough, and I'll ask you not to repeat it. I don't know what further implication you may have drawn, and I don't care to know. I think we should drop the matter."

Friend he may be, but Lucius is also of patrician blood; the cords that bind the rich together are made of gold, and are stronger than iron.

*   *   *

I made my way homeward, pondering the strange and fatal haunting of Titus and his wife. I had forgotten completely about the soldier until I heard him hissing at me from his garden wall.

"Yes, yes! You said you'd come back to help me, and here you are. Come inside!" He disappeared, and a moment later a little wooden door in the wall opened inward. I stooped and stepped inside to find myself in a garden open to the sky, surrounded by a colonnade. The scent of burning leaves filled my nostrils; an elderly slave was gathering leaves with a rake, arranging them in piles about a small brazier in the center of the garden.

The soldier smiled at me crookedly. I judged him to be not much older than myself, despite his bald head and the grey hairs that bristled from his eyebrows. The dark circles beneath his eyes marked him as a man who badly needed sleep and a respite from worry. He hobbled past me and pulled up a chair for me to sit on.

"Tell me, neighbor, did you grow up in the countryside?" he said. His voice cracked slightly, as if pleasant discourse was a strain to him.

"No, I was born in Rome."

"Ah. I grew up near Arpinum myself. I only mention it because I saw you staring at the leaves and the fire. I know how city folk dread fires and shun them except for heat and cooking. It's a country habit, burning leaves. Dangerous, but I'm careful. The smell reminds me of my boyhood. As does this garden."

I looked up at the tall, denuded trees that loomed in stark silhouette against the cloudy sky. Among them were some cypresses and yews that still wore their shaggy, grey-green coats. A weirdly twisted little tree, hardly more than a bush, stood in the corner, surrounded by a carpet of round, yellow leaves. The old slave walked slowly toward the bush and began to rake its leaves in among the others.

"Have you lived in this house long?" I asked.

"For three years. I cashed in the farm Sulla gave me and bought this place. I retired before the fighting was finished. My leg was crippled, and another wound made my sword arm useless. My shoulder still hurts me now and again, especially at this time of year, when the weather turns cold. This is a bad time of year, all around." He grimaced, whether at a phantom pain in his shoulder or at phantoms in the air I could not tell.

"When did you first see the lemures?" I asked. Since the man insisted on taking my time, there was no point in being subtle.

"Just after I moved into this house."

"Ah, then perhaps the lemures were here before you arrived."

"No," he said gravely. "They must have followed me here." He limped toward the brazier, stooped stiffly, gathered up a handful of leaves and scattered them on the fire. "Only a little at a time," he said softly. "Wouldn't want to be careless with a fire in the garden. Besides, it makes the pleasure last. A little today, a little more tomorrow. Burning leaves reminds me of boyhood."

"How do you know they followed you? The lemures, I mean."

"Because I recognize them."

"Who were they?"

"I never knew their names." He stared into the fire. "But I remember the Etruscan's face when my sword cut open his entrails and he looked up at me, gasping and unbelieving. I remember the bloodshot eyes of the sentries we surprised one night outside Capua. They had been drinking, the fools. When we stuck our swords into their bellies, I could smell the wine amid the stench that came pouring out. I remember the boy I killed in battle once—so young and tender my blade sliced clear through his neck. His head went flying off. One of my men caught it and cast it back at me, laughing. It landed at my feet. I swear, the boy's eyes were still open, and he knew what was happening to him. . . ."

He stooped, groaning at the effort, and gathered another handful of leaves. "The flames make all things pure again," he whispered. "The odor of burning leaves is the smell of innocence."

He watched the fire for a long moment. "They come at this time of year, the lemures. Seeking revenge. They cannot harm my body. They had their chance to do that when they were living, and they only succeeded in maiming me. It was I who killed their bodies, I who triumphed. Now they seek to drive me mad. They cast a spell on me. They cloud my mind and draw me into the pit. They shriek and dance about my head, they open their bellies over me and bury me in offal, they dismember themselves and drown me in a sea of blood and gore. Somehow I've always struggled free, but my will grows weaker every year. One day they will draw me into the pit and I will never come out again."

He covered his face. "Go now. I'm ashamed that you should see me like this. When you see me again, it will be more terrible than you can imagine. But you will come, when I send for you? You will come and see them for yourself? A man as clever as you might strike a bargain, even with the dead."

He dropped his hands. I would hardly have recognized his face—his eyes were red, his cheeks gaunt, his lips trembling. "Swear to me that you will come, Gordianus. If only to bear witness to my destruction."

"I do not make oaths—"

"Then promise me as a man, and leave the gods out of it. I beg you to come when I call."

"I will come," I finally sighed, thinking that a promise to a madman was not truly binding.

The old slave, clucking and shaking his head with worry, ushered me to the little door. "I fear that your master is already mad," I whispered. "These lemures are from his own imagination."

"Oh, no," said the old slave. "I have seen them, too."

"You?"

"Yes, just as he described."

"And the other slaves?"

"We have all seen the lemures."

I looked into the old slave's calm, unblinking eyes for a long moment. Then I stepped through the passage and he shut the door behind me.

"A veritable plague of lemures!" I said as I lay upon my couch taking dinner that night. "Rome is overrun by them."

Bethesda, who sensed the unease beneath my levity, tilted her head and arched an eyebrow, but said nothing.

"And that silly warning Lucius Claudius wrote in his note this morning! 'Do not bring the boy, the circumstances might frighten him'—ha! What could be more appealing to a twelve-year-old boy than the chance to see a genuine lemur!"

Eco chewed a mouthful of bread and watched me with round eyes, not sure whether I was joking or not.

"The whole affair seems quite absurd to me," ventured Bethesda. She crossed her arms impatiently. As was her custom, she had already eaten in the kitchen, and merely watched while Eco and I feasted. "As even the stupidest person in Egypt knows, the bodies of the dead cannot survive unless they have been carefully mummified according to ancient laws. How could the body of a dead man be wandering about Rome, frightening this Titus into jumping off a balcony? Especially a dead man who had his head cut off. It was a living fiend who *pushed* him off the balcony, that much is obvious. Ha! I'll wager it was his wife who did it!"

"Then what of the soldier's haunting? The old slave swears that the whole household has seen the lemures. Not just one, but a whole swarm of them."

"Fah! The slave lies to excuse his master's feeblemindedness. He is loyal, as a slave should be, but not necessarily honest."

"Even so, I think I shall go if the soldier calls me, to judge with my own eyes. And the matter of the lemur on the Palatine Hill is worth pursuing, if only for the handsome fee that Cornelia promises."

Bethesda shrugged. To change the subject, I turned to Eco. "And speaking of outrageous fees, what did that thief of a tutor teach you today?"

Eco jumped from his couch and ran to fetch his stylus and wax tablet.

Bethesda uncrossed her arms. "If you continue with these matters," she said, her voice now pitched to conceal her own unease, "I think that your friend Lucius Claudius gives you good advice. There is no need to take Eco along with you. He's busy with his lessons and should stay at home. He's safe here, from evil men and evil spirits alike."

I nodded, for I had been thinking the same thing myself.

The next morning I stepped quietly past the soldier's house. He did not spy me and call out, though I could tell he was awake and in his garden; I smelled the tang of burning leaves on the air.

I had promised Lucius and Cornelia that I would come again to the house on the Palatine, but there was another call I wanted to make first.

A few questions in the right ears and a few coins in the right hands were all it took to find the house of Furius's mother on the Caelian Hill, where his survivors had fled after he was proscribed, beheaded, and dispossessed. The house was small and narrow, wedged in among other small, narrow houses that might have been standing for a hundred years; the street had somehow survived the fires and the constant rebuilding that continually changes the face of the city, and seemed to take me into an older, simpler Rome, when rich and poor alike lived in modest private dwellings, before the powerful began to flaunt their wealth with great houses and the poor were pressed together into many-storied tenements.

A knock upon the door summoned a veritable giant, a hulking, thick-chested slave with squinting eyes and a scowling mouth—not the door slave of a secure and respectable home, but quite obviously a bodyguard. I stepped back a few paces so that I did not have to strain to look up at him, and asked to see his master.

"If you had legitimate business here, you'd know that there is no master in this house," he growled.

"Of course," I said, "I misspoke myself. I meant to say your mistress—the mother of the late Furius."

He scowled. "Do you misspeak yourself again, stranger, or could it be that you don't know that the old mistress had a stroke not long after her son's death? She and her daughter are in seclusion and see no one."

"What was I thinking? I meant to say, of course, Furius's widow—"

But the slave had had enough of me, and slammed the door in my face.

I heard a cackle of laughter behind me and turned to see a toothless old slavewoman sweeping the portico of the house across the street. "You'd have had an easier time getting in to see the dictator Sulla when he was alive," she laughed.

I smiled and shrugged. "Are they always so unfriendly and abrupt?"

"With strangers, always. You can't blame them—a house full of women with no man around but a bodyguard."

"No man in the house—ah, not since Furius was executed."

"You knew him?" asked the slavewoman.

"Not exactly. But I know of him."

"Terrible, what they did to him. He was no enemy of Sulla's. Furius had no stomach for politics or fighting. A gentle man, wouldn't have kicked a dog from his front step."

"But his brother took up arms against Sulla, and died fighting him."

"That was his brother, not Furius. I knew them both, from when they were boys growing up in that house with their mother. Furius was a peaceful child, and a cautious man. A philosopher, not a fighter. What was done to him was a terrible injustice—naming him an enemy of the state, taking all his property, cutting off his . . ." She stopped her sweeping and cleared her throat. She hardened her jaw. "And who are you? Another schemer come to torment his womenfolk?"

"Not at all."

"Because I'll tell you right now that you'll never get in to see his mother or sister. Ever since the death, and after that the old woman's stroke, they haven't stirred out of that house. A long time to be in mourning, you might say, but Furius was all they had. His widow goes out to do the marketing, with the little girl; but she still wears black. They all took his death very hard."

At that moment the door across the street opened. A blond woman emerged, draped in a black stola. Beside her, reaching up to hold her hand, was a little girl with haunted eyes and black curls. Closing the door and following behind was the giant, who saw me and scowled.

"On their way to market," whispered the old slavewoman. "She usually goes at this time of morning. Ah, look at the precious little one, so serious-looking yet so pretty. Not so much like her mother, not so fair; no, the very image of her aunt, I've always said."

"Her aunt? Not her father?"

"Him, too, of course . . ."

I talked with the old woman for a few moments, then hurried after the widow. I hoped for a chance to speak with her, but the bodyguard made it quite plain that I should keep my distance. I fell back and followed them in secret, observing her purchases as she did her shopping in the meat market.

At last I broke away and headed for the house on the Palatine.

Lucius and Cornelia hurried to the atrium even before the slave announced my arrival. Their faces were drawn with sleeplessness and worry.

"The lemur appeared again last night," said Lucius.

"The thing was in my bedchamber." Cornelia's face was pale. "I woke to see it standing beside the door. It must have been the smell that woke me—a horrible, fetid stench! I tried to rise and couldn't. I wanted to cry out, but my throat was frozen—the thing cast a spell on me. It said the words again: *Now you.* Then it disappeared into the hallway."

"Did you pursue it?"

She looked at me as if I were mad.

"But *I* saw the thing," offered Lucius. "I was in the bedchamber down the hall. I heard footsteps, and called out, thinking it might be Cornelia. There was no answer and the footsteps grew hurried. I leaped from my couch and stepped into the hall. . . ."

"And you saw it?"

"Only for an instant. I called out. The thing paused and turned, then disappeared into the shadows. I would have followed it—really, Gordianus, I swear I would have—but at that instant Cornelia cried out for me. I turned and hurried to her room."

"So the thing fled, and no one pursued it." I stifled a curse.

"I'm afraid so," said Lucius, wincing. "But when the thing turned and looked at me in the hallway, a bit of moonlight fell on its face."

"You had a good look at it, then?"

"Yes. Gordianus, I didn't know Furius well, but I had some dealings with him before his death, enough to recognize him across a street or in the Forum. And this creature—despite its broken teeth and the tumors on its flesh—this fiend most certainly bore the face of Furius!"

Cornelia suddenly gasped and began to stagger. Lucius held her up and called for help. Some of the household women gathered and escorted her to her bedchamber.

"Titus was just the same before his fall," sighed Lucius, shaking his head. "He began to faint and suffer fits, would suddenly lose his breath and be unable to catch another. They say such afflictions are frequently caused by spiteful lemures."

"Perhaps," I said. "Or by a guilty conscience. I wonder if the lemur left any other manifestations behind? Show me where you saw the thing."

Lucius led me down the hallway. "There," he said, pointing to a spot a few paces beyond the door to his room. "At night a bit of light falls just there; everything beyond is dark."

I walked to the place and looked about, then sniffed the air. Lucius sniffed as well. "The smell of putrefaction," he murmured. "The lemur has left its fetid odor behind."

"A bad smell, to be sure," I said, "but not the odor of a corpse. Look here! A footprint!"

Just below us, two faint brown stains in the shape of sandals had been left on the tiled floor. In the bright morning light other marks of the same color were visible, extending in both directions. Those toward Cornelia's bedchamber, where many other feet had traversed, quickly became confused and unreadable. Those leading away showed only the imprint of the forefeet of a pair of sandals, with no heel marks.

"The thing came to a halt here, just as you said. Then it began to run, leaving only these abbreviated impressions. Why should a lemur run on tiptoes, I wonder? And what is this stain left by the footsteps?"

I knelt down and peered closely. Lucius, shedding his patrician dignity, got down on his hands and knees beside me. He wrinkled his nose. "The smell of putrefaction!" he said again.

"Not putrefaction," I countered. "Common excrement. Come, let's see where the footprints lead."

We followed them down the hallway and around a corner, where the footprints ended before a closed door.

"Does this lead outside?" I asked.

"Why, no," said Lucius, suddenly a patrician again and making an uncomfortable face. "That door opens into the indoor toilet."

"How interesting." I opened it and stepped inside. As I would have expected in a household run by a woman like Cornelia, the fixtures were luxurious and the place was quite spotless, except for some telltale footprints on the limestone floor. There were windows set high in the wall, covered by iron bars. A marble seat surmounted the hole. Peering within, I studied the lead piping of the drain.

"Straight down the slope of the Palatine Hill and into the Cloaca Maxima, and thence into the Tiber," commented Lucius. Patricians may be prudish about bodily functions, but of Roman plumbing they are justifiably proud.

"Not nearly large enough for a man to pass through," I said.

"What an awful idea!"

"Even so . . ." I called for a slave, who managed to find a chisel for me.

"Now what are you doing? Here, those tiles are made of fine limestone, Gordianus! You shouldn't go chipping away at the corners."

"Not even to discover *this*?" I slid the chisel under the edge of one of the stones and lifted it up.

Lucius drew back and gasped, then leaned forward and peered down into the darkness. "A tunnel!" he whispered.

"So it appears."

"Why, someone must go down it!" Lucius peered at me and raised an eyebrow.

"Not even if Cornelia doubled my fee!"

"I wasn't suggesting that *you* go, Gordianus." He looked up at the young slave who had fetched the chisel. The boy looked slender and supple enough. When he saw what Lucius intended, he started back and looked at me imploringly.

"No, Lucius Claudius," I said, "no one need be put at risk; not yet. Who knows what the boy might encounter—if not lemures and monsters, then boobytraps or scorpions or a fall to his death. First we should attempt to determine the tunnel's egress. It may be a simple matter, if it merely follows the logical course of the plumbing."

Which it did. From the balcony on the western side of the house, it was easy enough to judge where the buried pipes descended the slope into the valley between the Palatine and the Capitoline, where they joined with the Cloaca Maxima underground. At the foot of the hill, directly below the house, in a wild, rubbish-strewn region behind some warehouses and granaries, I spied a thicket. Even stripped of their leaves, the bushes grew so thick that I could not see far into them.

Lucius insisted on accompanying me, though his bulky frame and expensive garb were ill-suited for traversing a rough hillside. We reached the foot of the hill and pushed our way into the thicket, ducking beneath branches and snapping twigs out of the way.

At last we came to the heart of the thicket, where our perseverance was rewarded. Hidden behind the dense, shaggy branches of a cypress tree was the tunnel's other end. The hole was crudely made, lined with rough dabs of cement and broken bricks. It was just large enough for a man to enter, but the foul smell that issued from within was enough to keep vagrants or even curious children out.

At night, hidden behind the storehouses and sheds, such a place would be quite lonely and secluded. A man—or a lemur, for that matter—might come and go completely unobserved.

"Cold," complained Lucius, "cold and damp and dark. It would have made more sense to stay in the house tonight, where it's warm and dry. We could lie in wait in the hallway and trap this fiend when he emerges from his secret passage. Why, instead, are we huddling here in the dark and cold, watching for who-knows-what and jumping in fright every time a bit of wind whistles through the thicket?"

"You need not have come, Lucius Claudius. I didn't ask you to."

"Cornelia would have thought me a coward if I didn't," he pouted.

"And what does Cornelia's opinion matter?" I snapped, and bit my tongue. The cold and damp had set us both on edge. A light drizzle began to fall, obscuring the moon and casting the thicket into even greater darkness. We had been hiding among the brambles since shortly after nightfall. I had warned Lucius that the watch was likely to be long and uncomfortable and possibly futile, but he had insisted on accompanying me. He had offered to hire some ruffians to escort us, but if my suspicions were correct we would not need them; nor did I want more witnesses to be present than was necessary.

A gust of icy wind whipped beneath my cloak and sent a shiver up my spine. Lucius's teeth began to chatter. My mood grew dark. What if I was wrong, after all? What if the thing we sought was not human, but something else . . .

"And as for jumping in fear every time a twig snaps," I whispered, "speak for yourself—"

I fell silent, for at that moment not one but many twigs began to snap. Something large had entered the thicket and was moving toward us.

"It must be a whole army!" whispered Lucius, clutching at my arm.

"No," I whispered back. "Only two persons, if my guess is right."

Two moving shapes, obscured by the tangle of branches and the deep gloom, came very near to us and then turned aside, toward the cypress tree that hid the tunnel's mouth.

A moment later I heard a man's voice, cursing: "Someone has blocked the hole!" I recognized the voice of the growling giant who guarded the house on the Caelian Hill.

"Perhaps the tunnel has fallen in." When Lucius heard the second voice he clutched my arm again, not in fear but surprise.

"No," I said aloud, "the tunnel was purposely blocked so that you could not use it again."

There was a moment of silence, followed by the noise of two bodies scrambling in the underbrush.

"Stay where you are!" I said. "For your own good, stay where you are and listen to me!"

The scrambling ceased and there was silence again, except for the sound of heavy breathing and confused whispers.

"I know who you are," I said. "I know why you've come here. I have no interest in harming you, but I must speak with you. Will you speak with me, Furia?"

"*Furia?*" whispered Lucius. The drizzle had ended, and moonlight illuminated the confusion on his face.

There was a long silence, then more whispering—the giant was trying to dissuade his mistress. Finally she spoke out. "Who are you?" she said.

"My name is Gordianus. You don't know me. But I know that you and your family have suffered greatly, Furia. You have been wronged, most unjustly. Perhaps your vengeance on Titus and Cornelia is seemly in the eyes of the gods—I cannot judge. But you have been found out, and the time has come to stop your pretense. I'll step toward you now. There are two of us. We bear no weapons. Tell your faithful slave that we mean no harm, and that to harm us will profit you nothing."

I stepped slowly toward the cypress tree, a great, shaggy patch of black amid the general gloom. Beside it stood two forms, one tall, the other short.

With a gesture, Furia bade her slave to stay where he was, then she stepped toward us. A patch of moonlight fell on her face. Lucius gasped and started back. Even though I expected it, the sight still sent a shiver through my veins.

I confronted what appeared to be a young man in a tattered cloak. His short hair was matted with blood and blood was smeared all around his throat and neck, as if his neck had been severed and then somehow fused together again. His eyes were dark and hollow. His skin was as pale as death and dotted with horrible tumors, his lips were parched and cracked. When Furia spoke, her sweet, gentle voice was a strange contrast to her horrifying visage.

"You have found out," she said.

"Yes."

"Are you the man who called at my mother's house this morning?"

"Yes."

"Who betrayed me? It couldn't have been Cleto," she whispered, glancing at the bodyguard.

"No one betrayed you. We found the tunnel this afternoon."

"Ah! My brother had it built during the worst years of the civil war, so that we might have a way to escape in a sudden crisis. Of course, when the monster became dictator, there was no way for anyone to escape."

"Was your brother truly an enemy of Sulla's?"

"Not in any active way, but there were those willing to paint him as such—those who coveted all he had."

"Furius was proscribed for no reason?"

"No reason but the bitch's greed!" Her voice was hard and bitter. I glanced at Lucius, who was curiously silent at such an assault on Cornelia's character.

"It was Titus whom you haunted first—"

"Only so that Cornelia would know what awaited her. Titus was a weakling, a nobody, easily frightened. Ask Cornelia; she frightened him into doing anything she wished, even if it meant destroying an innocent colleague from his younger days. It was Cornelia who convinced her dear cousin Sulla to insert my brother's name in the proscription lists, merely to obtain our house. Because the men of our line have perished, because Furius was the last, she thought that her calumny would go unavenged forever."

"But now it must stop, Furia. You must be content with what you have done so far."

"No!"

"A life for a life," I said. "Titus for Furius."

"No, ruin for ruin! The death of Titus will not restore our house, our fortune, our good name."

"Nor will the death of Cornelia. If you proceed now, you are sure to be caught. You must be content with half a portion of vengeance, and push the rest aside."

"You intend to tell her, then? Now that you've caught me at it?"

I hesitated. "First, tell me truly, Furia, did you push Titus from his balcony?"

She looked at me unwaveringly, the moonlight making her eyes glimmer like shards of onyx. "Titus jumped from the balcony. He jumped because he thought he saw the lemur of my brother, and he could not stand his own wretchedness and guilt."

I bowed my head. "Go," I whispered. "Take your slave and go now, back to your mother and your niece and your brother's widow. Never come back."

I looked up to see tears streaming down her face. It was a strange sight, to see a lemur weep. She called to the slave, and they departed from the thicket.

We ascended the hill in silence. Lucius stopped chattering his teeth and instead began to huff and puff. Outside Cornelia's house I drew him aside.

"Lucius, you must not tell Cornelia."

"But how else—"

"We will tell her that we found the tunnel but that no one came, that her persecutor has been frightened off for now, but may come again, in which case she can set her own guard. Yes, let her think that the unknown threat is still at large, always plotting her destruction."

"But surely she deserves—"

"She deserves what Furia had in store for her. Did you know Cornelia had placed Furius's name on the lists, merely to obtain his house?"

"I—" Lucius bit his lips. "I suspected the possibility. But Gordianus, what she did was hardly unique. Everyone was doing it."

"Not everyone. Not you, Lucius."

"True," he said, nodding sheepishly. "But Cornelia will fault you for not capturing the imposter. She'll refuse to pay the full fee."

"I don't care about the fee."

"I'll make up the difference," said Lucius.

I laid my hand on his shoulder. "What is rarer than a camel in Gaul?" Lucius wrinkled his brow. I laughed. "An honest man in Rome."

Lucius shrugged off the compliment with typical chagrin. "I still don't understand how you knew the identity of the imposter."

"I told you that I visited the house on the Caelian Hill this morning. What I didn't tell you was that the old slavewoman across the street revealed to me that Furius not only had a sister, but that this sister was the same age—his twin—and bore a striking resemblance to him."

"Ah! They must have been close, and her slightly softer features make her look younger than Furius."

"Who must have been quite handsome. Even through her horrid makeup . . ." I sighed. "Also, when I followed Furius's widow to market, I was struck by her purchase of a quantity of calf's blood. She also gathered a spray of juniper berries, which the little girl carried for her."

"Berries?"

"The cankers pasted on Furia's face—juniper berries cut in half. The blood was for matting her hair and daubing on her neck. As for the rest of her appearance, her ghastly makeup and costuming, you and I can only guess at the ingenuity of a household of women united toward a single goal. Furia has been in seclusion for months, which explains the almost uncanny paleness of her flesh—and the fact that she was able to cut off her hair without anyone taking notice."

I shook my head. "A remarkable woman. I wonder why she never married? The turmoil and confusion of the civil war, I suppose, and the deaths of her brothers ruined her prospects forever. Misery is like a pebble cast into a pond, sending out a wave that spreads and spreads."

*   *   *

I headed home that night weary and wistful. There are days when one sees too much of the world's wickedness, and only a long sleep in the safe seclusion of one's home can restore an appetite for life. I thought of Bethesda and Eco, and tried to push the face of Furia from my thoughts. The last thing on my mind was the haunted soldier and his legion of lemures, and yet I was destined to encounter them all before I reached my house.

I passed by the wall of his garden, smelled the familiar tang of burning leaves, but thought no more about the soldier until I heard the little wooden door open behind me and the voice of his old retainer crying out my name.

"Thank the gods you've finally returned!" he whispered hoarsely. He seemed to be in the grip of a strange malady or spell, for even though the door allowed him more room to stand, he remained oddly bent, his eyes gleamed dully, and his jaw was slack. "The master has sent messenger after messenger to your door—always they are told you are out, that your return is expected at any moment. But when the lemures come, time stops. Please, come! Save the master—save us all!"

From beyond the wall I heard the sound of moaning, not from one man but from many. I heard a woman shriek, and the sound of furniture overturned. What madness was taking place within the house?

"Please, help us! The lemures, the lemures!" The old slave made a face of such horror that I started back and turned to make my escape. My house was only a few steps up the pathway. But I turned back. I reached inside my tunic and felt for the handle of my dagger before I thought how little use a dagger would be to deal with those already dead.

It took no small amount of courage to step through the little door. My heart pounded like a hammer in my chest.

The air within was dank and smoky. After the brief drizzle a clammy cold had descended upon the hills of Rome, such as holds down plumes of smoke and makes the air unwholesome and stagnant. I breathed in an acrid breath and coughed.

The soldier came running from within the house. He tripped and staggered forward on his knees, wrapped his arms around my waist and looked up at me in abject terror. "There!" He pointed back toward the house. "They pursue me! Gods have mercy—the boy without a head, the soldier with his belly cut open, all the others!"

I peered into the hazy darkness, but saw nothing except a bit of whorling smoke. I suddenly felt dizzy and lightheaded. It was because I had not eaten all day, I told myself; I should have been less proud and presumed upon Cornelia's hospitality for a meal. Then, while I watched, the whorl of smoke began to expand and change shape. A face emerged from the murky darkness—a boy's face, twisted with agony.

"See!" cried the soldier. "See how the poor lad holds his own head in his fist, like Perseus holding the head of the Gorgon! See how he stares, blaming me!"

Indeed, out of the darkness and smoke I began to see exactly what the wretched man described, a headless boy in battle garb clutching his dismembered head by the hair and holding it aloft. I opened my mouth in awe and terror. Behind the boy, other shapes began to emerge—first a few, then many, then a legion of phantoms covered with blood and writhing like maggots in the air.

It was a terrifying spectacle. I would have fled, but I was rooted to the spot. The soldier clutched my knees. The old slave began to weep and babble. From within the house came the sound of others in distress, moaning and crying out.

"Don't you hear them?" cried the soldier. "The lemures, shrieking like harpies!" The great looming mass of corpses began to keen and wail—surely all of Rome could hear it!

Like a drowning man, the mind in great distress will clutch at anything to save itself. A bit of straw will float, but will not support a thrashing man; a plank of wood may give him respite, but best of all is a steady rock within the raging current. So my mind clutched at anything that might preserve it in the face of such overwhelming and inexplicable horror. Time had come to a stop, just as the old slave had said, and in that endlessly attenuated moment a flood of images, memories, schemes, and notions raged through my mind. I clutched at straws. Madness pulled me downward, like an unseen current in black water. I sank—until I suddenly found the rock for which I sought.

"The bush!" I whispered. "The burning bush, which speaks aloud!"

The soldier, thinking I spied something within the mass of writhing lemures, clutched at me and trembled. "What bush? Ah yes, I see it, too . . ."

"No, the bush here in your garden! That strange, gnarled tree among the yews, with yellow leaves all around. But now the leaves have all been swept in among the others . . . burnt with the others in the brazier . . . the smoke still hangs in the air . . ."

I pulled the soldier out of the garden, through the small door, and onto the pathway. I returned for the old slave, and then, one by one, for the others. They huddled together on the cobblestones, trembling and confused, their eyes wide with terror and red with blood.

"There are no lemures!" I whispered hoarsely, my throat sore from the smoke—even though I could see them hovering over the wall, cackling and dangling their entrails in the empty air.

The slaves pointed and clutched one another. The soldier hid behind his hands.

As the slaves grew more manageable, I led them in groups to my house, where they huddled together, frightened but safe. Bethesda was perplexed and displeased at the sudden invasion of half-mad strangers, but Eco was delighted at the opportunity to stay up until dawn under such novel circumstances. It was a long, cold night, marked by fits of panic and orgies of mutual reassurance, while we waited for sanity to return.

The first light of morning broke, bringing a cold dew that was a tonic to senses still befuddled by sleeplessness and poisoned by smoke. My head pounded like thunder, with a hangover far worse than any I had ever gotten from wine. A ray of pale sunlight was like a knife to my eyes, but I no longer saw visions of lemures or heard their mad shrieking.

The soldier, haggard and dazed, begged me for an explanation. I agreed readily enough, for a wise man once taught me that the best relief for a pounding headache is the application of disciplined thought, which brings blood to the brain and flushes evil humors from the phlegm.

"It came to me in a flash of inspiration, not logic," I explained. "Your autumnal ritual of burning leaves, and the yearly visitation of the lemures . . . the smoke that filled your garden, and the plague of spirits . . . these things were not unconnected. That odd, twisted tree in your garden is not native to Rome, or to the peninsula. How it came here, I have no idea, but I suspect it came from the East, where plants which induce visions are quite common. There is the snake plant of Aethiopia, the juice of which causes such terrible visions that it drives men to suicide; men guilty of sacrilege are forced to drink it as a punishment. The rivergleam plant that grows on the banks of the Indus is also famous for making men rave and see weird visions. But I suspect that the tree in your garden may be a specimen of a rare bush found in the rocky mountains east of Egypt. Bethesda tells a tale about it."

"What tale?" said Bethesda.

"You remember—the tale your Hebrew father passed on to you, about his ancestor called Moses, who encountered a bush that spoke aloud to him when it burned. The leaves of your bush, neighbor, not only spoke but cast powerful visions."

"Yet why did I see what I saw?"

"You saw that which you feared the most—the vengeful spirits of those you killed fighting for Sulla."

"But the slaves saw what I saw! And so did you!"

"We saw what you suggested, just as you began to see a burning bush when I said the words."

He shook his head. "It was never so powerful before. Last night was more terrible than ever!"

"Probably because, in the past, you happened to burn only a few of the yellow leaves at a time, and the cold wind carried away much of the smoke; the visions came upon some but not all of the household, and in varying degrees. But last night the smoke hovered in the garden and the haze spread through the house; and perhaps you happened to burn a great many of the yellow leaves at once. Everyone who breathed the smoke was intoxicated and stricken with a kind of madness. Once we escaped the smoke, with time the madness passed, like a fever burning itself out."

"Then the lemures never existed?"

"I think not."

"And if I uproot that accursed bush and cast it in the Tiber, I will never see the lemures again?"

"Perhaps not," I said. *Though you may always see them in your nightmares,* I thought.

"So, it was just as I told you," said Bethesda, bringing a cool cloth to lay upon my forehead that afternoon. Flashes of pain still coursed through my temples from time to time, and whenever I closed my eyes alarming visions loomed in the blackness.

"Just as you told me? Nonsense!" I said. "You thought that Titus was pushed from his balcony—and that his wife Cornelia did it!"

"A woman pretending to be a lemur drove him to jump—which is just the same," she insisted.

"And you said the soldier's old slave was lying about having seen the lemures himself, when in fact he was telling the truth."

"What I said was that the dead cannot go walking about unless they have been properly mummified, and I was absolutely right. And it was I who once told you about the burning bush that speaks, remember? Without that, you never would have figured the cause."

"Fair enough," I admitted, deciding it was impossible to win the argument.

"This quaint Roman idea about lemures haunting the living is completely absurd," she went on.

"About that I am not sure."

"But with your own eyes you have seen the truth! By your own wits you have proved in two instances that what everyone thought to be lemures were not lemures at all, only makeup and fear, intoxicating smoke and guilty consciences!"

"You miss the point, Bethesda."

"What do you mean?"

"Lemures *do* exist—perhaps not as visitors perceptible to the senses, but in another way. The dead do have power to spread misery among the living. The spirit of a man can carry on and cause untold havoc from beyond the grave. The more powerful the man, the more terrible his legacy." I shivered—not at lurid visions remembered from the soldier's garden, but at the naked truth, which was infinitely more concrete and terrible. "Rome is a haunted city. The lemur of the dictator Sulla haunts us all. Dead he may be, but not departed. His wickedness lingers on, bringing despair and suffering upon his friends and foes alike."

To this Bethesda had no answer. I closed my eyes and saw no more monsters, but slept a dreamless sleep until dawn of the following day.

THE PRINCE WHO WAS
A THIEF

Theodore Dreiser

*Full of treachery, danger, and the magic of the Orient, the courts of ancient Arabia
have inspired great storytelling since Scheherazade spun her thousand and one tales
for Schariar, a king of Islamic Samarkand. Similar to the* Arabian Nights *in style,
in content Theodore Dreiser's story of the prince who was a thief is at heart a crime
tale. The great American novelist was by no means the only author of his stature
to pen a crime story, but he is in a more fanciful mood here than in his better-known
works, under the influence perhaps of those bewitching Arabian night skies.*

As they gathered about him in the marketplace, Gazzar-al-Din, the
mendicant storyteller, thumped his tambour louder and louder,
exclaiming: "A marvelous tale, O Company of the Faithful! A
marvelous tale! Hearken! A tale such as has never yet been told in all
Hodeidah—no, not in all Yemen! 'A Prince Who Was a Thief.' For a score
of anna—yea, the fourth part of a rupee—I begin. As jasmine, it is fragrant;
as khat, soothing. A marvelous tale!"

"Ay-ee, but how is one to know that," observed Ahmed, the carpet
weaver, to Chudi, the tailor, with whom he had drawn near. "There are
many who promise excellent tales but how few who tell them."

"It is even as thou sayst, O Ahmed. Often have I hearkened and given
anna in plenty, yet few there are whose tales are worth the hearing."

"Why not begin thy tale, O Kowasji?" inquired Soudi, the carrier.
"Then if, as thou sayst, it is so excellent, will not anna enough be thine?
There are tellers of tales, and tellers of tales—"

"Yea, and that I would," replied the mendicant artfully, "were all as
honest as thou lookest and as kind. Yet have I traveled far without food,

and I know not where I may rest this night. . . . A tale of the great caliph and the Princess Yanee and the noble Yussuf, stolen and found again. And the great treasury sealed and guarded, yet entered and robbed by one who was not found. Anna—but a score of anna, and I begin! What? Are all in Hodeidah so poor that a tale of love and pleasure and danger and great palaces and great princes and caliphs and thieves can remain untold for the want of a few anna—for so many as ten dropped into my tambour? A marvelous tale! A marvelous tale!"

"Begin then," said Azad Bakht, the barber. "Here is an anna for thee," and he tossed a coin in the tambour.

"And here is another for thee," observed Haifa, the tobacco vendor, fishing in his purse. "I do not mind risking it."

Gazzar then crouched upon his rags, lifted his hand for silence, and began:

"Know then, O excellent citizens of Hodeidah, that once, many years since, there lived in this very Yemen where now is Taif, then a much more resplendent city, a sultan by the name of Kar-Shem, who had great cities and palaces and an army, and was beloved of all over whom he ruled. When he—wilt thou be seated, O friend? And silence!—when he was but newly married and ruling happily, a son was born to him, Hussein, an infant of so great charm and beauty that he decided he should be carefully reared and wisely trained and so made into a fit ruler for so great a country. But, as it chanced, there was a rival claimant to this same throne by another line, a branch long since deposed by the ancestors of this same king, and he it was, Bab-el-Bar by name, who was determined that the young Prince Hussein should be stolen and disposed of in some way so that he should never return and claim the throne. One day, when the prince was only four years of age, the summer palace was attacked and the princeling captured. From thence he was carried over great wastes of sand to Baghdad, where he was duly sold as a slave to a man who was looking for such, for he was a great and successful thief, one who trained thieves from their infancy up so that they should never know what virtue was."

"Ay-ee, there are such," interrupted Ahmed, the carpetweaver, loudly, for his place had only recently been robbed.

"Once the Prince Hussein was in the hands of this thief, he was at once housed with those who stole, who in turn taught him. One of the tricks which Yussuf, the master thief, employed was to take each of his neophytes in turn at the age of seven, dress him in a yarn jacket, lower him into a dry cistern from which there was no means of escape, place a large ring-cake upon a beam across the top and tell him to obtain the cake or starve. Many starved for days and were eventually dismissed as unworthy of his skill. But when the young Prince Hussein was lowered he meditated upon his state. At last he unraveled a part of his yarn jacket, tied a pebble to it and threw it so that it fell through the hole of the cake, and thus he was able to pull it down. At this Yussuf was so pleased that he had him drawn up and given a rare meal.

"One day Yussuf, hearing good reports from those who were training Hussein in thieving, took him to the top of a hill traversed by a road, where, seeing a peasant carrying a sheep on his back approaching, Yussuf Ben Ali asked of Hussein, now renamed Abou so that he might not be found: 'How shall we get the sheep without the peasant learning that we have taken it?' Trained by fear of punishment to use his wits, Abou, after some thought replied: 'When thou seest the sheep alone, take it!' Stealing from the thicket, he placed one of his shoes in the road and then hid. The peasant came and saw the shoe, but left it lying there because there was but one. Abou ran out and picked up the shoe, reappearing from the wood far ahead of the peasant where he put down the mate to the first shoe and then hid again. The peasant came and examined the shoe, then tied his sheep to a stake and ran back for the first one. Yussuf, seeing the sheep alone, now came out and hurried off with it, while Abou followed, picking up the last shoe. The peasant, coming back to where he had seen the first shoe, and not finding it, was dazed and ran back to his sheep, to find that that and the second shoe were gone. Yussuf was much pleased and when they returned to the city Yussuf decided to adopt Abou as his son." Gazzar now paused upon seeing the interest of his hearers and held out his tambour. "Anna, O friends, anna! Is not the teller of tales, the sweetener of weariness, worthy of his hire? I have less than a score of anna, and ten will buy no more than a bowl of curds or a cup of kishr, and the road I have traveled has been long. So much as the right to sleep in a stall with the camels is held at ten anna, and I am no longer young." He moved the tambour about appealingly.

"Dog!" growled Soudi. "Must thy tambour be filled before we hear more?"

"Bismillah! This is no storyteller but a robber," declared Parfi.

Some three of the listeners who had not yet contributed anything dropped each an anna into his tambour.

"Now," continued Gazzar somewhat gloomily, seeing how small were his earnings for all his art, "aside from stealing and plundering caravans upon the great desert, and the murdering of men for their treasure, the great Yussuf conducted a rug bazaar as a blind for more thievery and murder. Once he had adopted Abou as his son, Yussuf dressed him in silks and took him to his false rug market, where he introduced him with a great flourish as one who would continue his affairs after he, Yussuf, was no more. He called his slaves and said: 'Behold thy master after myself. When I am not here, or by chance am no more—praise be to Allah, the good, the great!—see that thou obey him, for I have found him very wise.'

"Soon Yussuf disguised himself as a dervish and departed upon a new venture; and soon after there happened to Abou a great thing. For it should be known that at this time there ruled in Baghdad the great and wise Yianko I, Caliph of the Faithful in the valleys of the Euphrates and the Tigris and master of provinces and principalities, and the possessor of an enormous treasury of gold, which was in a great building of stone. Also he possessed a palace of such beauty that travelers came from many parts and far countries to see. It was here, with his many wives and concubines and slaves and courtiers, and many wise men come from far parts of the world to advise with him and bring him wisdom, that he ruled and was beloved and admired.

"Now by his favorite wife, Atrisha, there had been born to him some thirteen years before the beautiful and tender and delicate and loving and much-beloved Yanee, the sweetest and fairest of all his daughters, whom from the very first he designed should be the wife of some great prince. Her hair was as spun gold, her teeth as pearls of the greatest price, lustrous and delicate; her skin as the bright moon when it rises in the east, and her hands and feet as petals in full bloom. Her lips were as the pomegranate when it is newly cut, and her eyes as those deep pools into which the moon looks when it is night."

"Yea, I have heard of such, in fairytales," sighed Chudi, the baker, whose wife was as parchment that has cracked with age.

"Now at the time that Abou was in charge of the dark bazaar it chanced that the caliph, who annually arranged for the departure of his daughter for the mountains which are beyond Azol in Bactria, where he maintained a summer palace, sent forth a vast company mounted upon elephants and camels out of Ullar and Cerf and horses of the rarest blood from Taif. This company was caparisoned and swathed in silks and thin wool and the braided and spun cloth of Esher and Bar with their knitted threads of gold. And it made a glorious spectacle indeed, and all paused to behold. But it also chanced that as this cavalcade passed through the streets of Baghdad, Abou, hearing a great tumult and the cries of the multitude and the drivers and the tramp of the horses' feet and the pad of the camels', came to the door of his bazaar, his robes of silk about him, a turban of rare cloth knitted with silver threads upon his head. He had now grown to be a youth of eighteen summers. His hair was as black as the wing of the uck, his eyes large and dark and sad from many thoughts as is the pool into which the moon falls. His face and hands were tinted as with henna when it is spread very thin, and his manners were graceful and languorous. As he paused within his doorway he looked wonderingly at the great company as it moved and disappeared about the curves of the long street.

"Yet, even as he gazed, so strange are the ways of Allah, there passed a camel, its houdah heavy with rich silks, and ornaments of the rarest within, but without disguised as humble, so that none might guess. And within was the beautiful Princess Yanee, hidden darkly behind folds of fluttering silk, her face and forehead covered to her starry eyes, as is prescribed, and even these veiled. Yet so strange are the ways of life and of Allah that, being young and full of wonder, she was at this very moment engaged in peeping out from behind her veils, the while the bright panorama of the world was passing. And as she looked, behold, there was Abou, gazing upon her fine accoutrements. So lithe was his form and so deep his eyes and so fair his face that, transfixed as by a beam, her heart melted and without thought she threw back her veil and parted the curtains of the houdah the better to see, and the better that he might see. And Abou, seeing the curtains put to one side and the vision of eyes that were as pools and the cheeks as the leaf of the rose shine upon him, was transfixed and could no longer move or think.

"Then bethinking himself that he might never more see her, he awoke and ran after, throwing one citizen and another to the right and the left. When at last he came up to the camel of his fair one, guarded by eunuchs and slaves, he drew one aside and said softly: 'Friend, be not wrathful and I will give thee a hundred dinars in gold do thou, within such time as thou canst, report to me at the bazaar of Yussuf, the rug merchant, who it is that rides within this houdah. Ask thou only for Abou. No more will I ask.' The slave, noting his fine robes and the green-and-silver turban, thought him to be no less than a noble, and replied: 'Young master, be not overcurious. Remember the vengeance of the caliph.' . . . 'Yet dinars have I to give.' . . . 'I will yet come to thee.'

"Abou was enraptured by even so little as this, and yet dejected also by the swift approach and departure of joy. 'For what am I now?' he asked himself. 'But a moment since, I was whole and one who could find delight in all things that were given me to do; but now I am as one who is lost and knows not his way.'

"Thereafter, for all of a moon, Abou was as one in a dream, wandering here and there drearily, bethinking him how he was ever to know more of the face that had appeared to him through the curtains of the houdah. And whether the driver of the camel would ever return. As day after day passed and there was no word, he grew thin and began to despair and to grow weary of life. At last there came to his shop an aged man, long of beard and dusty of garb, who inquired for Abou. And being shown him said: 'I would speak with thee alone.' And when Abou drew him aside he said: 'Dost thou recall the procession of the caliph's daughter to Ish-Pari in the mountains beyond Azol?' And Abou answered, 'Ay, by Allah!' 'And dost thou recall one of whom thou madest inquiry?' 'Aye,' replied Abou, vastly stirred. 'I asked who it was that was being borne aloft in state.' 'And what was the price for that knowledge?' 'A hundred dinars.' 'Keep thy dinars—or, better yet, give them to me that I may give them to the poor, for I bring thee news. She who was in the houdah was none other than the Princess Yanee, daughter of the caliph and heir to all his realm. But keep thou thy counsel and all thought of this visit and let no one know of thy inquiry. There are many who watch, and death may yet be thy portion and mine. Yet, since thou art as thou art, young and without knowledge of life, here is a spray of the myrtles of Ish-Pari—but thou art to think no further on anything thou hast seen or heard. And thou dost not—death!" He made the sign of three fingers to the forehead and the neck and gave Abou the spray, receiving in return the gold.

"Knowing that the myrtle was from the princess, and that henceforth he might seek but durst not even so much as breathe of what he thought or knew, Abou sighed and returned to his place in the bazaar.

"But now, Yussuf, returning not long after from a far journey, came to Abou with a bold thought. For it related to no other thing than the great treasury of the caliph, which stood in the heart of the city before the public market, and was sealed and guarded and built of stone and carried the wealth of an hundred provinces. Besides, it was now the time of the taking of tithes throughout the caliphate, as Yussuf knew, and the great treasury was filled to the roof, or so it was said, with golden dinars. It was a four-square building of heavy stone, with lesser squares superimposed one above the other after the fashion of pyramids. On each level was a parapet, and upon each side of every parapet as well as on the ground below there walked two guards, each first away from the centre of their side to the end and then back, meeting at the centre to reverse and return. And on each side and on each level were two other guards. No two of these, of any level or side, were permitted to arrive at the centre or the ends of their parapet at the same time as those of the parapets above or below, lest any portion of the treasury be left unguarded. There was but one entrance, which was upon the ground and facing the market. And through this no one save the caliph or the caliph's treasurer or his delegated aides might enter. The guards ascended and descended via a guarded stair. Anna, O friends," pleaded Gazzar once more, "for now comes the wonder of the robbing of the great treasury—the wit and subtlety of Abou—and craft and yet confusion of the treasurer and the caliph—anna!—A few miserable anna!"

"Jackal!" shouted Azad Bakht, getting up. "Thou robbest worse than any robber! Hast thou a treasury of thine own that thou hopest to fill?"

"Be not unkind, O friends," pleaded Gazzar soothingly. "As thou seest, I have but twenty annas—not the price of a meal, let alone of a bed. But ten—but—five—and I proceed."

"Come, then, here they are," cried Al Hadjaz, casting down four; and Zad-el-Din and Haifa and Chudi each likewise added one, and Gazzar swiftly gathered them up and continued:

"Yussuf, who had long contemplated this wondrous storehouse, had also long racked his wits as to how it might be entered and a portion of the gold taken. Also he had counseled with many of his pupils, but in vain. No one had solved the riddle for him. Yet one day as he and Abou passed the treasury on their way to the mosque for the look of honor, Yussuf said to Abou: 'Bethink thee, my son; here is a marvelous building, carefully constructed and guarded. How wouldst thou come to the store of gold within?' Abou, whose thoughts were not upon the building but upon Yanee, betrayed no look of surprise at the request, so accustomed was he to having difficult and fearsome matters put before him, but gazed upon it so calmly that Yussuf exclaimed: 'How now? Hast thou a plan?' 'Never have I given it a thought, O Yussuf,' replied Abou, 'but if it is thy wish, let us go and look more closely.'

"Accordingly, through the crowds of merchants and strangers and donkeys and the veiled daughters of the harem and the idlers generally, they approached and surveyed it. At once Abou observed the movement of the guards, saw that as the guards of one tier were walking away from each other those of the tiers above or below were walking toward each other. And although the one entrance to the treasury was well guarded, still there was a vulnerable spot, which was the crowning cupola, also four-square and flat, where none walked or looked. 'It is difficult,' he said after a time, 'but it can be done. Let me think.'

"Accordingly, after due meditation and without consulting Yussuf, he disguised himself as a dispenser of fodder for camels, secured a rope of silk, four bags, and an iron hook. Returning to his home he caused the hook to be covered with soft cloth so that its fall would make no sound, then fastened it to one end of the silken cord and said to Yussuf: 'Come now and let us try this.' Yussuf, curious as to what Abou could mean, went with him and together they tried their weight upon it to see if it would hold. Then Abou, learning by observation the hour at night wherein the guards were changed, and choosing a night without moon or stars, disguised himself and Yussuf as watchmen of the city and went to the treasury. Though it was as well guarded as ever they stationed themselves in an alley nearby. And Abou, seeing a muleteer approaching and wishing to test his disguise, ordered him away and he went. Then Abou, watching the guards who were upon the ground meet and turn, and seeing those upon the first tier still in the distance but pacing toward the centre, gave a word to Yussuf and they ran forward, threw the hook over the rim of the first tier and then drew themselves up quickly, hanging there above the lower guards until those of the first tier met and turned. Then they climbed over the wall and repeated this trick upon the guards of the second tier, the third and fourth, until at last they were upon the roof of the cupola where they lay flat. Then Abou, who was prepared, unscrewed one of the plates of the dome, hooked the cord over the side and whispered: 'Now, master, which?' Yussuf, ever cautious in his life, replied: 'Go thou and report.'

"Slipping down the rope, Abou at last came upon a great store of gold and loose jewels piled in heaps, from which he filled the bags he had brought. These he fastened to the rope and ascended. Yussuf, astounded by the sight of so much wealth, was for making many trips, but Abou, detecting a rift where shone a star, urged that they cease for the night. Accordingly, after having fastened these at their waists and the plate to the roof as it had been, they descended as they had come."

"A rare trick," commented Zad-el-Din.

"Thus for three nights," continued Gazzar, "they succeeded in robbing the treasury, taking from it many thousands of dinars and jewels. On the fourth night, however, a guard saw them hurrying away and gave the alarm. At that, Abou and Yussuf turned here and there in strange ways, Yussuf betaking himself to his home, while Abou fled to his master's shop. Once there he threw off the disguise of a guard and reappeared as an aged vendor of rugs and was asked by the pursuing guards if he had seen anybody enter his shop. Abou motioned them to the rear of the shop, where they were bound and removed by Yussuf's robber slaves. Others of the guards, however, had betaken themselves to their captain and reported, who immediately informed the treasurer. Torches were brought and a search made, and then he repaired to the caliph. The latter, much astonished that no trace of the entrance or departure of the thieves could be found, sent for a master thief recently taken in crime and sentenced to be gibbeted, and said to him:

" 'Wouldst thou have thy life?'

" 'Aye, if thy grace will yield it.'

" 'Look you,' said the caliph. 'Our treasury has but now been robbed and there is no trace. Solve me this mystery within the moon, and thy life, though not thy freedom, is thine.'

" 'O Protector of the Faithful,' said the thief, 'do thou but let me see within the treasury.'

"And so, chained and in care of the treasurer himself and the caliph, he was taken to the treasury. Looking about him he at length saw a faint ray penetrating through the plate that had been loosed in the dome.

" 'O Guardian of the Faithful,' said the thief wisely and hopefully, 'do thou place a cauldron of hot pitch under this dome and then see if the thief is not taken.'

"Thereupon the caliph did as advised, the while the treasury was resealed and fresh guards set to watch and daily the pitch was renewed, only Abou and Yussuf came not. Yet in due time, the avarice of Yussuf growing, they chose another night in the dark of the second moon and repaired once more to the treasury, where, so lax already had become the watch, they mounted to the dome. Abou, upon removing the plate, at once detected the odor of pitch and advised Yussuf not to descend, but he would none of this. The thought of the gold and jewels into which on previous nights he had dipped urged him, and he descended. However, when he neared the gold he reached for it, but instead of gold he seized the scalding pitch, which when it burned, caused him to loose his hold and fall. He cried to Abou: 'I burn in hot pitch. Help me!' Abou descended and took the hand but felt it waver and grow slack. Knowing that death was at hand and that should Yussuf's body be found, not only himself but Yussuf's wife and slaves would all suffer, he drew his scimitar, which was ever at his belt, and struck off the head. Fastening this to his belt, he re-ascended the rope, replaced the plate and carefully made his way from the treasury. He then went to the house of Yussuf and gave the head to Yussuf's wife, cautioning her to secrecy.

"But the caliph, coming now every day with his treasurer to look at the treasury, was amazed to find it sealed and yet the headless body within. Knowing not how to solve the mystery of this body, he ordered the thief before him, who advised him to hang the body in the marketplace and set guards to watch any who might come to mourn or spy. Accordingly, the headless body was gibbeted and set up in the marketplace where Abou, passing afar, recognized it. Fearing that Mirza, the wife of Yussuf, who was of the tribe of the Veddi, upon whom it is obligatory that they mourn in the presence of the dead, should come to mourn here, he hastened to caution her. 'Go thou not thither,' he said; 'or, if thou must, fill two bowls with milk and go as a seller of it. If thou must weep, drop one of the bowls as if by accident and make as if thou wept over that.' Mirza accordingly filled two bowls and passing near the gibbet in the public square dropped one and thereupon began weeping as her faith demanded. The guards, noting her, thought nothing—'for here is one,' said they, 'so poor that she cries because of her misfortune.' But the caliph, calling for the guards at the end of the day to report to himself and the master thief, inquired as to what they had seen. 'We saw none,' said the chief of the guard, 'save an old woman so poor that she wept for the breaking of a bowl!' 'Dolts!' cried the master thief. 'Pigs! Did I not say take any who came to mourn? She is the widow of the thief. Try again. Scatter gold pieces under the gibbet and take any that touch them.'

"The guards scattered gold, as was commanded, and took their positions. Abou, pleased that the widow had been able to mourn and yet not be taken, came now to see what more might be done by the caliph. Seeing the gold he said: 'It is with that he wishes to tempt.' At once his pride in his skill was aroused and he determined to take some of the gold and yet not be taken. To this end he disguised himself as a ragged young beggar and one weak of wit, and with the aid of an urchin, younger than himself and as wretched, he began to play about the square, running here and there as if in some game. But before doing this he had fastened to the sole of his shoes a thick gum so that the gold might stick. The guards, deceived by the seeming youth and foolishness of Abou and his friend, said: 'These are but a child and a fool. They take no gold.' But by night, coming to count the gold, there were many pieces missing and they were sore afraid. When they reported to the caliph that night he had them flogged and new guards placed in their stead. Yet again he consulted with the master thief, who advised him to load a camel with enticing riches and have it led through the streets of the city by seeming strangers who were the worse for wine. 'This thief who eludes thee will be tempted by these riches and seek to rob them.'

"Soon after it was Abou who, prowling about the marketplace, noticed this camel laden with great wealth and led by seeming strangers. But because it was led to no particular market he thought that it must be of the caliph. He decided to take this also, for there was in his blood that which sought contest, and by now he wished the caliph, because of Yanee, to fix his thought upon him. He filled a skin with the best of wine, into which he placed a drug of the dead Yussuf's devising, and dressing himself as a shabby vendor, set forth. When he came to the street in which was the camel and saw how the drivers idled and gaped, he began to cry, 'Wine for a para! A drink of wine for a para!' The drivers drank and found it good, following Abou as he walked, drinking and chaffering with him and laughing at his dumbness, until they were within a door of the house of Mirza, the wife of the dead Yussuf, where was a gate giving into a secret court. Pausing before this until the wine should take effect, he suddenly began to gaze upward and then to point. The drivers looked but saw nothing. And the drug taking effect they fell down; whereupon Abou quickly led the camel into the court and closed the gate. When he returned and found the drivers still asleep he shaved off half the hair of their heads and their beards, then disappeared and changed his dress and joined those who were now laughing at the strangers in their plight, for they had awakened and were running here and there in search of a camel and its load and unaware of their grotesque appearance. Mirza, in order to remove all traces, had the camel killed and the goods distributed. A careful woman and housewifely, she had caused all the fat to be boiled from the meat and preserved in jars, it having a medicinal value. The caliph, having learned how it had gone with his camel, now meditated anew on how this great thief, who mocked him and who was of great wit, might be taken. Calling the master thief and others in council he recited the entire tale and asked how this prince of thieves might be caught. 'Try but one more ruse, O master,' said the master thief, who was now greatly shaken and feared for his life. 'Do thou send an old woman from house-to-house asking for camel's grease. Let her plead that it is for one who is ill. It may be that, fearing detection, the camel has been slain and the fat preserved. If any is found, mark the door of that house with grease and take all within.'

"Accordingly an old woman was sent forth chaffering of pain. In due time she came to the house of Mirza, who gave her of the grease, and when she left she made a cross upon the door. When she returned to the caliph he called his officers and guards and all proceeded toward the marked door. In the meantime Abou, having returned and seen the mark, inquired of Mirza as to what it meant. When told of the old woman's visit he called for a bowl of the camel's grease and marked the doors in all the nearest streets. The caliph, coming into the street and seeing the marks, was both enraged and filled with awe and admiration for of such wisdom he had never known. 'I give thee thy life,' he said to the master thief, 'for now I see that thou art as nothing to this one. He is shrewd beyond the wisdom of caliphs and thieves. Let us return,' and he retraced his steps to the palace, curious as to the nature and soul of this one who could so easily outwit him.

"Time went on and the caliph one day said to his vizier: 'I have been thinking of the one who robbed the treasury and my camel and the gold from under the gibbet. Such an one is wise above his day and generation and worthy of a better task. What think you? Shall I offer him a full pardon so that he may appear and be taken—or think you he will appear?' 'Do but try it, O Commander of the Faithful,' said the vizier. A proclamation was prepared and given to the criers, who announced that it was commanded by the caliph that, should the great thief appear on the marketplace at a given hour and yield himself up, a pardon full and free would be granted him and gifts of rare value heaped upon him. Yet it was not thus that the caliph intended to do.

"Now, Abou, hearing of this and being despondent over his life and the loss of Yanee and the death of Yussuf and wishing to advantage himself in some way other than by thievery, bethought him how he might accept this offer of the caliph and declare himself and yet, supposing it were a trap to seize him, escape. Accordingly he awaited the time prescribed, and when the public square was filled with guards instructed to seize him if he appeared he donned the costume of a guard and appeared among the soldiers dressed as all the others. The caliph was present to witness the taking, and when the criers surrounding him begged the thief to appear and be pardoned, Abou called out from the thick of the throng: 'Here I am, O Caliph! Amnesty!' Whereupon the caliph, thinking that now surely he would be taken, cried: 'Seize him! Seize him!' But Abou, mingling with the others, also cried: 'Seize him! Seize him!' and looked here and there as did the others. The guards, thinking him a guard, allowed him to escape, and the caliph, once more enraged and chagrined, retired. Once within his chambers he called to him his chief advisers and had prepared the following proclamation:

" 'BE IT KNOWN TO ALL

Since within the boundaries of our realm there exists one so wise that despite our commands and best efforts he is still able to work his will against ours and to elude our every effort to detect him, be it known that from having been amazed and disturbed we are now pleased and gratified that one so skillful of wit and resourceful should exist in our realm. To make plain that our appreciation is now sincere and our anger allayed it is hereby covenant with him and with all our people to whom he may appeal if we fail in our word, that if he will now present himself in person and recount to one whom we shall appoint his various adventures, it will be our pleasure to signally distinguish him above others.

YIANKO I'

"This was signed by the caliph and cried in the public places. Abou heard all but because of the previous treachery of the caliph he was now unwilling to believe that this was true. At the same time he was pleased to know that he was now held in great consideration, either for good or ill, by the caliph and his advisers, and bethought him that if it were for ill perhaps by continuing to outwit the caliph he might still succeed in winning his favor and so to a further knowledge of Yanee. To this end he prepared a reply which he posted in the public square, reading:

" 'PROCLAMATION BY THE
ONE WHOM THE
CALIPH SEEKS

Know, O Commander of the Faithful, that the one whom the caliph seeks is here among his people free from harm. He respects the will of the caliph and his good intentions, but is restrained by fear. He therefore requests that instead of being commanded to reveal himself, the caliph devise a way and appoint a time where in darkness and without danger to himself he may behold the face of the one to whom he is to reveal himself. It must be that none are present to seize him.

THE ONE WHOM THE CALIPH SEEKS.'

"Notice of this reply being brought to the caliph he forthwith took counsel with his advisers and decided that since it was plain the thief might not otherwise be taken, recourse must be had to a device that might be depended upon to lure him. Behind a certain window in the palace wall known as 'The Whispering Window,' and constantly used by all who were in distress or had suffered a wrong, which owing to the craft of others there was no hope of righting, sat at stated times and always at night, the caliph's own daughter Yanee, whose tender heart and unseeking soul were counted upon to see to it that the saddest of stories came to the ears of the caliph. It was by this means that the caliph now hoped to capture the thief. To insure that the thief should come it was publicly announced that should anyone that came be able to tell how the treasury had been entered and the gold pieces taken from under the gibbet or the camel stolen and killed, he was to be handed a bag of many dinars and a pardon in writing; later, should he present himself, he would be made a councillor of state.

"Struck by this new proclamation and the possibility of once more beholding the princess, Abou decided to match his skill against that of the caliph. He disguised himself as a vendor of tobacco and approached the window, peered through the lattice which screened it and said: 'O daughter of the great caliph, behold one who is in distress. I am he whom the caliph seeks, either to honor or slay, I know not which. Also I am he who, on one of thy journeys to the mountain of Azol and thy palace at Ish-Pari thou beheldest while passing the door of my father's rug market, for thou didst lift the curtains of thy houdah and also thy veil and didst deign to smile at me. And I have here,' and he touched his heart, 'a faded spray of the myrtles of Ish-Pari, or so it has been told me, over which I weep.'

"Yanee, shocked that she should be confronted with the great thief whom her father sought and that he should claim to be the beautiful youth she so well remembered, and yet fearing this to be some new device of the vizier or of the women of the harem, who might have heard of her strange love and who ever prayed evil against all who were younger or more beautiful than they, she was at a loss how to proceed. Feeling the need of wisdom and charity, she said: 'How says thou? Thou are the great thief whom my father seeks and yet the son of a rug merchant on whom I smiled? Had I ever smiled on a thief, which Allah forbid, would I not remember it and thee? Therefore, if it be as thou sayst, permit it that I should have a light brought that I may behold thee.' 'Readily enough, O Princess,' replied Abou, 'only if I am thus to reveal myself to thee must I not know first that thou art the maiden whom I saw? For she was kind as she was fair and would do no man an ill. Therefore if thou wilt lower thy veil, as thou didst on the day of thy departure, so that I may see, I will lift my hood so that thou mayst know that I lie not.'

"The princess replied: 'So will I, but upon one condition: should it be that thou art he upon whom thou sayst I looked with favor and yet he who also has committed these great crimes in my father's kingdom, know that thou mayst take thy pardon and thy gold and depart; but only upon the condition that never more wilt thou trouble either me or my father.'

"At this Abou shrank inwardly and a great sorrow fell upon him; for now, as at the death of Yussuf, he saw again the horror of his way. Sadly punished for his deeds, Abou promised, and when the torch was brought the princess lifted her veil. Then it was that Abou again saw the face upon which his soul had dwelt and which had caused him so much unrest. He was now so moved that he could not speak. He drew from his face its disguise and confronted her. And Yanee, seeing for the second time the face of the youth upon whom her memory had dwelt these many days, her heart misgave her and she dared not speak. Instead she lowered her veil and sat in silence, the while Abou recounted the history of his troubled life and early youth; how he had been trained in evil ways; of how he came to rob the treasury, and how the deeds since, of which the caliph complained, had been in part due to his wish to defeat the skill of the caliph. At last the princess said: 'Go, and come no more, for I dare not look upon thee, and the caliph wishes thee only ill. Yet let me tell my father that thou wilt trouble him no more,' to which Abou replied: 'Know, O Princess, thus will I do.' Then opening the lattice, Yanee handed him the false pardon and the gold, which Abou would not take. Instead he seized and kissed her hand tenderly and then departed.

"Yanee returned to her father and recounted to him the story of the robbery of the treasury and all that followed, but added that she had not been able to obtain his hand in order to have him seized because he refused to reach for the gold. The caliph, once more chagrined by Abou's cleverness in obtaining his written pardon without being taken, now meditated anew on how he might be trapped. His daughter having described Abou as both young and handsome, the caliph thought that perhaps the bait of his daughter might win him to capture and now prepared the following and last pronunciamento, to wit:

" 'TO THE PEOPLE OF
BAGHDAD

Having been defeated in all our contests with *The One Whom the Caliph Seeks,* and yet having extended to him a full pardon signed by our own hand and to which has been affixed the caliphate seal, we now deign to declare that if this wisest of lawbreakers will now present himself in person before us and accept of us our homage and good will, we will, assuming him to be young and of agreeable manners, accept him as the affiant of our daughter. To this end we have ordered that the third day of the seventh moon be observed as a holiday, that a public feast be prepared and that our people assemble before us in our great court. Should this wisest of fugitives appear and declare himself we will there publicly reaffirm and do as is here written and accept him into our life and confidence. I have said it.

                                                                YIANKO I'

"The caliph showed this to his daughter and she sighed, for full well she knew that the caliph's plan would prove vain—for had not Abou said that he would return no more? But the caliph proceeded, thinking this would surely bring about Abou's capture.

"In the meantime in the land of Yemen, of which Abou was the rightful heir, many things had transpired. His father, Kar-Shem, having died and the wretched pretender, Bab-el-Bar, having failed after a revolution to attain to Kar-Shem's seat, confessed to the adherents of Kar-Shem the story of the Prince Hussein's abduction and sale into slavery to a rug merchant in Baghdad. In consequence, heralds and a royal party were at once sent forth to discover Hussein. They came to Baghdad and found the widow of Yussuf, who told them of the many slaves Yussuf had owned, among them a child named Hussein to whom they had given the name of Abou.

"And so, upon Abou's return from 'The Whispering Window,' there were awaiting him at the house of Mirza the representatives of his own kingdom, who, finding him young and handsome and talented, and being convinced by close questioning that he was really Hussein, he was apprised of his dignity and worth and honored as the successor of Kar-Shem in the name of the people of Yemen.

"And now Hussein (once Abou), finding himself thus ennobled, bethought him of the beautiful Yanee and her love for him and his undying love for her. Also he felt a desire to outwit the caliph in one more contest. To this end he ordered his present entourage to address the caliph as an embassy fresh from Yemen, saying that having long been in search of their prince they had now found him, and to request of him the courtesy of his goodwill and present consideration for their lord. The caliph, who wished always to be at peace with all people, and especially those of Yemen, who were great and powerful, was most pleased at this and sent a company of courtiers to Hussein, who now dwelt with his entourage at one of the great caravanseries of the city, requesting that he come forthwith to the palace that he might be suitably entertained. And now Abou, visiting the caliph in his true figure, was received by him in great state, and many and long were the public celebrations ordered in his honor.

"Among these was the holiday proclaimed by Yianko in order to entrap Abou. And Yianko, wishing to amuse and entertain his guest, told him the full history of the great thief and of his bootless efforts thus far to take him. He admitted to Hussein his profound admiration for Abou's skill and ended by saying that should any one know how Abou might be taken he would be willing to give to that one a place in his council, or, supposing he were young and noble, the hand of his daughter. At this Hussein, enticed by the thought of so winning Yanee, declared that he himself would attempt to solve the mystery and now prepared to appear as a fierce robber, the while he ordered one of his followers to impersonate himself as prince for that day.

"The great day of the feast having arrived and criers having gone through the streets of the city announcing the feast and the offer of the caliph to Abou, there was much rejoicing. Long tables were set in the public square, and flags and banners were strung. The beautiful Yanee was told of her father's vow to Hussein, but she trusted in Abou and his word and his skill and so feared naught. At last, the multitude having gathered and the caliph and his courtiers and the false Hussein having taken their places at the head of the feast, the caliph raised his hand for silence. The treasurer, taking his place upon one of the steps leading to the royal board, reread the proclamation and called upon Abou to appear and before all the multitude receive the favor of the caliph or be forever banned. Abou, or Hussein, who in the guise of a fierce mountain outlaw had mingled with the crowd, now came forward and holding aloft the pardon of the caliph announced that he was indeed the thief and could prove it. Also, that as written he would exact of the caliph his daughter's hand. The caliph, astounded that one so uncouth and fierce-seeming should be so wise as the thief had proved or should ask of him his daughter's hand, was puzzled and anxious for a pretext on which he might be restrained. Yet with all the multitude before him and his word given, he scarce knew how to proceed or what to say. Then it was that Yanee, concealed behind a lattice, sent word to her father that this fierce soul was not the one who had come to her but an impostor. The caliph, now suspecting treachery and more mischief, ordered this seeming false Abou seized and bound, whereupon the fictitious Hussein, masquerading in Hussein's clothes, came forward and asked for the bandit's release for the reason that he was not a true bandit at all but the true prince, whom they had sought far and wide.

"Then the true Hussein, tiring of the jest and laying aside his bandit garb, took his place at the foot of the throne and proceeded to relate to Yianko the story of his life. At this the caliph, remembering his word and seeing in Abou, now that he was the Prince of Yemen, an entirely satisfactory husband for Yanee, had her brought forward. Whereupon the caliph declared that he would gladly accept so wise a prince, not only as his son by marriage but as his heir, and that at his death both he and Yanee were jointly to rule over his kingdom and their own. There followed scenes of great rejoicing among the people, and Hussein and Yanee rode together before them.

"And now, O my hearers," continued Gazzar most artfully, although his tale was done, "ye have heard how it was with Abou the unfortunate, who came through cleverness to nothing but good—a beautiful love, honor and wealth and the rule of two realms—whereas I, poor wanderer that I am—"

But the company, judging that he was about to plead for more anna, and feeling, and rightly, that for so thin a tale he had been paid enough and to spare, arose and as one man walked away. Gazzar counted his small store of anna and tucking his tambour into his rags, turned his steps wearily toward the mosque, where before eating it was, as the Koran commanded, that he must pray.

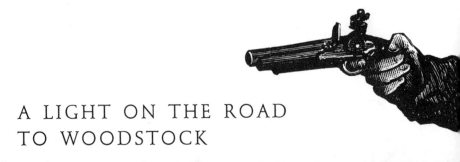

A LIGHT ON THE ROAD
TO WOODSTOCK

Ellis Peters

A deeply religious age may prove as fruitful to the crime writer as an age of licentiousness and debauchery, for at such a time the contrast between good and evil will be starker, while the existence of high ideals will allow those who would defraud and dupe better opportunities to find an unsuspecting mark. No series character more successfully combines a knowledge of the world at its most corrupt with the aspiration to goodness than Ellis Peters's medieval Benedictine monk Brother Cadfael, a soldier initiated into the religious life late, after a career as a crusader and free knight. The author of this most successful of all historical crime series, who took the name Ellis Peters to set her crime writings apart from the mainstream work published under her given name, Edith Pargeter, resembles her character in having begun this seminal work of her career late, with many published books behind her.

The king's court was in no hurry to return to England, that late autumn of 1120, even though the fighting, somewhat desultory in these last stages, was long over, and the enforced peace sealed by a royal marriage. King Henry had brought to a successful conclusion his sixteen years of patient, cunning, relentless plotting, fighting, and manipulating, and could now sit back in high content, master not only of England but of Normandy, too. What the Conqueror had misguidedly dealt out in two separate parcels to his two elder sons, his youngest son had now put together again and clamped into one. Not without a hand in removing from the light of day, some said, both of his brothers, one of whom had been shovelled into a hasty grave under the tower of Winchester, while the other was a prisoner in Devizes, and unlikely ever to be seen again by the outer world.

The court could well afford to linger to enjoy victory, while Henry trimmed into neatness the last loose edges still to be made secure. But his fleet was already preparing at Barfleur for the voyage back to England, and he would be home before the month ended. Meantime, many of his barons and knights who had fought his battles were withdrawing their contingents and making for home, among them one Roger Mauduit, who had a young and handsome wife waiting for him, certain legal business on his mind, and twenty-five men to ship back to England, most of them to be paid off on landing.

There were one or two among the miscellaneous riffraff he had recruited here in Normandy on his lord's behalf whom it might be worth keeping on in his own service, along with the few men of his household, at least until he was safely home. The vagabond clerk turned soldier, let him be unfrocked priest or what he might, was an excellent copyist and a sound Latin scholar, and could put legal documents in their best and most presentable form, in good time for the king's court at Woodstock. And the Welsh man-at-arms, blunt and insubordinate as he was, was also experienced and accomplished in arms, a man of his word, once given, and utterly reliable in whatever situation on land or sea, for in both elements he had long practice behind him. Roger was well aware that he was not greatly loved, and had little faith in either the valour or the loyalty of his own men. But this Welshman from Gwynedd, by way of Antioch and Jerusalem and only God knew where else, had imbibed the code of arms and wore it as a second nature. With or without love, such service as he pledged, that he would provide.

Roger put it to them both as his men were embarking at Barfleur, in the middle of a deceptively placid November, and upon a calm sea.

"I would have you two accompany me to my manor of Sutton Mauduit by Northampton, when we disembark, and stay in my pay until a certain lawsuit I have against the abbey of Shrewsbury is resolved. The king intends to come to Woodstock when he arrives in England, and will be there to preside over my case on the twenty-third day of this month. Will you remain in my service until that day?"

The Welshman said that he would, until that day or until the case was resolved. He said it indifferently, as one who has not business of any importance anywhere in the world to pull him in another direction. As well Northampton as anywhere else. As well Woodstock. And after Woodstock? Why anywhere in particular? There was no identifiable light beckoning him anywhere, along any road. The world was wide, fair, and full of savour, but without signposts.

Alard, the tatterdemalion clerk, hesitated, scratched his thick thatch of grizzled red hair, and finally also said yes, but as if some vague regret drew him in another direction. It meant pay for some days more, he could not afford to say no.

"I would have gone with him with better heart," he said later, when they were leaning on the rail together, watching the low blue line of the English shore rise out of a placid sea, "if he had been taking a more westerly road."

"Why that?" asked Cadfael ap Meilyr ap Dafydd. "Have you kin in the west?"

"I had once. I have not now."

"Dead?"

"I am the one who died." Alard heaved lean shoulders in a helpless shrug, and grinned. "Fifty-seven brothers I had, and now I'm brotherless. I begin to miss my kin, now I'm past forty. I never valued them when I was young." He slanted a rueful glance at his companion and shook his head. "I was a monk of Evesham, an *oblatus,* given to God by my father when I was five years old. When I was fifteen I could no longer abide to live my life in one place, and I ran. Stability is one of the vows we take—to be content in one place, and go abroad only when ordered. That was not for me, not then. My sort they call *vagus*—frivolous minds that must wander. Well, I've wandered far enough, God knows, in my time. I begin to fear I can never stand still again."

The Welshman drew his cloak about him against the chill of the wind. "Are you hankering for a return?"

"Even you seamen must drop anchor somewhere at last," said Alard. "They'd have my hide if I went back, that I know. But there's this about penance, it pays all debts, and leaves the record clear. They'd find a place for me, once I'd paid. But I don't know . . . I don't know . . . The *vagus* is still in me. I'm torn two ways."

"After twenty-five years," said Cadfael, "a month or two more for quiet thinking can do no harm. Copy his papers for him and take the case until his business is settled."

They were much of an age, though the renegade monk looked the elder by ten years, and much knocked about by the world he had coveted from within the cloister. It had not paid him well in goods or gear, for he went threadbare and thin, but in wisdom he might have got his fair wages. A little soldiering, a little clerking, some horsetending, any labour that came to hand, until he could turn his hand to almost anything a hale man can do. He had seen, he said, Italy as far south as Rome, served once for a time under the Court of Flanders, crossed the mountains into Spain, never abiding anywhere for long. His feet still served him, but his mind grew weary of the road.

"And you?" he said, eyeing his companion, whom he had known now for a year in this last campaign. "You're something of a *vagus* yourself, by your own account. All those years crusading and battling corsairs in the midland sea, and still you have not enough of it, but must cross the sea again to get buffeted about Normandy. Had you no better business of your own, once you got back to England, but you must enlist again in this muddled mêlée of a war? No woman to take your mind off fighting?"

"What of yourself? Free of the cloister, free of the vows!"

"Somehow," said Alard, himself puzzled, "I never saw it so. A woman here and there, yes, when the heat was on me, and there was a woman by and willing, but marriage and wiving . . . it never seemed to me I had the right."

The Welshman braced his feet on the gently swaying deck and watched the distant shore draw nearer. A broad-set, sturdy, muscular man in his healthy prime, brown-haired and brown-skinned from eastern suns and outdoor living, well-provided in leather coat and good cloth, and well-armed with sword and dagger. A comely enough face, strongly featured, with the bold bones of his race—there had been women, in his time, who found him handsome.

"I had a girl," he said meditatively, "years back, before ever I went crusading. But I left her when I took the Cross, left her for three years and stayed away seventeen. The truth is, in the east I forgot her, and in the west she, thanks be to God, had forgotten me. I did enquire, when I got back. She'd made a better bargain, and married a decent, solid man who had nothing of the *vagus* in him. A guildsman and counsellor of the town of Shrewsbury, no less. So I shed the load from my conscience and went back to what I knew, soldiering. With no regrets," he said simply. "It was all over and done, years since. I doubt if I should have known her again, or she me." There had been other women's faces in the years between, still vivid in his memory, while hers had faded into mist.

"And what will you do," asked Alard, "now the king's got everything he wanted, married his son to Anjou and Maine, and made an end of fighting? Go back to the east? There's never any want of squabbles there to keep a man busy."

"No," said Cadfael, eyes fixed on the shore that began to show the solidity of land and the undulations of cliff and down. For that, too, was over and done, years since, and not as well done as once he had hoped. This desultory campaigning in Normandy was little more than a postscriptum, an afterthought, a means of filling in the interim between what was past and what was to come, and as yet unrevealed. All he knew of it was that it must be something new and momentous, a door opening into another room. "It seems we have both a few days' grace, you and I, to find out where we are going. We'd best make good use of the time."

There was stir enough before night to keep them from wondering beyond the next moment, or troubling their minds about what was past or what was to come. Their ship put into the roads with a steady and favourable wind, and made course into Southampton before the light faded, and there was work for Alard checking the gear as it was unloaded, and for Cadfael disembarking the horses. A night's sleep in lodgings and stables in the town, and they would be on their way with the dawn.

"So the king's due in Woodstock," said Alard, rustling sleepily in his straw in a warm loft over the horses, "in time to sit in judgement on the twenty-third of the month. He makes his forest lodges the hub of his kingdom; there's more statecraft talked at Woodstock, so they say, than ever at Westminster. And he keeps his beasts there—lions and leopards—even camels. Did you ever see camels, Cadfael? There in the east?"

"Saw them and rode them. Common as horses there, hard-working and serviceable, but uncomfortable riding, and foul-tempered. Thank God it's horses we'll be mounting in the morning." And after a long silence, on the edge of sleep, he asked curiously into the straw-scented darkness: "If ever you do go back, what is it you want of Evesham?"

"Do I know?" responded Alard drowsily, and followed that with a sudden sharpening sigh, again fully awake. "The silence, it might be . . . or the stillness. To have no more running to do . . . to have arrived, and have no more need to run. The appetite changes. Now I think it would be a beautiful thing to be still."

The manor which was the head of Roger Mauduit's scattered and substantial honour lay somewhat southeast of Northampton, comfortably under the lee of the long ridge of wooded hills where the king had a chase, and spreading its extensive fields over the rich lowland between. The house was of stone, and ample, over a deep undercroft, and with a low tower providing two small chambers at the eastern end, and the array of sturdy byres, barns, and stables that lined the containing walls was impressive. Someone had proved a good steward while the lord was away about King Henry's business.

The furnishings of the hall were no less eloquent of good management, and the men and maids of the household went about their work with a brisk wariness that showed they went in some awe of whoever presided over their labours. It needed only a single day of watching the Lady Eadwina in action to show who ruled the roost here. Roger Mauduit had married a wife not only handsome, but also efficient and masterful. She had had her own way here for three years, and by all the signs had enjoyed the dominance. She might, even, be none too glad to resign her charge now, however glad she might be to have her lord home again.

She was a tall, graceful woman, ten years younger than Roger, with an abundance of fair hair, and large blue eyes that went discreetly half-veiled by absurdly long lashes most of the time, but flashed a bright and steely challenge when she opened them fully. Her smile was likewise discreet and almost constant, concealing rather than revealing whatever went on in her mind; and though her welcome to her returning lord left nothing to be desired, but lavished on him every possible tribute of ceremony and affection from the moment his horse entered at the gate, Cadfael could not but wonder whether she was not, at the same time, taking stock of every man he brought in with him, and every article of gear or harness or weaponry in their equipment, as one taking jealous inventory of his goods and reserves to make sure nothing was lacking.

She had her little son by the hand, a boy of about seven years old, and the child had the same fair colouring, the same contained and almost supercilious smile, and was as spruce and fine as his mother.

The lady received Alard with a sweeping glance that deprecated his tatterdemalion appearance and doubted his morality, but nevertheless was willing to accept and make use of his abilities. The clerk who kept the manor roll and the accounts was efficient enough, but had no Latin, and could not write a good court hand. Alard was whisked away to a small table set in the angle of the great hearth, and kept hard at work copying certain charters and letters, and preparing them for presentation.

"This suit of his is against the abbey of Shrewsbury," said Alard, freed of his labours after supper in the hall. "I recall you said that girl of yours had married a merchant in that town. Shrewsbury is a Benedictine house, like mine of Evesham." His, he called it still, after so many years of abandoning it; or his again, after time had brushed away whatever division there had ever been. "You must know it, if you come from there."

"I was born in Trefriw, in Gwynedd," said Cadfael, "but I took service early with an English wool merchant, and came to Shrewsbury with his household. Fourteen, I was then—in Wales fourteen is manhood, and as I was a good lad with the short bow, and took kindly to the sword, I suppose I was worth my keep. The best of my following years were spent in Shrewsbury, I know it like my own palm, abbey and all. My master sent me there a year and more, to get my letters. But I quit that service when he died. I'd pledged nothing to the son, and he was a poor shadow of his father. That was when I took the Cross. So did many like me, all afire. I won't say what followed was all ash, but it burned very low at times."

"It's Mauduit who holds this disputed land," said Alard, "and the abbey that sues to recover it, and the thing's been going on four years without a settlement, ever since the old man here died. From what I know of the Benedictines, I'd rate their honesty above our Roger's, I tell you straight. And yet his charters seem to be genuine, as far as I can tell."

"Where is this land they're fighting over?" asked Cadfael.

"It's a manor by the name of Rotesley, near Stretton, demesne, village, advowson of the church and all. It seems when the great earl was just dead and his abbey still building, Roger's father gave Rotesley to the abbey. No dispute about that, the charter's there to show it. But the abbey granted it back to him as tenant for life, to live out his latter years there undisturbed, Roger being then married and installed here at Sutton. That's where the dispute starts. The abbey claims it was clearly agreed the tenancy ended with the old man's death, that he himself understood it so, and intended it should be restored to the abbey as soon as he was out of it. While Roger says there was no such agreement to restore it unconditionally, but the tenancy was granted to the Mauduits, and ought to be hereditary. And so far he's hung on to it tooth and claw. After several hearings they remitted it to the king himself. And that's why you and I, my friend, will be off with his lordship to Woodstock the day after tomorrow."

"And how do you rate his chances of success? He seems none too sure himself," said Cadfael, "to judge by his short temper and nailbiting this last day or so."

"Why, the charter could have been worded better. It says simply that the village is granted back in tenancy during the old man's lifetime, but fails to say anything about what shall happen afterwards, whatever may have been intended. From what I hear, they were on very good terms, Abbot Fulchered and the old lord, agreements between them on other matters in the manor book are worded as between men who trusted each other. The witnesses are all of them dead, as Abbot Fulchered is dead. It's one Godefrid now. But for all I know the abbey may hold letters that have passed between the two, and a letter is witness of intent, no less than a formal charter. All in good time we shall see."

The nobility still sat at the high table, in no haste to retire, Roger brooding over his wine, of which he had already drunk his fair share and more. Cadfael eyed them with interest, seen thus in a family setting. The boy had gone to his bed, hauled away by an elderly nurse, but the Lady Eadwina sat in close attendance at her lord's left hand, and kept his cup well filled, smiling her faint, demure smile. On her left sat a very fine young squire of about twenty-five years, deferential and discreet, with a smile somehow the male reflection of her own. The source of both was secret, the spring of their pleasure or amusement, or whatever caused them so to smile, remained private and slightly unnerving, like the carved stone smiles of certain very old statues Cadfael had seen in Greece, long ago. For all his mild, amiable, and ornamental appearance, combed and curled and courtly, he was a big, well-set-up young fellow, with a set to his smooth jaw. Cadfael studied him with interest, for he was plainly privileged here.

"Goscelin," said Alard by way of explanation, following his friend's glance. "Her right-hand man while Roger was away."

Her left-hand man now, by the look of it, thought Cadfael. For her left hand and Goscelin's right were private under the table, while she spoke winningly into her husband's ear; and if those two hands were not paddling palms at this moment Cadfael was very much deceived. Above and below the drapings of the board were two different worlds. "I wonder," he said thoughtfully, "what she's breathing into Roger's ear now."

What the lady was breathing into her husband's ear was, in fact: "You fret over nothing, my lord. What does it matter how strong his proofs, if he never reaches Woodstock in time to present them? You know the law; if one party fails to appear, judgement is given for the other. The assize judges may allow more than one default if they please, but do you think King Henry will? Whoever fails of keeping tryst with him will be felled on the spot. And you know the road by which Prior Heribert must come." Her voice was a silken purr in his ear. "And have you not a hunting lodge in the forest north of Woodstock, through which that road passes?"

Roger's hand had stiffened round the stem of his wine cup. He was not so drunk but he was listening intently.

"Shrewsbury to Woodstock will be a two- or three-day journey to such a rider. All you need do is have a watcher on the road north of you, to give warning. The woods are thick enough, masterless men have been known to haunt there. Even if he comes by daylight, your part need never be known. Hide him but a few days, it will be long enough. Then turn him loose by night, and who's ever to know what footpads held and robbed him? You need not ever touch his parchments—robbers would count them worthless. Take what common thieves would take, and theirs will be the blame."

Roger opened his tight-shut mouth to say in a doubtful growl: "He'll not be travelling alone."

"Hah! Two or three abbey servants—they'll run like hares. You need not trouble yourself over them. Three stout, silent men of your own will be more than enough."

He brooded, and began to think so, too, and to review in his mind the men of his household, seeking the right hands for such work. Not the Welshman and the clerk, the strangers here; their part was to be the honest onlookers, in case there should ever be questions asked.

They left Sutton Mauduit on the twentieth day of November, which seemed unnecessarily early, though as Roger had decreed that they should settle in his hunting lodge in the forest close by Woodstock, which meant conveying stores with them to make the household habitable and provision it for a party for, presumably, a stay of three nights at least, it was perhaps a wise precaution. Roger was taking no chances in his suit, he said; he meant to be established on the ground in good time, and have all his proofs in order.

"But so he has," said Alard, pricked in his professional pride, "for I've gone over everything with him, and the case, if open in default of specific instructions, is plain enough and will stand up. What the abbey can muster, who knows? They say the abbot is not well, which is why his prior comes in his place. My work is done."

He had the faraway look in his eye, as the party rode out and faced westward, of one either penned and longing to be where he could but see, or loose and weary and being drawn home. Either a *vagus* escaping outward, or a penitent flying back in haste before the doors should close against him. There must indeed be something desirable and lovely to cause a man to look towards it with that look on his face.

Three men-at-arms and two grooms accompanied Roger, in addition to Alard and Cadfael, whose term of service would end with the session in court, after which they might go where they would. Cadfael horsed, since he owned his own mount, Alard afoot, since the pony he rode belonged to Roger. It came as something of a surprise to Cadfael that the squire Goscelin should also saddle up and ride with the party, very debonair and well-armed with sword and dagger.

"I marvel," said Cadfael drily, "that the lady doesn't need him at home for her own protection, while her lord's absent."

The Lady Eadwina, however, bade farewell to the whole party with the greatest serenity, and to her husband with demonstrative affection, putting forward her little son to be embraced and kissed. Perhaps, thought Cadfael, relenting, I do her wrong simply because I feel chilled by that smile of hers. For all I know she may be the truest wife living.

They set out early and before Buckingham made a halt at the small and penurious priory of Bradwell, where Roger elected to spend the night, keeping his three men-at-arms with him, while Goscelin with the rest of the party rode on to the hunting lodge to make all ready for their lord's reception the following day. It was growing dark by the time they arrived, and the bustle of kindling fire and torches, and unloading the bed linen and stores from the sumpter ponies went on into the night. The lodge was small, stockaded, well-furnished with stabling and mews, and in thick woodland, a place comfortable enough once they had a roaring fire on the hearth and food on the table.

"The road the prior of Shrewsbury will be coming by," said Alard, warming himself by the fire after supper, "passes through Evesham. As like as not they'll stay the last night there." With every mile west, Cadfael had seen him straining forward with mounting eagerness. "The road cannot be far away from us here, it passes through the forest."

"It must be nearly thirty miles to Evesham," said Cadfael. "A long day's riding for a clerical party. It will be night by the time they ride past into Woodstock. If you're set on going, stay at least to get your pay, for you'll need it before the thirty miles is done."

They went to their slumber in the warmth of the hall without a word more said. But he would go, Alard, whether he himself knew it yet or not. Cadfael knew it. His friend was a tired horse with the scent of the stable in his nostrils; nothing would stop him now until he reached it.

It was well into the middle of the day when Roger and his escort arrived, and they approached not directly, as the advance party had done, but from the woods to the north, as though they had been indulging in a little hunting or hawking by the way, except that they had neither hawk nor hound with them. A fine, clear, cool day for riding, there was no reason in the world why they should not go roundabout for the pure pleasure of it—and indeed, they seemed to come in high content!—but that Roger's mind had been so preoccupied and so anxious concerning his lawsuit that distractions seemed unlikely. Cadfael was given to thinking about unlikely developments, which from old campaigns he knew to prove significant in most cases. Goscelin, who was out at the gate to welcome them in, was apparently oblivious to the direction from which they came. That way lay Alard's highway to his rest. But what meaning ought it to have for Roger Mauduit?

The table was lavish that night, and lord and squire drank well and ate well, and gave no sign of any care, though they might, Cadfael thought, watching them from his lower place, seem a little tight and knife-edged. Well, the king's court could account for that. Shrewsbury's prior was drawing steadily nearer, with whatever weapons he had for the battle. But it seemed rather an exultant tension than an anxious one. Was Roger counting his chickens already?

The morning of the twenty-second of November dawned, and the noon passed, and with every moment Alard's restlessness and abstraction grew, until with evening it possessed him utterly, and he could no longer resist. He presented himself before Roger after supper, when his mood might be mellow from good food and wine.

"My lord, with the morrow my service to you is completed. You need me no longer, and with your goodwill I would set forth now for where

I am going. I go afoot and need provision for the road. If you have been content with my work, pay me what is due, and let me go."

It seemed that Roger had been startled out of some equally absorbing preoccupation of his own, and was in haste to return to it, for he made no demur, but paid at once. To do him justice, he had never been a grudging paymaster. He drove as hard a bargain as he could at the outset, but once the agreement was made, he kept it.

"Go when you please," he said. "Fill your bag from the kitchen for the journey when you leave. You did good work, I give you that."

And he returned to whatever it was that so engrossed his thoughts, and Alard went to collect the proffered largesse and his own meagre possessions.

"I am going," he said, meeting Cadfael in the hall doorway. "I must go." There was no more doubt in voice or face. "They will take me back, though in the lowest place. From that there's no falling. The blessed Benedict wrote in the Rule that even to the third time of staying a man may be received again if he promise full amendment."

It was a dark night, without moon or stars but in fleeting moments when the wind ripped apart the cloud covering to let through a brief gleam of moonlight. The weather had grown gusty and wild in the last two days, the king's fleet must have had a rough crossing from Barfleur.

"You'd do better," urged Cadfael, "to wait for morning, and go by daylight. Here's a safe bed, and the king's peace, however well enforced, hardly covers every mile of the king's highroads."

But Alard would not wait. The yearning was on him too strongly, and a penniless vagabond who had ventured all the roads of Christendom by day or night was hardly likely to flinch from the last thirty miles of his wanderings.

"Then I'll go with you as far as the road, and see you on your way," said Cadfael.

There was a mile or so of track through thick forest between them and the highroad that bore away west-northwest on the upland journey to Evesham. The ribbon of open highway, hemmed on both sides by trees, was hardly less dark than the forest itself. King Henry had fenced in his private park at Woodstock to house his wild beasts, but maintained also his hunting chase here, many miles in extent. At the road they parted, and Cadfael stood to watch his friend march steadily away towards the west,

eyes fixed ahead, upon his penance and his absolution, a tired man with
a rest assured.

Cadfael turned back towards the lodge as soon as the receding shadow
had melted into the night. He was in no haste to go in, for the night,
though blustery, was not cold, and he was in no mind to seek the
company of others of the party now that the one best known to him was
gone, and gone in so mysteriously rapt a fashion. He walked on among
the trees, turning his back on his bed for a while.

The constant thrashing of branches in the wind all but drowned the
scuffling and shouting that suddenly broke out behind him, at some
distance among the trees, until a horse's shrill whinny brought him about
with a jerk, and set him running through the underbrush towards the spot
where confused voices yelled alarm and broken bushes thrashed. The
clamour seemed some little way off, and he was startled as he shouldered
his way headlong through a thicket to collide heavily with two entangled
bodies, send them spinning apart, and himself fall asprawl upon one of
them in the flattened grass. The man under him uttered a scared and angry
cry, and the voice was Roger's. The other man had made no sound at all,
but slid away very rapidly and lightly to vanish among the trees, a tall
shadow swallowed in shadows.

Cadfael drew off in haste, reaching an arm to hoist the winded man.
"My lord, are you hurt? What in God's name is to do here?" The sleeve
he clutched slid warm and wet under his hand. "You're injured! Hold fast,
let's see what harm's done before you move . . ."

Then there was the voice of Goscelin, for once loud and vehement in
alarm, shouting for his lord and crashing headlong through bush and brake
to fall on his knees beside Roger, lamenting and raging.

"My lord, my lord, what happened here? What rogues were those,
loose in the woods? Dared they waylay travellers so close to the king's
highway? You're hurt—here's blood . . ."

Roger got his breath back and sat up, feeling at his left arm below the
shoulder, and wincing. "A scratch. My arm . . . God curse him, whoever
he may be, the fellow struck for my heart. Man, if you had not come
charging like a bull, I might have been dead. You hurled me off the point
of his dagger. Thank God, there's no great harm, but I bleed . . . Help me
back home!"

"That a man may not walk by night in his own woods," fumed
Goscelin, hoisting his lord carefully to his feet, "without being set upon

by outlaws! Help here, you, Cadfael, take his other arm . . . Footpads so close to Woodstock! Tomorrow we must turn out the watch to comb these tracks and hunt them out of cover, before they kill . . ."

"Get me withindoors," snapped Roger, "and have this coat and shirt off me, and let's staunch this bleeding. I'm alive, that's the main!"

They helped him back between them, through the more open ways towards the lodge. It dawned on Cadfael, as they went, that the clamour of furtive battle had ceased completely, even the wind had abated, and somewhere on the road, distantly, he caught the rhythm of galloping hooves, very fast and light, as of a riderless horse in panic flight.

The gash in Roger Mauduit's left arm, just below the shoulder, was long but not deep, and grew shallower as it descended. The stroke that marked him thus could well have been meant for his heart. Cadfael's hurtling impact, at the very moment the attack was launched, had been the means of averting murder. The shadow that had melted into the night had no form, nothing about it rendered it human or recognisable. He had heard an outcry and run towards it, a projectile to strike attacked and attacker apart; questioned, that was all he could say.

For which, said Roger, bandaged and resting and warmed with mulled wine, he was heartily thankful. And indeed, Roger was behaving with remarkable fortitude and calm for a man who had just escaped death. By the time he had demonstrated to his dismayed grooms and men-at-arms that he was alive and not much the worse, appointed the hour when they should set out for Woodstock in the morning, and been helped to his bed by Goscelin, there was even a suggestion of complacency about him, as though a gash in the arm was a small price to pay for the successful retention of a valuable property and the defeat of his clerical opponents.

In the court of the palace of Woodstock the king's chamberlains, clerks, and judges were fluttering about in a curiously distracted manner, or so it seemed to Cadfael, standing apart among the commoners to observe their antics. They gathered in small groups, conversing in low voices and with anxious faces, broke apart to regroup with others of their kind, hurried in and out among the litigants, avoiding or brushing off all questions, exchanged documents, hurried to the door to peer out, as if looking for some late arrival. And there was indeed one litigant who had not kept to his time, for there was no sign of a Benedictine prior among those assembled, nor had anyone appeared to explain or justify his absence. And Roger Mauduit, in spite of his still and painful arm, continued to relax, with ever-increasing assurance, into shining complacency.

The appointed hour was already some minutes past when four agitated fellows, two of them Benedictine brothers, made a hasty entrance, and accosted the presiding clerk.

"Sir," bleated the leader, loud in nervous dismay, "we here are come from the abbey of Shrewsbury, escort to our prior, who was on his way to plead a case at law here. Sir, you must hold him excused, for it is not his blame nor ours that he cannot appear. In the forest some two miles north, as we rode hither last night in the dark, we were attacked by a band of lawless robbers, and they have seized our prior and dragged him away . . ."

The spokesman's voice had risen shrilly in his agitation, he had the attention of every man in the hall by this time. Certainly he had Cadfael's. Masterless men some two miles out of Woodstock, plying their trade last night, could only be the same who had happened upon Roger Mauduit and all but been the death of him. Any such gang, so close to the court, was astonishing enough, there could hardly be two. The clerk was outraged at the very idea.

"Seized and captured him? And you four were with him? Can this be true? How many were they who attacked you?"

"We could not tell for certain. Three at least—but they were lying in ambush, we had no chance to stand them off. They pulled him from his horse and were off into the trees with him. They knew the woods, and we did not. Sir, we did go after them, but they beat us off."

It was evident they had done their best, for two of them showed bruised and scratched, and all were soiled and torn as to their clothing.

"We have hunted through the night, but found no trace, only we caught his horse a mile down the highway as we came hither. So we plead here that our prior's absence be not seen as a default, for indeed he would have been here in the town last night if all had gone as it should."

"Hush, wait!" said the clerk peremptorily.

All heads had turned towards the door of the hall, where a great flurry of officials had suddenly surged into view, cleaving through the press with fixed and ominous haste, to take the centre of the floor below the king's empty dais. A chamberlain, elderly and authoritative, struck the floor loudly with his staff and commanded silence. And at sight of his face silence fell like a stone.

"My lords, gentlemen, all who have pleas here this day, and all others present, you are bidden to disperse, for there will be no hearings today. All suits that should be heard here must be postponed three days, and will be heard by His Grace's judges. His Grace the king cannot appear."

This time the silence fell again like a heavy curtain, muffling even thought or conjecture.

"The court is in mourning from this hour. We have received news of desolating import. His Grace with the greater part of his fleet made the crossing to England safely, as is known, but the *Blanche Nef,* in which His Grace's son and heir, Prince William, with all his companions and many other noble souls were embarked, put to sea late, and was caught in gales before ever clearing Barfleur. The ship is lost, split upon a rock, foundered with all hands, not a soul is come safe to land. Go hence quietly, and pray for the souls of the flower of this realm."

So that was the end of one man's year of triumph, an empty achievement, a ruinous victory, Normandy won, his enemies routed, and now everything swept aside, broken apart upon an obstinate rock, washed away in a malicious sea. His only lawful son, recently married in splendour, now denied even a coffin and a grave, for if ever they found those royal bodies it would be by the relenting grace of God, for the sea seldom put its winnings ashore by Barfleur. Even some of his unlawful sons, of whom there were many, gone down with their royal brother, no one left but the one legal daughter to inherit a barren empire.

Cadfael walked alone in a corner of the king's park and considered the foolishness of mortal vainglory, that was paid for with such a bitter price. But also he thought of the affairs of little men, to whom even a luckless king owed justice. For somewhere there was still to be sought the lost prior of Shrewsbury, carried off by masterless men in the forest, a litigant who might still be lost three days hence, when his suit came up again for hearing, unless someone in the meantime knew where to look for him.

He was in little doubt now. A lawless gang at liberty so close to a royal palace was in any case unlikely enough, and Cadfael was liable to brood on the unlikely. But that there should be two—no, that was impossible. And if one only, then that same one whose ambush he had overheard at some distance, yet close enough, too close for comfort, to Roger Mauduit's hunting lodge.

Probably the unhappy brothers from Shrewsbury were off beating the wilds of the forest afresh. Cadfael knew better where to look. No doubt

Roger was biting his nails in some anxiety over the delay, but he had no reason to suppose that three days would release the captive to appear against him, nor was he paying much attention to what his Welsh man-at-arms was doing with this time.

Cadfael took his horse and rode back without haste towards the hunting lodge. He left in the early dusk, as soon as the evening meal was over in Mauduit's lodging. No one was paying any heed to him by that time of day. All Roger had to do was hold his tongue and keep his wits about him for three days, and the disputed manor would still be adjudged to him. Everything was beautifully in hand, after all.

Two of the men-at-arms and one groom had been left behind at the hunting lodge. Cadfael doubted if the man they guarded was to be found in the house itself, for unless he was blindfolded he would be able to gather far too much knowledge of his surroundings, and the fable of the masterless men would be tossed into the rubbish heap. No, he would be held in darkness, or dim light at best, even during the day, in straw or the rush flooring of a common hut, fed adequately but plainly and roughly, as wild men might keep a prisoner they were too cautious to kill, or too superstitious, until they turned him loose in some remote place, stripped of everything he had of value. On the other hand, he must be somewhere securely inside the boundary fence, otherwise there would be too high a risk of his being found. Between the gate and the house there were trees enough to obscure the large holding of a man of consequence. Somewhere among the stables and barns, or the now empty kennels, there he must be held.

Cadfael tethered his horse in cover well aside from the lodge and found himself a perch in a tall oak tree, from which vantage point he could see over the fence into the courtyard.

He was in luck. The three within fed themselves at leisure before they fed the prisoner, preferring to wait for dark. By the time the groom emerged from the hall with a pitcher and a bowl in his hands, Cadfael had his night eyes. They were quite easy about their charge, expecting no interference from any man. The groom vanished momentarily between the trees within the enclosure, but appeared again at one of the low buildings tucked under the fence, set down his pitcher for a moment while he hoisted clear a heavy wooden bar that held the door fast shut, and vanished within. The door thudded to after him, as though he had slammed it shut with his back braced against it, taking no chances even with an elderly monastic. In a few minutes he emerged again empty-handed, hauled the bar into place again, and returned, whistling, to the hall and the enjoyment of Mauduit's ale.

Not the stables nor the kennels, but a small, stout hay-store built on short wooden piles raised from the ground. At least the prior would have fairly snug lying.

Cadfael let the last of the light fade before he made a move. The wooden wall was stout and high, but more than one of the old trees outside leaned a branch over it, and it was no great labour to climb without and drop into the deep grass within. He made first for the gate, and quietly unbarred the narrow wicket set into it. Faint threads of torchlight filtered through the chinks in the hall shutters, but nothing else stirred. Cadfael laid hold of the heavy bar of the storehouse door, and eased it silently out of its socket—opening the door by cautious inches, and whispering through the chink: "Father . . .?"

There was a sharp rustling of hay within, but no immediate reply.

"Father Prior, is it you? Softly . . . Are you bound?"

A hesitant and slightly timorous voice said: "No." And in a moment, with better assurance: "My son, you are not one of these sinful men?"

"Sinful man I am, but not of their company. Hush, quietly now! I have a horse close by. I came from Woodstock to find you. Reach me your hand, Father, and come forth."

A hand came wavering out of the hay-scented darkness to clutch convulsively at Cadfael's hand. The pale patch of a tonsured crown gleamed faintly, and a small, rounded figure crept forth and stepped into the thick grass. He had the wit to waste no breath then on questions, but stood docile and silent while Cadfael re-barred the door on emptiness, and taking him by the hand, led him softly along the fence to the unfastened wicket in the great gate. Only when the door was closed as softly behind them did he heave a great, thankful sigh.

They were out, it was done, and no one would be likely to learn of the escape until morning. Cadfael led the way to where he had left his horse tethered. The forest lay serene and quiet about them.

"You ride, Father, and I'll walk with you. It's no more than two miles into Woodstock. We're safe enough now."

Bewildered and confused by so sudden a reversal, the prior confided and obeyed like a child. Not until they were out on the silent highroad did he say sadly, "I have failed of my mission. Son, may God bless you for this kindness, which is beyond my understanding. For how did you know of me, and how could you divine where to find me? I understand nothing of what has been happening to me. And I am not a very brave man . . . But my failure is no fault of yours, and my blessing I owe you without stint."

"You have not failed, Father," said Cadfael simply. "The suit is still unheard, and will be for three days more. All your companions are safe in Woodstock, except that they fret and search for you. And if you know where they will be lodging, I would recommend that you join them now, by night, and stay well out of sight until the day the case is heard. For if this trap was designed to keep you from appearing in the king's court, some further attempt might yet be made. Have you your evidences safe? They did not take them?"

"Brother Orderic, my clerk, was carrying the documents, but he could not conduct the case in court. I only am accredited to represent my abbot. But, my son, how is it that the case still goes unheard? The king keeps strict day and time, it's well known. How comes it that God and you have saved me from disgrace and loss?"

"Father, for all too bitter reason the king could not be present."

Cadfael told him the whole of it, how half the young chivalry of England had been wiped out in one blow, and the king left without an heir. Prior Heribert, shocked and dismayed, fell to praying in a grieving whisper for both dead and living, and Cadfael walked beside the horse in silence, for what more was there to be said? Except that King Henry, even in this shattering hour, willed that his justices should still prevail, and that was virtue in any monarch. Only when they came into the sleeping town did Cadfael again interrupt the prior's fervent prayers with a strange question.

"Father, was any man of your escort carrying steel? A dagger, or any such weapon?"

"No, no, God forbid!" said the prior, shocked. "We have no use for arms. We trust in God's peace, and after it in the king's."

"So I thought," said Cadfael nodding. "It is another discipline, for another venture."

By the change in Mauduit's countenance Cadfael knew the hour of the following day when the news reached him that the prisoner was flown. All the rest of that day he went about with nerves at stretch and ears pricked for any sensational rumours being bandied around the town, and eyes roving anxiously in dread of the sight of Prior Heribert in court or street, braced to pour out his complaint to the king's officers. But as the hours passed and still there was no sign, he began to be a little eased in his mind, and to hope still for a miraculous deliverance. The Benedictine brothers were seen here and there, mute and sombre-faced; surely they could have had no word of their superior. There was nothing to be done but set his teeth, keep his countenance, wait and hope.

The second day passed, and the third day came, and Mauduit's hopes had soared again, for still there was no word. He made his appearance before the king's judge confidently, his charters in hand. The abbey was the suitor. If all went well, Roger would not even have to state his case, for the plea would fail of itself when the pleader failed to appear.

It came as a shattering shock when a sudden stir at the door, prompt to the hour appointed, blew into the hall a small, round, unimpressive person in the Benedictine habit, hugging to him an armful of vellum rolls, and followed by his black-gowned brothers in close attendance. Cadfael, too, was observing him with interest, for it was the first time he had seen him clearly. A modest man of comfortable figure and amiable countenance, rosy and mild. Not so old as that night journey had suggested, perhaps forty-five, with a shining innocence about him. But to Roger Mauduit it might have been a fire-breathing dragon entering the hall.

And who would have expected, from that gentle, even deprecating presence, the clarity and expertise with which that small man deployed his original charter, punctiliously identical to Roger's, according to the account Alard had given, and omitting any specific mention of what should follow Arnulf Mauduit's death—how scrupulously he pointed out the omission and the arguments to which it might give rise, and followed it up with two letters written by that same Arnulf Mauduit to Abbot Fulchered, referring in plain terms to the obligatory return of the manor and village after his death, and pledging his son's loyal observance of the obligation.

It might have been want of proofs that caused Roger to make so poor a job of refuting the evidence, or it might have been craven conscience. Whatever the cause, judgement was given for the abbey.

Cadfael presented himself before the lord he was leaving barely an hour after the verdict was given.

"My lord, your suit is concluded, and my service with it. I have done what I pledged, here I part from you."

Roger sat sunk in gloom and rage, and lifted upon him a glare that should have felled him, but failed of its impact.

"I misdoubt me," said Roger, smouldering, "how you have observed your loyalty to me. Who else could know . . ." He bit his tongue in time, for as long as it remained unsaid no accusation had been made, and no rebuttal was needed. He would have liked to ask: How *did* you know? But he thought better of it. "Go, then, if you have nothing more to say."

"As to that," said Cadfael meaningly, "nothing more need be said. It's over." And that was recognisable as a promise, but with uneasy implications, for plainly on some other matter he still had a thing to say.

"My lord, give some thought to this, for I was until now in your service, and wish you no harm. Of those four who attended Prior Heribert on his way here, not one carried arms. There was neither sword nor dagger nor knife of any kind among the five of them."

He saw the significance of that go home, slowly but with bitter force. The masterless men had been nothing but a children's tale, but until now Roger had thought, as he had been meant to think, that that dagger-stroke in the forest had been a bold attempt by an abbey servant to defend his prior. He blinked and swallowed and stared, and began to sweat, beholding a perilous gulf into which he had all but stumbled.

"There were none there who bore arms," said Cadfael, "but your own."

A double-edged ambush that had been, to have him out in the forest by night, all unsuspecting. And there were as many miles between Woodstock and Sutton Mauduit returning as coming, and there would be other nights as dark on the way.

"Who?" asked Roger in a grating whisper. "Which of them? Give him a name!"

"No," said Cadfael simply. "Do your own divining. I am no longer in your service, I have said all I mean to say."

Roger's face had turned grey. He was hearing again the plan unfolded so seductively in his ear. "You cannot leave me so! If you know so much, for God's sake return with me, see me safely home, at least. You, I could trust!"

"No," said Cadfael again. "You are warned, now guard yourself."

It was fair, he considered: it was enough. He turned and went away without another word. He went, just as he was, to Vespers in the parish church, for no better reason—or so he thought then—than that the dimness within the open doorway beckoned him as he turned his back on a duty completed, inviting him to quietness and thought, and the bell was just sounding. The little prior was there, ardent in thanksgiving, one more creature who had fumbled his way to the completion of a task, and the turning of a leaf in the book of his life.

Cadfael watched out the office, and stood mute and still for some time after priest and worshippers had departed. The silence after their going was deeper than the ocean and more secure than the earth. Cadfael breathed and consumed it like new bread. It was the light touch of a small hand on the hilt of his sword that startled him out of that profound isolation. He looked down to see a little acolyte, no higher than his elbow, regarding him gravely from great round eyes of blinding blue, intent and challenging, as solemn as ever was angelic messenger.

"Sir," said the child in stern treble reproof, tapping the hilt with an infant finger, "should not all weapons of war be laid aside here?"

"Sir," said Cadfael hardly less gravely, though he was smiling, "you may very well be right." And slowly he unbuckled the sword from his belt, and went and laid it down, flatlings, on the lowest step under the altar. It looked strangely appropriate and at peace there. The hilt, after all, was a cross.

Prior Heribert was at a frugal supper with his happy brothers in the parish priest's house when Cadfael asked audience with him. The little man came out graciously to welcome a stranger, and knew him for an acquaintance at least, and now at a breath certainly a friend.

"You, my son! And surely it was you at Vespers? I felt that I should know the shape of you. You are the most welcome of guests here, and if there is anything I and mine can do to repay you for what you did for us, you need but name it."

"Father," said Cadfael, briskly Welsh in his asking, "do you ride for home tomorrow?"

"Surely, my son, we leave after Prime. Abbot Godefrid will be waiting to hear how we have fared."

"Then, Father, here am I at the turning of my life, free of one master's service, and finished with arms. Take me with you!"

WITCH HUNT

Terry Mullins

No tour stopping in the Middle Ages would be complete without a tale of witchcraft, that "black art" that virtually all the population of Europe believed in and feared. Under the guise of this art, many wicked men manipulated their terrified neighbors, and it was a daring sleuth indeed who would pursue to the end an investigation in which whispers were circulated of the devil's influence. The historical mystery is a natural vehicle for retired Philadelphia editor Terry Mullins, a graduate of Edgar Allan Poe's alma mater, the University of Virginia, who revels in historical facts and quotations.

The witches' terror fell upon Liege with a suddenness that left the citizens—all but a few—shuddering helplessly. A warm summer passed and the crops were good. Levo the innkeeper got three large casks of beer from Germany, and Julien Feys, the head weaver, sent goods south. Then, just when everything was serene, the witches came.

Alain Schram was among the last to hear of their presence. A handsome young merchant, he had no wife to give him news. Sir John Mandeville, the world traveler who was recuperating in Liege, was perhaps the last person in all of Flanders to learn of the witches. People in Liege listened to him, for he had much wisdom and even greater knowledge; but they seldom had opportunity to tell him much. Had these two received word of the presence of witches earlier, much terror might have been averted.

A murky spring outside the city was called the Spring of Beelzebub. It was on land owned by the Bishop of Liege, but no amount of ecclesiastical activity could cleanse it of its reputation. An earlier bishop had built a small shrine in a grove of trees surrounding the spring. The shrine, never popular with the people, became a gathering place for robbers. When the bishop, with the help of soldiers of the local nobility, acted to clear the robbers out, he destroyed the trees which concealed them. What he found when he came upon the shrine was never openly told, but he had the shrine burned and its ashes cast into the spring.

That spring, then, was where the coven of witches gathered in the year of our Lord 1352.

Farmers told about it on Saturday when they came into town for market. They told of weird sounds and strange lights and of owls flying through the air the night before. On Sunday a priest heard of it and led some of his bolder parishioners to the spring. They found the destroyed grove grown up into a thick and rambling copse. There was no sign of the burned shrine. But there were other things.

Sir John Mandeville lived at the inn, so he was usually among the first customers at its tavern after dusk. On a cool September evening, Tuesday, the third of the month, he was especially convivial. People crowded in, seeking light and warmth and companionship. As on many recent occasions, they looked to the one man in the city who would know how to deal with arcane events.

Mandeville received them gladly. He told them of the race of Cyclops, huge men with one eye in the middle of their foreheads, of others who had no heads at all but had eyes in their shoulders, of the damsel changed into the likeness of a dragon—all scary tales from distant lands. But of the horror at home, no one spoke.

Then Alain entered. Hankin Levo, the innkeeper, greeted Alain with enthusiasm. Patrons of the tavern were even more obsequious. After all, Alain was an *echevin,* a member of the municipal governing council, and a man of undetermined but considerable wealth.

Only Mandeville failed to show pleasure at his entry. The old man was in the middle of one of his yarns and hated distractions. He paused, waved Alain to an empty chair at his table, and resumed his narrative. "It has been told, though I myself have not seen them, that there are Pygmies only a cubit tall who marry and beget children when they are only three years old and who grow old when they are five. They are nourished solely by the aroma of apples. . . ."

The traveler's story continued but Alain's thoughts were on Louise de Broux.

He had seen her only once, last May. He had found her, a beautiful child of fourteen, screaming in terror as a large rat alternately lunged at her and then retreated when she kicked at it and flapped her skirts. The rat had her cornered and was attacking out of simple meanness.

Alain didn't bother to scare it away. He drew a dagger and hurled it at the beast, killing it at once. The girl calmed immediately. She smiled at him and laughed, a wonderful smile and a happy laugh. "You must be Alain the rat killer," she said.

He admitted that he was.

"How lucky for me it was you who came by."

"And how lucky for me," he replied.

The unconscious gallantry brought about a subtle change in the girl. Her hands, which had been clutching her skirt, let it drop and smoothed it out. Her smile softened from delight to pleasure and her eyes spoke messages which no daughter of the nobility would ever put into words to a commoner, even a wealthy *echevin*.

Laughter in the tavern brought Alain back to the present.

Mandeville had finished his story and was looking at him with mock disgust. "You don't have to laugh at my stories," he said, "but at least you might listen. Where was your mind? You have been staring at that glass of wine for ten minutes. Wine is meant for drinking, not for crystal gazing, though there is a certain Spanish wine that can conjure up five friendly familiar spirits if one gazes intently enough and says the right charm."

"I wasn't crystal gazing. I was thinking of a rat I killed last summer."

"It must have been some rat. What made it different from the hundreds you kill every week?"

"Not hundreds. The people exaggerate. Still, hardly a day goes by that I don't kill at least one. I hate the creatures."

The last was said with such passion that Mandeville couldn't ignore it. "Some special reason?"

"When I was a child," Alain began, then moved his hand across his eyes to dismiss the subject. "Let's not talk about rats. I hate them. How's your gout?"

Mandeville smiled and drained the last of his wine. "The gout is much better," he said. "The climate of Liege suits my old bones."

Mandeville's beard of three colors began to bristle. Alain knew this to be a sign of curiosity. The man who had traveled all over the world never lost his inquisitiveness. "When will Freddy Pluys return?" he asked.

"Not until November. We are delivering tapestries to Genoa for Julien Feys. Freddy is to come back with olive oil. Why?"

"I asked Freddy to make notes for me on the increase of rats in Paris, Naples, and other places. I'm puzzled at the increase. I'd like to know where it is greatest and why. Your mention of killing a rat reminded me."

"That brings up another matter. Those daggers of yours, they are especially made for throwing, aren't they?"

"Yes. I can generally kill a rat with any dagger or knife, but I never miss with these."

"And I bet I could name the man who made them for you. He lives in Milan, doesn't he?"

"He does. I met him in my youth. Freddy and I delivered him enough Flemish wine to make the whole city drunk. He saw me throw at a rat in his kitchen. I pinned its back leg to the floor. He said I could do better with a well-balanced dagger and he made me one. I've had him make me a half dozen more since. He's a craftsman."

Mandeville concurred and added, "He made my sword."

It was perhaps well for Alain that his mind was absorbed with pleasant thoughts of Louise when he called on Eugene Latteur. He had scarcely entered the house when Eugene's young wife Denise burst into the room and said, "Alain Schram! I knew I heard your voice!" She turned to her husband. "He is just the man to kill that rat in our pantry."

Eugene, thirty and more years older than his wife, responded slowly but with increasing agreement. "It's a wily rodent," he said, "only moderate in size but with teeth that cut their way through two inches of wood in half an hour. We chased him away from the flour box a dozen times, but while we were at dinner yesterday he gnawed through and had a dinner for himself."

They rose and headed for the back door, Denise chattering spiritedly and leading the way, Eugene following slowly. The pantry was a small shed behind the house. It was windowless, so Denise threw the door wide open to let in as much as possible of the orange light reflected from clouds overhead.

Alain walked to the entrance and peered in, giving his eyes time to become accustomed to the dimness. Denise pressed close behind, leaning against him and pointing to the right. "That hole is where he gets in," she said, "and the chest farther on is where he does his thieving."

The chest had been repaired, but even as he watched, Alain could hear the splintering of wood. "He's at it now," he said. He drew and balanced his dagger.

Two steps freed him from Denise's body. A third step and the rat scooted from behind the chest and made for the hole. It got not quite halfway there before Alain's dagger struck it.

"He killed it!" Denise shouted, moving in and blocking out most of the fading light.

Alain picked up the rat, removed and cleaned his dagger, and offered the dead rat to Denise. She quickly moved out of his way and called to her husband, who stood watching from the back doorway of the house.

Husband and wife congratulated Alain and they went in to celebrate.

Denise went into the kitchen, made sure the servants were proceeding properly with the dinner, and then ran upstairs. She came down with her three-year-old son and the duenna who had been with the Latteurs as long as Alain could remember. While Alain and Eugene talked, the child walked over to his father and climbed up on one leg. Eugene bounced him with a measured and steady beat. "We're worried," Eugene said. "Witches have been covening by the spring on Friday nights. First they killed chickens, then pigs. Last Friday night it was a goat. They'll kill a child soon. Friday after next is the thirteenth. They'll steal a child before then and sacrifice it. We're worried."

Thus Alain learned about the witches.

The women sat with several items of Eugene's clothing piled before them. As the men talked, the women searched the coats and breeches for tears and holes. On finding any, they proceeded to mend them. From time to time they would find dead fleas in the garments. These they would carefully shake into a large basin placed between them for that purpose. It was a cozy domestic scene. The men should have been talking about weather, crops, and business. Instead they grappled with dark fears and ominous forebodings.

"Why doesn't the bailie take some men up to the spring on a Friday night and seize the witches?" Alain asked.

"The bailie? You wouldn't find Pierre going near that spring with an army. And he couldn't raise an army in Liege to fight witches. I wouldn't go and I guess I'm as brave as any man hereabouts."

"I've seen a few witches burned in Italy. They were poor old women. They babbled and people said they were talking in Satan's tongue. I don't know. Most of them just seemed to be short on wits. Before they died some of them were grinning and waving to the crowds. They seemed to enjoy the attention they were getting. I doubt that anyone had paid any attention to them in a long time. Frankly, they seemed to be harmless."

"That's in the light of day. At night they change shape and Satan gives them power to fly through the air and enter locked rooms and steal children or bewitch healthy people so they die."

"There is one more Friday night before the thirteenth. This Friday let's go to the Spring of Beelzebub and watch for them. If there's a coven of witches meeting there, we'll grab them and bring them to the bishop for trial."

Eugene was astounded. "You'd never do that," he said. "They anoint themselves with magical potions so they can become invisible at will. Or they could change themselves into a cat or an owl. Anyway, you'll never get me or any of the other citizens of Liege to go with you to a coven on a Friday night. Satan himself might be there!"

Alain looked at the women. The duenna had stopped sewing and was staring at him as if he had suggested going to hell and fighting with the demons. Denise continued sewing, her eyes intent on her work, but her usually cheerful face was ashen. The young child had left its father's knee and gone to clutch its mother's skirts.

Alain turned back to Eugene, but at that moment a servant entered. Supper was ready. Plans for putting an end to the witch scare would have to be postponed. And then it would be to Mandeville that he talked.

They settled at table as two servants brought in the first course: Flemish wine and veal pasties, black puddings and sausages.

Once the subject of witchcraft is brought up, it does not die easily. Eugene might shy away from discussing plans for going after witches, but he was willing to elaborate on the danger witches posed to the community.

"We want to protect our son," he said, "but how do you guard against a force of evil which cannot be kept out by locks or frightened away by dogs?"

Alain temporized. Like most of the rest of the world, he had been brought up with a lively fear of those who practiced the black art. But as a merchant he dealt with men on all levels and he observed that the best educated held witches in contempt. Sir John Mandeville in particular felt pity rather than fear for them.

"What precautions have you taken?" he asked.

"The only one I know," Eugene replied. "I keep arrows smeared with hog's blood and hellebore within easy reach. It's the only thing that can kill a witch. If I see one, she's dead. But their power to become invisible is what defeats me."

"You seem to have done all you can do. You have a crucifix above the boy's bed?"

"Naturally."

At this point the second course arrived: hares in civey, pea soup, salt meat, and a soringue of eels.

When conversation resumed, it centered on the harm witches do. To Alain's relief, it moved away from the killing of children at witches' Sabbat and dealt with their charms and spells.

"The floods which devastated this country in my youth were generally considered the work of witches," Eugene said. "And once a young woman was accused by the priest of St. Denis of trying to take holy bread away from the Mass to desecrate it. The weavers' guild rose to her defense since her husband was one of their leading members. The bishop was won over and the woman was not harmed."

Alain told of stories he had heard in Avignon of women going to witches for spells which would cause their husbands to be faithful. Such spells appeared to have made witches fairly popular in that city.

The third course was served: a roast of partridges and capons; luce, carp, and pottage.

"You could never catch a witch," Eugene said. "A witch will carry a quarterstaff to beat off pursuers. They use it to help them leap over walls and other obstacles. If you pursue them closely, they put the staff between their legs and fly off to their meeting place."

Alain didn't disagree. He had heard such arguments all his life, but he had never met anyone who had seen such things happen.

Eugene brooded. "You'll never catch them, but if I see one, I'll put a smeared arrow through its ribs."

The fourth course brightened him a bit. He looked at the fish à la dondine, the savory rice, and the bourrey in hot sauce and smiled. "I'll protect my son against Satan himself," he said.

"Who first reported the witches?" Alain asked.

"Some peasants in one of the count's villages. Since the lights and such were on cathedral land, they brought the word with them into town instead of telling Count de Broux."

"And, of course, the count wouldn't lead his knights onto the bishop's land even if he was willing to go after the witches."

"That's it. The church or the town must deal with the coven. And you won't find anyone willing to take on the task."

With the fifth course—lark pasties, rissoles, larded milk, and sugared flawns—Eugene broke off talking about witches and began to recount events connected with the rat in the flour box. Here for the first time the women joined in the talk. Denise told of its first appearance and her futile attempts to get the dogs after it. Eugene marveled at its ability to gnaw its way into the pantry. He told of blocking the rat hole, of nailing boards over it, and of hurling a pitchfork at it. "I feared we'd never be rid of it, but rat killer here got it the first time."

Denise took up the narrative, telling it in detail for the benefit of the duenna and boy, neither of whom had witnessed any part of the affair. Eugene's son demanded to see the rat and was promised that after dinner he might.

He squealed with joy as the final course—pears and comfits, medlars and peeled nuts, hippocras and wafers—arrived.

When the meal was over they went out to show him the rat. "It isn't very large," he observed.

"No," said Eugene, "and that made him all the harder to kill. He was quick and wily."

As Alain was leaving, Eugene clapped him on the shoulder and said, "I'm glad you came by today."

Denise hugged him and kissed his cheek, saying, "Come more often."

He promised them he would and left determined to do something about the witches. It was not right that good people like the Latteurs should worry about the safety of their son.

It was partly youthful impatience, partly a feeling that if he delayed acting immediately, something awful might happen that he could have prevented, and partly a knowledge that if he let Mandeville get going on his tavern yarns, serious conversation might be impossible. For a combination of reasons, therefore, Alain set out to find Mandeville early the next morning.

Shortly after noon he found him at the house occupied by the notary, Jean d'Outremeuse. Mandeville was helping the latter fashion a chronicle of the life of Ogier de Danois. They had reached that point in collaboration where any interruption is welcomed, so Alain was greeted warmly.

His story about the witches produced two different results. Mandeville shared Alain's view that they must take action. His friend shrank from the idea. "Only a great hero like Ogier could battle witches," he said. "And even he would not attempt to do so unless they had worked great devastation. Let us instead go down to the Church of the Holy Cross and pray to be rescued from this evil."

The notary dumped a lap full of verses into a chest and prepared to leave. Alain and Mandeville followed him, discussing plans for deeds of a more mundane sort.

An hour later Alain and Mandeville were alone in the latter's room. "You've seen a few witches," Mandeville said, "and I've seen more—mostly when they were being burned, of course. For the greater part they are old women without money or charm, completely powerless but willing to give anything, even their souls, for ability to control someone or something. Some are very young girls who cannot wait for life to bring them its fruits. All are easy victims of false promises made by others or imagined by themselves. It is ridiculous that people like Jean should tremble before them."

"He is not the only one. How many men in Liege do you think will join us?"

"You have a point. And we ought not tell the whole city we plan to go after the coven. Do you think we could do it by ourselves?"

"I'm willing to try."

"Good. We'll see if we can get help from a few discreet people, then Friday we go witch hunting."

With the decision made, reaction set in. It was all very well for Mandeville to picture witches as pitiful persons seeking some way to make their dull lives more interesting. But evil did exist.

Alain had seen Grimoria, books of black magic. He had read parts of them: bizarre and confused instructions of pointless ritual, garbled names, and extravagant claims of demonic results. He could reject the comical pictures of horned devils, of fanged furies, of naked women with talons and serpentine hair. But he could not cast off the sinister intent of the books. Evil might express itself poorly, but it existed. And out by the Spring of Beelzebub evil had hold of someone. Evil, or Satan himself, took control of human beings and drove them to diabolical actions.

Alain was silent, moodily pondering such thoughts as he walked with Mandeville to see the bishop and tell him of their plans. As they entered the episcopal palace, an elderly priest met and led them to the bishop's chambers.

The bishop was delighted to see Sir John Mandeville. He was surprised to see Alain Schram and at first thought that the *echevin* had come on official business. He thawed a bit when he found that this was not so. Mandeville began to tell the bishop about the witches, only to find out that he was many weeks too late.

The bishop, a short, sturdy man with a square head and a strong jaw, laughed before Mandeville had got well started. "My dear Sir John," he interrupted, "are you just finding out about that outrage? The town has been talking about little else for over a month." He pulled at his long beaklike nose with stubby fingers. Then he pounded a powerful fist into the palm of his other hand. Black hairs on the back of his fingers shook like antennae. "I have been preaching against those witches every Sunday. I won't have witches in Liege!"

"I'm glad to hear that," Mandeville replied. "Alain and I want to break up this little game, but since they are your witches . . ."

"They are not my witches!"

"Well, they are on your property. They meet out where the little shrine used to be. We thought we ought to get your permission to go after them, and perhaps your help."

"Permission? You have not only my permission but my injunction to get them. Bring them to me and we'll put an end to this deviltry. Alas, I have no knights and I cannot personally accompany you, but you have my blessing."

His object attained, Mandeville relaxed and began sparring with the bishop. "Why didn't you get the count to take his knights out there and drive the witches away?"

The bishop, always on better terms with the nobility than the town government, looked at Alain and hesitated before replying. Finally his outrage overcame his caution. "The count told me he wouldn't waste his knights on witches. His knights will fight humans and the Church must fight spiritual dangers. Since I have no knights of my own, I must listen to stories of animals being dismembered and parts of their bodies left at the gates of the city, at crossroads, even on the steps of St. Denis."

He looked at Alain and added, "I even spoke to the town and got the same answer I did from the count. So much for democracy."

Alain, as an *echevin,* could understand the town's reply. Under Charlemagne the counties had been jointly governed by a bishop and a count. But Liege had received a charter from the king and was governed by merchants. The Church had long ago come to terms with this arrangement, but few bishops liked it. Still, he refused to be drawn into the argument.

Mandeville had no such qualms. He almost purred, "But didn't Aquinas say that the state is a kind of pact between the king and the people?"

The bishop snorted. "In *De Regimine Principii* Thomas declared that monarchy is the best government. The body has one head, not many."

When Mandeville replied with a quotation from the *Summa Theologica* Alain's attention wandered. He wondered that Mandeville could deal with so many men, all on their own level. He himself had profited from Mandeville's knowledge of trade, from how and where to get the best wool from England to where and how to find buyers in Italy. The only statement Alain knew from Aquinas, he had learned from Mandeville: Man does not sin in using moderate gains acquired in trade for the support of his household. Since he had a broad understanding of what was meant by support of his household, Alain felt no guilt as his wealth increased.

This was, to Alain's surprise, one time when Mandeville was not disposed to debate at length. He had got the permission he wanted. Now he thanked the bishop and took Alain back into the dark, narrow streets of Liege to seek a few brave men to help them attack the coven.

Three hours later they had found no recruits. Everyone wanted the witches caught. No one wanted to catch them.

"There is no help in the town," Mandeville said, "so let us turn to the castle."

Alain was glad to do so.

As they left the city wall behind them and rode toward the castle, Alain's thoughts were all on the count's daughter. He had hoped for an excuse to see her again. None had presented itself until now. He felt lightheaded. His heart palpitated in a strange manner. He felt as if life could give him no greater gift than to see and perhaps speak with Louise de Broux.

Approaching the castle they passed two knights slowly riding their mounts around the exercise ground. They saluted them and entered. The gate leading to the lists was narrow and Mandeville preceded Alain. In this manner they crossed the drawbridge and entered the castle. In its bailey, beyond the stables and smithy, was the count's chapel. The Count de Broux, his wife, daughter, and seneschal came out of the chapel before Mandeville and Alain reached the castle's inner wall. The count hailed them. His marshal called several stable boys to tend their horses and the count invited his guests into the palace.

Alain, however, was claimed by Louise. The rat killer must help them, she said. Rats were threatening their stores of grain. She had her way, as she apparently usually did.

So, while Mandeville and the count went into the palace to talk, Alain, led by Louise and accompanied by the countess, the seneschal, the marshal, and several servants, set out to protect the castle food supply.

Across the bailey from the chapel was their bakehouse. This, Louise said, was the area infested by rats. The seneschal, a grizzled knight in his fifties, ordered the door thrown open. Two servants obeyed him and they all saw three rats scurrying about inside.

The marshal, oblivious to everyone around him, grabbed a club and charged in after the rats. With him rushing about in the bakehouse, Alain could not throw at the rats. The seneschal called to the marshal to get out of the way, but the marshal, a little man who scampered about like a dog chasing a rabbit in an open field, ignored the words. He seemed to be a person who could keep only one thing on his mind at a time, and killing rats was his fixed idea.

The seneschal laughed. "Georges Delfose is a wild man," he said. "He'll kill one of those pests if it takes him all day." It seemed as if it might. The man was so comical that everyone laughed. He heard the laughter and his fury increased. None of his blows came within a foot of any of the rats but the rodents were as frantic as he was. Their raucous squeals mixed with his curses and the thunder of the club pounding the earthen floor.

A fourth rat crept from somewhere to see what was going on and quickly disappeared again. The marshal was nimble, strong, indefatigable, and thoroughly inaccurate. One final two-handed blow shattered his club. The seneschal ran in and grabbed the frustrated marshal. "That's the third club you've broken in two weeks," he said, "and you've never killed a rat yet. You stay with trapping them. Now go outside and let Mr. Schram get at them." He half led and half dragged him out.

Alain walked into the bakehouse. Dust filled the air. The rats were quiet, but Alain could see two of them. One had been running between the oven and a large baking tray in the corner. It was by the oven now in plain sight, waiting to dodge another blow. Alain's wrist came forward and his dagger accounted for one rat.

Behind him there were cheers. A small crowd of knights, squires, peasants, and servants had gathered to watch the marshal's antics. Now they applauded the first kill. Louise was so excited that she lost all sense of being a young woman and became the girl he had first seen kicking at the rat which attacked her.

With the first sign of success, several servants volunteered to beat on the side of the bakehouse to scare rats into the open. A rousing hour and a half followed. At the end, seven rats had been killed and no more could be found.

There seemed little point to intruding on the count and Mandeville, so Alain waited out in the bailey, talking with Louise, the countess, and the seneschal.

Louise showed him the stables where the knights' steeds were being groomed. Most of the stalls were empty. "There are only six knights serving the count now," the seneschal said. "Once there were half a hundred."

The smithy was equally spacious. One smith and two assistants were at work. The count's retainers formed a small community now. As the town had grown, the castle and its villages had become less important. But for Alain the castle held one thing the town could not match, Louise de Broux.

When the count and Mandeville returned, Louise changed again. Her artless chattering became witty. Her careless gestures became graceful. Her frank admiration of Alain's skill with the dagger became warm appreciation as she told her father what had been going on.

The count was gracious in his thanks. As Alain and Mandeville prepared to leave, the count ordered his seneschal to give each a purse of money. "No guest ever leaves without a gift," he said.

As they rode toward Liege, Alain noted the small farms they passed. "The count's wealth comes from these serfs, peasants, and freemen," he commented to Mandeville, "and they live in huts without windows and at most a table and chair or two within. I feel I should return the count's gift to them."

"Which ones?"

"That is the problem. I would probably cause jealousy and stir up trouble if I tried."

"And the count would be mortally insulted. You are wealthier than he is anyway. Would you give your own money to them?"

"I see what you mean. Still, I don't feel right about it. How did your talk with the count go?"

"He and his knights want nothing to do with witches. They'll fight against the King of England or the Emperor of Germany, but they want no part of the Prince of Darkness."

"Then we'll go it alone."

That effectively ended their attempt to enlist others. Church, town, and castle had refused to aid them. In high spirits they made their plans.

That Friday was overcast. Mandeville buckled on his sword. Alain, though he wore a sword, too, strapped four daggers on at convenient places. Things you can't reach with a sword, you can with a well-aimed dagger. They set out shortly before sunset.

They reached the copse, a tangled mass of low bushes and half-grown trees. It looked dark and impenetrable. As they rode around it, however, they found several places where secret paths entered. The openings had been covered with branches in a clumsy effort to disguise them.

"There are several ways in," Alain said.

"And ways out," Mandeville added significantly. "But we can't ride our horses in. If we leave them out here, we might scare the witches away."

"And we'd find the horses killed, too."

A small stream which flowed from the spring and eventually reached the Meuse River had wild bits of green growing along its banks. From place to place there would be large clusters of bushes and an occasional very old tree. About half a mile downstream there was a large clump of ancient yews which could hide the animals. They tethered them among the yews and returned to the copse.

Entering one of the paths and covering it behind them, they worked their way toward the center. It took them no more than ten minutes to find the spring.

In a small clearing beside it they found a rude pulpit built. A human skull and a short sword lay on the ground inside the pulpit. Two feet in front of the pulpit was a pile of flat stones arranged to form a sort of altar. Beside the altar was a large basket.

Other than that the cleared area was bare, but there was a rustling in the rue bushes behind the pulpit. Tied there and grazing quite peacefully was a two-month-old lamb.

Mandeville looked worried. "I don't like this at all," he said. "The farmers were right. Something has been going on here and it looks as if these aren't just silly people gathering together for immoral thrills. There is organization of a sort here, someone planning and setting the scene beforehand."

"That's an ugly weapon," Alain said.

"It's an ancient short sword," Mandeville replied, "one carried by nobles into battle during the Crusades of St. Louis. It looks sharp. I could guess which noble owns it."

Alain didn't wish to hear the name, yet no power on earth could have kept him from asking, "Which?"

"Count de Broux."

Alain winced. He remembered too well Mandeville's saying that old women and very young girls were particularly susceptible to the lure of Satanism. He tried to focus his mind on the innocent beauty of Louise de Broux, but a tough strain of honesty made him admit that there was something other than innocence in the way her smile had changed, the way her whole attitude had changed when he had blurted out, "How lucky for me." There was no wantonness, he would swear, but there was nothing childlike in her eyes. Even in the present macabre circumstances, the memory of that brief encounter sent blood pounding in his ears.

Their first meeting had been brief but more intimate than his recent tour of the castle's bailey. The presence of a couple of dozen of the count's retainers had sounded a convivial but not a personal note on the latter occasion.

He looked with loathing at the short sword. It cast a pall over him.

"Not having second thoughts, are you?" Mandeville asked.

"No! This thing has got to be stopped."

There was nothing more to be found in the clearing. The setting sun cast formless shadows and the place grew dim. The stone altar took on the appearance of a coffin. The rude pulpit seemed to change shapes in the enfolding dark. One moment it was a poorly built screen thrown up to hide the sword and the skull. The next it was a monstrous cage which might hold feral creatures steeped in forbidden craft of human and inhuman lore. And the next it would disappear altogether, a blank space merged with the surrounding blackness.

Mandeville motioned to some thick bushes at the edge of the clearing. "We can hide there," he said. "If we crouch down, no one will see us even if there are lights; and I'm sure there will be lights."

They beat their way into the brush, cutting down small plants which might trip them if they needed to leave their hiding place quickly. Soon they had a safe, if not altogether comfortable, blind from which to watch the clearing.

They had less than an hour to wait. They heard snappings and rustlings, then the sound of people walking over dead leaves and brittle sticks. Then they saw the flickering of small lights. The sounds and glimmers came closer.

Three naked figures entered the clearing from the side opposite the watchers. Two men and a woman approached and touched the altar. They had a single torch which they fixed in the ground at one corner. Then they lay face down in front of the altar.

A few minutes later others came by threes. When four torches had been set at the altar, there were six men and six women prostrate in the clearing. One more and the coven would be complete.

He appeared with a suddenness that surprised Alain. A man with a horned mask rose behind the pulpit and shouted in a high falsetto voice. The coven shouted reply.

All the witches wore masks, crude caps of cloth or poorly woven straw or leaves and twigs tied together covering half their faces. Mostly the effect was bizarre rather than awesome. But the leader's mask, a leather hood with eye holes and three horns, was grotesque enough to appall. Around the face it had obscene shapes which danced and dangled when he moved.

The leader, speaking as Satan himself, led the coven in a litany of blasphemy. The crowd swayed and stamped.

The men were ill-nourished specimens past middle age. Five women were ancient crones with shriveled breasts and sagging flesh which flopped loosely on their bones. The sixth was a young girl. She it was who walked up to the altar and lay down on it. The Satan figure, carrying the human skull, left his pulpit and approached the altar. He placed the skull on the young girl's navel and she held it in place. Then he disappeared into the darkness and reappeared with the lamb and a sword.

Four men came forward, two on each side of the altar. They each took one leg of the animal and held it over the skull. The leader seized the lamb's head, pulled it back, and cut its throat. Blood gushed forth, filling the skull, and pouring out over the young girl's body. The Satan figure took the lamb and skinned it quickly and expertly. He cut its skin into thirteen parts and called the coven forward.

He took the skull from the girl and, beginning with her, made each to taste of it. Then they all took a part of the lamb's skin and rubbed the blood and grease all over their bodies. They kept up a monotonous chant.

As they were doing this, the leader cut off the left back leg of the slaughtered animal and waved it about, dancing frenetically and beating the altar with the lamb's leg. He continued in a mad passion even after the coven had finished anointing themselves.

When the chanting ended, he signaled for two men to hold the girl. He put on a pair of heavy gauntlets and reached behind the pulpit, drawing forth a huge ferocious rat. He held it up, shouting, "This is Judas and this shall be the Judas kiss." The rat bit viciously at the gauntlets as the man approached the girl.

When she realized that he meant for her to kiss the rat, the girl screamed and tried to break free, but the men tightened their grip on her arms and held her head so she couldn't move it.

Mandeville said, "The rat will bite off her nose." He seized his sword and started to rise. But Alain had moved sooner. He was already standing clear of the bushes with a dagger in each hand. The rat was still two feet from the girl when it died.

The coven was stunned. Its leader dropped the rat and vanished behind the pulpit. Others started to run. Alain, clearly visible in the torchlight, held the second dagger poised to throw. "Stand still, all of you!" he shouted.

They were transfixed with fear.

Mandeville looked behind the pulpit, but the leader was gone. He herded the others together. "Where are your clothes?" he asked. One man replied that they removed them as soon as they entered the copse.

Since they had come by two different paths, Mandeville drove one group and Alain the other back as they had come. Outside the copse they came together again, dressed and unmasked. Alain recognized the men and three old women as poor townspeople. The young girl was no one he had ever seen before. Two old women said they lived on farms of the count's estate.

Alain got the horses and he and Mandeville marched the coven to the town and woke the bishop.

No one in the coven knew who the leader was. They all thought he was Satan. They had never seen him without his mask.

Mandeville shook his head. "These are just miserable victims of the man who posed as Satan," he said. "Until we find him, we have not crushed the menace. He will find more dupes and start over."

"I think I can find him," Alain replied.

The next day Alain, Mandeville, and the bishop rode to the castle. The bailey was filled with knights, squires, peasants, and servants. Word of the night's events had got around.

The count himself came out with his seneschal. Mandeville and the bishop spoke with him. They motioned for Alain to take over. He moved through the crowd to the stables. There he found the marshal, whom he turned over to the bishop.

A crew of the count's servants rummaged through old equipment from days when the count's knights numbered half a hundred. Under a pile of saddles they found the gauntlets, rat-gnawed and bloodstained. Further down they discovered the mask of Satan. Since none would touch it, Alain hauled it out and gave it to the bishop.

As they carried the marshal to the cathedral for ecclesiastical trial, Mandeville asked Alain, "How could you recognize the marshal with that mask on?"

"You weren't there," Alain responded, "when he tried to kill the rats. Once you have seen him in a frenzy, you can't mistake it. The weird gyrations with the lamb's leg gave him away as if he had on no mask at all."

GATHER NOT THY ROSE

Miriam Grace Monfredo

Beneath the surface of prosperous and flourishing Elizabethan England lay lingering insecurities. Only two generations removed from the dynastic Wars of the Roses, the Virgin Queen sat on her throne with an eye to potential claimants to her crown at home, and very real threats abroad. It was a time for undercover work, the stuff of spy fiction. As Miriam Grace Monfredo offers her solution to the true unsolved mystery of the death of Amy Robsart Dudley, the wife of the queen's horsemaster Robert Dudley, we see just how stealthy the political maneuverings of the age were. The author is almost exclusively a writer of historical crime, having made her debut in Ellery Queen's Mystery Magazine's *Department of First Stories in 1989, and subsequently authoring two critically acclaimed historical novels and more stories.*

A breeze off the Thames ruffled the hemlocks bordering the stone-walled terrace; it swung the hoop frame of a lady-in-waiting's wide bell skirt, yet the lady herself stood fixed, staring down a flight of marble stairs. Sprawling over the bottom step lay Amy Robsart, wife of Robert Dudley, mistress of Cumnor Place, Oxfordshire. Late mistress. The young woman's head was twisted grotesquely above a once graceful neck, her body had crumpled like a marionette come unstrung.

Lady Margaret drew in her breath sharply, thinking of a plaything carelessly tossed aside.

With shaking hands she lifted her skirts to make her way down the stairs, stepping gingerly over a silk slipper, lost halfway. At the bottom, Margaret stood beside her mistress, gazing at the tumbled hair sprinkled with yew and hemlock needles, stripped from boughs overhanging the steps. A small, bare branch was still clutched in the curled fingers.

Margaret sighed and raised her eyes over the manor house rose gardens, which her mistress had loved, to a darkening twilight sky. It was almost over, this late summer day in the year of our Lord, 1560. And the servants would soon be returning from Abingdon Fair, where the mistress herself had sent them. Well, let *them* discover her. Raise the cry that would echo throughout all of England.

Margaret kneeled over the woman, searching through folds of silken gown; her hand closed around a roll of vellum. Standing upright again, she glanced about quickly, then slipped the note inside her own sleeve. She would go back inside, stoke the fire. And wait.

Some minutes later Margaret sat shivering on a stool before the hearth; the flames furling around beechwood logs had not yet warmed the withdrawing room. Flanders tapestries, covering tawny ironstone walls, gave off a musty odor of damp wool. The tapestry over the fireplace had woven in it a small brown doe trapped by hunters, their arrows glinting with metallic thread. Margaret's spare frame shuddered and she wrapped her arms tightly around herself. Her memory slipped back to three days past. It seemed a hundred years ago.

Like a brilliant pendant, the moon had hung over the manor house: Margaret could even pick out, in a field beyond, the flecks that were tough little Cotswold sheep. Clouds above Oxfordshire's hills swelled, creamy as court-ladies' breasts spilling over whalebone corsets. Margaret's lips tightened; she straightened the high-collared bodice of her cambric gown. Concealed by yews that thrust against the manor walls, she ran her hands briskly up and down her arms, then drew her thin mantle of wool closely around herself. The only sound was a mill wheel creaking farther down the Thames.

Hoofbeats pounded the cobblestone drive. A horse whinnied, and Margaret took a step forward, better to see Amy Robsart dart from the courtyard to meet a grey stallion and rider.

Margaret daubed her eyes, which watered in the chill of near frost. Had the sleeves of her mistress's cloak not been edged in ermine, she might have missed the exchange. A flash of white fur, the chink of a coin pouch tossed and caught, the rustle of parchment disappearing into a sleeve. That was all. No words passed. The stallion reared, pawing the sky, its thighs broader than her mistress's waist. The horse and rider galloped east toward London, disappearing at last beyond the massive oaks lining the drive of Cumnor Place. Slowly, the hoofbeats ebbed.

Satisfied that her mistress was in no danger, Margaret sheathed the dagger she had gripped, and made her way around the yews to the courtyard. Her shadow loomed in the flicker of torchlight, dwarfing the woman who stood before the gate with eyes cast downward. Cobblestones crunched under Margaret's feet.

Amy Robsart whirled around. "Margaret?" she whispered. "Margaret, is it you?"

"It is, Milady. Breathe easy now."

The young woman inclined her head to rest it briefly against Margaret's shoulder. Then she tugged the parchment from her sleeve and sighed. "Now I shall have the truth. For good or ill, Margaret, at least I will know. If the rumors are false, then I can rest. If they be true . . ."

"First inside, Milady, before we catch our death of cold. There'll be time enough after I stir the fire."

Margaret recognized the strong, round script of her niece Kat's hand. Kat Ashley who presided over Her Majesty's royal bedchamber. Who had stood in lieu of mother to the newly crowned Elizabeth since childhood.

Logs hissed in the fireplace. Amy Robsart sank into cushions on a bench, slumped against the back rail, and unrolled the parchment. Margaret lowered herself to a stool at her mistress's feet.

"To the Mistress Dudley," Amy began softly. "Milady, I pen this from the palace at Whitehall, on the fifth day of September, because my aunt Margaret has bid me give answer to the questions concerning your husband, Robert Dudley. This is a most delicate matter, Milady.

"You inquire as to Her Majesty's well-being. Since the coronation, the queen has been surrounded by suitors who vie for her attention. Worry over Her Majesty's health, which has never been strong, increases the longer she delays in choosing a husband and settling the succession. And Her Majesty seems melancholy, not at all herself; the court physicians bled her from the foot and arm in June, though why I cannot say. But I assure you the court rumours that the queen is with child are false.

"As to the other rumours which have so distressed you, Milady, I can only say that I have entreated Her Majesty to put a stop to them by quickly taking a suitable husband."

Here Amy's voice faltered. She let go the letter and lifted her hands to her face, her eyes hidden by a veil of fine brown hair.

Margaret reached for the letter, which had dropped to a woven foot-cloth. Her eyes swept it rapidly; again she blessed her father, a Protestant clergyman, who had insisted she learn to read. As she guessed, her niece implied nothing that was not already known by all the court. By all of Europe. That while Elizabeth sported, riding to hunt with her horsemaster Dudley, the affairs of England waited. And tongues wagged; not only English tongues, but Scot and French and Spanish. All had suitors at court. All were kept at bay by a queen whose horsemaster was said to have access to her private chambers.

Kat had been circumspect, but Margaret could read between the lines. And Amy Robsart Dudley, for all her naiveté, was not stupid: she had seen, as had Margaret, the headstrong Elizabeth riding in a flamboyant gold-covered litter on the way to her Westminster coronation. The January morning had been bleak; as Elizabeth was carried through cheering London streets, the clouds suddenly lifted. The sun streamed down. There were those who said the new queen had commanded it. As she had commanded that her horsemaster Dudley ride at the head of the royal procession.

That a man so handsome, so versed in charm as Dudley—a man who early in their marriage could make the sheltered Amy gasp with pleasure behind the bedchamber curtains—that he would remain merely this imprudent queen's horsemaster was unlikely. Just as it was unlikely that the ambitious Robert Dudley was riding only Her Majesty's horses.

Margaret became aware that Amy had lifted her face from her hands and was watching her. She felt a tremor run down her spine; her mistress's dark eyes were dry. The eyes Margaret had expected to be red and weeping, which had indeed been weeping for months, were instead glowing. They burned in her lovely face from a fire whose source Margaret could not begin to guess.

Amy abruptly stood and began to pace before the hearth. She twisted and untwisted her hands, wove them together again, while nodding her head as though agreeing with some inner wisdom. "So they are lovers," she said finally. "My Robert and the queen are lovers, and all Europe knows . . ."

"Milady," Margaret interrupted gently, "the queen and your husband were childhood companions. My niece does not say they are now lovers—"

"Oh, she didn't have to! What is more the point, Margaret, she didn't say they were *not*. Well, I wanted the truth. Now I have it."

She stopped pacing. Her eyes widened, gleamed with an expression Margaret could not read. "They want me dead. Robert and the queen. That's why—"

"Milady! Surely not." Margaret got to her feet and reached for her mistress's shoulder.

Amy jerked her shoulder away. "Yes," she whispered. Her face was ashen, only the eyes burning. "That is why the last time Robert was here, I became so ill. He tried to poison me, but put out the story that I wanted to take my own life. Don't you see, Margaret?"

Margaret gaped at her mistress. It was not possible. Even Dudley would not dare murder. That he wanted to wed Elizabeth, rule her and so England, Margaret had no doubt. His father, the Duke of Northumberland, had been executed when conspiring for power seven years before, during Queen Mary's reign. Bloody Mary. Elizabeth's half-sister by their father Henry's first wife, the Papist Catherine of Aragon.

Margaret's heart thudded, recalling the fear, the danger, of those terrible years. She clenched her hands, squeezed them until her fingers ached, trying to dispel the memory.

With effort, she brought herself back to her mistress. To be rid of Amy, for the queen and for power, would Robert Dudley kill his wife? Not possible! The scandal would destroy not only him—but the queen as well. He *must* know that.

Amy began to pace anew. Back and forth, back and forth, more and more swiftly across the floor. Color flooded her cheeks as she rubbed them fiercely with her knuckles. She reminded Margaret of a caged beast, clawing its own fur. This was not the gentle mistress she had served for ten years. This was a wild thing. Margaret again felt the tremor. Had her mistress, by abandonment and humiliation and now unreasoning fear for her life, been pushed over the edge into madness?

Yet *was* Amy's fear unreasonable? Dudley had enemies. Formidable enemies, who feared his favour with the queen. Could they be plotting his young wife's death, with the intention of placing the blame on Dudley? On the queen? And Amy truly had been ill. Vomiting, retching for twelve hours. At the time, Margaret had put it down to nervous vapours, concern over the rumours from London. But what if . . . ?

Margaret caught her breath. Within the past months, two new servants had been hired: a farrier and—a kitchen maid. Robert Dudley had done the hiring. Still, what if the maid had been directed to Cumnor Place by traitors? Margaret told herself she would dismiss the maid immediately, prepare her mistress's food with her own hands.

Amy was still pacing, now muttering softly. "She will not have him. No. I must find a way. A way to bring them both down before God and the world . . ."

"Milady, please. You need to rest. Please, come to bed . . ." Margaret cautiously took hold of her mistress's arm. Meeting no resistance, she guided the distraught woman toward the sleeping chamber.

For three days, Margaret watched her mistress pace the chamber. Amy never slept. Wringing her hands, her face feverish, she sought a plan, charging Margaret with secrecy. The other servants whispered among themselves and stayed away from the chamber door. Only the grounds-keeper dared knock, bearing bouquets of late summer roses for his mistress. Roses first brought west to England from the land of the Crusades, long before the Tudors' ascendency. Roses coaxed to bloom far beyond their season: Damask pinks, Moss and white Ayrshire, the Alba of York, the red Gallica of Lancaster. Their perfume scented the chamber. The mistress paced.

On the morning of the eighth day of September, when Margaret entered the inner bedchamber, Amy was propped against cushions beneath sheets and a down coverlet the white of virgin snow. Margaret saw with relief the pale face, the quiet hands, the calm eyes of her mistress.

"Margaret, I want you to give the servants leave to go to Abingdon Fair." This said with the mistress's customary sweet voice.

"All of them, Milady? Surely not the farrier, who has a score of horses to shoe . . ."

"*All* of them," her mistress said, the voice less sweet. "Save of course yourself."

Margaret felt a sudden prick of uneasiness, as from a thorn hidden inside her lady's good temper.

With the servants gone, the mistress Dudley emerged at last from her chamber. Margaret brushed the fine hair until it shone through its silver-threaded net caul like ripe chestnuts. Then, gowned in black silk, train sweeping behind her, Amy drifted slowly through the chambers of the manor house. She stroked each drowsing cat, touched each treasured object with loving fingers. She sat before the fire and plucked her pear-shaped lute; humming a simple French air, popular at court, a smile wandering over her face. Almost Margaret could believe that all was well. Almost.

The day was warm, sunny, the sky a stained-glass blue. Autumn must wait. In late afternoon, after napping in her chamber, her mistress bid Margaret accompany her for a stroll through the gardens. So she said. But when they stepped to the terrace, she caught Margaret's arm and faced her. Margaret saw eyes that burned again with the fire of three days past.

"I have done it, Margaret," she said, her voice a low whisper. She glanced about furtively, though they were alone. "I have made a plan. A plan of such cunning you will scarce believe it."

Margaret tried to pull away; her mistress's fingers gripped her wrist like iron tongs. "No, Margaret, you must help me now. I have done the rest, it is only to finish I need you."

"Milady, please . . ."

"It is too late to protest." Amy Robsart's voice became impatient. Defiant. "I have taken hemlock root. I shall die very soon . . ."

Margaret grabbed the hand that held her, wrenching it away. She couldn't speak, could barely breathe, and she stepped backward. Her mistress seemed not to notice and leaned toward Margaret, her tone conspiratorial. "Listen to me, Margaret. The poison will take yet some time to work. And no one will blame you—I have written a note, you see. A note that will exact from Robert his comely neck, and from the queen her throne."

From inside a puffed sleeve, she withdrew a rolled leaf of vellum. "Here I have written that my husband and the queen have plotted against me—"

"Milady! Milady, you cannot do this." Margaret heard her own voice as if from far away. This was mad. Elizabeth *would* lose the throne, perhaps her life, if the mistress's vengeance was successful.

"I cannot do this?" Amy's eyes shone. "I have done it. I have here written," she waved the note in Margaret's face, "that with only a short time left, I found the strength to name my assassins. The queen. My husband. I drank the cordial that Robert brought me on his last visit from London. Cordial from the palace wine cellars. Cordial poisoned by—"

"Your husband brought no cordial from London," Margaret cried, knowing this could not be vouchsafed by any but herself.

Amy's lips rounded in a wily smile. "Who is to say? After all, hemlocks," she gestured toward those along the terrace, "grow everywhere."

Still smiling, Amy tucked the note back in her sleeve and turned toward the stairs. "You couldn't know, dear Margaret, that I dug the root last night while you slept. No one will blame you . . ."

"Mistress Dudley—Wait!" Margaret's tongue felt thick, the words sticking in her throat. "I cannot let her enemies believe the queen had a hand in this."

"Oh, it matters not what you do." Amy waved her dismissal airily. "People will believe what they want, true or no. And Elizabeth's enemies will make them believe it *is* true."

"Milady—"

"No more, Margaret!" Amy spun to face her, the black silken train following like a shadow. "I go now to my rose gardens. The groundskeeper said there is but one bloom left—on the very bush Robert gave me for our betrothal day. I will pluck it from that bush, smell its perfume once more. And that is how I will be found: with the crimson-and-white Tudor rose clasped to my breast.

"What *you* must do, Margaret, is tell all who will listen from whence the rose came."

Margaret had no words. Amy began to walk toward the marble steps. Unable to do other than watch, Margaret saw in that instant more than her mistress's madness. She saw her father's agonized face as flames consumed him; him and three hundred others burned at the stake by Mary Tudor. With Elizabeth the persecution had ceased. But now Margaret saw Elizabeth's throne empty, awaiting her likely successor, Mary of Scotland. Another Papist. Margaret saw her brothers, those two who had escaped the first Mary, pursued, tortured, and burned. And her niece Kat. Kat's children.

Margaret felt herself moving, propelled forward, though her limbs were numb. No, Milady. Gather not thy rose.

Amy paused at the top of the stairs, half-turned to Margaret behind her, and smiled. Then she turned back and stepped off. Margaret lunged forward, caught the train under her slipper, and held it down. Just long enough for Amy Robsart Dudley to sway, totter, and begin a headlong plunge down the marble stairs.

The withdrawing room had grown warm. Margaret stirred on the stool before the leaping blue flames, brought back to the present by the sound of horses' hooves, wagon wheels rumbling. The servants returning from the fair. She glanced about her. All that she had speculated in this same room while with her mistress three days past, others would now speculate. If foul play should be suspected, there were many suspects. But who would guess at poison in a woman who had simply fallen down stairs? The mystery of Amy Robsart's death, if it was believed to *be* a mystery, would not be solved.

Margaret's lips curved. There might always be doubt, however, and Robert Dudley would never be free of suspicion; could never wed Elizabeth. Amy had at least succeeded in that.

There were the first frantic shouts from outside: the servants had found their mistress. Margaret leaned forward and carefully thrust the note into the fire. The flames caught it. It flared briefly before it curled like a petal, and blackened to ash.

DEATH OF A NOVERINT

William Bankier

In characterizing an age we rely on generalities, pictures that fix as one the ups and downs of decades. The London of the Elizabethan era is most often depicted as a fermenting, bubbling hive of activity, where the arts reached new heights, and commerce flourished. But there were years of plague when London was desolate and deserted, and it is to this city that William Bankier turns for his solution to the death of Marlowe. Modern London is a city the Canadian author knows well, having lived on its waterways for a number of years in a houseboat. Perhaps some echo from the past inspired him to reach back to a time when even great poets and dramatists were involved in London's world of espionage.

Peter Falconer coughed and closed the window. "It's stopped rain-ing," he said. "I think I'll go out and busk beside St. Paul's." He found his shawm under some scribbled pages on the writing desk. Moistening the split reed as well as he could with lips that were dry from the fever, he blew a trill. "Betty? Did you hear what I said?"

She was angry with him because he had failed to persuade Guy Kemp-ton to bring them with him to Richmond. "I heard. You'll be lucky if you collect a penny."

He wound a long scarf around his neck and struck a pose. It was the way he had stood last year when she gave it to him, having worked on it whenever she was not serving ale at the inn. Back then, she clapped her hands and her angel's face beamed under the halo of yellow hair. Now, she cast a frown from the couch where she lay sprawled under a cloud of smoke from her tiny silver pipe. Falconer inwardly cursed Raleigh for bringing back the weed from Virginia—and Kit Marlowe for giving them the pipe.

"I'm off," he said, chop-fallen.

"You'll kill yourself that much sooner."

"Don't blame me, Betty. I did my best with Guy. And don't blame Guy. His father drew the line. He'll accommodate his own son, but he dreads others bringing the plague from London."

"Friendship dies easy," was her comment.

Falconer stood in the doorway. He used the scarf to blot sweat from his cheek, discreetly. She was not watching. "Will you be here when I get back?"

"If you get back." Then, as he was groping his way down the dark stairs, the door burst open and she called, "Will you play something pretty?"

"I'll play the one you like," he said. "The galliard written by the queen's father. They always pay to hear that."

It was a funny old time to live in London. Peter Falconer, who had been here for all but twelve of his twenty-seven years, missed the usual turmoil. It was said that ten thousand had died in the past year. Leaving Ludgate Lane, heading for St. Paul's along streets nearly bereft of people, he could believe the death toll.

If a man might live a few more years, make it through to 1600, would everything be all right? Surely the wheel would turn. The plague would be over and done with.

A poster fluttered on a damp stone wall as Falconer shuffled past. He stopped to stare at it. As he rubbed his eyes, the scrawled lines swam into focus. They were poorly drawn in the opinion of a skilled noverint such as himself.

> "You strangers that inhabit in this land,
>   Note this same writing, do it understand;
>   Conceive it well for safeguard of your lives,
>   Your goods, your children, and your dearest wives."

With all his problems, Falconer realized he could be worse off. He could be the target of this threatening verse—one of the Huguenots newly arrived from Flanders, seeking the protection of England's Protestant queen while facing the enmity of much of the local population. Feeling guilty for no reason he could fathom, Falconer moved on. Some said there would be riots. Without the plague sapping so much energy, there might have been before now.

The bookstalls were busy in St. Paul's churchyard. You could count on people gathering here, as long as London had people. And the publishers would never stop publishing. Something about printed pages stirs in man a sense of immortality. Well, the mice would soon devour the paper, and there went your immortality. But it was a striving in that direction, Falconer believed. Not that he wrote anything himself. He only made clear copies of what other men wrote.

"Young Peter! Mind how you go!"

Falconer caught himself for he had, indeed, staggered. He turned and saw the distinguished figure of Christopher Marlowe. The famous poet was wearing a velvet cloak, drawn back to reveal the handle of the rapier at his side.

"I never thought to see you back in London," Falconer said.

"I come and go." Marlowe sniffed a clove-studded orange balanced in a gloved hand. "I don't stay."

"They said you were holed up with Walsingham in that pile of stone at Scadbury."

"You should flee this town yourself, Peter." Sensitive eyes displayed concern as Marlowe observed the tall, pale man before him. In height and general build, the two resembled each other. "While you can."

"I've been considering several offers." Falconer's laugh degenerated into a chesty wheeze.

Somebody inside the stall was trying to get Marlowe's attention. Falconer recognized Blount, the publisher. The poet signalled his availability in a moment. He said to the noverint, "I've a job for you."

"All donations gratefully received."

"Do you know the Anchor? On Bankside, close to Rose Alley, near the theater?"

"Ask me another. I've been thrown out of more taverns than you've had hot dinners."

"Meet me there at three o'clock." Marlowe used both hands to straighten Falconer's battered felt hat. "It's good pay, young Peter. I can promise you that."

* * *

Falconer went home, discarding the idea of busking that day. There was now money he could count on. Marlowe would never let him down. Why waste his breath blowing tunes for people who didn't care? When breath might so soon be cut off.

The door was propped open when he passed the inn. They were drunk inside, singing at eleven o'clock in the morning. Falconer saw Betty behind the bar in conversation with the owner, a Yorkshireman with arms like thighs.

She met him at the door; he knew better than to bring his symptoms inside. "You made your fortune quickly," she said.

"I'm going upstairs. To rest for an hour."

"You should never have gone out." Betty drew the scarf up across his chin. The backs of her fingers smoothed his ruffled hair.

"I saw Kit Marlowe. He's giving me a job. I'm to collect the work at three. At Rose Alley."

"That's over the bridge. You can't walk that far."

"I'll rest. Kit says the pay is good."

Betty was reassured but she said anyway, "You'll end up in Newgate. He'll have you killing people, that troublemaker."

"It was never true. Tom Watson killed Bradley, and it was self-defense. Marlowe just happened to be there."

"Calm down. I hate to see you get excited." She raised her voice in answer to the Yorkshireman's summons. "I'm coming!" Then she turned Falconer like a child and patted him on his way. "Slowly up the stairs. Be careful. I won't see you until you get back."

Falconer raised a hand in silent farewell, making his exit around the corner like Tamburlaine himself in that glorious production years ago. He and Kempton were getting paid to make music in the pit. They had just met Marlowe and it seemed that the good times were going to last forever.

He lay in Betty's hollow on the couch. The smell of ripe tobacco was sweet but he sensed it must be poison. Some day, surely, it would be forbidden to smoke. He wished he had Marlowe's orange to counteract the plague. All he had was Kellwaye's pamphlet. He snatched it from the floor and blinked at the index page. Botch—the general cure thereof. Carbunkle—how to know him. Chickens—how to apply them.

Peter's eyes began to close. The pamphlet fell. He was back in the thatched cottage outside Oxford, seven years old, seated at a refectory table in light from the open door, being taught to read by Falconer, his adoptive father. It was a rare opportunity for an orphan. Peter had never known his parents. Falconer held an administrative position at the university. He began instructing the boy when he became aware of his sketching talent and his quick mind.

Falconer's true son, Jason, heavy and dull at age ten, was watching from the doorway. His cold blue eyes were half-closed, the lower lip hung wetly.

Jason and his jealousy turned out to be Peter's ticket to London. As the boys grew older, exchanges became more physical. Peter was never a match for his brother. A bloody nose was one thing. The softly uttered threat of murder was another. "I'll beat your bloody brains out!" They were in the stable and Jason was holding an iron shoe.

That night, Peter packed ink pot, quills, and scrivener's knife, tied the copper coins he had saved in the corner of a kerchief, then set out after dark for Winchester. He was twelve years old.

Cart wheels racing over cobblestones in Ludgate Lane woke Peter up. There was a chorus of angry shouting. A woman was cursing in pain. Men were running after the offending vehicle, trying to get the driver to stop. Peter went to the window and looked down. They were lugging the woman away, one leg dragging. Drivers cared nothing for people in the street these days. It was every man for himself. *Sauve qui peut.*

The remainder of a joint of ham was on the sideboard, protected by a tin lid. Betty was able to rescue such items once in a while from downstairs. Peter was not hungry but he swallowed a few scraps and drank half a bottle of ale. His throat felt sore.

Down on the street, heading for the bridge, his spirits rose. Kit's assignment would give him something to do. He loved the smell of ink, the scratching sound of a quill's tip on paper. For too long, Peter had been idle, bereft of work in a city where many projects had been postponed due to the plague. Now his mind would be occupied. And with the money in his pocket, he and Betty could leave London. They might travel south into the Kentish hills where the air was fit to breathe.

Passing under the archway and entering the first multi-storied structure on London Bridge, Peter almost bumped into Guy Kempton, who was coming out. His friend was obviously embarrassed to see him. "Cheer up, Guy. It may never happen."

The portly musician clutched a framed portrait of a young man. "My father," he said, holding it up to pale sunlight. "When he was nineteen. It was damaged by mildew. I've had it retouched."

"He'll like that."

"He'd better. It cost me enough." Then, after a pause, "Peter, are you all right? You don't look all right."

"I'm soon to prosper. I'm on my way to see Marlowe about some work he wants done."

"Be careful. I wouldn't touch Marlowe with a barge pole."

"The Star Chamber? They questioned him and let him go. He's too important, got too many friends in high places."

"The Tower of London is a high place," Kempton said gloomily.

Falconer laughed. "That's the way, keep your sense of humor. You'll need it in Richmond when the old gentleman begins to drive you mad."

"I wish you and Betty could have come. I'd have given anything, truly."

"It wasn't your decision, Guy. We both know that."

As the young men parted, Kempton called, "You must flee London, Peter!"

"Give me a week," Falconer replied. "I'll be so far away you'll never hear from me again."

The Anchor seemed to be deserted. Falconer moved along Maiden Lane to the corner of Rose Alley. The empty theater was in sight, no flag flying from the staff atop the turret. And here came Christopher Marlowe at his usual vigorous pace and with him, the dashing figure of his friend and patron, Tom Walsingham.

"Good, you found us," Marlowe said. "They've closed the inn for fear of the pox."

"There's not much trade," Falconer conceded.

Walsingham said, "What was it Raleigh told me the other night? The coward dies a thousand times, the brave man dies but once."

"Raleigh steals most of what he says." Marlowe produced a rolled sheaf of manuscript. "This is what I want you to copy, young Peter. Will you be able to read my writing?"

The noverint scanned the familiar scrawl, finding the title page. "You surprise me, Kit," he said.

"Speak your mind."

"This play is censored. Banned. The Master of the Revels says *The Book of Sir Thomas More* cannot be produced." Falconer's heart was pounding. "Even I know that."

"Are we asking you to produce it?" Walsingham asked politely.

Mocking Falconer's alarm ever so gently, Marlowe said, "Your Master of the Revels did not say the play could not be worked over and improved. In any case, I'm only asking you to copy these lines in your elegant hand."

It intrigued Falconer to see how similar the young men were. Even though Walsingham belonged to the landed gentry, while Marlowe was the son of a Canterbury shoemaker. "I was concerned for your safety," he said. "But you appear long for his world."

"On the contrary," the poet said cheerfully. "There is a persistent feeling within me that I shall be dead before the week is out."

"I don't find that funny," Falconer said.

"Nor do I," murmured Walsingham.

Marlowe was searching inside his purse. He brought out a number of coins, handing them to the noverint. "Still, I feel it. And that is why I am paying you half in advance."

Falconer could hardly comprehend the money he was holding. It came to nearly three pounds. "This is far too much!"

"No, it is only enough." The poet remembered something. "That plus the other half to be paid on delivery is what I received for the completed script of *Tamburlaine the Great*. I had just arrived in London from Cambridge and handed it to The Lord Admiral's Company."

"One-tenth would be more than generous."

"Don't argue with me, young Peter. I want you to have the money. Now get you home and get to work."

Falconer was moving away when he thought to ask, "Where would you have me deliver the finished pages?"

"We'll be at Scadbury," Tom Walsingham said. "It's twelve miles, we'll send someone. Don't even consider coming there."

"You'll never survive the journey," Betty scolded, dropping a shawl across his shoulders for protection against the damp night air. Falconer was working at his desk. She tipped her head to admire the fine dark flow of script. His hand trembled like a bird's wing to and from the ink pot. But when he applied quill to paper, it became steady as a rock.

Falconer could feel strength dribbling out of him like the last half-inch of wine from a broken cask. The pox on his chest had spread to his neck; he wore his shirt collar turned up. With the dryness inside his mouth, it was not easy to speak. He could imagine his tongue soon beginning to swell.

There would be no escaping to the Kentish hills, he and Betty with their worldly goods bundled. They had ceased talking about it. Even the move to Richmond with Guy Kempton would have come too late. They both knew it.

"Nearly done!" He was on the final page of Marlowe's scrawl. "I want you to use this money to get out of London."

"We'll talk about that when we've got the other half."

"It will be in my hand tomorrow afternoon."

"The journey is too far," she argued for the tenth time.

"I mean to have that money," Falconer said flatly. "You've supported me long enough."

Horse and cart with driver was costing seven pence. It was money well spent, leading, as it would, to the collection of a further three pounds when they reached Tom Walsingham's estate. Falconer lay on a pile of empty hopsacks in the back of the cart, folio pages rolled and clutched in his hand. He had begun the journey seated beside the driver, a Ludgate acquaintance named Grief. But now that they were in the countryside, he was stretched flat on the sacks, trying to control fits of coughing triggered by the cart wheels bouncing along a rutted lane. Sunlight poured through leafy branches overhead; Falconer shielded his eyes with the back of one hand.

"He was a funny old man," the driver stated between whistles and clucks to the plodding horse.

"Who?"

"Sir Thomas More."

Falconer regretted now having told Grief the subject of Marlowe's script. "How so?"

"What he said to Sir Edmund Walsingham. The grandfather of the bloke I'm taking you to visit at Scadbury. Sir Edmund was Lieutenant of the Tower of London. So he was in charge of all the executions."

"Lovely." Falconer craved sleep.

"And when Sir Thomas More started up the stairs to have his head cut off, he said to Walsingham, 'I pray you, Master Lieutenant, see me safe up. As for my coming down, let me shift for myself.' "

The clopping of the horse's hoofs emphasized Falconer's lack of response. So the driver repeated, "Funny old man."

An hour later, Grief wakened his passenger by reaching back, clutching his hair, and giving his head a shake. "We're here," he announced as Falconer got onto hands and knees and stared at the moat, the gateway, and the massive Tudor beams. "I thought you were dead."

A servant came running with a pikestaff held at the port. "Who goes there? Where are you from? Who do you want to see?"

"I'm delivering some manuscript to Christopher Marlowe. He gave it me day before yesterday in London."

"Keep back!" The servant made a threatening gesture with the pike. "He's not here. They both went up to Deptford, to Mrs. Bull's Inn. Marlowe and my master Walsingham."

The driver gave his passenger a laconic stare. "What now?"

"We've no choice. We go to Deptford."

"It'll cost you more."

"It's only seven miles," Falconer protested. "And it's on our way back to London."

"You can pay me another three pence," the driver said. "Or you can get out and walk."

"Drive on," the noverint said. He began searching for three pennies in his cowhide purse.

Within an hour, they were breathing tangy air from the great tidal river. Rolling into Deptford, the driver said, "Those masts at the end of the street, they belong to *The Golden Hind*. I was here in '81 when the queen gave Drake his knighthood."

"Where is Mrs. Bull's Inn?"

"Don't get excited, it's just ahead. See the sign? Have I ever delivered you wrong?" As Falconer climbed down, Grief told him, "The Hind is now a floating tavern. I'll be there for a couple of hours if you should need me."

The inn seemed deserted. But it was not closed; the door creaked as Falconer went inside, bending to clear a low ceiling. It was like coming aboard a ship. Contrasted with the late-afternoon sunlight, it was dark between the papered walls where pewter tankards hung, glowing dully, above a close-packed flotilla of oak tables.

"Who's out there?" It was Marlowe's voice calling from an inner room. "It's me, Kit. Peter Falconer."

A door swung open, spilling lantern light from a room clouded with tobacco smoke. Marlowe, in shirt sleeves, filled the doorway. "What are you doing here?"

"I brought the pages." When the poet blinked at him, he added, "The assignment you gave me."

"Yes, of course. Come in, young Peter. You look at death's door. Why did you make the journey?"

"I wanted you to have my copy." Falconer proffered the scroll. He knew there would be no need to mention the additional money to Kit Marlowe.

The poet drew the pages open and held them to the light. "Splendid," he said. "Your usual elegant work. My poor sentences look quite worthy, being so professionally inscribed."

There were four men besides Marlowe in the room, seated around a table cluttered with tankards, plates, and bowls. Falconer saw the remnants of a feast, but he felt no hunger. He recognized Walsingham. The other three were strangers.

"Tom, you know," Marlowe said, introducing his noverint. "Meet Robert Poley, Ingram Frizer, and Nicholas Skeres." They nodded, but none of them seemed happy to have his name announced to this intruder.

Walsingham was impatient. "May I remind you, Christopher, we have little time."

"Always time to verify the welfare of a friend." Marlowe looked closely into Falconer's eyes. "Tell the truth, young Peter. You're on your last legs."

Falconer was ready to drop. He coughed and could not stop until he was given a drink. There was no strength in him. He leaned on Marlowe's arm. The man called Poley murmured, "Must he bring his pox in here?"

"I want you to rest before you go another step," Marlowe said. He led Falconer back to a couch against a wall in the darkened room. Peter fell onto it like a bundle of dried sticks. His eyes closed and he sighed deeply. "When it's time to go," the poet whispered, "I'll make arrangements for your transport." Then he went back into the smoky room, leaving the door ajar.

"Can we settle this?" Poley said. Drifting on the rim of sleep, Falconer heard their conversation in fragments. What they were saying amazed him. "Let's have done and get out of here."

"Why can't I just go on living?" Marlowe said. "I've done good work as a government agent. I spied on the Catholic exiles in Rheims, those who would return and bring down Her Majesty. I'm friends with Raleigh."

"You're a wise poet," Walsingham said, "but a political fool. You drink and then you babble. You can't restrain your tongue. You're not the only atheist among us, but you've flaunted it too often in public."

"*Quod me nutrit, me destruit,*" the poet said. Falconer had seen the Latin inscription on a portrait of Marlowe years ago on a visit to Cambridge, in happier times. He knew it meant, "That which nourishes me destroys me." Was he referring to the poetic muse which ruled his tongue? Or to alcohol?

"As for Raleigh," Walsingham went on, "he wants you 'dead' as much as any of us. When the Star Chamber summons you back for further questioning, and it will, they'll proceed to torture. They'll ask you about Raleigh's little academy of free thinkers. You'll name names, including his and mine."

"I'd never expose my friends."

"You would. They'll stretch you on the rack. They'll burn you. And you're no religious fanatic like old Francis Kett."

"I'd forgotten Kett," Marlowe mused. "I knew him only vaguely at Corpus Christi. They say he went in sackcloth, leaping and dancing into the fire. Twenty times all together, clapping his hands."

"But Marlowe will not appear before the Chamber again because Marlowe is going to be killed right now, in self-defense, by our good friend Frizer. In an argument over the payment for Mrs. Bull's meat and wine."

Falconer heard Marlowe's sarcastic laugh. "Will posterity believe such a flimsy motive?"

"They'll believe it," Walsingham said, "because these three will swear to it. Now I must go. I was never here."

"Wait," Poley said. "We haven't found our substitute. The man to be killed in Marlowe's place."

"It was decided. You'll choose some drunken sailor from the Deptford waterfront. It's gone dark, you can do it easily. Get on with it."

Marlowe's voice overrode the others. He sounded stubborn, as if a problem had given him pause for some time and was still unresolved.

"Wait. You speak as if the life of this unknown sailor is without value. Why should he die so that I may live?"

"Because," Walsingham hissed as if he were addressing a child, "you and not this anonymous man are about to be tortured, giving away the names of certain important people, myself included. After which, we too may be summoned to the Tower. And who knows what chaos might overwhelm England in the wake of such wholesale executions?"

"I believe," Marlowe said, "that England soon will enter into civil war, whatever you may do this day."

Poley interrupted, "Are we to debate this subject until daylight returns? It goes on and on, like one of your damned plays."

As Marlowe laughed out loud, Walsingham said, "And there's the bigger reason. You must leave this country tonight and never return. You must sail for safety in France or Italy. Christopher Marlowe has many more plays to write. Though they appear under another name."

"The victim," Poley said. "Let's go out and find our sailor."

Peter Falconer's heart was pounding. He was experiencing a sensation of inner sweetness. It was akin to the euphoria he had once felt late in the morning when, parched with thirst, he had poured down a foaming pint of brown October ale without drawing a breath. He lifted himself from the couch and went to the light. He staggered as he entered the room, catching the doorframe and leaning there.

"I could not help overhearing what was said," he whispered. He cleared his throat and said it again. Then, "You can see how it is with me. I have the plague. I won't last another week. Let your anonymous sailor live. Take me."

Marlowe said, "Don't be ridiculous, Peter."

"Listen to him," Poley snapped.

"It would be an honor to die in your place, Kit. I've been your noverint. Let me be your angel."

"I could never permit it."

"I'm an orphan. I've never known really who I am." Too weak to stand, Falconer settled onto a chair. "This act would identify me. Forever."

"He is the right size. Kit's clothes will fit him." Walsingham glanced from one to the other of the three conspirators. They nodded agreement. "Come with me, Kit," he said. "Your passage is arranged, you sail on the tide." He turned to Poley. "You remember the plan? Frizer is to have wounds, as if there was a fight."

Marlowe turned in the doorway. "You know not who you are, young Peter?" he said quietly. "I can tell you. You are as noble a man as was ever born. What can I do for you?"

"There is a woman in Ludgate Lane, her name is Betty Allingham. She works at the Golden Fleece. I was going to give her the balance of the fee you meant to pay me."

"She shall have three pounds," Marlowe said, "and a goodly sum beyond that."

The murder was done quickly. Bleeding from self-inflicted wounds on his arms, Ingram Frizer drove his knife deeply into Falconer's head above the right eye. The coroner, who had been paid in advance, falsified the required document. At the inquest, all three men described the drunken fight over money with Poley and Skeres doing their best to hold off Marlowe before Frizer, desperately, drove home the fatal thrust.

Two days later, there was a hurried burial in the yard of St. Nicholas Church in Deptford, by the north wall of the tower. In the years that followed, Marlowe was vilified by members of the establishment who resented his brilliance and feared his determination to describe people and attitudes as he saw them.

As for Peter Falconer, a brief reference to his existence was recorded in the manuscript of time. But the quill that inscribed his name was selected, as in only the rarest cases, from an angel's wing.

THE WILLIAM SHAKESPEARE MURDER CASE

George Baxt

As if combining comedy and mystery were not difficult enough, some few brave authors such as native New Yorker George Baxt presume to add a third element, history, to their brew. We need not wonder at the author's choice of the Elizabethan era as the backdrop for his wit, for his broad, rumbustious humor complements the liberality of the times. George Baxt is the author of seven comic mystery novels featuring historical personages, though none of his other subjects to date is as illustrious as that he chooses here.

Sixteen hundred and one was not a vintage year for the theater in London. The comedies were more vulgar than ever, attributed to this era of permissiveness. The melodramas were grislier and bloodier than the previous season, when even the most faithful of patrons took to booing and hissing and catcalling and throwing rotten vegetables, of which there was always an overabundance. The pageants and the pantomimes were growing longer and duller and it was a current joke that physicians with patients troubled by sleepless nights were recommending an evening at the theater as a remedy.

But all was not yet lost. There was one small hope. Master Will Shakespeare's *Hamlet*.

"I hear they are having fourth-act trouble," one gentleman in a tavern whispered to another.

Still another said, "I am told there is trouble with young Rutherford."

"Rutherford? But he was such a touching Juliet!"

"Aye, but now he plays, I am told, a character called Ophelia. It is a role in which he must grow mad and drown himself in a pool of water."

"Rutherford? But it is known he never goes near water!"

"That's not the half of it," said another gossip. "At yesterday's re-hearsal, the play ran for close to eight hours."

"*Eight* hours! But surely it will be cut!"

"Master Will does not allow it. You know playwrights."

"Actually, I don't, and I'm told I'm all the more fortunate for it."

Will Shakespeare was onstage at the Globe Theatre, glaring at the three men seated on a bench in the pit smoking clay pipes of various colors. To think, thought Shakespeare, to think those were my Christmas gifts. "I will not cut a line!" he shouted.

Matthew Miller leapt to his feet, took his purple pipe from his frothing mouth, and bellowed, "As the representative of the Lord Chamberlain, your benefactor—"

"It is Her Majesty Queen Elizabeth who is my benefactor!"

"And the Lord Chamberlain speaks for Her Exalted Majesty and I speak for the Lord Chamberlain!"

"So you admit you are a ventriloquist's dummy!"

"Apologize at once or *Hamlet* shall never open!"

Sir Ogden Willoughby arose and put an arm around Miller's shoulder, almost blinding him with his orange pipe, which he now remembered to remove from his mouth. "Come now, Miller, let cooler heads prevail."

"He does nothing but insult me and taunt me with jibes. I who supported him when everyone wished to cancel his *Titus Andronicus*!"

Sir Ogden sighed. "We certainly lost a bundle on that one. Gad, cutting off the heroine's hands—I shudder at the memory. Now, Willie—"

Here it comes, Shakespeare thought, he's calling me Willie. It will be the gallows next.

"Dear Willie, we are all pulling together for a success. London is sorely in need of a good drama."

"*Hamlet* is a *great* drama!" shouted Shakespeare in a rare display of egotism.

"That is for history to decide, Willie. But the fact remains, at eight hours, *Hamlet* is no longer a play, it is an ordeal. You saw yourself at yesterday's rehearsal how our audience paid little heed to the dramatics after the first two hours."

"It was a benefit!"

It was the turn of Nathaniel Rigby to rise to his feet, gesticulating wildly with his green pipe. "You must listen to reason, Shakespeare! Those monologues have got to go!"

"Never!"

"By the great lord Harry, they must! I mean, for crying out loud, man, 'To be or not to be'! Who gives a damn! And 'That this too, too solid flesh would melt!' or whatever the hell the words are. They're stage waits! The orange sellers will do a healthy business and there'll be peel flying about."

"I will hear no more of this! You pierce my heart with your words!"

"And you pierce our purses with yours! Eight hours! Do you know what that will cost us in overtime?"

Shakespeare began tearing at his hair. "Where is Burbage? He is the star! He revels in my words! Why is he not here to help defend me against these philistines?"

Sir Ogden drew himself up haughtily. "I am not a philistine. I am Church of England."

Roger Lansing, the stage manager, hurried onstage. "Burbage is at the Boar's Head Inn tearing a pigeon to tatters."

"Fetch him, damn it! Fetch him at once! And while you're there, bring me a ham on whole wheat and a tankard of beer."

Young Rutherford sat before a dressing-room mirror trying on a variety of wigs. He couldn't decide which would best suit the character of Ophelia. The one he favored he had already worn in *As You Like It* and he knew the bitches in the audience would recognize it and make loud comments. He thought to himself with a sigh, How difficult are London audiences, they begrudge a boy his livelihood. And soon, very soon (he was studying his face in the mirror), he would be too old to play ingenues. What next? The nurse in *Romeo and Juliet*? Oh, what the hell, she had the funniest lines. He caught the reflection of Olivia Lansing in the mirror, standing in the doorway. She was the stage manager's sister.

"Why do you smirk, mistress Olivia? Do I somehow displease you?"

Hands on hips, the slim young beauty with the unwashed hair sashayed into the room. "All men impersonating women displease me."

"Then you suffer centuries of displeasure."

"Someday, my young bucko growing older before my eyes, women will take their rightful place in the theater. There will be an end to this disgraceful discrimination."

"Not in our time, mistress. There will be no progress this century."

"Are you also a soothsayer, master Rutherford?"

"I rarely sooth, but I often say. How do you like this wig?"

"It makes you look too Danish."

A swarthy and unkempt man, hat in hand, was led to William Shakespeare by one of the theater assistants. "Master Will, this person says he has a message for you."

Shakespeare glared at the slob. "Well? Out with it."

"It's your wife, sir."

"My wife? What wife? Oh, you mean Anne Hathaway. You come all the way from Stratford-on-Avon?"

"No, sir," said the man with a hearty laugh that made all assembled avert their faces, "she is at the Prawn and Pullet. She just got off the afternoon stagecoach."

Shakespeare shook a fist. "Is there never to be any peace for me? What brings the accursed wench to London? I told her to stay home until I read the reviews!"

"She said if you don't come to her, she will come to you."

"Od bodkins and fie! This is what I get for marrying a Hathaway, a slut descended from a long line of shirt manufacturers!" Will turned to his three antagonists and shouted, "My wife's in town!" They groaned. "I must away to her at once. But I beg you remain until I return and then we shall settle the matter!"

As Shakespeare fled, Sir Ogden said to his two allies, "Face it, gentlemen, Shakespeare's slipping. 'Neither a borrower nor a lender be.' Oh, boy, won't the libraries love that one?"

In her room at the Prawn and Pullet, Anne Hathaway rummaged in her carpetbag. She unpacked swiftly. A bodice, a jerkin, her second-best frock, a hastily wrapped half-eaten leg of mutton, and a lethal-looking snee. Her husband burst into the room as she held the snee in her hand.

"Is that a snee I see?" asked Shakespeare suavely, assuming the manner of a man of the world, any world.

"It is a family heirloom. I carry it everywhere, you know that."

"No, I don't. You never go anywhere. Why are you here? Why have you chosen to displeasure me again?"

She reached for her handbag. From it she withdrew a slightly tattered book leaf. Shakespeare recognized her fingermarks. Mutton grease. They were all over the walls and furniture and their three children back in the thatched-roof cottage in Stratford-on-Avon. She waved the paper under his nose. "Who is she?"

"Who is who?"

"The Dark Lady, you cheating son of a bitch!"

"I know no Ethiopes save my own *Othello,* and he is fiction—along with your jealousies."

"Who is the Dark Lady of this sonnet, Will? I demand you tell me! It is obviously written to some person of whom you are enamored!"

He glowered. "It is good to see your grammar has improved, wife. Now if we could only do something about the way you suck on your teeth."

"Don't you change the subject!"

"I wish I could change the wife."

"So you choose to insult me. Who is my rival for your affections? Who is the hyena? Is it Lansing's sister Olivia? Is it she? I am told she fawns over you like a cocker spaniel in heat."

"If she does, it is not for a position in my bedroom. She wishes to act on the stage. A fanciful notion but quite ridiculous."

She clutched her chest. "Oh, my God!"

"Heartburn?"

"The actors in your plays who portray the women—is it one of them? Is it, Will? Is it one of them who is your Dark Lady?"

"This is ridiculous. This scene is totally unplayable—thank heaven it will never be attributed to me. I must return to the theater at once. And you, madam, I pray you return to Stratford and our three dear little kiddies."

"Hypocrite. You can't stand the sight of them."

He pointed an index finger at her with a stern look on his face. "Be gone, madam, to my second best bed!"

"You're repeating yourself!" she shouted as he slammed the door behind him.

She raged about the room and then came to a decision. She placed the snee in her handbag and left the room.

In the cellar of the Globe Theatre, Olivia Lansing paced back and forth in the dimly lit place (one solitary candle was all the theater allowed in the budget) while her brother Roger attempted to placate her violent person. She wiped spittle from the corners of her mouth with one hand and tears from the corners of her eyes with the other. "Olivia, Olivia, make peace with yourself. They will never allow you to act in this company or any other company in the queendom. Such a revolution will never take place in our time! Wed yourself to Anthony Bedgood. True, he is elderly but he is wealthy and heir to an even greater fortune."

"I thought you despised him. You have urged me to marry some other heir, one younger and more to your liking."

"No, no, no—I have changed my mind! Don't change an heir for me!"

"You are such a fool, Roger. You have seen me act in the privacy of our tatterdemalion shack in the meanest district of the city. You have told me I am brilliance itself!"

"Indeed, I will never go back on that opinion, for we both know I am one of those most hopeless and idiotic of persons, an honest man."

"It is I who should be playing Ophelia, not young Rutherford. Young— ha! I'll wager you he is almost one and twenty if not a year more and he *looks* it. Do you see the lines about his mouth?"

"I am told they are from laughter."

"There's nothing funny about *Hamlet,* brother!"

Richard Burbage, the great star of the theater who was intent on making his greatest triumph as the prince of Denmark, said to young Rutherford as they stood face to face in the wings of the theater, "I warn you for the last time, laddie, if you once again try to queer it when I say 'Get thee to a nunnery,' I shall stick you with a dirk!"

Young Rutherford folded his arms, tapped one foot ominously, narrowed his eyes, which had never been his best feature as they were grown too closely together, and responded, "You fat oaf!" Burbage reddened. "You boar without tusks. You boneless ham. You toothless beaver—"

"Go on." Burbage's eyes flashed murder.

"Thank you, I shall." He took a breath and continued. "You tasteless suet pudding. You—"

Shakespeare entered out of breath as Olivia Lansing and her brother emerged from the cellar, Olivia holding the candle, tallow dripping on her flowing skirt.

Sir Ogden asked charitably, "Well, Will, what of your wife?"

Shakespeare flipped his wrist with disdain and said, "Leave her to heaven.—Burbage! Burbage, have you heard? These three claypipe smokers wish to assassinate us. They wish to cut your monologues!"

"Fie and away with them!" cried Burbage at his fruitiest. "What knaves and scoundrels would so unhand us? Who are these servants of Satan who plague us with the scourge of stupidity? Cut the monologues? I'd sooner cut— Well, on second thought—"

No one saw Anne Hathaway slip into the theater. She hid behind a convenient curtain until she saw young Rutherford flap his hands in disgust and return to the dressing room. Then she hurried after him, shut the door, and leaned against it.

"Well, madam? And what, pray, may I do for you?"

"You know who I am."

"From your heaving chest, I assume you are a wronged wife."

"This has got to stop!"

"What nonsense you speak. The show must go on!"

"I am talking about the way you inspire Will to write these love sonnets. They must stop!"

"Could you cause the tides to go in but one direction? A waterfall to flow upstream?"

"Oh, shut up and listen to me!" She was rummaging in her handbag and swiftly menaced him with the snee. "Do you know what this is?"

"A foul-looking appendage."

"Its thrust is fatal. I have a keen hand with a snee."

"I have no reason to doubt you. But mind, madam, if you dispatch me with dispatch, there will be no performance. I am the only actor who has committed Ophelia's lines to memory. There was no money to hire someone to study under me. This production is being produced on what in ancient Greece they called a shoestring. Cut off my life and you cut off your income. I know master Shakespeare's financial condition—all England knows it. So I beg you, madam, take leave of your senses if you will, but while you're at it also take leave of me."

He was at her side and opened the door. The two fell in the line of vision of Olivia and Roger Lansing, who saw Anne replace the snee in her handbag.

As she left the dressing room, she said viciously over her shoulder to Rutherford, "I hope you fall flat on your face."

He slammed the door shut and she moved to a bench—and, sitting, she placed her handbag on a table beside her and covered her face with her hands.

*   *   *

Onstage, Nathaniel Rigby waved his green pipe and shouted, "Very well, you two rapscallions, have it your way! But mark my words, this is the last the world will ever hear of your accursed prince!"

Shakespeare snorted. "That's what you said about my *Henry the Fifth,* and there are six companies of that touring the hinterlands and the continent—albeit it is getting mixed notices in France." He sighed the sigh of a very tired man. "All Gaul is divided. Let us go on with the rehearsal!" He clapped his hands. "We shall turn now to Ophelia's mad scene." He said in an aside to Burbage, "We must find a way to prevent Rutherford getting indigestion from chewing the scenery." He shouted, "Where is Rutherford? Time diminishes rapidly or something like that. I seem to lack for memorable quotes today. It has been such a terrible day."

Someone screamed. "He is dead! Young Rutherford is dead! There is a snee in his heart!"

"A snee," echoed Shakespeare, sounding like the ghost of Hamlet's father.

All converged at the door to Rutherford's dressing room. He was lying flat on his back, arms outstretched, eyes lifeless as the rest of him, the hilt of the snee indeed protruding from his person where one might accurately suppose the heart was placed. Shakespeare knelt and recognized his wife's snee. "Oh, my God, what hath this Hathaway wrought? What treachery is committed in the despicable name of jealousy? My wife! My wife! A kingdom for my wife!"

Anne entered of her own volition. She recognized the accusation in her husband's eyes.

"I did not perform this foul deed," she said in a husky voice. "I swear upon our children's heads."

"Sure, you do," said her husband with an unbecoming sneer. "With them out of the way, you would have more time to entertain your petty jealousies."

"I did not murder him. I admit I threatened him, but I did not murder him. An alien hand stole the weapon from my handbag while I sat on yonder bench."

She flung a thumb over her shoulder in the general direction of the bench. "I swear this, Will. On another's body rests the burden of the guilt."

"Oh, fie," shouted Richard Burbage, "the catastrophe is even worse than one can imagine! Will! Will! Who now is to play Ophelia?"

Shakespeare gasped and clutched his chest.

"Heartburn?" asked his wife coyly and then retreated, sucking on her teeth.

Olivia Lansing came forward. "I have committed every line of Ophelia's to memory. I have watched every rehearsal and know every movement. The costumes will fit me, for I am as willowy and slender as once was the deceased. And I don't need a wig, I have my own natural tresses."

Anne Hathaway thought, They'll need a thorough washing, my young vixen. And then she wondered what her husband was wondering (and, oh, what joy would have filled her dark being if she knew that for once in their lifetime they were at last in agreement!). Did this wench murder young Rutherford to further her own ambition?

Not a word was spoken for several moments. Glances were exchanged and chins were stroked, the tips of noses were scratched, hands were run through hair under perukes, and throats were cleared.

But Will Shakespeare knew this was an historical moment. He knew that on this night of financial necessity, a woman would appear on a London stage in a major role. He could see by the looks on the faces of the three troublesome ones that they could not afford to cancel the production. Olivia Lansing would take her place in history alongside the first person who ate an oyster, the first person who ate a tomato, the first person who organized a bacchanalian orgy.

Sir Ogden Willoughby spoke for them all. "Very well, wench. But prithee, remember this well—tonight you go onstage an anonymous young nobody, you have to come back a star!"

A star, thought Shakespeare. A murderess more than likely. If so, her career will be short-lived. There will be no garland around her neck, there will be the hangman's noose.

Roger Lansing eagerly took Will's right hand and shook it effusively. "I know my sister will do well for you, Will. She has acted for me in the privacy of our terrible home and she is wonderful. You won't be disappointed, I know you won't! Oh, thank you for clasping my hand so tightly, Will. I know in your heart of hearts you know I'm right."

Shakespeare indeed held Roger Lansing's hand in a tight clasp as his wife and the others looked at his face, which was one they now did not recognize. The features were familiar, but the shadings were black and ominous.

"What have you eaten today, Roger?"

"What? What do you mean?"

Shakespeare repeated the question, enunciating each word very slowly and very clearly, the way he spoke dialogue when he himself acted onstage.

"I've eaten nothing much, really. An apple. Some cheese and bread. That's all."

"You are sure of this?"

"Yes, Will, yes! You're hurting my wrist!"

"You did not eat mutton?"

"Mutton? Who can afford mutton on my salary?"

He turned to the others. "You all know the price of mutton is prohibitive."

"You did not eat mutton," said Shakespeare stentoriously as he held up Lansing's hand for all to see, "yet look at these fingers! Are they not greasy with mutton fat? Is it not obvious that he has had plenty of mutton?"

There was a susurrus of murmurs interlarded with some clicking of tongues, and from Sir Ogden a very studious "Yea, verily."

"My wife brought with her to London a leg of mutton—cooked, of course—on which she chomped to sustain her through the long and arduous journey. Her hands were larded with mutton grease. When first she showed me the snee back at the Prawn and Pullet, she transferred this grease to the hilt. And you, Roger Lansing, when you purloined the weapon from her handbag, you grasped the hilt and covered yourself not with glory, but with mutton grease! I charge you with the murder of young Rutherford!"

Roger Lansing screamed as he sank to his knees and Sir Ogden sent a boy to find a person of authority to take the culprit into custody. "I did it for Olivia! I could not stand her frustration and her suffering! I know her to be a fine actress and she deserved her chance! I will go gladly to the gallows or to the headsman or whatever is fashionable when I am sentenced! I am not sorry! I am not sorry, and I know that God will forgive me for striking this blow against the discrimination of women!"

Shakespeare looked at him coldly and said, "Murder Will out."

THE EARL'S NIGHTINGALE
(AS TOLD BY JAMES BOSWELL,
1779)

Lillian de la Torre

Occasionally a particular historical figure proves more important than period in the genesis of an historical mystery. Such was the case with the Dr. Sam: Johnson detective stories first introduced by Lillian de la Torre in 1943 in the pages of Ellery Queen's Mystery Magazine. *A lifelong devotee of the Sherlock Holmes stories, the author realized that in the English lexicographer Johnson and his biographer Boswell she had something like a real-life counterpart to Holmes and Watson. In fictionalizing the pair for the purposes of the crime story, she created one of the first and unquestionably one of the best historical mystery series. Sadly, there will be no more Dr. Sam: Johnson stories, for the author died in 1993 at the age of ninety-one.*

I was the first to find them, in the darkest nook of a dead wall backwards of Drury Lane playhouse, whence she had come. If I had not had a linkboy lighting my way, I should have passed them by. Felicia Faye had been shot through the head at point-blank range. Beside her in his blood, like a knight of old fallen in her defence, lay the ardent young clergyman. The miscreant's weapons, cast down beside them, remained; but the miscreant was nowhere to be seen . . .

It had all started so agreeably.

I had had, indeed, some trouble in perswading my good friend and mentor, Dr. Sam: Johnson, to pay that first visit to Inchbrooke.

The great man, sage, lexicographer, and *detector,* sat four-square in his old-stile armed chair and would not budge.

"How, Mr. Boswell, Inchbrooke?" he growled. "The seat of the Earl of Sandsea? What have I to do with Earls?"

"Sir, sir," I remonstrated, "the First Lord of the Admiralty, the patron of our South Sea explorers! Of whom Jem Burney as well you know is one, and it is he who urgently desires that we may accept of the Earl's polite invitation and join him in a visit to Inchbrooke."

Jem Burney! That was a different matter, for next to Jem's novelizing sister Fanny, seafaring Jem was a prime favourite of Dr. Johnson. In the end, Jemmy's perswasions prevailed, and he carried us off with him in his carriage to Inchbrooke.

The sun was low in the west when we entered the park gates. The mansion of Inchbrooke rose before us. Pleasantly built of stone, it displayed a crenellated roof-line, a Gothick tower, and the gryphon coat of arms of Sandsea carven in stucco over the arched entrance way.

As our carriage neared the arch, we were startled to be joined by an astonishing escort, a dusky youth with wild black hair, unclad save for his breeches. He rode a large bay horse and discharged a brace of pistols in the air as he galloped. He circled us and made off again, whooping. We were still staring, and Jemmy was laughing, as we pulled up under the gryphon.

A tall man, gold-laced in sea-green, was there to welcome us—the Earl himself! Noel Mountavon, sixth Earl of Sandsea, had clever eyes in a sun-bronzed face, and his own sandy hair tied back with a wide ribband. He was smiling broadly.

"Don't mind Omiah, sirs," he said. "He is from Otaheite in the South Seas, and he had never seen a horse or a pistol until I furnished him with both. You see the result! Leftenant Burney knows him of old, not so, Leftenant? But, come, gentlemen, make ready, for the concert is about to begin."

A neat serving-maid led us to our rooms. She had a provocative dimple and a roving eye, and gave me the benefit of both, which I noted for future exploration.

Soon we were established in the white-and-gold drawing room ready for the concert, Dr. Johnson, decent in mulberry broadcloth with large white wig of state, I in my bloom-coloured breeches and silver-laced coat. The young leftenant, bronzed and eager of eye, squared his broad shoulders in naval blue.

Mr. Omiah, no longer a half-naked savage, was now presented to us. He wore the costume of his country, a voluminous sort of toga in some biscuit-coloured stuff. Executing a bow that would have done credit to a dancing master, he uttered sedately, "Howdydo?"

It was now that a latecomer made an entrance, a strong-set gentleman with a keen, mobile face and flashing eyes.

"What, David!" exclaimed Dr. Johnson, embracing him.

"I perceive that you know Mr. Garrick, Dr. Johnson."

"None better, my Lord, for years ago we two came up to London together in search of fame and fortune, and Davy found both at Drury Lane, playhouse, did you not, Davy?"

"I did, sir," replied the great actor-manager in his rich player's voice, "and so did you, sir, among the booksellers."

Now came in our *prima donna*. She was handed by her chaplain, a slender youth in black broadcloth and bands.

"Miss Felicia Faye, gentlemen, my protegee and the nightingale of our concerts."

This lady I regarded with a lively interest, Dr. Johnson with a dubious eye, for everybody knew that Miss Faye was not only protegee but *maitresse en titre* to the musical Earl.

Felicia Faye curtsied low. Her oval face mantled with rosy colour and her large dark eyes were pensive. She wore blush-coloured tissue cut low and cunningly draped, and her own hair piled high and powdered.

The young chaplain handed her to the harpsichord. She gave him a smile and without ceremony began to play. She played with taste and feeling. The soft-eyed young clergyman beside her hung on her every note, and Mr. Omiah, moving up close on the other hand, peered at the action of the harpsichord in silent amazement.

Miss Faye began to sing, giving us "Cockles and Mussels" in a voice unaffectedly sweet and pure. Then Jem Burney, being one of the "musical Burneys," rendered a sea chanty in his strong baritone. To follow Garrick was called upon, but so eloquently did he plead off that Omiah was called in his stead.

Nothing loath, the islander settled his draperies and launched into a song in the manner of his country, a sort of ballad that told of an amorous contest between an old woman and a pretty maiden for the favour of a beautiful youth. The voice was harsh, but so spirited was the action, so insinuating the glances, that even Dr. Johnson burst into plaudits.

Not to be outdone, Miss Faye now gave us "The Jolly Milkmaid" with exquisite comic effect, and turned to us laughing.

"Brava, brava!" cried Garrick. "What a treasure you have hidden here, my Lord! Say, may we not have her for Drury Lane?"

"I cannot spare her," replied the Earl, smiling, his eye resting fondly upon her, "but you may have Omiah."

"Omiah! Done! I'll make a pantomime of Omiah, the King of Otaheite!"

"Ver' good!" cried the youth, and performed a creditable *pas seul,* "Omiah dance!"

"Not Omiah! Harlequin shall dance, and Omiah shall have the first box and invite us all to share it with him. Good, that's settled. Now, Miss Faye, what will you sing next? Give us a sad song!"

"I will give you 'The Unfortunate Lovers,' if Mr. Lidley will join me."

The young clergyman bowed, and the duet began.

So sad was the story, so haunting the harmonies, and so feeling the glances exchanged that I could scarce forbear a tear. But a frown drew down the Earl's sandy brows and his bluff voice cut into the last minor note as he cried roughly:

"Sorry stuff, Felicia! Come, let us have a martial tune! Give us 'The Galland Grenadiers'!"

This selection, it soon appeared, was designed to display the noble Earl's prowess on the kettle drums, which he smote furiously with great flourishing of lace ruffles and drumsticks.

I wished much that I had brought my flute. I could indeed have sung a comic song of my own composing, but nobody asked me.

As it turned out, the singing was near its end. Miss Faye had barely begun "As Cupid One Morning," when suddenly at the window opposite appeared a face, a face pale and gaunt in the reflected candlelight, framed by tangled dark hair and distorted with hatred and fury. Miss Faye rose in alarm, wavered a moment, and swooned into the young clergyman's arms.

The Earl was white with rage. "Kate! How has she got loose? Secure her at once!"

Footmen scurried, the face disappeared, and the company broke up.

"I wonder," remarked Dr. Johnson as we sought our beds, "that my Lord lets his deranged tenants thus roam the estate."

"Alas, do you not know, sir?" said Jem Burney. "That was no tenant, but the Earl's Countess. She is quite out of her wits and lives under restraint in a remote corner of the estate. But she is wily, as you see, and hard to hold. I pity his Lordship."

The next morning Dr. Johnson elected to lie late, but I rose betimes and followed the shooting party. Mr. Omiah now appeared in English garb, armed with his English pistols. With these he blazed away gleefully, tho unsuccessfully, at everything with feathers, not sparing the dunghill cocks and the ducks on the pond. His marksmanship was not improved by the fact that, in too slavish imitation of his patron the Earl, he persisted in shooting with his left hand.

But I took little note of his feats, for a sudden the pretty serving-maid appeared in the grounds, heading for the lime-tree walk. I made haste to follow and caught her up in the topiary garden. From behind a clipped boxwood bird, I suddenly confronted her.

"Whither away, pretty maid?"

She gasped, turned, and fled. I would not give over now, but followed close on her heels. Against a wall of clipped box, suddenly she vanished. The Inchbrooke maze! Without an Ariadne, without a clew of thread, rashly I followed the sound of her footsteps inside. I was well in when I heard them no more. She was out and away, and I—I was trapped in the maze! Cursing my own folly, I began to run around like a rat in a trap. Then, finding a rustick seat against the boxwood barrier, I sat down and drew breath.

"Dear Miss Faye," said a mellifluous voice from somewhere outside, tantalizingly close to my ear, "pray let us sit here and repose a while. I have much to say to you."

Shall I hear more, or shall I speak at this? But what a fool I should look, begging for rescue like a lost child! Better stop my ears and be silent.

"A sermon, Mr. Lidley?" said the lady lightly.

"Why not? I cannot bear it any longer, to see you living in concubinage, doxy to a notorious rake—"

"Dear Mr. Lidley," said the lady gently, "I am no doxy. My Lord took me from the milliner's counter when I was sixteen, and sent me to France to learn musick and become a lady. And like a lady he has cherished me since. You have no call to put such words on me."

"I have a sacred call, for your soul's sake!" cried the clergyman passionately. "Miss Faye—Felicia! Leave this life of infamy and turn to me. Be my wife, Felicia!"

"No, Adam, it is too late. Give up such a mad thought, for I never can be yours."

"I will never give you up!" cried the clergyman. "I will be your protector in spite of yourself—to the death if need be, I swear it!"

By this time I had abandoned all thought of stopping my ears. What a scene of sentiment!

But the scene was over. There was a rustle of petticoats as the lady rose. "Enough, Adam. You know his Lordship's temper. I dare not linger more. Farewell."

As their footsteps receded, I realized—there went rescue! In desperation, I chose an alley at random, turned a crochet or two—and found myself in the open at last.

I never did catch up with the dimpled serving lass, but as we returned to London next day, I found myself otherwise well pleased with our entertainment at Inchbrooke.

David Garrick was as good as his word. Soon the papers bore news of his grand new pantomime, *Harlequin Omiah,* with Wright as Harlequin and scenes and machines of unimaginable splendour by the famous Mr. de Loutherberg.

"We must be there!" I cried.

"Stuff and nonsense!" growled the sage. "You may be there if you chuse. Little Davy Garrick's pantomime is very well, sir, for fribbles and moony-eyed Misses and South Sea savages, but not for philosophers. Pray, sir, hold me excused." This time there was no Jemmy Burney to perswade him otherwise, for Jem was off again to the other side of the world.

Boswell proposes, but Johnson disposes. However, a more compelling proposal soon arrived, as a footman handed in an obliging card from the Earl, desiring us to dine with him at his townhouse in company with Mr. Omiah and proceed thence to the pantomime. There is no refusing an Earl. On the night appointed, we duly presented ourselves.

We sat down six at table. His Lordship presided at the head, smiling complaisantly, arrayed in garnet velvet. Miss Faye at the foot wore sea-green French gauze cut low and a high powdered head picked out with golden posies. Mr. Omiah as the guest of honour outdid her in splendour in his cream-coloured brocade richly gold-laced. I was another bird of bright plumage in my silver-laced scarlet coat. Only Dr. Johnson in sober earth-brown and the young clergyman in his clerical black struck a darker note.

Indeed the feast started on a rather dark note when the young chaplain, invited to say grace, waxed prolix, inviting the Almighty to forgive us our sins in terms rather too specific to please the Earl.

"Pray, Mr. Lidley," he snapped when Amen finally sounded, "attend to your own sins."

"So I do, your Lordship," replied the youth mournfully, fixing his brooding gaze on Miss Faye.

Arrival of a tureen filled with green turtle soup created a diversion, and we all fell to.

Since the centerpiece of the feast was a mighty baron of beef, and among the side dishes was a succulent veal pye with plums and sugar, it was definitely, in Dr. Johnson's view, "a meal to ask a man to."

Mr. Omiah, in high fettle, obviously concurred. When the beef appeared, he cheered loudly and, producing his precious pistols from his capacious pockets, he brandished them as one who intends to fire a salvo; an intent which was quickly repressed by the Earl.

"Omiah cel-ebrate," he muttered, putting up his weapons reluctantly.

"Later, Omiah."

"Later, cel-ebrate." Omiah cheered up, and soon his wild laughter was ringing out freely again.

We could not linger over the walnuts and wine, for the theatre called. As we left the table, the Earl muttered testily to Miss Faye in a carelessly audible undertone:

"I tell you, Felicia, I will not be cuckolded."

"What nonsense, Noel," said she with a laugh.

"Hornified, I say, by a lovesick puppy in canonicals, and then sit still while he piously directs the Lord to forgive *my* sins!"

They passed out of earshot.

Our party was soon assembled on the doorstep, where the Earl's crested coach was waiting. A light mist was falling. We mounted with dispatch, handing in Miss Faye, propelling bulky Dr. Johnson up the high step, Mr. Omiah and myself springing in after. His Lordship was the last to mount. He had his foot on the step when a breathless boy ran up with a billet and stayed him. My Lord scanned it with a face of dismay.

"Kate again! I should never have brought her up to London!"

"For surgeons," urged Miss Faye gently. "For her own good, sir."

"Even so. I must go at once."

He turned back. As the coach started off, I glimpsed the devoted eyes of Adam Lidley following us from the pavement.

Mr. Omiah was in high spirits.

"*Now* cel-ebrate!" he cried, and forthwith produced his pistols, immediately taking aim at a passing playhouse pigeon.

"No!" cried Miss Faye sharply. "Disarm him, Mr. Boswell!"

"Put it up, Mr. Omiah!" said Dr. Johnson peremptorily, and the youth reluctantly did so as the coach drew to a halt before the playhouse door.

To us who had seen Mr. de Loutherberg's stage effects before, watching the dazzled Omiah afforded more entertainment than the pantomime itself. It opened with the wing-ladder candles all dark and a chymically glowing moon traversing the sky over Otaheire. Then Harlequin Omiah came on with a leap that made the real Omiah gasp, and the action began.

The next scene shewed the arrival of Captain Cook's ship. It was pretty to see how the painted waves rose and fell as de Loutherberg's stage servants, unseen, turned the crank, and when they drew the painted ship across, Omiah stuttered with excitement.

He approved of Columbine's neat form and gauzy skirts, and urged Harlequin audibly to embrace her. The pageantry as the wedding of the pair was celebrated enchanted him, when Venus and Cupid in their golden car descended on the flyings, his excitement mounted, and he fell a-cheering when the wedded pair was by the same means wafted heavenwards.

Then it was over. As the applause started, the youth leaped to his feet, and though Miss pulled at his coattails, he persisted in bowing elaborately from the box, waving to the crowd and loudly uttering "Howdydo? Howdydo? Howdydo?" until the curtains finally closed.

We came out of the theatre into a scene of confusion. The mist had thickened into black fog, and the departing crowd was elbowing and jostling. In the press we somehow lost Miss Faye, and stood a moment baffled and anxious. Then we separated to seek her in several directions.

It was I who found her by the backward wall, dead beside her faithful protector, who had thus, I saw with emotion, kept his promise to the death. What prescient uneasiness had prompted him to follow her hither?

Many hands took up the dead lady and her fallen champion and bore them to the Earl's coach, while other bystanders ran for the surgeon and the magistrate.

The Earl was still from home. The victims were carried in and laid out on their beds. The lady was quite dead. But when Mr. Hardiman, the surgeon, turned to Adam Lidley he found him to be, tho insensible, still in life.

"Fortuitous!" rumbled tall Saunders Welch, the magistrate. "Then we have but to wait and he will tell us what pernitious malefactor has perpetrated this execrable atrocity!"

Still the same old Welch, with his sesquipedalian terms!

Suppressing a smile, Dr. Johnson asked: "Have you the weapon, Mr. Welch?"

Welch produced a pair of much used naval officer's pistols and shook his white head over them dubiously. Then he laid them on the table. The surgeon scrutinized them knowledgeably.

"The story is clear, sirs," he said. "The ball from the first pistol did the lady's business. The second pistol missed fire, and the assailant immediately clubbed it to beat out the gentleman's brains. A left-handed ruffian, we observe, as his victim is bloodied over the right temple. The young man has defended the lady with his bare hands, for see this hand, begrimed as it is and bedabbled with blood."

"A brave young man," I said. "He deserved a better fate."

"I doubt not that he will come to himself in time," said the surgeon reassuringly.

"Then we must wait," said humane Dr. Johnson. "Go home to bed, gentlemen. Boswell and I will do the waiting."

At last the clergyman opened bewildered blue eyes. He looked blankly about, and fixed on Dr. Johnson.

"Who are you?" he demanded faintly.

"I am your friend, Sam: Johnson, who is waiting for you to tell him what happened to Miss Faye."

"What happened—*What happened to Miss Faye?*"

"Miss Faye is dead."

The youth turned his bandaged face to the wall and burst into a storm of weeping.

"Poor lad. We must wait until he quiets."

But when he was quiet, he was asleep.

"Sleeping is healing. Let us leave him. There are others to be questioned. Come, Bozzy."

We tiptoed away.

At this moment, at last, the Earl came home. He was disshevelled and grim.

"What a goose-chase!" he exclaimed, doffing his gold-laced hat and mopping his brow. "And where do you think we found her at last? Outside the playhouse with the stragglers, squatting there like a child, listening to the ballad-woman."

Something in our silence adverted him.

"What is it, Dr. Johnson?" he demanded quickly.

Gently my friend told him of his loss. He stood stock-still, giving no sign save a tightening of the lips as the story came out.

"But, my Lord," concluded Dr. Johnson, "when Mr. Lidley rouses, he will name the miscreant, who will then pay for his crimes."

"I desire it," said the Earl through stiff lips. "Pray, Dr. Johnson, stand by me, remain in my house until this thing is unravelled."

"I will do so, my Lord."

There was but little more to say; and so having said it, we began all three to ascend. But on the stair Dr. Johnson remarked quietly to me:

"And all this while, where is Mr. Omiah? What may he not have seen as he sought Miss Faye alone in the backward regions? We must enquire. Come, Boswell."

Accordingly, instead of proceeding to our temporary quarters, we made our way to the youth's bedchamber. Our quiet knock went unanswered. When Dr. Johnson pushed the door, it gave. What a sight met our eyes!

On the floor squatted the islander, but how changed! Brocade and fine linen lay discarded. His brown chest and clustering inky curls were streaked with ashes. He was singing to himself on a mournful, wailing note as he cast spices on the dying embers of his fire. The chamber smelled of cinnamon and nutmeg.

"Pray attend me, Mr. Omiah," Dr. Johnson said.

But the islander, absorbed in his song, would not attend. We had perforce to give over the attempt and leave him to his savage rites. So at last we sought our temporary beds.

We were awakened too soon by an alarm in the house. Rising hastily, we followed the running feet where they led, to the young clergyman's bedchamber. There around the bed the household was assembled. The chambermaid who had found him was still there in hystericks, ministered to by the housekeeper with the hartshorn bottle. The Earl was there in his padded, brocaded nightgown, and Omiah beside him still half-naked and daubed with ashes. The surgeon, summoned in haste, was there, and the magistrate was expected. On the bed the young clergyman lay bleeding, and the surgeon was staunching the flow.

"Ah, Dr. Johnson," he said, "another attack! This time the murderer has attempted to cut his victim's throat, and with Mr. Lidley's own razor! Again a left-handed assailant, you observe, again an arm too weak to finish the business. The same assassin, without doubt."

"Left-handed!" I cried. "Omiah! Mr. Omiah is left-handed!"

"Me no!" cried the islander in alarm.

"Be quiet, Omiah," said the Earl, "and we shall hear truth. Dr. Johnson?"

"Very well, my Lord. Let us ponder the facts in order." Dr. Johnson spoke in measured tones. "There are clear marks by which this murderer may be known. First, as said, he is left-handed. Second, he came from this house."

"How do you make that out, sir?"

For answer, Dr. Johnson took the assassin's bloody pistol from the table and silently pointed to the Earl's gryphon crest impressed on the butt.

"I have been remiss," muttered the Earl, "that anybody could come at my pistols."

"So the murderer came from here, and here he remained to make a second attack on his victim. Now, what moved him to such terrible deeds? Miss Faye died. Who resented her to the death? Countess Kate, whom she replaced? Mr. Omiah, the pistoleer?"

The savage broke out in vehement Otaheitian, but the Earl silenced him.

"Or someone else who cherished a secret anger against the pair?"

"Get on, Dr. Johnson!" snapped the Earl. "Leave speculation! Get on!"

"I will, my Lord. Let us scan this villain's proceedings. He shoots Miss

Faye dead at point-blank range. Obviously he is someone whose approach she has no reason to fear. Then he turns the second pistol against her protector. It fails, and he clubs his weapon and attempts to beat out his victim's brains with the butt. His arm is too weak and he fails. He casts down his useless weapons and takes to flight.

"But what a foolish assassin! He finds Miss has a protector. Does he make away with him first? No, he shoots Miss forthwith, leaving her defender to cry murder!, to spoil his aim, to foil the attempt.

"But there was no cry of murder, his aim was true, the attempt succeeded. What was Adam Lidley doing all that while?"

"Adam!"

All eyes turned to the bed, where the pale young clergyman lay in silent tears.

"Surely not Adam!" cried the Earl. "The murderer has attacked him twice!"

"Look at him," said Dr. Johnson quietly. "Say, Adam. Did you not shoot her yourself? Tell us."

There was no reply as the tears continued to flow.

"Then *I* will tell *you.* Seizing the Earl's pistols, you followed Miss to the playhouse and waited for her to come out. You drew her aside unperceived, put the pistol to her head, and shot her dead."

"Why would he do so?" I exclaimed. "He loved her!"

"He will tell us presently. Then, Adam, you put the pistol to your own head. It missed fire. Desperate, you attempted to beat out your own brains with the butt. You battered your own right temple with your right hand, giving the appearance of a left-handed attack by another. No man can beat out his own brains. You flinched. But such awful efforts struck you insensible and erased memory. Just so did a comparable shock, you will remember, Boswell, blank the mind of that disappearing servant wench, Elizabeth Canning."

"I remember, sir. A morbid oblivion."

"Then, Adam, as the night passed, memory came back to you, and you attempted your own life again, this time with your own razor. Why did you kill her, Adam?"

"How else," whispered the young divine passionately, "could I have saved her from her life of sin? Only her blood could atone, and mine for her. But neither bludgeon nor razor has availed, and what will become of me now?"

As if in answer to his question, Welch, the magistrate, now appeared in the doorway.

"Ah, Mr. Welch," said Dr. Johnson, "you come in good time, sir. Here is your man (indicating the pale young clergyman where he lay in tears). Take him. But mark you, sir, let him be gently used, for the unfortunate young man is not right in his wits."

"I am not mad," protested the unhappy clergyman, "and I desire to die. Take me to Newgate."

So in fact it was done, and Adam Lidley attained his desire upon Tyburn Tree . . .

All was over when next we adverted to this sad affair. Over dinner at the Mitre I began:

"I marvel, sir, that in this late tragedy of love and madness our usually keen friend Saunders Welch failed to perceive that the Earl's mark was on the pistols."

"Nor did he fail, sir," replied Dr. Johnson with a smile. "You may depend upon it. But when it comes to Earls, Saunders knows his place, while I do not."

"And say, sir," I pursued the subject, "if you knew that Lidley was guilty, why did you play cat and mouse with him before denouncing him?"

"Sir, I did not *know*," replied the sage, "but I had Master Adam in my eye. Mixed with the blood on his right palm were the grimy marks of powder such as speckle the hand of him who fires a pistol, especially if it be fouled and misfires. Had he fired those pistols himself? I put him to the test. Rehearsing the facts of the case, I observed him. When in my lucubrations I began to approach the truth, his face told me so. And thus does guilt detect itself."

"Impelled thereto," I replied, "by Dr. Sam: Johnson, Detector!"

AUTHOR'S AFTERWORD

The hardest thing about this story was explaining temporary traumatic amnesia in Eighteenth Century terms.

Amnesia aside, this story really happened. On April 7, 1779, the Reverend James Hackman shot his inamorata, Martha Raye, outside Covent Garden Theatre. Although she had been the mistress of the Earl of Sandwich for nineteen years, and had borne him nine children, Hackman still wanted to marry her. Refused repeatedly, he finally resolved to end it all. He seized a brace of pistols, followed her to the theatre, and shot her down. But the pistol he had reserved for himself missed fire and the attempt to beat out his own brains proved futile.

The love-crazed clergyman was a great popular success. James Boswell found his case so fascinating that he paid him a visit in the condemned cell. He did *not* ride with him to the gallows, although the newspapers alleged that he did.

The Earl of Sandwich, as everybody knows, invented the sandwich rather than leave the gambling table long enough to dine. But he did much more than that. He ruled the Admiralty, he patronized South Sea exploration. A lover of music, he performed on the kettle drums, promoted concerts of Handel's music, and took a musical mistress when his wife went mad.

The Earl's guest from Tahiti, Omiah, was in his own way as great a popular success as Hackman. David Garrick did once propose to put the picturesque youth into a pantomime, but he never did. It was left for John O'Keefe, ten years later, to do so.

Saunders Welch was a real Bow Street magistrate. He liked to use big words, according to Boswell, in imitation of his good friend, Dr. Sam: Johnson.

For more about Sandwich and Miss Raye, read George Martelli's *Jemmy Twitcher* (Jonathan Cape, 1962).

For Omiah, see Thomas Blake Clark's *Omai* (The Colt Press, 1940).

CHINOISERIE

Helen McCloy

Old Pekin is the setting for Helen McCloy's classic crime story; members of the Russian legation, an Englishman, a Tartar, and their Chinese hosts are the key players in the drama. It is a time of intense sensitivity over questions of nationality, when understanding national-character traits figures as intimately in the solution to the mystery as recognizing universal human motives such as greed, lust, and envy. The author, an American critic and novelist who published more than two dozen books, integrates these several elements in a topnotch whodunit, while also providing a thoroughly evocative portrait of the age.

This is the story of Olga Kyrilovna and how she disappeared in the heart of old Pekin.

Not Peiping, with its American drugstore on Hatamen Street. Pekin, capital of the Manchu Empire. Didn't you know that I used to be language clerk at the legation there? Long ago. Long before the Boxer Uprising. Oh, yes, I was young. So young I was in love with Olga Kyrilovna . . . Will you pour the brandy for me? My hand's grown shaky the last few years . . .

When the nine great gates of the Tartar City swung to at sunset, we were locked for the night inside a walled, mediaeval citadel, reached by camel over the Gobi or by boat up the Pei-ho, defended by bow and arrow and a painted representation of cannon. An Arabian Nights' city where the nine gate towers on the forty-foot walls were just ninety-nine feet high so they would not impede the flight of air spirits. Where palace eunuchs kept harems of their own to "save face." Where musicians were blinded because the use of the eye destroys the subtlety of the ear. Where physicians prescribed powdered jade and tigers' claws for anaemia brought on by malnutrition. Where mining operations were dangerous because they opened the veins of the Earth Dragon. Where felons were slowly sliced to death and beggars were found frozen to death in the streets every morning in the winter.

It was into this world of fantasy and fear that Olga Kyrilovna vanished as completely as if she had dissolved into one of the air spirits or ridden away on one of the invisible dragons that our Chinese servants saw in the atmosphere all around us.

It happened the night of a New Year's Eve ball at the Japanese Legation.

When I reached the Russian Legation for dinner, a Cossack of the Escort took me into a room that was once a Tartar General's audience hall. Two dozen candle flames hardly pierced the bleak dusk. The fire in the brick stove barely dulled the cutting edge of a North China winter. I chafed my hands, thinking myself alone. Someone stirred and sighed in the shadows. It was she.

Olga Kyrilovna . . . How can I make you see her as I saw her that evening? She was pale in her white dress against walls of tarnished gilt and rusted vermilion. Two smooth, shining wings of light brown hair. An oval face, pure in line, delicate in color. And, of course, unspoiled by modern cosmetics. Her eyes were blue. Dreaming eyes. She seemed to live and move in a waking dream, remote from the enforced intimacies of our narrow society. More than one man had tried vainly to wake her from that dream. The piquancy of her situation provoked men like Lucien de L'Orges, the French *chargé*.

She was just seventeen, fresh from the convent of Smolny. Volgorughi had been Russian minister in China for many years. After his last trip to Petersburg, he had brought Olga back to Pekin as his bride, and . . . Well, he was three times her age.

That evening she spoke first. *"Monsieur* Charley . . ."

Even at official meetings the American minister called me "Charley." Most Europeans assumed it was my last name.

"I am glad you are here," she went on in French, our only common language. "I was beginning to feel lonely. And afraid."

"Afraid?" I repeated stupidly. "Of what?"

A door opened. Candle flames shied and the startled shadows leaped up the walls. Volgorughi spoke from the doorway, coolly. "Olga, we are having sherry in the study . . . Oh!" His voice warmed. "*Monsieur* Charley, I didn't see you. Good evening."

I followed Olga's filmy skirts into the study, conscious of Volgorughi's sharp glance as he stood aside to let me pass. He always seemed rather formidable. In spite of his grizzled hair, he had the leanness of a young man and the carriage of a soldier. But he had the weary eyes of an old man. And the dry, shrivelled hands, always cold to the touch, even in summer. A young man's imagination shrank from any mental image of those hands caressing Olga . . .

In the smaller room it was warmer and brighter. Glasses of sherry and vodka had been pushed aside to make space on the table for a painting on silk. Brown, frail, desiccated as a dead leaf, the silk looked hundreds of years old. Yet the ponies painted on its fragile surface in faded pigments were the same lively Mongol ponies we still used for race meetings outside the city walls.

"The Chinese have no understanding of art," drawled Lucien de L'Orges. "Chinese porcelain is beginning to enjoy a certain vogue in Europe, but Chinese painters are impossible. In landscape they show objects on a flat surface, without perspective, as if the artist were looking down on the earth from a balloon. In portraits they draw the human face without shadows or thickness, as untutored children do. The Chinese artist hasn't enough skill to imitate nature accurately."

Lucien was baiting Volgorughi. "Pekin temper" was as much a feature of our lives as "Pekin throat." We got on each other's nerves like a storm-stayed house party. An unbalanced party where men outnumbered women six to one.

Volgorughi kept his temper. "The Chinese artist doesn't care to 'imitate' nature. He prefers to suggest or symbolize what he sees."

"But Chinese art is heathen!" This was Sybil Carstairs, wife of the English Inspector General of Maritime Customs. "How can heathen art equal art inspired by Christian morals?"

Her husband's objection was more practical. "You're wastin' money, Volgorughi. Two hundred Shanghai *taels* for a daub that will never fetch sixpence in any European market!"

Incredible? No. This was before Hirth and Fenollosa made Chinese painting fashionable in the West. Years later I saw a fragment from Volgorughi's collection sold in the famous *Salle Six of the Hôtel Drouot*. While the *commissaire-priseur* was bawling: *On demande quatre cent mille francs* . . . I was seeing Olga again, pale in a white dress against a wall of gilt and vermilion in the light of shivering candle flames . . .

Volgorughi turned to her just then. "Olga, my dear, you haven't any sherry." He smiled as he held out a glass. The brown wine turned to gold in the candlelight as she lifted it to her lips with an almost childish obedience.

I had not noticed little Kiada, the Japanese minister, bending over the painting. Now he turned sleepy, slant-eyes on Volgorughi and spoke blandly. "This is the work of Han Kan, greatest of horse painters. It must be the finest painting of the T'ang dynasty now in existence."

"You think so, Count?" Volgorughi was amused. He seemed to be yielding to an irresistible temptation as he went on. "What would you say if I told you I knew of a T'ang painting infinitely finer—a landscape scroll by Wang Wei himself?"

Kiada's eyes lost their sleepy look. He had all his nation's respect for Chinese art, tinctured with jealousy of the older culture. "One hears rumors now and then that these fabulous masterpieces still exist, hidden away in the treasure chests of great Chinese families. But I have never seen an original Wang Wei."

"Who, or what, is Wang Wei?" Sybil sounded petulant.

Kiada lifted his glass of sherry to the light. "Madame, Wang Wei could place scenery extending to ten thousand *li* upon the small surface of a fan. He could paint cats that would keep any house free from mice. When his hour came to pass above, he did not die. He merely stepped through a painted doorway in one of his own landscapes and was never seen again. All these things indicate that his brush was guided by a god."

Volgorughi leaned across the table, looking at Kiada. "What would you say if I told you that I had just added a Wang Wei to my collection?"

Kiada showed even, white teeth. "Nothing but respect for Your Excellency's judgment could prevent my insisting that it was a copy by some lesser artist of the Yüan dynasty—possibly Chao Mēng Fu. An original Wang Wei could not be bought for money."

"Indeed?" Volgorughi unlocked a cabinet with a key he carried on his watch chain. He took something out and tossed it on the table like a man throwing down a challenge. It was a cylinder in an embroidered satin cover. Kiada peeled the cover and we saw a scroll on a roller of old milk-jade.

It was a broad ribbon of silk, once white, now ripened with great age to a mellow brown. A foot wide, sixteen feet long, painted lengthwise to show the course of a river. As it unrolled a stream of pure lapis, jade and turquoise hues flowed before my enchanted eyes, almost like a moving picture. Born in a bubbling spring, fed by waterfalls, the river wound its way among groves of tender, green bamboo, parks with dappled deer peeping through slender pine trees, cottages with curly roofs nestling among round hills, verdant meadows, fantastic cliffs, strange wind-distorted trees, rushes, wild geese, and at last, a foam-flecked sea.

Kiada's face was a study. He whispered brokenly. "I can hear the wind sing in the rushes. I can hear the wail of the wild geese. Of Wang Wei truly is it written—his pictures were unspoken poems."

"And the color!" cried Volgorughi, ecstasy in his eyes.

Lucien's sly voice murmured in my ear. "A younger man, married to Olga Kyrilovna, would have no time for painting, Chinese or otherwise."

Volgorughi had Kiada by the arm. "This is no copy by Chao Mēng Fu! Look at that inscription on the margin. Can you read it?"

Kiada glanced—then stared. There was more than suspicion in the look he turned on Volgorughi. There was fear. "I must beg your excellency to excuse me. I do not read Chinese."

We were interrupted by a commotion in the compound. A gaunt Cossack, in full-skirted coat and sheepskin cap, was coming through the gate carrying astride his shoulders a young man, elegantly slim, in an officer's uniform. The Cossack knelt on the ground. The rider slipped lightly from his unconventional mount. He sauntered past the window and a moment later he was entering the study with a nonchalance just this side of insolence. To my amazement I saw that he carried a whip which he handed with his gloves to the Chinese boy who opened the door.

"Princess, your servant. Excellency, my apologies. I believe I'm late."

Volgorughi returned the greeting with the condescension of a Western Russian for an Eastern Russian—a former officer of *Chevaliers Gardes* for an obscure Colonel of Oussurian Cossacks. Sometimes I wondered why such a bold adventurer as Alexei Andreitch Liakoff had been appointed Russian military *attaché* in Pekin. He was born in Tobolsk, where there is Tartar blood. His oblique eyes, high cheek bones, and sallow, hairless skin lent color to his impudent claim of descent from Genghis Khan.

"Are Russian officers in the habit of using their men as saddle horses?" I muttered to Carstairs.

Alexei's quick ear caught the words. "It may become a habit with me."

He seemed to relish my discomfiture. "I don't like Mongol ponies. A Cossack is just as sure-footed. And much more docile."

Olga Kyrilovna roused herself to play hostess. "Sherry, Colonel Liakoff? Or vodka?"

"Vodka, if Her Excellency pleases." Alexei's voice softened as he spoke to Olga. His eyes dwelt on her face gravely as he took the glass from her hand.

The ghost of mockery touched Volgorughi's lips. He despised vodka as a peasant's drink.

Alexei approached the table to set down his empty glass. For the first time, his glance fell on the painting by Wang Wei. His glass crashed on the marble floor.

"You read Chinese, don't you?" Volgorughi spoke austerely. "Perhaps you can translate this inscription?"

Alexei put both hands wide apart on the table and leaned on them studying the ideographs. "*Wang Wei*. And a date. The same as our 740 A.D."

"And the rest?" insisted Volgorughi.

Alexei looked at him. "Your Excellency really wishes me to read this? Aloud?"

"By all means."

Alexei went on. "*At an odd moment in summer I came across this painting of a river course by Wang Wei. Under its influence I sketched a spray of peach blossom on the margin as an expression of my sympathy for the artist and his profound and mysterious work. The Words of the Emperor. Written in the Lai Ching summerhouse, 1746.*"

Kiada had been frightened when he looked at that inscription. Alexei was angry. Why I did not know.

Carstairs broke the silence. "I don't see anything 'mysterious' about a picture of a river!"

"Everything about this picture is . . . mysterious." Kiada glanced at Volgorughi. "May one inquire how Your Excellency obtained this incomparable masterpiece?"

"From a pedlar in the Chinese City." Volgorughi's tone forebade further questions. Just then his Number One Boy announced dinner.

There was the usual confusion when we started for the ball at the Japanese Legation. Mongol ponies had to be blindfolded before they would let men in European dress mount and even then they were skittish. For this reason it was the custom for men to walk and for women to drive in hooded, Pekin carts. But Sybil Carstairs always defied this convention, exclaiming: "Why should I be bumped black and blue in a springless cart just because I am a woman?" She and her husband were setting out on foot when Olga's little cart clattered into the compound driven by a Chinese groom. Kiada had gone on ahead to welcome his early guests. Volgorughi lifted Olga into the cart. She was quite helpless in a Siberian cloak of blue fox paws and clumsy Mongol socks of white felt over her dancing slippers. Her head drooped against Volgorughi's shoulder drowsily as he put her down in the cart. He drew the fur cloak around her in a little gesture that seemed tenderly possessive. She lifted languid eyes.

"Isn't Lady Carstairs driving with me?"

"My dear, you know she never drives in a Pekin cart. You are not afraid?" Volgorughi smiled. "You will be quite safe, Olga Kyrilovna. I promise you that."

Her answering smile wavered. Then the hood hid her face from view as the cart rattled through the gateway.

Volgorughi and Lucien walked close behind Olga's cart. Alexei and I followed more slowly. Our Chinese lantern boys ran ahead of us in the darkness to light our way like the linkmen of mediaeval London. Street lamps in Pekin were lighted only once a month—when the General of the Nine Gates made his rounds of inspection.

The lantern light danced down a long, empty lane winding between high, blank walls. A stinging Siberian wind threw splinters of sleet in my face. We hadn't the macadamized roads of the Treaty Ports. The frozen mud was hard and slippery as glass. I tried to keep to a ridge that ran down the middle of the road. My foot slipped and I stumbled down the slope into a foul gutter of sewage frozen solid. The lanterns turned a corner. I was alone with the black night and the icy wind.

I groped my way along the gutter, one hand against the wall. No stars, no moon, no lighted windows, no other pedestrians. My boot met something soft that yielded and squirmed. My voice croaked a question in Mandarin: "Is this the way to the Japanese Legation?" The answer came in sing-song Cantonese. I understood only one word: "Alms . . ."

Like Heaven itself I saw a distant flicker of light coming nearer. Like saints standing in the glow of their own halos I recognized Alexei and our lantern boys. "What happened?" Alexei's voice was taut. "I came back as soon as I missed you."

"Nothing. I fell. I was just asking this—"

Words died on my lips. Lantern light revealed the blunted lion-face, the eyeless sockets, the obscene white stumps for hands—"mere corruption, swaddled man-wise." A leper. And I had been about to touch him.

Alexei's gaze followed mine to the beggar, hunched against the wall. "She is one of the worst I've ever seen."

"She?"

"I think it's a woman. Or, shall I say, it was a woman?" Alexei laughed harshly. "Shall we go on?"

We rounded the next corner before I recovered my voice. "These beggars aren't all as wretched as they seem, are they?"

"What put that idea into your head, Charley?"

"Something that happened last summer. We were in a market lane of the Chinese City—Sybil Carstairs and Olga Kyrilovna, Lucien and I. A beggar, squatting in the gutter, stared at us as if he had never seen Western men before. He looked like any other beggar—filthy, naked to the waist, with tattered, blue cotton trousers below. But his hands were toying with a little image carved in turquoise matrix. It looked old and valuable."

"He may have stolen it."

"It wasn't as simple as that," I retorted. "A man in silk rode up on a mule leading a white pony with a silver embroidered saddle. He called the beggar 'elder brother' and invited him to mount the pony. Then the two rode off together."

Alexei's black eyes glittered like jet beads in the lantern light. "Was the beggar the older of the two?"

"No. That's the queer part. The beggar was young. The man who called him 'elder brother' was old and dignified . . . Some beggars at home have savings accounts. I suppose the same sort of thing could happen here."

Again Alexei laughed harshly. "Hold on to that idea, Charley, if it makes you feel more comfortable."

We came to a gate where lanterns clustered like a cloud of fireflies. A piano tinkled. In the compound, lantern boys were gathering outside the windows of a ballroom, tittering as they watched barbarian demons "jump" to Western music.

Characteristically, the Japanese Legation was the only European house in Pekin. Candle flames and crystal prisms. Wall mirrors and a polished *parquet* floor. The waltz from *Traviata*. The glitter of diamonds and gold braid. Punch *à la Romaine*.

"Where is Princess Volgorughi?" I asked Sybil Carstairs.

"Didn't she come with you and Colonel Liakoff?"

"No. Her cart followed you. We came afterward."

"Perhaps she's in the supper room." Sybil whirled off with little Kiada.

Volgorughi was standing in the doorway of the supper room with Lucien and Carstairs. "She'll be here in a moment," Carstairs was saying.

Alexei spoke over my shoulder. "Charley and I have just arrived. We did not pass Her Excellency's cart on the way."

"Perhaps she turned back," said Lucien.

"In that case she would have passed us," returned Alexei. "Who was with her?"

Volgorughi's voice came out in a hoarse whisper. "Her groom and lantern boy. Both Chinese. But Kiada and the Carstairs' were just ahead of her; *Monsieur* de L'Orges and I, just behind her."

"Not all the way," amended Lucien. "We took a wrong turning and got separated from each other in the dark. That was when we lost sight of her."

"My fault." Volgorughi's mouth twisted bitterly. "I was leading the way. And it was I who told her she would be . . . safe."

Again we breasted the wind to follow lanterns skimming before us like will o' the wisps. Vainly we strained our eyes through glancing lights and broken shadows. We met no one. We saw nothing. Not even a footprint or wheel rut on that frozen ground. Once something moaned in the void beyond the lights. It was only the leper.

At the gate of the Russian Legation, the Cossack guard sprang to attention. Volgorughi rapped out a few words in Russian. I knew enough to understand the man's reply. "The *baryna* has not returned, Excellency. There has been no sign of her or her cart."

Volgorughi was shouting. Voices, footfalls, lights filled the compound. Alexei struck his forehead with his clenched hand. "Fool that I am! The leper!"

He walked so fast I could hardly keep up with him. The lantern boys were running. A Cossack came striding after us. Alexei halted at the top of the ridge. The leper had not moved. He spoke sharply in Mandarin. "Have you seen a cart?" No answer. "When she asked me for alms, she spoke Cantonese," I told him. He repeated his question in Cantonese. Both Volgorughi and Alexei spoke the southern dialects. All the rest of us were content to stammer Mandarin.

Still no answer. The Cossack stepped down into the gutter. His great boot prodded the shapeless thing that lay there. It toppled sidewise.

Alexei moved down the slope. "Lights!" The lanterns shuddered and came nearer. The handle of a knife protruded from the leper's left breast.

Alexei forced himself to drop on one knee beside that obscene corpse. He studied it intently, without touching it.

"Murdered . . . There are many knives like that in the Chinese City. Anyone might have used it—Chinese or European." He rose, brushing his knee with his gloved hand.

"Why?" I ventured.

"She couldn't see." His voice was judicious. "She must have heard . . . something."

"But what?"

Alexei's Asiatic face was inscrutable in the light from the paper lanterns.

Police? Extra-territorial law courts? That was Treaty Port stuff. Like pidgin English. We had only a few legation guards. No gunboats. No telegraph. No railway. The flying machine was a crank's daydream. Even cranks hadn't dreamed of a wireless telegraphy . . . Dawn came. We were still searching. Olga Kyrilovna, her cart and pony, her groom and lantern boy, had all vanished without trace as if they had never existed.

As character witnesses, the Chinese were baffling. "The Princess's groom was a Manchu of good character," Volgorughi's Number One Boy told us. "But her lantern boy was a Cantonese with a great crime on his conscience. He caused his mother's death when he was born which the Ancients always considered unfilial."

At noon some of us met in the smoking room of the Pekin Club. "It's curious there's been no demand for ransom," I said.

"Bandits? Within the city walls?" Carstairs was skeptical. "Russia has never hesitated to use *agents provocateurs*. They say she's going to build a railway across Siberia. I don't believe it's practical. But you never can tell what those mad Russians will do. She'll need Manchuria. And she'll need a pretext for taking it. Why not the abduction of the Russian minister's wife?"

Kiada shook his head. "Princess Volgorughi will not be found until 'The

River' is restored to its companion pictures, 'The Lake,' 'The Sea,' and 'The Cloud.' "

"What do you mean?"

Kiada answered me patiently as an adult explaining the obvious to a backward child. "It is known that Wang Wei painted this series of pictures entitled Four Forms of Water. Volgorughi has only one of them—The River. The separation of one painting from others in a series divinely inspired is displeasing to the artist."

"But Wang Wei has been dead over a thousand years!"

"It is always dangerous to displease those who have passed above. An artist as steeped in ancient mysteries as the pious Wang Wei has power over men long after he has become a Guest On High. Wang Wei will shape the course of our lives into any pattern he pleases in order to bring those four paintings together again. I knew this last night when I first saw 'The River' and—I was afraid."

"I wonder how Volgorughi did get that painting?" mused Carstairs. "I hope he didn't forget the little formality of payment."

"He's not a thief!" I protested.

"No. But he's a collector. All collectors are mad. Especially Russian collectors. It's like gambling or opium."

Lucien smiled unpleasantly. "Art! Ghosts! Politics! Why go so far afield? Olga Kyrilovna was a young bride. And Volgorughi is . . . old. Such marriages are arranged by families, we all know. 'Women,' as Balzac said, 'are the dupes of the social system.' When they consent to marriage, they have not enough experience to know what they are consenting to. Olga Kyrilovna found herself in a trap. She has escaped, as young wives have escaped from time immemorial, by taking a lover. Now they've run off together. *Sabine a tout donné, sa beauté de colombe, et son amour . . .*"

"*Monsieur* de L'Orges."

We all started. Alexei was standing in the doorway. His eyes commanded the room. "What you say is impossible. Do I make myself clear?"

"Of course, Alexei. I—I was only joking." Lucien sounded piteous.

But Alexei had no pity. "A difference of taste in jokes has broken many friendships. . . . Charley, will you come back to the Russian Legation with me?"

The Tartar General's audience hall had never seemed more shabby. Volgorughi sat staring at the garish wall of red and gilt. He was wearing an overcoat, carrying hat and gloves.

"News, Excellency?" queried Alexei.

Volgorughi shook his head without looking up. "I've been to the *Tsungli Yamên.*" He spoke like a somnambulist. "The usual thing. Green tea. Melon seeds. A cold stone pavilion. Mandarins who giggle behind satin sleeves. I asked for an audience with the emperor himself. It was offered— on the usual terms. I had to refuse—as usual. By the time a gunboat gets to the mouth of the Pei-ho, they may agree to open another seaport to Russian trade by way of reparation, but . . . I shall never see Olga Kyrilova again. Sometimes I think our governments keep us here in the hope that something will happen to give them a pretext for sending troops into China . . ."

We all felt that. The *Tsungli Yamên* or Foreign Office calmly assumed that our legations were vassal missions to their emperor like those from Thibet. The emperor would not receive us unless we acknowledged his sovereignty by kowtowing, the forehead to strike the floor audibly nine times. Even if we had wished to go through this interesting performance for the sake of peace and trade, our governments would not let us compromise their sovereignty. But they kept us there, where we had no official standing, where our very existence was doubted. "It may be there are as many countries in the West as England, France, Germany and Russia," one mandarin had informed me. "But the others you mention—Austria, Sweden, Spain and America—they are all lies invented to intimidate the Chinese."

Alexei was not a man to give up easily. "Excellency, I shall find her."

Volgorughi lifted his head. "How?"

Alexei shouted. The study door opened. An old man in workman's dress came in with a young Chinese. I knew the old man as Antoine Billot, one of the Swiss clockmakers who were the only western tradesmen allowed in Pekin.

"Charley," said Alexei. "Tell Antoine about the fingering piece you saw in the hands of a beggar last summer."

"It was turquoise matrix, carved to represent two nude figures embracing. The vein of brown in the stone colored their heads and spotted the back of the smaller figure."

"I have seen such a fingering piece," said Antoine. "In the Palace of Whirring Phoenixes. It is in that portion of the Chinese City known as the Graveyard of the Wu Family, in the Lane of Azure Thunder."

"It is the Beileh Tsai Heng who lives there," put in Antoine's Chinese apprentice. "Often have we repaired his French clocks. Very fine clocks of Limoges enamel sent to the Emperor Kang Hsi by Louis XIV. The Beileh's grandmother was the Discerning Concubine of the Emperor Tao Kwang."

"An old man?" asked Alexei.

"The Beileh has not yet attained the years of serenity. Though the name Heng means 'Steadfast' he is impetuous as a startled dragon. He memorialized the late emperor for permission to live in a secluded portion of the Chinese City so that he could devote his leisure to ingenious arts and pleasures."

I looked at Alexei. "You think the beggar who stared at us was a servant of this prince?"

"No. Your beggar was the prince himself. 'Elder Brother' is the correct form for addressing a Manchu prince of the third generation."

"It is the latest fad among our young princes of Pekin," explained the apprentice, "to haunt the highways and taverns dressed as beggars, sharing the sad life of the people for a few hours. They vie with each other to see which can look the most dirty and disreputable. But each one has some little habit of luxury that he cannot give up, even for the sake of disguise. A favorite ring, a precious fan, an antique fingering piece. That is how you can tell them from the real beggars."

Alexei turned to me. "When a taste for the exquisite becomes so refined that it recoils upon itself and turns into its opposite—a taste for the ugly—we call that decadence. Prince Heng is decadent . . . bored, curious, irresponsible, ever in search of a new sensation." Alexei turned back to the apprentice. "Could the Beileh be tempted with money?"

"Who could offer him anything he does not already possess?" intoned the young Chinese. "His revered father amassed one hundred thousand myriad snow-white *taels* of silver from unofficial sources during his benevolent reign as Governor of Kwantung. In the Palace of Whirring Phoenixes even the wash bowls and spitting basins are curiously wrought of fine jade and pure gold, for this prince loves everything that is rare and strange."

Alexei hesitated before his next question. "Does the Beileh possess any valuable paintings?"

"His paintings are few but priceless. Four landscape scrolls from the divine brush of the illustrious Wang Wei."

Volgorughi started to his feet. "What's this?"

"You may go, Antoine." Alexei waited until the door had closed. "Isn't it obvious, sir? Your Wang Wei scroll was stolen."

Volgorughi sank back in his chair. "But . . . I bought it. From a pedlar in the Chinese City. I didn't ask his name."

"How could a nameless pedlar acquire such a painting from such a prince honestly?" argued Alexei. "Your pedlar was a thief or a receiver. Such paintings have religious as well as artistic value to the Chinese. They are heirlooms, never sold even by private families who need the money. Last night the moment I saw the marginal note written by the Emperor Ch'ien Lung I knew the picture must have been stolen from the Imperial Collection. I was disturbed because I knew that meant trouble for us if it were known you had the painting. That's why I didn't want to read the inscription aloud. It's easy to see what happened. The thief was captured and tortured until he told Heng you had the painting. Heng saw Olgo Kyrilovna with Charley and Lucien in the Chinese City last summer. He must have heard then that she was your wife. When he found you had the painting, he ordered her abduction. Now he is holding her as hostage for the return of the painting. All this cannot be coincidence."

Volgorughi buried his face in his hands. "What can we do?"

"With your permission, Excellency, I shall go into the Chinese City tonight and return the painting to Heng. I shall bring back Olga Kyrilovna . . . if she is still alive."

Volgorughi rose, shoulders bent, chin sunk on his chest. "I shall go with you, Alexei Andreitch."

"Your Excellency forgets that special circumstances make it possible for me to go into the Chinese City after dark when no other European can do so with safety. Alone I have some chance of success. With you to protect, it would be impossible."

"You will need a Cossack Escort."

"That would strip the legation of guards. And it would antagonize Heng. Olga Kyrilovna might be harmed before I could reach her. I prefer to go alone."

Volgorughi sighed. "Report to me as soon as you get back . . . You are waiting for something?"

"The painting, Excellency."

Volgorughi walked with a shuffling step into the study. He came back with the scroll in its case. "Take it. I never want to see it again."

At the door I looked back. Volgorughi was slumped in his seat, a figure of utter loneliness and despair.

Alexei glanced at me as we crossed the compound. "Something is puzzling you, Charley. What is it?"

"If this Beileh Heng is holding Olga Kyrilovna as a hostage for the painting, he wants you to know that he has abducted her. He has nothing to conceal. Then why was the leper murdered? If not to conceal something?"

Alexei led the way into a room of his own furnished with military severity. "I'm glad Volgorughi didn't think of that question, Charley. It has been troubling me too."

"And the answer?"

"Perhaps I shall find it in the Palace of Whirring Phoenixes. Perhaps it will lead me back to one of the men who dined with us yesterday evening. Except for the Carstairses, we were all separated from each other at one time or another in those dark streets—even you and I . . ."

Alexei was opening a cedar chest. He took out a magnificent robe of wadded satin in prismatic blues and greens. When he had slipped it on he turned to face me. The Tartar cast of his oblique eyes and sallow skin was more pronounced than I had ever realized. Had I passed him wearing this costume in the Chinese City I should have taken him for a Manchu or a Mongol.

He smiled. "Now will you believe I have the blood of Temudjin Genghis Khan in my veins?"

"You've done this before!"

His smile grew sardonic. "Do you understand why I am the only European who can go into the Chinese City after dark?"

My response was utterly illogical. "Alexei, take me with you tonight!"

He studied my face. "You were fond of Olga Kyrilovna, weren't you?"

"Is there no way?" I begged.

"Only one way. And it's not safe. You could wear the overalls of a workman and carry the tools of a clockmaker. And stay close to me, ostensibly your Chinese employer."

"If Antoine Billot will lend me his clothes and tools . . ."

"That can be arranged." Alexei was fitting a jewelled nail shield over his little finger.

"Well? Is there any other objection?"

"Only this." He looked up at me intently. His pale face and black eyes were striking against the kingfisher blues and greens of his satin robe. "We are going to find something ugly at the core of this business, Charley. You are younger than I and . . . will you forgive me if I say you are rather innocent? Your idea of life in Pekin is a series of dances and dinners, race meetings outside the walls in spring, charades at the English Legation in winter, snipe shooting at Hai Tien in the fall. Your government doesn't maintain an Intelligence Service here. So you can have no idea of the struggle that goes on under the surface of this pleasant social life. Imperialist ambitions and intrigues, the alliance between politics and trade, even the opium trade—what do you know of all that? Sometimes I think you don't even know much about the amusements men like Lucien find in the Chinese City . . . Life is only pleasant on the surface, Charley. And now we're going below the surface. Respectability is as artificial as the clothes we wear. What it hides is as ugly as our naked bodies and animal functions. Whatever happens tonight, I want you to remember this: under every suit of clothes, broadcloth or rags, there is the same sort of animal."

"What are you hinting at?"

"There are various possibilities. You said Heng stared at your party as if he had never seen Western men before. Are you sure he wasn't staring at Olga Kyrilovna as if he had never seen a Western woman before?"

"But our women are physically repulsive to Chinese!"

"In most cases. But the Chinese are not animated types. They are individuals, as we are. Taste is subjective and arbitrary. Individual taste can be eccentric. Isn't it possible that there are among them, as among us, men who have romantic fancies for the exotic? Or sensual fancies for the experimental? I cannot get those words of Antoine's apprentice out of my mind: *this prince loves everything that is rare and strange . . .*"

A red sun was dipping behind the Western Hills when we passed out a southern gate of the Tartar City. In a moment all nine gates would swing shut and we would be locked out of our legations until tomorrow's dawn. It was not a pleasant feeling. I had seen the head of a consul rot on a pike in the sun. That was what happened to barbarian demons who went where they were not wanted outside the Treaty Ports.

The Chinese City was a wilderness of twisting lanes, shops, taverns, theaters, teahouses, opium dens, and brothels. Long ago conquering Manchu Tartars had driven conquered Chinese outside the walls of Pekin proper, or the Tartar City, to this sprawling suburb where the conquered catered to the corruption of the conqueror. The Chinese City came to life at nightfall when the Tartar City slept behind its walls. Here and there yellow light shone through blue dusk from a broken gateway. Now and then we caught the chink of porcelain cups or the whine of a *yuehkin* guitar.

Alexei seemed to know every turn of the way. At last I saw why he was Russian military *attaché* at Pekin. Who else would learn so much about China and its people as this bold adventurer who could pass for a Manchu in Chinese robes? When we were snipe-shooting together, he seemed to know the Pei-chih-li plain as if he carried a military map of the district in his head. Years afterward, when the Tsar's men took Port Arthur, everyone learned about Russian Intelligence in China. I learned that evening. And I found myself looking at Alexei in his Chinese dress as if he had suddenly become a stranger. What did I know of this man whom I had met so casually at legation parties? Was he ruthless enough to stab a beggar already dying of leprosy? Had he had any reason for doing so?

We turned into a narrower lane—a mere crack between high walls. Alexei whispered: "The Lane of Azure Thunder."

A green-tiled roof above the dun-colored wall proclaimed the dwelling of a prince. Alexei paused before a gate, painted vermilion. He spoke Cantonese to the gatekeeper. I understood only two words—"Wang Wei." There were some moments of waiting. Then the gate creaked open and we were ushered through that drab wall into a wonderland of fantastic parks and lacquered pavilions blooming with all the colors of Sung porcelain.

I was unprepared for the splendor of the audience hall. The old palaces we rented for legations were melancholy places, decaying and abandoned by their owners. But here rose, green, and gold rioted against a background of dull ebony panels, tortured by a cunning chisel into grotesquely writhing shapes. There were hangings of salmon satin embroidered with threads of gold and pale green, images of birds and flowers carved in jade and coral and malachite. The slender rafters were painted a poisonously bright jade-green and on them tiny lotus buds were carved and gilded. There was a rich rustle of satin and the Beileh Heng walked slowly into the room.

Could this stately figure be the same rude fellow I had last seen squatting in the gutter, half naked in the rags of a beggar? He moved with the deliberate grace of the grave religious dancers in the Confucian temples. His robe was lustrous purple—the "myrtle-red" prescribed for princes of the third generation by the Board of Rites. It swung below the paler mandarin jacket in sculptured folds, stiff with a sable lining revealed by two slits at either side. Watered in the satin were the Eight Famous Horses of the Emperor Mu Wang galloping over the Waves of Eternity. His cuffs were curved like horseshoes in honor of the cavalry that set the Manchu Tartars on the throne. Had that cavalry ridden west instead of south, Alexei himself might have owed allegiance to this prince. Though one was Chinese and one Russian, both were Tartar.

Heng's boots of purple satin looked Russian. So did his round cap faced with a band of sable. His skin was a dull ivory, not as yellow as the southern Chinese. His cheeks were lean; his glance, searching and hungry. He looked like a pure-bred descendant of the "wolf-eyed, lantern-jawed Manchus" of the Chinese chronicles. A conqueror who would take whatever he wanted, but who had learned from the conquered Chinese to want only the precious and fanciful.

Something else caught my eye. There was no mistake. This was the beggar. For, pale against his purple robe, gleamed the fingering piece of turquoise matrix which his thin, neurotic fingers caressed incessantly.

No ceremonial tea was served. We were being received as enemies during a truce. But Alexei bowed profoundly and spoke with all the roundabout extravagance of Mandarin politeness.

"An obscure design of destiny has brought the property of your highness, a venerable landscape scroll painted by the devout Wang Wei, into the custody of the Russian minister. Though I appear Chinese in this garb, know that I am Russian and my minister has sent me in all haste and humility to restore this inestimable masterpiece to its rightful owner."

Heng's eyes were fixed on a point above our heads for, Chinese or barbarian, we were inferiors, unworthy of his gaze. His lips scarcely moved. "When you have produced the scroll, I shall know whether you speak truth or falsehood."

"All Your Highness's words are unspotted pearls of perpetual wisdom." Alexei stripped the embroidered case from the jade roller. Like a living thing the painted silk slipped out of his grasp and unwound itself at the Beileh's feet.

Once again a faery stream of lapis, jade, and turquoise hues unrolled before my enchanted eyes. Kiada was right. I could hear the wind sing in the rushes and the wail of the wild geese, faint and far, a vibration trembling on the outer edge of the physical threshold for sound.

The hand that held the fingering piece was suddenly still. Only the Beileh's eyeballs moved, following the course of Wang Wei's river from its bubbling spring to its foam-flecked sea. Under his cultivated stolidity, I saw fear and, more strangely, sorrow.

At last he spoke. "This painting I inherited from my august ancestor the ever-glorious Emperor Ch'ien Lung who left his words and seal upon the margin. How has it come into your possession?"

Alexei bowed again. "I shall be grateful for an opportunity to answer that question if Your Highness will first condescend to explain to my mean intelligence how the scroll came to leave the Palace of Whirring Phoenixes?"

"Outside Barbarian, you are treading on a tiger's tail when you speak with such insolence to an Imperial Clansman. I try to make allowances for you because you come of an inferior race, the Hairy Ones, without manners or music, unversed in the Six Fine Arts and the Five Classics. Know then that it is not your place to ask questions or mine to answer them. You may follow me, at a distance of nine paces, for I have something to show you."

He looked neither to right nor left as he walked soberly through the audience hall, his hands tucked inside his sleeves. At the door he lifted one hand to loosen the clasp of his mandarin jacket, and it slid from his shoulders. Before it had time to touch the ground, an officer of the Coral Button sprang out of the shadows to catch it reverently. The Beileh did not appear conscious of this officer's presence. Yet he had let the jacket fall without an instant's hesitation. He knew that wherever he went at any time there would always be someone ready to catch anything he let fall before it was soiled or damaged.

We followed him into a garden, black and white in the moonlight. We passed a pool spanned by a crescent bridge. Its arc of stone matched the arc of its reflection in the ice-coated water, completing a circle that was half reality, half illusion. We came to another pavilion, its roof curling up at each corner, light filtering through its doorway. Again we heard the shrill plaint of a guitar. We rounded a devil-screen of gold lacquer and the thin sound ended on a high, feline note.

I blinked against a blaze of lights. Like a flight of parti-colored butterflies, a crowd of girls fluttered away from us, tottering on tiny, mutilated feet. One who sat apart from the rest, rose with dignity. A Manchu princess, as I saw by her unbound feet and undaunted eyes. Her hair was piled high in the lacquered coils of the Black Cloud Coiffure. She wore hairpins, earrings, bracelets and tall heels of acid-green jade. Her gown of sea-green silk was sewn with silver thread worked in the Pekin stitch to represent the Silver Crested Love Birds of Conjugal Peace. But when she turned her face, I saw the sour lines and sagging pouches of middle age.

Princess Heng's gaze slid over us with subtle contempt and came to rest upon the Beileh with irony. "My pleasure in receiving you is boundless and would find suitable expression in appropriate compliments were the occasion more auspicious. As it is, I pray you will forgive me if I do not linger in the fragrant groves of polite dalliance, but merely inquire why Your Highness has seen fit to introduce two male strangers, one a barbarian, into the sanctity of the Inner Chamber?"

Heng answered impassively. "Even the Holy Duke of Yen neglected the forms of courtesy when he was pursued by a tiger."

A glint of malice sparkled in the eyes of the Beileh's Principal Old Woman. "Your Highness finds his present situation equivalent to being pursued by a tiger? To my inadequate understanding that appears the natural consequence of departing from established custom by attempting to introduce a barbarian woman into the Inner Chamber."

Heng sighed. "If the presence of these far-travelled strangers distresses you and my Small Old Women you have permission to retire."

Princess Heng's jade bangles clashed with the chilly ring of ice in a glass as she moved towards the door. The Small Old Women, all girls in their teens, shimmered and rustled after the Manchu princess who despised them both as concubines and as Chinese.

Heng led us through another door.

"Olga!"

The passion in Alexei's voice was a shock to me. In my presence he had always addressed her as "excellency" or "princess" . . . She might have been asleep as she lay there on her blue fox cloak, her eyes closed, her pale face at peace, her slight hands relaxed in the folds of her white tulle skirt. But the touch of her hands was ice and faintly from her parted lips came the sweet, sickish odor of opium.

Alexei turned on Heng. "If you had not stolen her, she would not have died!"

"Stolen?" It was the first word that had pierced Heng's reserve. "Imperial Clansmen do not steal women. I saw this far-travelled woman in a market lane of the Chinese City last summer. I coveted her. But I did not steal her. I offered money for her, decently and honorably, in accord with precepts of morality laid down by the Ancients. Money was refused.

Months passed. I could not forget the woman with faded eyes. I offered one of my most precious possessions. It was accepted. The painting was her price. But the other did not keep his side of the bargain. For she was dead when I lifted her out of her cart."

The lights were spinning before my eyes. "Alexei, what is this? Volgorughi would not . . ."

Alexei's look stopped me.

"You . . ." Words tumbled from my lips. "There was a lover. And you were he. And Volgorughi found out. And he watched you together and bided his time, nursing his hatred and planning his revenge like a work of art. And finally he punished you both cruelly by selling her to Heng. Volgorughi knew that Olga would drive alone last night. Volgorughi had lived so long in the East that he had absorbed the Eastern idea of women as well as the Eastern taste in painting. The opium must have been in the sherry he gave her. She was already drowsy when he lifted her into the cart. No doubt he had planned to give her only a soporific dose that would facilitate her abduction. But at the last moment he commuted her sentence to death and let her have the full, lethal dose. He gave her goodbye tenderly because he knew he would never see her again. He promised her she would be safe because death is, in one sense, safety—the negation of pain, fear, and struggle . . .

"There was no pedlar who sold him the painting. That was his only lie. He didn't prevent your coming here tonight because he wanted you to know. That was your punishment. And he saw that you could make no use of your knowledge now. Who will believe that Olga Kyrilovna, dead of a Chinese poison in the Chinese City, was killed by her own husband? Some Chinese will be suspected—Heng himself, or his jealous wife, or the men who carry out his orders. No European would take Heng's story seriously unless it were supported by at least one disinterested witness. That was why the leper had to die last night, while Volgorughi was separated from Lucien through a wrong turning that was Volgorughi's fault. The leper must have overheard some word of warning or instruction from Volgorughi to Olga's lantern boy that revealed the whole secret. That word was spoken in Cantonese. Olga's lantern boy was Cantonese. Volgorughi spoke that dialect. The leper knew no other tongue. And Lucien, the only person who walked with Volgorughi, was as ignorant of Cantonese as all the rest of us, save you."

Heng spoke sadly in his own tongue. "The treachery of the Russian minister in sending this woman to me dead deserves vengeance. But one thing induces me to spare him. He did not act by his own volition. He was a blind tool in the skillful hand of the merciless Wang Wei. Through this woman's death 'The River' has been restored to its companion pictures, 'The Lake,' 'The Sea,' and 'The Cloud.' And I, who separated the pictures so impiously, have had my own share of suffering as a punishment . . .''

. . . Yes, I'll have another brandy. One more glass. Olga? She was buried in the little Russian Orthodox cemetery at Pekin. Volgorughi was recalled. The breath of scandal clung to his name the rest of his life. The Boxer Uprising finally gave the West its pretext for sending troops into China. That purple satin Epicurean, the Beileh Heng, was forced to clean sewers by German troops during the occupation and committed suicide from mortification. The gay young bloods of Pekin, who had amused themselves by playing beggar, found themselves beggars in earnest when the looting was over. Railways brought Western businessmen to Pekin and before long it was as modern as Chicago.

Alexei? He became attentive to the wife of the new French minister, a woman with dyed hair who kept a Pekinese sleeve dog in her bedroom. I discovered the distraction that can be found in study of the early Chinese poets. When I left the service, I lost track of Alexei. During the Russian revolution, I often wondered if he were still living. Did he join the Reds, as some Cossack officers did? Or was he one of the Whites who settled in Harbin or Port Arthur? He would have been a very old man then, but I think he could have managed. He spoke so many Chinese dialects . . .

The scroll? Any good reference book will tell you that there are no Wang Wei scrolls in existence today, though there are some admirable copies. One, by Chao Mēng Fu, in the British Museum, shows the course of a river. Scholars have described this copy in almost the same words I have used tonight to describe the original. But they are not the same. I went to see the copy. I was disappointed. I could no longer hear the song of the wind in the rushes or the wail of the wild geese. Was the change in the painting? Or in me?

THE NOTORIOUS
SNOWMAN

James Powell

Magnets for the dignitaries of many nations, the cities of great empires seethe with opportunities for diplomatic crimes of potentially disastrous proportions. The St. Petersburg of the 1870s was just such a place. To it Canadian author James Powell dispatches his celebrated detective Ambrose Ganelon, to be inducted into an imperial musical society, and to solve crimes along the way. Mr. Powell's Ganelon series is unique among crime historicals in following four generations of a family-run private detective agency, tracing a history of crime from 1840 to World War I.

O n a December afternoon in 1875 Ambrose Ganelon, a black forelock carefully arranged across his impressive brow, stood at a window of his suite in St. Petersburg's fashionable Hotel du Nord, his short, stout frame shaking with laughter. Below him in the broad windswept gloom of the Nevsky Prospekt a slender young cavalry officer stepping from an open droshky had reminded the detective of the most recent joke about that arrogant and empty-headed breed making the rounds in intelligent society: "Have you heard of the cavalry officer who was so stupid the other cavalry officers were starting to notice?"

Detective Ganelon was still smiling when his attention was drawn across the boulevard to a limping figure in a greasy, padded overcoat who had just hurried up from the same direction as the droshky. This new arrival stopped right opposite the hotel and stroked his long ragged beard with an expression of wild cunning and calculation.

As Ganelon marveled at the contrast between this face and that of the cavalry officer, the dome of St. Isaac's Cathedral caught the last rays of the scanty winter light and glowed as bright and golden as Ganelon's own sun, conjuring him back to San Sebastiano and his comfortable armchair and his beloved Prattmann oboe. A knock interrupted this pleasant reverie.

Sergeant Lucas, Ganelon's bodyguard, answered the door and brought over a visiting card sent up from the lobby. Ganelon read it and nodded. A minute later Lieutenant Paul Orlovsky of the Chevalier Guards, the same officer whose arrival Ganelon had noted from the window, strode into the room, tossing his coat, hat, and gloves to the startled Lucas without a sideward glance.

Ganelon offered Orlovsky a chair and endured polite conversation until the arrival of the steaming glass of tea the hotel presented to winter visitors. When the officer set down his glass he still appeared in no hurry to state his business. Screwing a monocle into his eye he regarded the detective languidly, as he might a curiosity on display. Ganelon knew what the man was waiting for. People expected him to look them up and down and make some astonishing deduction based on the mud on their instep or where they carried their pocket handkerchief.

Having no desire to prolong the interview, Ganelon gave the man a penetrating look. There really wasn't much to deduce. Russian officers had scores of batmen to keep their kits impeccable, which was to say clueless. The man's drawing room pallor was understandable. The Chevalier Guards were attached to the Imperial household and this was the season of balls and social gatherings.

Then Ganelon smiled to himself, noting the arc of angry teeth marks between the officer's right thumb and forefinger. The empress always kept a short-tempered throng of Pekinese about her, each of which she would soothe and fondle in turn and pass on to an equerry. Orlovsky must have gotten a wrong handle on one. And that bite was too fresh to have come from Moscow where the empress had gone to attend the accouchement of a daughter. Therefore the empress had returned. Therefore the child had been delivered.

"So tell me, Lieutenant, does Russia have a new grand duke or a new grand duchess?"

Orlovsky blinked so stupidly that Ganelon made no attempt to conceal his impatience as he described his reasoning.

"Amazing!" declared the officer. "All that from a little doggy bite. And of course you're right. A fine baby boy."

"Now then, what can I do for you, Lieutenant?"

"I've just now come from the livery stable that supplies the coaches that cross the ice to Kronstadt," said Orlovsky. "They informed me that you have engaged their last vehicle for a trip there this afternoon. As one gentleman to another I am hoping I can get you to share your coach with my sister who has passage on a ship leaving this evening."

Ganelon had come to St. Petersburg to be formally inducted into the Imperial Society of Amateur Woodwind Virtuosi. He had only intended to spend a week in the Russian capital. But his archrival, the wily Dr. Ludwig Fong, had chosen that moment to offer Ganelon's weight in louis d'or to the man who could rid Fong of the one he hated most in all the world. This bounty sent professional assassins swarming over every train out of Russia.

Fearing for Ganelon's safety, San Sebastiano's Prince Feinhart had dispatched the royal steam yacht, the *Guido Tancredi* then at Cowes, to pick up Ganelon at the Russian island naval base at Kronstadt which served as the icebound St. Petersburg's winter port. This required Ganelon to extend his visit. During this time, if police reports were correct, a pair of highbinders from Fong's Young Fu Brotherhood had reached the city.

Ganelon explained this situation to Orlovsky, adding, "By departing without fanfare we hope to minimize the chance of Fong's people making a move against me. But why subject your sister to the slightest risk when, I have no doubt, she can delay her departure by a day or two without any great inconvenience?"

"I'm afraid that's impossible," said the officer. "You see, my sister recently returned from several years abroad completing her education. She left with a quick mind and while away she added a quick tongue to it. Last night at the Bal des Palmiers she made an indiscreet remark concerning the Princess Dolgoruki, an intimate friend of the emperor himself. Our table must have included an informant for the Third Section."

"The Secret Police?"

Orlovsky nodded. "Early this morning two of their agents appeared at my sister's door and informed her she had twenty-four hours to leave Russia and could not return for a year." Ganelon's black scowl drawn from that arsenal of dark looks which had earned him the nickname, the Genghis Khan of Detection, obliged the officer to explain. "However unjust in my sister's case, such summary sentences of exile are part of the new law the State has enacted to save us from the anarchists and other illegal elements in our midst."

"An excessive law, sir," insisted Ganelon.

Orlovsky shrugged. "Anyone can obey a reasonable law. The truly faithful subject obeys the unreasonable ones with even greater zeal." The philosophical ring of these words pleased the officer immensely.

Ganelon pulled himself to his feet with a weary chuckle. "I think I admire your sister's spirit, Lieutenant. She is welcome to share our fate if she wishes. We leave in two hours."

After showing Orlovsky to the door, Ganelon returned to the window. But the dome of St. Isaac's was dim. Snow was falling across the city. Ganelon saw Orlovsky emerge from the hotel and step into his droshky. As the vehicle moved off, a gray shape stepped from a doorway across the street and limped after it.

A hard snow was slanting out of the early darkness and into the glow of the streetlights when a coach on runners, with baggage lashed to the roof, pulled away from a side entrance of the Hotel du Nord and turned onto the hard-packed surface of the Nevsky Prospekt.

Ganelon sat at a window seat, bundled up in a long raccoon-skin coat with huge lapels, a wolf-skin cap with earflaps, and immense fur mittens. Experiencing his first taste of Russian winter on his arrival from Berlin, Ganelon had gone right from the railroad station to the furrier. But, even at sixty-five, Ganelon possessed a deep wellspring of vanity and he suspected the outfit made him look the fool.

This concern was aggravated by the presence of Miss Vera Orlovsky, the Lieutenant's sister. The handsome young woman with large, sad, green eyes sat with her arms out of the sleeves of her fur coat, a buffalo-skin lap robe across her knees, staring intently at the frost on the window. A green and white enamel heater hung from the ceiling beside her. Hot coals put into this box through an outside metal trap beneath the coachman's bench were supposed to warm the coach and the coachman's feet as well.

On the other side of the heater sat a small Tartar-looking man with a consequential air that belied the condition of his brown melon hat or his shabby overcoat. He had arrived with the Orlovskys and presented himself to Ganelon in the hotel lobby. "Putiatin of the Third Section," he announced. "I must accompany this lady to the gangplank." Mistaking Ganelon's stony stare for incredulity the man pulled out his credentials. "Probationary agent Putiatin."

But the detective waved the proof away. "Who would claim to belong to the Russian Secret Police if he did not?'' he asked. Before Ganelon turned away, he noticed the bibulous cheek veins which might explain the man's probationary status.

Of course the everwatchful Lucas who now sat across from Putiatin had checked the man's papers. Lucas was a phenomenon. In all the years since Ganelon's power of ratiocination had been named a Treasure of the Principality, First Class, and Sergeant Lucas had been assigned to him as a bodyguard, he had never once caught the man when his mind was not exactly where his body was. Ganelon sometimes feared Lucas had no dreams. But the man just preferred to keep them for his time off. Two nights ago, for example, while Ganelon and the other Fellows of the Imperial Society of Amateur Woodwind Virtuosi attended a private and well-guarded dinner at the Restaurant Dunon hosted by the bassoon-playing Tsarevitch Alexis, Lucas had spent his free night at one of the final performances of a touring American Wild West show.

With darkness falling fast the coach reached the end of the boulevard and turned to the northeast to avoid the spired Admiralty and skirt the immense pile of the Winter Palace. As the heater blunted the chill it misted up the windows. Ganelon used a mitten tip to clean a section of glass. The coach was descending an elegant ramp walled in gray granite. Then it reached the frozen surface of the Neva itself and the runners gave off a cleaner, more tempered sound. The coach swung wide around a hippo-drome with bleachers and a clubhouse built on the ice, the racecourse marked out with cut fir trees set upright in the snow. Beyond, in the gloaming, stood the Stock Exchange and its rostral columns.

Before the coach completed its arc, Ganelon got a glimpse of the towers of the intimidating Fortress of St. Peter and St. Paul. Then the crowded lights on the islands grew sparser. Then the shore itself fell back behind them as the coach moved out onto the Gulf of Finland. The driving snow was horizontal now in the light given off by the lanterns which marked each quarter mile of their route across the ice. The twenty-mile trip to Kronstadt would take two hours.

Putiatin pulled out a pint bottle of vodka and cleared his throat sol-emnly. ''Third Section regulations do permit an agent on duty to take alcohol for his stomach's sake when serving on the high seas.'' Laughing at his joke, he pounded the floor with his foot. The cork came out of the bottle with a pop. Putiatin offered it to the viceless Lucas who declined with a gesture of the hand. Ganelon refused as well, and Miss Orlovsky, still staring into the darkness, didn't even notice the offer.

Putiatin gave an indifferent shrug. "It comes from a little vodka shop in a side street near your hotel. They flavor it with woodruff like in the village where I grew up." Putiatin took a long pull on the bottle. He smacked his lips appreciatively and searched for something else to drink to. "A toast to our glorious police!" he exclaimed. "The Snowman's days are numbered!" He drank again. Then he pounded the floor, giggled, and turning his back on his companions he burrowed down into the buffalo robe for a nap.

As Ganelon knew, the Snowman was the daring thief who had been stealing jewels by the double handfuls at the bals des palmiers, the court dinner dances for the last three winter seasons. The newspapers called him the Snowman because he seemed to melt away each spring. Rumor had it that the jewels financed *The Tocsin,* a liberal journal published abroad and smuggled back into Russia.

Ganelon had come to St. Petersburg half expecting the police would request his assistance in the case. But just before his arrival, Markov, one of the Snowman's gang, was caught trying to cross by train into Germany carrying sixteen emeralds, eight diamonds, and twenty-five rubies in his stomach. The Russian police reportedly acted on a tip from the German authorities. Apparently Markov did not know who the Snowman really was. But under police questioning—of what sort Ganelon had no doubt— he betrayed another gang member named Bunin who was later shot in a police ambush, returning over the rooftops to his room near the Hay Market. According to Markov, this Bunin, now lying unconscious in the hospital, did know the real identity of the Snowman. Yet in spite of this, last night the thief had struck again.

Thinking this Snowman might prove a worthy adversary, Ganelon asked, "Miss Orlovsky, could you tell me a little about these bals des palmiers?"

Vera Orlovsky brushed an eyelash with a fingertip before turning from the frosted pane. "I beg your pardon?"

Ganelon repeated his question.

"Ah," she said, half smiling. "Well, Mr. Ganelon, when winter comes we Russians like to pretend we are living in the tropics. Picture a South Sea island inhabited by the brightest parrots and most sparkling hummingbirds imaginable and there is your bal des palmiers. The hussars in their velvet slung jackets of every hue, and the women, their hair, throats, wrists, and waists aglitter with jewels all spinning together in the dance among the rows of live palm trees from the greenhouses at Tsarskoe Selo. And all the while on the other side of the tall windows of the Nicholas Hall snow sweeps across the Neva ice and the temperature is five below."

"Suppose you and I pass the time to Kronstadt by solving this Snowman business," said Ganelon, "who he is and how he does it. You were at the ball last night. You could be my eyes and ears."

The woman shook her head. "You honor me. But you'll need better eyes and ears than those of a foolish woman in love. I saw no one but Prince Waldemar and heard no voice but his."

"I understand," said Ganelon. "Please don't disturb yourself. Old detectives like to have their riddles to chew on."

Vera Orlovsky laughed bitterly. "Then try explaining why I was denounced to the Secret Police by a man who said he loved me."

"Prince Waldemar? But your brother said the whole table overheard your remark."

"That isn't quite accurate," said Vera Orlovsky. "Do you know the story of Catherine the Great and the violet, Mr. Ganelon? Walking about her estate at Tsarskoe Selo one day the empress discovered the first spring violet pushing up through the snow and ordered a soldier posted there to protect it. Since the order was never rescinded, one hundred and fifty years later a soldier still stands there through rain or shine.

"Well, as my brother, the prince, and I were going in to dinner, we were discussing current gossip about the jealousy of the emperor regarding the Princess Dolgoruki. As we sat down I compared the concern of a certain unnamed august gentleman for the honor of a certain titled lady to this tragic sentry standing guard over a bloom long departed. A cruel remark meant to be humorous. But no one but the prince and my brother knew whom I was referring to. Though my brother grows sillier every day, I don't doubt his affection for a moment. Therefore it must have been Prince Waldemar."

"Then tell me about him," asked Ganelon.

"Our families were always close. He was like an older brother to me." She smiled. "An older and more responsible one. When silly Paul ran off and joined a traveling show at seventeen, it was Waldemar who brought him back. Then Waldemar inherited an estate of many souls, as they used to say. In the south near Odessa. Not long after that a well-to-do aunt bought Paul a commission in the Chevalier Guards and sent me abroad to finish my education. When I returned, Prince Waldemar was up here on a visit. We saw a great deal of each other. He delayed his departure. Then he delayed it again. Commitments were made. Now suddenly he has me sent away. Why, Mr. Ganelon?"

The detective spread his mittens. "I'm still too young to try to unravel the mysteries of the heart." But Ganelon thought about it, his mind still half on the bal-des-palmiers business. Of course that might be the explanation for Prince Waldemar's conduct. Suppose he was the Snowman. He's lost his regular way of getting the jewels out of the country. He denounces her to the Secret Police, knowing it wouldn't be difficult to slip the jewels into her baggage and not much chance the baggage would be examined by customs when she was escorted out of the country by the Secret Police. "Miss Orlovsky, did Prince Waldemar come up for the winter season each year?"

"No," she said. "This was his first season in years. He only stayed on my account. He said he wanted to dance every dance at every ball with me. And he did."

Ganelon gave a dismal sigh. It couldn't be Waldemar. The silence lengthened. Vera Orlovsky turned back to her frozen window. Lucas crossed his legs. Putiatin snored beneath the buffalo robe.

Many minutes later a sudden jangle of bells and wind-muffled shouts and curses dashed by them out of the night and just as quickly were gone. Their coach swerved, tottered, rose into the air, and then fell back down with a heavy jolt and a sharp crack. The vehicle spun a quarter turn before dragging to a halt. Lucas's side of the coach was three feet higher than Ganelon's.

The policeman threw open his door and hoisted himself outside to see what had happened. Putiatin woke up, emptied his bottle in one gulp, added Lucas's buffalo robe to his own, and went back to sleep. Ganelon pushed his door open with his shoulder and fought his way forward to the horses through the driving snow and howling wind. A marker light ten feet away cast a shallow light across the accident. The horse down on the ice gasped for breath. The other three stamped in their harness. The left coach runner had been shattered to kindling.

At the edge of the darkness, staring out across the ice, Lucas shouted, "The coachman bolted with a small green leather piece of luggage. I think he was hurt. He was limping." Lucas drew his pistol and turned back to the injured horse.

Ganelon remained where Lucas had been standing, staring off into the darkness. He heard the pistol shot behind him.

"I'll have to ride for help," shouted Lucas, cutting the remaining lead horse out of its traces. "I'll be back in two hours." He pressed his pistol into Ganelon's hand, swung up onto the horse's back, and galloped off into the darkness.

Ganelon led the other horses around to the lee side of the coach and tied them there. Then he rejoined Vera Orlovsky. He explained their predicament, adding, "There's nothing to worry about. We're just in for a bit of a wait." He sat back down without unbuttoning his coat and pulled the lap robe up over his knees. With all the coming and going the air was chill and the coals in the heater were old. The wind seemed to pipe in at every crack now. "Did you have a green case among your things, Miss Orlovsky?" asked the detective. "A gift from your brother, perhaps?"

"Why, yes," she marveled. "My new vanity case. A going-away present."

"Forgive me for not elaborating," said Ganelon. "I don't have all the facts and probably never will. But I can tell you this: Prince Waldemar did not betray you to the Secret Police. And your brother does love you."

Without another word he buried his chin in his upturned lapels to hide a fierce scowl. Diable, how neatly the preposterous cavalry officer had hooked the patronizing detective and reeled him in like a fat, stupid fish! Lieutenant Paul Orlovsky, alias the St. Petersburg Snowman, had convinced the great Ambrose Ganelon himself to escort the stolen jewels and his sister, whom he wanted out of harm's way, to the boat.

Vera Orlovsky interrupted this dark brooding with an earnest, "Listen!" Other sounds were crowding in on the wind. "Wolves," said the woman with a grimace. "I thought I heard them five minutes ago. Now they're closer. In hard winters they sometimes come south out of the forests of Finland. Welcome to Russia, Mr. Ganelon. The dead horse will draw them like flies."

"Well, when the horse is finished we'll throw them Putiatin here," said Ganelon lightly. The Secret Police agent's snores were growing louder by the minute. "Anyway, we'll be safe in here," said the detective. "They're not going to come in through the windows." But the reassurance he hoped for didn't come.

"The subject's too shrouded in myth and legend for a Russian to give you an answer on that," she said.

Ganelon stood up and drew Lucas's pistol out of his overcoat pocket. "I'm going to have to let the horses loose and give them a chance to run for it," he said. "I might even get a shot off at a wolf."

As Ganelon reached for the door it burst open and a large gray shape lunged inside. Ganelon was knocked across the seat. The pistol flew up in the air and landed in Vera Orlovsky's lap. In an instant she had it aimed squarely and unwaveringly at the head of the bearded man in the padded overcoat, the coachman, who lay moaning with fear on the floor of the coach.

Snow swirled about them. Ganelon got to his feet and closed the door. Then he stepped around the new arrival's body and over to Putiatin. The snoring man had brought a second bottle for the return trip. He passed the bottle down to the man who, chest heaving, had just propped himself up on one elbow and looked the very personification of winter, his beard all matted with frost and hung with icicles around the mouth. It was the man with the limp, the one who had watched Orlovsky from the other side of the Nevsky Prospekt.

Ganelon crossed back to the door. "Shoot if you have to, Miss Orlovsky," he said and stepped outside into the wind and blinding snow. He found his way around the coach to the horses. A slap on the rump sent them thundering off down the ice to Kronstadt. Ganelon stood there for a moment, a good ten miles out to sea on the ice of the Gulf of Finland with the wind and the wolves howling all around him. Then he turned back inside where a mystery waited to be fully unraveled.

A third of the vodka in the bottle was gone. When Ganelon took back the bottle, the bearded man watched him less in fear now than with shrewdness. When the detective pointed to Lucas's place on the seat the man got up, dragged off one of Putiatin's buffalo robes, wrapped himself in it, and sat down. Then he said something in Russian.

"He says in his village they flavor the vodka with anise," translated Vera Orlovsky. "He says anise is better."

"Ask him about the bal-des-palmier jewels."

Her eyes grew large but she did. Ganelon did not have to wait for a translation of the man's claim of ignorance. He gestured toward the door. "Then tell him he isn't welcome here," he said. As if on cue a wolf howled nearby.

The man's eyes found their fear again. As he talked, Vera Orlovsky translated. "The jewels are lost out there on the ice, sir. I ran from the accident meaning to work my way to the lanterns and follow them to Kronstadt. But I became lost in the storm. Then I heard the wolves. I fell several times running from the sound. I lost the green leather case. I didn't dare stop to look for it. The howling was all around me. I ran through the wind and darkness with the wolves on my scent, I know. I ran until I stumbled onto the roadway again, right out here. I'd come full circle."

"And what of the real coachman?" demanded Ganelon.

The man smiled craftily and nodded at the vodka. "Among us, sir, there's no trick to getting to do another man's job."

"Start at the beginning," ordered the detective.

The man looked across at his snoring neighbor. He made his thumb and forefinger into a pair of pincers and demonstrated it to Ganelon questioningly. When the detective nodded, the man reached over and applied the pincer to Putiatin's nostrils. The snoring stopped.

With his hand to Putiatin's nose the man continued his story. "I am a poor carter, sir, though years ago, in a traveling show, I wore bright cardboard armor and drove a Roman chariot with five horses abreast, holding the reins in my teeth. But I was a slave to drink. There was this bad accident and I was let go with a limp for a pension. Later I found work as a carter at the emperor's estate at Tsarskoe Selo. During the wintertime the day before each of these Palm Balls of theirs we would drive the trees to town in a caravan of wagons and two days later we would drive them back."

An outburst of snarls told us that the wolves had reached the coach. Something—it might have been a strong gust of wind—butted against the door. The carter looked from Ganelon to the vodka. Ganelon passed over the bottle. The carter took a long drink before continuing. "Three years ago an old comrade from the traveling-show days, a man named Bunin, asked me if I was above making a little extra on the side. Sometimes I was to work it so I was the last vehicle in the caravan and I was to stop on the outskirts of St. Petersburg, as if one of my team had a stone in its hoof.

"Bunin would come out of the bushes with a suitcase and bring it into the back of the van. After a minute he'd bring it out again. Two days later on my way back we'd do the same thing again. I soon realized I was part of the jewel thefts reported in the newspapers. But the pay was good and the risks seemed small enough.

"Suddenly two weeks ago I read of the arrest of another acquaintance from the traveling-show days. Markov the stone eater. That was his act, sir, swallowing rocks and broken glass and pieces of sardine cans. There's a knack to it. After the show he would regurgitate it all up again. I never cared much for Markov."

"And what was this Bunin's act?" asked Ganelon.

The carter toasted Ganelon's question with the bottle. "An animal act, sir. A yodeling goat, a dancing pig, a—"

"A monkey," supplied Ganelon bitterly, remembering Orlovsky's smooth "doggy bite" reference.

"A marvel of a monkey, sir. It marched about in a soldier's uniform with a little rifle and a pack on its back." He drank and sputtered with laughter. "Just think about it, sir. There is our Snowman dancing those fast foreign dances with all those beauties and popping the jewels out of their settings like peas out of a pod. And there's the trained monkey following him from palm tree to palm tree under the ceiling. And he feeds the jewels up to it as smooth as glass!"

At that moment Ganelon heard the most blood-curdling sound of his lifetime, the hard relentless claws of a wolf at the ice on the window right beside his head. Vera Orlovsky swallowed a scream.

The carter was too far into his story and his vodka to notice. "When they nabbed Markov," he continued, "I figured Bunin would skip and there'd be no one to lead the police to me. But bold as brass Bunin arrived to say we were doing our number one last time. Well, thought I, why not? Here's my chance to steal the jewels and run before Bunin collects the monkey. So I stopped my van and he put the monkey inside."

The carter shook his head with great distress. "Oh, sir, I should have run when the police shot Bunin the next day. But think of it. Think of all the wealth in that monkey's little pack if only I could wait and collect that last load of trees! Fear and greed struggled together in my brain as our caravan drove into St. Petersburg today. By luck I saw the lieutenant leave the main entrance of the Winter Palace in a droshky as we passed. Chief Double Eagle. I'd never have recognized him if Markov and Bunin hadn't set my mind on those traveling-show days. The young of the well-off sometimes do for adventure what necessity demands of the poor.

"Still, the young gentleman had been a good horseman and a crack shot. He'd gallop into the arena in red Indian warpaint and feathers, shoot a line of twenty kopeck pieces dead center, and after, when the trick riding was done, he'd bend the coins double and throw them to the crowd. Now there he was wearing the uniform of a fancy regiment."

Here Miss Orlovsky's translation faltered. Ganelon motioned her on. A brief racket of snarls and claws at the coach door gave way to growls and snuffling.

"One look at that officer's face and I knew I'd been beaten to the jewels, sir," said the carter. "I jumped down from my van and took off after that droshky, not really knowing what I was going to do. First he stopped at a luggage shop and bought a small green case. Then I followed him into a livery stable yard and stood warming myself at the hostlers' bonfire while he asked about the coach to Kronstadt. From there he went to your hotel. Clearly my bird was about to take flight. But perhaps all was not lost.

"I would take the coachman's place and ransack Chief Double Eagle's luggage on the trip across the ice. Did I say I can drive a team with the reins in my teeth? Imagine how I felt when I discovered that my man wasn't making the trip but the lady here. But then I saw the little green case. I was trying to find out where the jewels were hidden in it when that damned hack troyka spooked the horses and caught me with a mouthful of leather. Some naval officers on their way to a gypsy café, I'll bet. The rest you know, sir."

"And suppose you'd gotten away with it, what would you have done?" demanded Ganelon.

"I'd have signed on a freighter for South America."

"And would you take such a ship right now, tonight?" asked the detective. "Or should we turn you over to Mr. Putiatin here of the Secret Police?"

The horrified carter pulled back his fingers. Putiatin's fierce snoring outburst drew frightened yelps from the departing wolves. "I swear I would sail, sir," said the carter.

Bells swept into earshot. There was a clatter of rifle fire. Soon Lucas's anxious face was in the doorway. On the road he had met two troykas of naval bandsmen delighted to come to the assistance of a Member of the Imperial Society of Amateur Woodwind Virtuosi. And would that worthy gentleman like a wolf-skin trophy? He would not.

* * *

An hour and a half later Ganelon was settled in his steam-heated state-room on board the *Guido Tancredi,* having sworn a mighty oath to Lucas to remain there until they reached the clement waters of the Mediterranean. "I advised Miss Orlovsky to cable her prince," he said. "I expect he'll be there when she disembarks."

"And her brother, sir?" asked Lucas.

"I rather imagine your Wild West show will depart for home with an extra Indian in the troupe." Ganelon settled back in his easy chair and sipped on his glass of hot grog, feeling the satisfaction of a riddle solved. Then he thought of Putiatin. Sobered by the bone-chilling ride in the troyka with the baggage, the man would be stamping his feet at the bottom of Miss Orlovsky's gangplank. Ganelon pointed to his furry outer-wear heaped on the bed. "Lucas," he said, "please present those superfluous items to Putiatin with my compliments. And don't forget the mittens."

Back in San Sebastiano, Ganelon would scowl darkly, remembering this gesture, for among the accumulated newspapers he would discover a short St. Petersburg item: "Our correspondent reports a deterioration of Sino-Russian relations due to the murder in broad daylight near the Hotel du Nord of Arkady Vassilyitch Putiatin, an agent (posthumous grade) of the Third Section. His assassins, arrested on the spot, are believed to be agents of the Celestial Empire."

They were not. They were members of the Young Fu Brotherhood.

Ganelon threw down the newspaper. When next he and Dr. Ludwig Fong met, the detective pledged he would remember Putiatin.

A STATESMAN'S TOUCH

Robert Barnard

Politics being a favorite subject of satirists, what better setting could one of mystery's best satirists of all have chosen than the Paris Peace Conference of 1919, where gathered together under one roof we find all the major statesmen of the time. Robert Barnard's barbed wit has been delighting mystery readers since his first book appeared in 1974. The genre suits the former professor of literature to a tee, for if you have a talent for lampooning, a murder investigation will oblige by turning up all manner of embarrassing little secrets.

M ais c'est incroyable!"
The hotel manager looked down towards his beautifully shod feet with an expression more of distaste than of disbelief. The head porter, who had summoned him, thought to himself that if you find a trickle of blood seeping under the door of one of the bedrooms into the corridor, it is not altogether surprising to discover a corpse behind the door, or to find that the corpse was murdered. But, as an intelligent man, he held his peace.

"It's that man Radovan Radič," said the manager, his mouth twisting as he looked down at the body with the gaping wound between its shoulders.

"A Bulgarian, wasn't he?" the porter asked.

"Serbian, I believe. But Serbian, Bulgarian, Hungarian—they're all the same. Brutes!" He looked around the spare, ill-furnished room, one of their cheapest. "I only know of this creature because the police were around asking about him last week."

"Illegal resident?"

"Worse, much worse. Apparently he was a thoroughly unsavoury character. All sorts of activities, including blackmail. He had been touting letters from Marie of Romania."

"Ah—to Prince Stirbey?"

"No, not that old story. Something more recent. They thought it possible he was an agent of the King of Serbia, but on balance they thought he was acting for his own ends. I was all for throwing him out onto the street at once, but the Sûreté begged me not to. Here they could keep an eye on him, they said. I wish now that I had insisted, but when the Sûreté begs . . ."

"Of course. In our position one obeys. Who have we in the hotel tonight?"

"Ah, that is the question."

It was indeed. The Hôtel George IV, formerly the Impérial, situated on the Avenue Decazes, had carved for itself a minor but vital role in the diplomatic comings and goings of that year 1919, the year of the Peace Conference. Paris was awash with kings, statesmen, and mere politicians, not to mention the attendant diplomats, secretaries, and the inevitable newspapermen. Behind the ceremonial and the open negotiations there mushroomed encounters of a more personal nature. The George IV catered, discreetly, for any assignation, whether political, romantic, or frankly sexual, that the participants wished to keep from the gaze of the public or of rival statesmen. The hotel's system of backstairs access and private corridors was unrivalled in the French capital, and the manager was formidably discreet. He already regretted the renaming of the hotel, which had been done in the hope of profiting by a confusion with the new and magnificent George V. The hotel had found a quite different and much more lucrative identity, and would have benefited from a more anonymous name. That very morning an English visitor had commented cheerily that the only connection George IV had had with France had been his delusion that he led the allied troops at the Battle of Waterloo. The manager's demeanour had been glacial. It was the height of bad taste to mention the Battle of Waterloo in Paris.

He now enumerated the hotel's more sensitive guests, strictly in order of rank.

"The King of Spain is in Suite Fifteen with a woman who is not his mistress."

"Madame Grigot would raise hell if she knew."

"Quite . . . Alfonso XIII—such an *unlucky* number. I'm surprised his mother chose the name."

The head porter caught his drift.

"Spain remained neutral during the course of the war," he remarked.

"Very profitably neutral. His Majesty was a noncombatant, at least on the field of battle. . . . I think, you know, that we need take no special steps where His Majesty is concerned."

The head porter nodded sage agreement.

"Then there is the president of the United States. He is in Suite Seven with the prime minister of Italy."

"There is no question of—?"

"No, no. Out of the question. The president has no such inclinations. Mrs. Wilson would never allow it. They are engaged in extremely sensitive discussions concerning Italy's new borders in the Tyrol. They will have to be informed."

"Of course."

"And then there is the prime minister of Great Britain . . ."

"Ah yes. Mr. Lloyd-George."

The head porter of the George IV naturally managed "George" more or less in the English manner, but "Lloyd" came out as "Lo-id." He was, nevertheless, extremely familiar with the name.

"Yes. With a most attractive woman of a certain age. I escorted them personally to Suite Twelve, his favourite suite. The prime minister's patronage is of course an honour to the hotel. . . ."

"Naturally."

"Though it is not an honour we can proclaim. . . ."

"Except discreetly."

"Exactly. We proclaim it discreetly. Mr. Lloyd-George must of course be told before the police are summoned. . . . Who else? The Belgian ambassador, the Latvian chargé d'affaires, the Australian foreign minister, all with ladies. They can be informed. For the rest, diplomats, members of various parliaments—they must take their chance. We will inform them if we can, but before too long, for our good name, we must summon the Sûreté. *Mon dieu!* They said they wished to keep an eye on him! What an eye!"

And leaving the head porter on guard outside the door, with instructions to inform any curious guests that there had been an unfortunate accident, the manager bustled off in his stately fashion to alert his guests.

*   *   *

In Suite Fifteen, the young dancer whose name was unknown to him lay under the King of Spain and thought rapturously that it really was something, to be pleasured by a king. The pleasure was undisturbed by any call from the hotel management.

In Suite Seven, the president of the United States of America put down the telephone and rose.

"Mr. Prime Minister, this has been a most interesting and productive meeting, and we have made real, very real progress, but I regret that it must come to an end."

The president's interpreter, who looked like a Mafia boss but who was in fact a Harvard professor, rose to his feet, but the Italian prime minister remained seated and looked petulant.

"But Mr. President, I wish to protest about Merano—"

"I'm afraid that there has been a murder in the hotel. Some scruffy little Balkan muckraker. It would greatly harm me in the American press if it were thought that I were making secret deals—coming to unofficial understandings—with a foreign power. No doubt the Italian press feels similarly strongly."

It didn't, but the Italian prime minister got to his feet.

"Of course. And my king is very touchy about his prerogative in matters of foreign policy."

"Ah, I think I have met your king. A very small man, I seem to recollect."

"But touchy accordingly. You are right, Mr. President: we should be gone."

"Why don't you stay, Giuliano? You could go through what we've already agreed on. No scandal in your being here."

And the president and the prime minister opened the door onto the backstairs corridors and scuttled out. In minutes they were in two taxis which the manager had summoned for them, speeding back to their respective hotels.

In Suite Twelve, the British prime minister was more relaxed than the American president.

"Yes, I'm alone." He flicked his tongue around his lips. His companion for the night had just returned from her maid's room, and had said with a coquettish smile: "Ten minutes!" He could hardly wait. "The lady is preparing herself," he told the manager.

"Mr. Lloyd-George, I am desolated to have to tell you that there has been a murder—"

"A murder? In this hotel?"

"Yes indeed. A Balkan adventurer of the most dubious kind."

"A Balkan adventurer? Do you mean a gigolo?"

"No, no. A Serbian with a criminal bent. Perhaps it is best for you not to know the details."

"Perhaps it is."

"So I wondered whether you and the most charming lady would wish to . . . remove yourselves from any intrusiveness on the part of the police?"

"Hmmm. . . . You have not yet called the police?"

"No indeed. I informed you first, Mr. Prime Minister."

"Obliged to you. Hmmmm. I have a certain . . . experience in handling tricky matters of this kind."

"Your statesmanship is known to all, sir."

"Leave it with me for ten minutes or so. I may be able to advise you how to handle this. Suggest something to . . . to safeguard the reputation of the hotel."

"Of the hotel, of course, Mr. Prime Minister."

In his office on the ground floor of the George IV, the manager fumed at the well-known hypocrisy of the English. To pretend that he was thinking of a solution to the hotel's crisis, when all he wanted from the period of grace was—what he had come for in the first place. How truly perfidious was Albion!

In Suite Fifteen, the nameless young dancer, once more under the King of Spain, was deciding that it was even more extraordinary than she had thought, being pleasured by a king.

In Suite Seven, Professor Giuliano, master now of a luxurious suite, wished he could have taken advantage of the well-known freedoms of the Hôtel George IV. But with police in the offing that was hardly on the cards. With a sigh he returned to the maps of Southern Europe that had been occupying his master and his guest. He took hold of the carafe of barley water that Mr. Wilson had been drinking, then changed his mind and poured a glass of the prime minister's French champagne. As he sipped, he looked down at the maps on the desk and a new expression came over his face.

In Suite Twelve, Mr. Lloyd-George took up the phone.

"Mr. Manager? Suite Twelve here. Now, you said this Johnnie was Serbian, did you not?"

"Yes, Mr. Lloyd-George. What I believe we are now to call Yugo-slavian."

"Well, we shall see about that. But it's a good point. Got any of his fellow-countrymen on your staff, have you? Or anyone else from the Balkans? Very quarrelsome people, the Eastern Europeans. Or even a North African might do."

"I believe there is someone in the kitchens—let me see, I think there is somebody from Croatia."

"Capital. Part of the new kingdom."

"I seem to remember he is one of the meat chefs."

"With the skills of a butcher, then? Even better. I wouldn't mind betting his passport is not in order."

"It does often happen that people will work for less if we . . . turn a blind eye."

"Quite. Well, offer him a good sum of money—what's a thousand pounds in francs?—and tell him to disappear."

"Ah, you mean—?"

"It will be unimaginable riches to him. He'll take himself off and become a rich man in his own country. You don't need to do anything more. Tell the police he's disappeared, and they'll jump at it. Crime solved, with no effort. Suspicious foreigner—everyone's happy. They won't trouble anyone else, if the solution's handed to them on a plate."

"I do believe, Mr. Prime Minister, that you're right."

"Of course I am. And there'll be no scandal attached to the hotel. We all want that, don't we? Let me know how things go."

As he put down the phone, the door to the bedroom opened, and a vision in rustling silks swept through.

"My *dear*!" said Mr. Lloyd-George appreciatively.

The men from the Sûreté behaved in a way that at first bordered on the surly.

"This is the man Radič," said the inspector, looking at the body on the floor with disgust.

"It is. I wanted to throw him out."

"We told you to keep an eye on him."

"You said that you would keep an eye on him."

"That's what we meant. My God! With this man's record it could be anyone—and possibly one of the highest in Europe. Or of course one of their hirelings. . . ."

"It occurred to me—" began the manager.

"Yes?"

"Did you not say that the man was possibly in the pay of the King of Serbia?"

"It was one of the possibilities."

"And has he not recently proclaimed himself king of a country called Yugoslavia?"

"Lord knows. Who understands what goes on down there? I have an idea you're right."

"It is a very quarrelsome part of the world. . . ."

"They're always at it. Love, war, love, war."

"It is, after all, where the late conflict began."

The inspector nodded sagely.

"It is. If the archduke were alive today, so would a hell of a lot more people be."

"Exactly. So I wondered if someone of one of the other nationalities that the king has annexed to his new kingdom, perhaps in a quarrel with this unsavoury character . . ."

The inspector considered.

"You have someone from the region staying in the hotel?"

"Staying here? Heavens above, one was enough! It is, I believe, a poverty-stricken hole. But in our kitchens . . ."

"Ah. Someone without papers, no doubt."

The manager gesticulated.

"His papers *seemed* in order—"

"Who is this man?"

"He is one of the assistant meat chefs—a lowly position."

"I think we must talk to this man. What nationality did you say he was?"

"I believe Croatian."

"Who knows where these places are? But it is down there somewhere. Lead on, Mr. Manager."

Preceded by the manager, the policemen trooped along dingy corridors, up staircases and then more staircases until they came to a long, low attic which served as a sort of dormitory for the lower members of staff. Watched surreptitiously by Turkish, Portuguese, Bulgarian, and Algerian eyes, silently beseeching that their papers not be asked for, fearful of being sent back from the squalor that they lived in to the greater squalor they had come from, the little army marched nearly the length of the dimly lit room.

"Ah, see!" said the manager, greatly surprised. "He is gone!"

The bed was neatly made. From the rough cupboard beside it all trace of the occupant had been removed.

"This, evidently, is our man. Come, Mr. Manager, and give us all the details on him that you have."

The little army turned, walked the narrow space between the rows of beds, and began the long trek down to the manager's office. As the door to the attic closed, there could be heard a great sigh of relief in several languages.

In Suite Fifteen, the admiration of the nameless dancer had gradually turned to rage. This was too much! How many times was it now? She had lost count. Bang, snore, bang, snore, bang, snore. She felt like a leaky bicycle tyre. This was being treated like a common prostitute. And at the end, she wouldn't even get paid, probably. Come the dawn and it would be, "*Adieu, ma petite,*" and that would be that. *Le roi le veut.* Well, she'd had enough. What had been an honour had become a tedious hassle. Fortunately, the king was now in a snore phase.

She got up, but before she put her clothes on she peeped out the door. The first things that met her eye were the backs of two stalwart gendarmes bearing something covered with a sheet away on a stretcher. Turning her head, she saw two more gossiping at the other end of the corridor. Police in the hotel! An inconspicuous departure would be quite impossible. She sighed. Better stick it out.

On the bed, the snores lessened in volume. The king stirred.

In Suite Seven, Professor Giuliano contemplated his handiwork. The map the president and the prime minister had worked on lay to his left hand, a red line stretching halfway across the thigh at the top of the leg of Italy, breaking off when their work had been interrupted. The new border between Italy and the defeated Austria. At Professor Giuliano's right hand was a duplicate map, unused in the negotiations, on which he had drawn a new red line, mostly identical, but which now veered north at a crucial point, to put on the Italian side Merano and a rich area of Alpine villages, woods, and grazing lands. He took the map on his left and the suite's heavy table lighter over to the grate and set fire to a corner. When he was satisfied it was entirely burned, he went back to the desk and poured himself another glass of champagne. Being born in New York did not mean he was not still a patriotic Italian. He smiled with professorial self-esteem: it was a brilliant stroke, worthy of his father, the Mafia boss.

As the first rays of dawn struck the Avenue Decazes, the phone rang in Suite Twelve. The British prime minister had always impressed on the manager that, should anything of importance arise, he should always be rung. "If I am busy, I simply don't answer," he had said. Now he was already dressed and in the sitting room, while his companion completed her morning toilette in the bedroom.

"Mr. Prime Minister?" said the manager. "I thought I should tell you that, thanks to your brilliant suggestion, everything went like a dream."

"Glad to hear it. All it needed was a touch of statesmanship."

"The police accepted absolutely my interpretation of the unfortunate event and the man's disappearance."

"Of course they did. Less trouble."

"The man will by now have evaporated, and the case is in effect closed."

"Splendid."

"The police have now left the hotel, and you and your charming guest can leave without arousing any impertinent curiosity."

"Excellent. I think I hear her coming now. Call two taxis, will you?"

The door from the bedroom had indeed opened, and sailing through, dressed for her morning activities, came the lovely woman of a certain age who had shared the prime minister's night. He gazed at her appreciatively: splendid figure, regal carriage, gorgeous clothes and hat. Odd to think of her as granddaughter of that dumpy little woman. She, like him, would from now be caught up in the great public events of the time. He saw the reddish-brown tip of a hatpin poking through the too-small evening bag: typical of her and her kind always to be prepared for an emergency!

"I've just had a call from the manager," he said. "The emergency's over. The police have gone."

"Excellent," she said. "I have a very full morning of engagements. Civil of him to let you know."

"Naturally he did," said Mr. Lloyd-George, swelling to his full adiposity. "I advised him how to go about things."

"I do love a clever man."

"And I *am* the Prime Minister of Great Britain."

She paused before disappearing through the door.

"And I am Marie of Romania."

EDITOR'S NOTE: Readers of Dorothy Parker may recognize the allusion in the last line of this story to her verse "Comment," collected in *Not So Deep as a Well* (The Viking Press, 1938).

SMILING JOE AND THE TWINS

Florence V. Mayberry

No historical crime anthology would be complete without a tale of gangsters in America's roaring twenties. Romanticized in novels and movies, organized crime has tame and folksy beginnings in Florence Mayberry's story of Reno, Nevada and its homegrown resistance to the big boys in Chicago. The author has been writing for Ellery Queen's Mystery Magazine since 1964, often in the historical field, and always employing a variety of locales, a legacy of her own wide experience as a traveler.

1.

It is doubtful that any two people were more unlike than the Galway twins, Geraldine and Patricia. Their mother, an extremely pretty, very feminine blond lady, named them. That occurred in the early morning at the hospital as the babies nuzzled at her breast. That evening their names were shortened on the hospital records to Jerry and Pat by bellowing demand of their father. Mr. Dion Galway had had his heart set on fine big Irish sons. But other than getting a divorce and finding a new wife, which twenty years' residence in Reno, Nevada, had soured him on, plus his strong attachment to the wife he had, it seemed that boyish nicknames were as close as he could reach to that goal. For unfortunately the birth of the twins had turned into a touch and go crisis and the doctors announced that these two husky little females had ended childbearing in this Galway family.

It soon became evident that Jerry was a true matchup for a boy designation. One afternoon when she was no more than two and a half, the

Galway ranch hands were alerted by hysterics from the normally calm Indian nursemaid as she raced through the stables screeching that Jerry was not only lost but likely trampled by Dion's high-strung racehorses. A mass search spread out until one of the men looked into the Shetland pony's stall and found Jerry tippytoed on a box, yanking on the pony's mane, determined to go horsie-back. When the rescuer tried to pick her off, she loosed a banshee yell, kicked, and bit, demanding to be put aboard.

Her command obeyed, her pudgy hands grabbed the pony's mane and to the admiring amazement of all, except her mother, nursemaid, and sister Pat, the latter quietly dressing dollies in the nursery, Jerry proudly trotted her steed up to the front veranda of the sprawling ranch house.

In strong contrast to the stocky, black-eyed, red-haired Jerry, Pat continued to grow up into a replica of her mother, graceful, slender, blond, and very feminine. Also terrified of horses. Even at the advanced age of six she had to be dragged by her father to the stables and boosted and strapped into the saddle of the fat lazy Shetland long forsaken by the bronc-riding Jerry, then led weeping around the corral, while Jerry, astride a quarter horse or one of her father's Arabs, raced around the cow pasture intent on lassoing some indignant bovine.

"Run that heifer down, baby!" Jerry's adoring father might be yelling. "Not a boy in Washoe County can match you! Keep it up, you'll be running this place by the time you're ten." And if the ranch foreman was nearby Dion might say, "Wouldn't you think being twins with that little redheaded spitfire, Pat might show some of that spunk. I tell you, the way that Jerry even sasses me around she'll not only run the ranch, by twenty-one she'll be pushing to take over some of my clubs around Nevada."

Dion Galway's antecedents had a way of being black-haired and black-eyed, or fiery redheads and black-eyed, scarce a blue eye or blond among them. The males were grudge-bearing, fist-flying roisterers back in Ireland who eventually fought their way onto an emigrant boat for America and kept up the good fight after they landed. In various profitable ways, and hanging together as a family, they bunched up a sizeable Galway fortune. Dion's particular generation had produced him as the lone male among eight vivid and demanding females, his sisters and cousins, which strongly motivated his desire for a son. The family inheritance had therefore been cut nine ways. A very comfortable legacy for each, but to the expansive Dion merely piddling. Consequently, in his early twenties he ventured west and joyfully discovered that Nevada and Reno in the early nineteen-twenties offered fascinating possibilities of turning his inheritance into a great deal of money. Discovered love, too, with a calm Nordic beauty devoted to cooking, keeping house, and loving her husband.

During Dion's second year in Reno he caught the eye of the Old Man, who was often referred to on Commercial Row and the Lake and Center streets gambling habitats as the King of Nevada, said title arising from the fact that the Old Man owned controlling interest in Nevada's more successful gambling clubs. In those days this did not include Las Vegas, since that little sun-roasted town was barely on the map as far as the sophisticates of the Biggest Little City in the World were concerned. Tomorrow maybe, but take care of that when tomorrow shows up.

The Old Man and the engaging young Irisher took to each other right off, became mutual admirers as well as stockholders. By the time the twins came along Dion was occasionally referred to as the "crown prince." As years passed, so did the references increase. It was a profitable association, income arising largely from the legal gambling clubs, plus "et cetera" covering a shadowy field of enterprise. Their business soared along with prohibition and the world's rising divorce rate. In keeping with this, Dion acquired a fine big ranch in the mountain-bordered, green-pastured Washoe Valley, which spread between Reno and Carson City. Dion soon crowned the ranch with a luxurious two-story house where Inga, his blond, blue-eyed wife, contentedly threw parties for Reno's upper crust plus numerous newsworthy wealthy ladies temporarily resident in Reno while awaiting freedom from tiresome husbands.

Smiling Joe Clancy also hit Reno in the nineteen-twenties. Somewhat younger than Dion Galway, Smiling Joe was only twenty-six, but very advanced in the world's ways, as the former had been upon his own arrival in the Biggest Little City. Back in those twenties the "Mob," whether stemming from Chicago, New York, Kansas City, wherever or whatever, hadn't yet eased into town to grab off juicy chunks of Nevada. The Nevada crooks were home folks, family folks, steady churchgoers, with unpretentious homes, first up for charity donations. Leaders of this home-grown sovereignty amounted to a modest handful, topped by the "king," and maybe a crown prince. Their moral standards leaned heavily toward old-fashioned conservative, with a downright fetish about protecting their womenfolk, with heavy emphasis on "their." It was a matter of public boasting that all Reno's businessmen of any stature were making "damn sure" Reno's women would be safe on any street, day or night.

Fooling around by randy local males was strictly limited to the Line, a string of cabins tucked into a hollow at the outskirts of town, said cabins rented out to strictly professional ladies. Considerable guessing went on among Reno's less informed population segments as to who, singular or plural, owned the Line and pocketed a big slice of its income. No guessing took place as to whether or not it was lucrative. It was.

Prohibition fostered those past happy days in Reno. The big depression of 1929 seemed to scoot right past the Biggest Little City; the Old Man and Dion, plus the lucky handful of public-spirited citizens, felt real special about their town and its good business. Hence, so far, no mob.

When Smiling Joe hit town Reno was in great condition, ripe for the taking for anyone who could slip in. Joe's smile kept getting wider and wider.

Now what about those two little Nevada princesses, the Galway twins?

Steadily growing up. Jerry was winning prizes for riding and jumping, plus breeding and bartering her own string of mounts, plus begging her dad to let her have a go at broncobusting. Made Dion about the proudest man in Nevada. Eased his disappointment in her sister Pat, who spent most of her time in tippytoe ballet classes, blond hair piled high in ribbons, saucy tutus bouncing over ruffled pants.

"Lemme tell you, Mr. Galway, your Jerry sits those big Arabians like she and the horse came into the world thataway, all of a piece," the ranch foreman reported.

"Yessiree, got me a boy all right," Dion boasted. "Anything ever happens to me, that kid's already got the guts to take over everything I got."

Truth is, that took a weight off Dion, since lately there were times when he grew anxious that he actually might not live forever. It took hard-core struggle to stay crown prince with money-hungry applicants nibbling at that shadowy title. Then too, the king was getting up in years and the uncertainty of age was making him tricky and very, very shrewd. He got a kick out of playing one contender against another, back and forth, like with the king's sudden, all-out friendship with that big, chuckling, grinning Joe. Where the hell did that guy come from anyway? And now the Old Man was confiding in Dion that it was downright wonderful the way that happy guy Joe could lift an old man's spirits, make him feel young again.

The twins were about twelve when Joe surfaced in Reno.

Joe was kind of a mystery to everybody. Hailed from somewhere in the

Midwest, sidestepped giving out precisely where. At the start, who cared? Guys from somewhere or nowhere were always stopping off at Reno, leaving the same way. Soon gone. But Joe; Joe stayed.

During his first few days in Reno, Joe wandered in and out of the various gambling clubs. Then he began to show up regularly in the largest of the Old Man's establishments, in which Dion also held heavy financial interest. Just kind of routine visits. Then one night became special. Joe shot a wad, lost himself a real bundle, but never blinked an eye. He grinned, reached in his pocket, pulled out hundred-dollar bills like they were pennies, and put down five of them. It was noted that this pocket was on the inside of his coat and had a button on it.

Well, it turned out that this crazy galoot, carrying all that cash around, won five thousand that night. All on the up and up, for sure. Sharp-eyed, suspicious floor managers testified to that. Joe didn't act proud, or cocky, or anything, just widened his smile into a big bashful grin, bought drinks for the table, eased off into the night. "Be back," he promised cheerily.

He was. Not the next night, he saved it up for later. Instead he went to the neighboring club, which happened to be under the same management. Lost five hundred. Shook his head like an embarrassed kid. "Try, try again," he said, then lost a couple times more. Shook his head again, his grin kind of twisted and goofy, put another bill on the table. And blamed if he didn't end up with four, maybe it was six, thousand to the good. He took it real low-key, pleased but quiet, kind of like a kid getting an unexpected present at a Sunday school program.

Joe didn't push it too far, just showed up now and then, spread himself around different clubs. Once in a while he lost, and took that like a man. He took his winnings the same way, which, if anyone bothered to keep track, considerably overbalanced the losses.

The management of the clubs bothered.

Dion himself carried word of the new arrival to the Old Man, who wisely suggested that a few telegrams be sent off asking questions. Like to Chicago, New York, Kansas City, New Orleans, Detroit, since the stranger was reputed to be from the Midwest or back East.

None of the sources had heard of a Joe Clancy.

"Could be a name change took place," Dion suggested to the Old Man. So more telegrams were sent, this time with a description: SIX FEET TWO OVER TWO HUNDRED POUNDS BROWN WAVY HAIR BLUE EYES MAYBE 25 TO 30 YEARS SMILES A LOT.

The "smiles a lot" pinned Joe. Back came a telegram from Kansas City: COULD BE SMILING JOE FORSHEY NOT CLANCY RAN TULSA CABARET SHOT MAN CHEATING POKER CHARGES DROPPED GUY LIVED BESIDES X CON BUT BUDDIES HOLD GRUDGE JOE HARD BUT STRAIGHT KEEPS WORD.

The Old Man took a fancy to this character reference and had Dion bring Joe up to the palace on the hill overlooking the Truckee River for a little royal hospitality. Joe gave a wide grin, said it made him real proud to accept.

2.

The Old Man's fancy for Joe increased at that first meeting. He told Dion afterwards he hadn't laughed that much in years, said Joe's down-home humor and way of looking at things relaxed him. He'd slept that night straight through, first time in ages.

At the time, this admiring comment slipped right past Dion on account of he'd laughed a lot too. It was only later, after five or six similar comments, that he started thinking about it.

Joe started out as kind of a flunky, translate that bodyguard, driving the Old Man all over Nevada to inspect his multiple investments, some of them in areas where the king was not real popular. But all that riding around can be pretty hard on an old man, and in a couple of years it was Joe showing up to check the clubs and bars while his boss stayed home. Dion also stayed home, in a fine new administrative office above the main club. "I knew you wouldn't want to be doing all that driving around, being away from your family," the Old Man had pointed out to Dion. "Besides, I need you to keep the store here in Reno. Those back-east mobs are itching to take over Nevada and they'll hit Reno first. Joe can watch the outskirts. If they try to sneak in the back door, he already knows some of their boys."

Dion felt a light sweat pop out on his forehead. "Yeah, I know, but remember, Joe's a newcomer himself. Maybe I oughta go with him some of the time, keep an eye—"

"Joe's got great eyes," the Old Man broke in. "The kind sees backwards and forwards at the same time. So have you, Dion, so why put two four-eyed guys on the same job? If Joe blows it, then I'll take a hand and

I've still got you. Besides, you got your family here, you don't need to be running around.''

About then whispers started up and down Commercial Row and around Lake and Center streets that there was a runner-up for crown prince. Dion didn't catch the whispers right away, it took him awhile. Which was a good thing for Joe's social life. Because by that time he had become real popular with the Galway females. Both Jerry and Pat were into a teenage crush on big, handsome, fun-fun "Uncle" Joe, who was keeping them supplied with expensive chocolates and wall-to-wall stuffed animals. Inga, their mother, considered Joe a darling lonely man who kept smiling to cover secret sorrow that he did not have his own wonderful children like her daughters. To fill this vacancy in his life she made a point of inviting him to all her lavish parties, determined that some lovely, also lonely, rich divorcee would latch onto him and eventually fill his need. She was cheered to discover that a number of almost-unattached ladies were quite ready to do this.

Joe was at the Galway home so regularly, always loaded with flowers for Inga and teddy bears and chocolates for the kids, dancing with pretty ladies including Inga and the twins in the big recreation room, that Dion began to brood about it. To aggravate this brooding, he kept remembering how relaxed and good-natured the Old Man always became when Joe showed up.

By the time the twins reached nineteen, and Joe his early thirties, practically the only thing Pat and Jerry agreed on was their deep affection for Uncle Joe. Both attended university, Jerry aiming for animal husbandry, Pat dreaming of stardom on Broadway via a drama major. Both were very grown-up, except when Uncle Joe was around. Then they were still kids, wrestling for his attention.

As he observed his daughters smother Joe with hugs and kisses upon his every arrival at the Galway spread, then squabble heatedly over which would dance with him first, Dion's brooding matured into hot-eyed suspicion. Particularly painful to note was that Jerry, his pride and joy surrogate son, always seemed to win. Extra heft and muscle gave her the advantage against the willowy Pat. Then before Pat could grab her turn on the dance floor, Jerry would rush Uncle Joe, arm in arm, out to the stables to admire her beloved horses. Pat, her underlip thrust out, would hasten after them to claim Joe's arm on the way back.

Hot-eyed suspicion eventually effloresced into convinced reality, accompanied by rage, when word reached Dion from his and the Old Man's main club that its next-door subsidiary dining room was having the honor of Pat's presence almost every weekday noon, accompanied by a hungry coterie of university football hunks, Pat the generous hostess. Or was she? But no; a not so generous fatherly review of the meal ticket revealed that it had been signed by Joe. "Was Joe hiding inside those hulks?" Dion demanded of the maître d'. No, Joe just popped in, signed, and popped out, generous guy that he was.

"Oh sure, big-hearted snake," Dion mumbled to himself. "Cover up, that's what. Just one more play for my kids. I got to do something about Joe."

Inga innocently brought something else to Dion's attention. With motherly concern she reported that Jerry was getting strange, locking herself in her room, then seemingly for no reason bursting out to quarrel with Pat. Once even wrestling Pat to the floor while Pat screamed, "Jealous fat old thing! You hate me because Uncle Joe buys my lunch!" Then Jerry had bounced Pat's head on the floor, yelling back, "You asked him! You keep asking him! You bring those boys along for camouflage!"

"My little girls are growing up," worried Inga. "And poor Joe caught in the middle because he's so kind."

I know where I'd like to catch him, Dion thought as he ran the information through his mind on his drive back to town. It's time I put the bastard out of the picture.

That night he tracked Joe down by telephone and invited him to his office for a little chat. When Joe showed up the handshake he got was big cordial stuff, but Dion's black eyes burning through slitted lids were not. Joe noticed.

"Joe, I'll waste no time. Plunge right in. I been noticing you and my girls are pretty damn chummy."

"What's new?" Joe asked easily, all good-natured. "Always been. Those kids are like my own, that is if I had any."

"You're a little short of their daddy age, Joe, unless you started daddying in early teens. So I'm laying it on the line. You're damn always at my house loading those girls with goodies, chatting up a storm, God only knows what you talk to them about. Because now you've got them fighting about you. Pat down at our restaurant every day, you feeding her, by God. I don't need nobody feeding my girls, she's got an allowance better'n most men make a month, to say nothing about she could put it on the house—"

"That's nothing but a kid stunt!" Joe broke in. "She wants a free lunch for that football team that's always trailing her. Kid stuff. She thinks you might put up a holler at the repeat bill or get too fatherly about the muscle she's running around with. Top of that, it makes her a big girl on campus, showing off about her dad's place of business."

"Yeah! That's not the way I see it! Neither does the maître d'. Don't try to con a man who wrote the book on conning. You been leading her on and Pat's picked up the boys for you to hide behind. Somehow my Jerry got roped in on that, now she's acting like some silly lovesick girl, lost interest in the ranch, you inveigling her down to the club trailing the ranch boys, maybe getting them to rough up the college kids, make a comedy outa my business."

Joe threw back his head and laughed.

Dion jumped to his feet. "By God, a crook like you, leading on my girls! I'll—"

"Ease off, Dion," Joe said softly. "Don't push this into something both of us will be sorry about. Those girls are just growing up. My sisters turned peculiar around that age, brooding around, crying if you pointed a finger at them, all kinds of weird female things. And as for Jerry, I don't think you can face the fact that she's a girl, not a boy."

"Don't tell me Jerry's just growing up. You been stuffing Inga with that kind of rot? Jerry's already grown-up, ready to take over the ranch. Two-three more years and I'll ease her into bigger responsibility. She's smart, she can run these clubs. Rides like a man, thinks like a man, she's got no business wasting time trying to be a fool girl. Now I'm a reasonable kinda man, Joe, you may be a little right about Pat and her gang at lunch. Pat's a girl all the way, doesn't hit things straight on, sidesteps the female way. Look how she may be cutting you out from her sister by corralling you down here at the club, handy as Jerry can cut out a horse from a herd. My Jerry comes out fighting, slam-bang, all up front."

"Dion, I'd never hurt those girls. They're great kids, but to me, kids. And I think it's outa line to dream up something like that to come between you and me, not in this business. The Old Man won't go for that kind of flying off on some kiddie ride. We're grown-up. On my part—"

Mention of the Old Man stirred up the banked fire in Dion, and it flared out. "Then get this straight—on my part I want you the hell out of Reno! Ask the Old Man to give you a jump start in Elko, Ely, maybe Las Vegas, Vegas is a comer, it'll be ready for the picking before long. Give you a big future, and I'll help you talk it up with the Old Man."

"The Old Man put you up to this?" Joe asked quietly.

Dion's head tipped back, as though reading an answer on the ceiling. "Haven't brought it up with him. Yet."

Joe smiled. "Wouldn't."

"Why not?"

"Like I said, kid stuff. Make him bust out laughing. Only not jolly. More like he'd be wondering what kinda guys he's got working with him, handling his money."

"Don't try to sidetrack me, Joe, you been building things up until I'm sick—all those damn teddy bears, candy, flowers, jollying the women, cracking jokes with the Old Man until he can't think straight for laughing, it's gone on too long!"

Joe's smile held, but his blue gaze was hard and straight. "Figured there was something deeper with you than teddy bears and free lunches."

"Cut the gaff! I'm gonna deal with something real simple. Like I'll be a helluva lot happier with you anywhere that's not Reno."

Joe nodded as though something in his mind had become clear, said, "I'll be as straight with you as you're trying to be with me. I've always admired you, partly because you're a good family man, really care about your wife and kids. One of these days I'd like to try for the same. But be reasonable, Dion. I'm a grown man. Won't make me feel good to be run outa Reno by teddy bears. No stuffed toys run me outa Tulsa; it was too many tricky characters hiding around too many corners. Anyway, Vegas and Elko are not my kinda towns, I like a town green with trees and a river running down its middle. If I had my druthers I'd even like to stay here long enough to be buried in Reno." He hesitated, let his grin get wider. "Naturally I want to be real old when that happens."

Dion's eyes flashed. "Some kinda meaning in that?"

The grin tightened. "Well, you read the papers same's I do. And they print about sometimes peculiar things that happen around Reno. Like that prominent business guy we both knew—fact is, he did business with you and the Old Man—and one afternoon with all the stores still open he vanished right off Virginia Street. Downtown, in broad daylight. Sheriff, police, everybody searched the whole damn state, big reward offered.

Never did find the guy. Could be he trusted somebody too much and now he's paving the bottom of some godforsaken mine shaft. Or something. So if I get my druthers I don't want to leave town that way."

"I'd like to know what the hell that's got to do with moving on!"

"Like you suggested, Dion, let's cut the gaff. Here's my suggestion. You keep your girls home, out of anywhere near these clubs where I might be. If you can. Tell Inga not to invite me to your house no more, same for the girls. And from here on everything between you and me is strictly business. And my business is mine, same for you."

"I want you the hell outa town!"

Joe sighed, shook his head seemingly in wonderment, stood up. "Still seems to me it's more than your house and your girls you're anxious about. Could it be because my piece of business arrangements with the Old Man recently got a little bigger?"

Irish temper scalded Dion's cheeks. He sprang to his feet and flung open the office door. "The hell out!"

Joe took his time to the door. Stopped. "I meant it when I said I admired you. So this is a pretty dumb way for men who been friends to act."

"Who said we were friends!"

"I did." The grin crept back. "Did I ever mention what they used to call me at school? That dumb ox. Guess I never outgrowed it."

Out on the sidewalk, headed for his parked car, he warned himself, "Joe, here on out better watch your back and dark alleys. Maybe even in daylight. And be careful not to lean over any bridge to watch the fish swim down toward Pyramid Lake."

3.

After Joe's departure Dion paced the floor, also talking to himself. "By God, all I've done is give that damn poker face ideas. Can't ever tell what he's cooking up, eyes like a smile froze in blue glass. I better get Inga and the girls outa town, send 'em to Europe, keep 'em there all summer."

He sat at his desk, cogitating, then grabbed his hat, headed for the street and his car, and turned the car toward the Old Man's big gabled house above the river.

When he reached it he swore fervently. Joe's car was parked in its driveway. "Beat me," Dion muttered. "Inside, spouting jokes, maybe even about what we discussed, have the Old Man in stitches."

Furious, he turned back to his office. There, a slow, meditative search through files produced the number he sought and he put in a long-distance call to Tulsa. After that he telephoned Inga, informing her that she and the twins would soon have a big treat, would be on their way for a lengthy stay in Europe. "In the name of God, what put that idea in your head? I'm not having an affair, this is a special treat because those kids need to get a wider view of the world, not just concentrate on Reno. Get yourselves some nice travel things, shoot the works. Hey, I may even join you later along the way."

Near midnight Jerry clumped into the house, exhausted but triumphant. "Mom, I'm sure happy the boys got me down to the stables tonight," she announced, "because I got the first look at my future champion, a filly! Real beauty, bearing all the marks of her sire. She and I are going to prove a filly can outrace all the boys. I'm going to train her, bring her up right from this day one. Good thing university vacation is coming up, give me lots of free time."

"But, darling, you can't, not this summer—I have such great news, Daddy is giving us a marvelous gift. He just called insisting that Pat, you, and I go to Europe this summer as a special education for you girls, isn't that wonderful? Jerry, don't stick out your underlip, it's a marvelous opportunity and ever so much better than staying down in that smelly stable. Jerry, stop shaking your head—we'll have such fun shopping: designer clothes, museums and things, purses and belts in Italy—"

"No! I will not!"

"Don't go into one of your stubborn tantrums! Really, darling, you'll hurt Daddy's feelings when he's trying to be so good to us. The sudden trip surprised me too, but already I love the idea. We'll go on the biggest liner, dance and swim on board, have fun all the way."

"Won't! I'm afraid of boats and oceans, I love deserts and horses, and I won't leave my new filly!"

Inga reached Dion by phone at his office. "So, darling, you know how Jerry can get, and I really have to say you've always encouraged her to be—" she almost said "like you," changed it to "—independent. Now she has caused such a fuss that Pat is refusing to go too, says she's going to take a summer course at the U, some special drama project. I think maybe she was planning that as a surprise for us. She'll star in the play, and Jerry has this new female horse—"

"To hell with surprises and we got more horses than we need. I don't need any more surprises or horses. For God's sake, Inga, you're their mother, why haven't you seen this coming? Both those girls have fallen for that grinning, teddy-bear-toting Joe who's forever cluttering up our house! Refigure their plans to include Joe and you'll have a squabble over which one gets him for their very own teddy bear. Tonight I warned him never to enter our house again. I called the ranch foreman, told him to throw him off the place if he turns up. And you tell Pat not to set foot near our clubs or the restaurant; if she does I'll have her brought straight up to my office. And if any of Joe's presents arrive at the house, send 'em back. And as for Jerry—" His voice trailed off, got lost somewhere deep in his chest. "Inga, tomorrow first thing make those reservations for Europe."

Next morning, after a late-night argument between mother and daughters, Pat, a pouting angel, blond curls tied high on her head with a blue ribbon, came downstairs for breakfast. "Ooh, Pattie, how pretty you look, feel better this morning? Sweetheart, Daddy and I had another talk last night and, well, Daddy says you mustn't go down by the clubs or the restaurant anymore because—well, I dislike even mentioning it, but because he thinks you might, well, be fond of Uncle Joe, I mean too fond. Of course you're fond, but you mustn't ever be too fond. You're so young and, well, Uncle Joe is not actually your *uncle*. He's a *man*. Daddy said for me to make that clear."

"What in hell does Dad think we thought he was?" That question zoomed upon Inga and Pat from Jerry, leaning over the stair balustrade, glaring fiercely upon them. "Have we ever called him *Auntie*?"

"Don't be impudent, dear. It's just because he loves you that your father takes such interest. You girls are almost women and anything can—I mean might—"

"I'm already a woman, and it sure might!" Jerry proclaimed with deep conviction.

"Me too!" Pat echoed.

"Now you girls listen, Daddy is very determined. Now Pat, you must not take your friends to lunch at the club restaurant anymore, you have plenty of money to go some other place. And Jerry, you're not to take Joe to the stables again, that is if he gets past the ranch hands, the ranch is off limits and that's very disappointing to me, he's such a help when I have friends here, so you see Mother's also—" She gave a troubled sigh. "It's too bad this came up, but you girls must have brought it on yourselves, always making over Uncle—I mean, Joe. And maybe Joe feels bad too, because Daddy says Joe has to move to Las Vegas or somewhere."

"No!" Jerry shouted.

Pat began to cry.

4.

Dion took his turn at discussing this unhappy state of affairs with the Old Man. To his grave disappointment the Old Man chuckled—it made Dion flinch, his chuckle sounded so much like Joe's—and said he had to agree with Joe that Dion's concern, although laudable in a loving father, was pretty far-fetched. "Besides—and get this straight, Dion—our business don't need my two closest associates at loggerheads. Especially right now. We need a strong front. Talk reached me that some of those back-east hoods are on the way to muscle in on Reno. Now Reno's mine, been that way a long time and I want it to stay that way. Sure, once in a while we've borrowed some of their thugs for special jobs here and there, to keep our boys clean. But in our organization, no. So we've got to have solidarity, full cooperation. You and Joe make up."

Dion nodded. Inwardly his mind raced on how to give the Old Man what he wanted. Minus Joe.

On the same evening that Dion was worrying that around back in his office, Jerry was standing tiptoe in Joe's apartment living room, arms wrapped around Joe's neck, begging, "Please, please, Uncle Joe, marry me! I've been in love with you forever and ever." Her head nuzzled against his chin. "I'm nineteen now, I'm a woman, I can marry who I want. And I'm not going to Europe! I'm not even going back to university. I don't need a degree, I can hire veterinarians. I just want you, Uncle Joe. You and my horses."

"Looky here, honey, to me you're still a little girl, a wonderful little girl, and you got lots of time to pick out a man. I'm nothing but a poor old knockabout fake uncle. So you better just stick to your horses. Your daddy and I decided—"

"Damn what you decided! I do my own deciding!"

"Baby, be sensible. You and your little sister are like my own—"

"I am NOT like your kid! Pat maybe, but NOT ME! I've been grown-up all my life, riding, roping, cussing with the best ever since I could walk. Dad liked that, he wanted me for his boy. Well, I'm no boy, I'm all girl. I know all about mares and stallions, I know all—"

He gently pushed her away. "Jerry, baby, you don't know nothing about men. Or you wouldn't be here, hanging on my neck. Now you go on downstairs, climb in your car, and drive home. I'm due at the club to check things out. Be a good girl, git!" His wide, affectionate grin turned the order into a caress. He led her to his outer door, eased her into the hallway, closed the door. Then put his shoulders against it and took a deep, stretching breath. "Oh Christ!"

Give Joe credit. He tried.

After he finished his usual checkup down at the club, he wandered out to Center Street, looking up appreciatively at the colored electric signs over the club's doorways, at pedestrians hurrying in and out of the next-door hotel, intent on various destinations. "Reno's a great town," he thought. "I'd like to stay."

He noticed Dion's big sedan drive slowly by the club entrance. Joe grinned, waved. *Out hound-dogging, planning to catch him a damn rabbit named Joe.* He pulled a packet of chewing gum from his pocket, unwrapped a couple of sticks, poked them in his mouth. Chewed ruminatively. *That little Jerry, never thought of her that way before, sure a beauty, fire and spunk.* Another thought edged beside it, *Mind this, Joe, pasture even a good strong stallion out in a cold lonely winter too long and he could end up crippled with rheumatism, fit for nothing.*

He stopped thinking and headed up Center Street to get his car, halted as a distressed wisp of a female voice called, "Uncle Joe!"

He bent and peered at the parked cars. A small white hand waved above the door of a low sports roadster with a canvas top. In back of it he glimpsed a pale heart-shaped face. "Here, Uncle Joe! Please!" It was Pat.

"What you doing here alone this time of night, honey? Saw your daddy just drive by, you looking for him?"

The heart-shaped face moaned. "No, no! Please, Uncle Joe, just get in the car! I don't want Daddy to see me, I have to talk to you." She threw open the car door. "Hurry! Before he sees me."

"Honey, your daddy and I kinda decided—"

"Get in!"

He slid in beside her. The car snorted and took off toward Virginia Street, then turned west along the light-flecked Truckee River, finally parked on a quiet side street.

"Okay, little girl, what's the trouble?"

"It's the Horse!" Pat sobbed.

He was startled. Jerry and horses, yes. But Pat, drama, ballet, dresses so form-fitting it'd be hard to climb aboard even a Shetland pony. What did Pat have to do with horses?

What could he say about horses? "Well, honey, you get throwed, pick yourself up, get right back on."

"He threatens to leave Reno and never see me again if I won't run away with him!"

Joe patted the sobbing girl. *This ain't no regular horse, this is some smooth-talking bastard of a stud who—*

"But if I do, Daddy has such a terrible temper he may kill the Horse and keep me in Europe forever, maybe in a monastery!"

"Honey, monasteries are for priests, they ain't—"

"I love him, simply love him! Don't you remember him, Uncle Joe? That handsome, curly-headed boy I always sat beside at lunch. I brought the other boys along so no one would guess the Horse was special. Actually his name is Herschel, but he hates that, so the team calls him the Horse on account of he's always galloping down the field to make touchdowns—he's marvelous, absolutely thrilling! Another university is trying to get him but I can't bear to have him leave me and our U, so Uncle Joe, please help me keep him here. If you help me tell Daddy about the Horse, that I want to marry him, that I never ever wanted to marry you, he'd be so relieved he'd agree to almost anything. Please, please!" and her arms twined around his neck.

He tugged gently at her arms. "Pat, you gotta talk to your mama about this, then she can talk to your dad; this is family stuff. Your dad might think I put you up to this."

She pushed his hands away and her grip around his neck tightened. She buried her face against his chest. "Please, please, please!"

Headlights rounded the corner behind them. A long black car slid in front of the roadster, parked. Dion Galway stepped out, walked back, thrust his face close to the two heads. "Clancy—Forshey, whoever the hell you are, you lied! Said you never bothered my girls. I'm through with this fooling around, I want you the hell and gone by morning. Anywhere, just gone! And don't go whining to the Old Man. Won't do any good after I tell him I caught you tonight!"

He yanked open the door, grabbed his daughter. She clung to Joe, whimpering, "It's not Uncle Joe's fault, I asked him, I was the one—"

"Shut up!" Dion dragged her out of the car to his automobile, started the motor, shot down the street.

Joe sat quietly, listening to tires screech out of hearing. Then he pulled out the car keys, tucked them under the seat, and walked to the center of town where his own car was parked. He had enough time, he figured. Likely Dion would first take Pat home, deposit her with Inga, then head back to the Old Man's house to spill his story. "Catch him before he gets inside, explain the facts," he decided. "Maybe I can get his head screwed on right."

He drove across the river, up the tree-lined hill, parked beside the entrance to the Old Man's driveway. Eased into the padded leather seat, moved his big shoulders back and forth to relieve tension, rolled down his window to better hear any approaching car. Street light filtering through the leafy branches turned their shadows into a dizzy, mesmerizing dance over the sidewalk. Pretty sight, restful. Joe watched it, leaned back his head, let the evening's strain drift away.

He awakened at the touch of cold metal against his nose. "One yelp and it's over," warned Dion's equally cold voice. "I'll swear you came here to pick a bone with the Old Man, claiming he and I were plotting to kick you outa the business. All I did was protect him and myself. You're the Johnny-come-lately in Reno, Joe, been in trouble before, even shot a man. The cops will believe me. So will the Old Man after I tell him about finding you hugging my girl out in a parked car—get your damn hands up, keep 'em up!" With his free hand he opened the car door. "Nice and easy, out in the street!"

Joe raised his hands, slowly edged to the opening. "No sweat, Dion. I know how you'd feel if what you're thinking was true. Only it's not."

"Can it!"

"You've got it wrong." Joe's left foot felt for the pavement, set the sole of his shoe solidly upon it. "Your Irish temper's getting in the way."

"Shut up!"

"Okay, okay," Joe said meekly. His upper body braced against the seat back, his right leg pulled free of the steering shaft to join the left. But instead of joining it, the right leg, with 220 pounds of self-preservation behind it, slammed against the door, drove it and Dion into the car's hood. Pinned Dion between two pieces of hard metal. Joe stood over his captive gripping his gun hand. "Dion, the Old Man's sure gonna be boiled, having his right- and left-hand men fighting in his front yard, runs down the neighborhood." His voice was gentle, one friend to another. "Besides how it's gonna look in the papers. All over the country maybe. Give a whole bunch of crooks big confidence about taking over Reno."

He gave the wrist a mild twist and stood erect, hefting the pistol. "Damn! You sure picked a cannon, didn't aim to miss."

Dion arose, his face a ghost's in the shadowed light, crouched to spring. "Hold it!" Joe warned coldly. "We already had our fun. Now listen good before one of us gets splashed all over the street. Your Pat is itching to get married, but not to me. To one of those football players I been feeding. I told you it was kid stuff. So tonight she asked old big-hearted Uncle Joe the sucker to help her nail this boy. Otherwise he threatens to leave town and her with her heart broke. She was begging me to talk to you about it, she's too scared. That's as far as she got when you showed up. You gonna commit murder for that? With Pat going hysterical, spilling to the world the real story? Then getting married anyway, only her daddy not at the wedding because he's in the pen?"

Brief silence.

"Which football player?"

"Better ask her."

"I don't think he's got a name. I think it's your cock-and-bull story to save your hide. I still want you gone. Besides, true or not, I've got more than one girl."

Joe switched off his mental flashback of the encounter with Jerry earlier that night.

"This is all a bunch of damn foolishness, Dion. We're businessmen, not feisty kids. Now slide to one side off that car hood. Easylike, no need for this car door to take another swing. While you're at it, think this over. I'm not leaving."

Once Dion was standing free, Joe broke open the pistol, removed the bullets, dropped them in his pocket, and tossed the gun against the curb. He got in his car, steadied the broken door with his left hand, turned the key, swung around Dion, and drove off.

As he headed home he remembered Jerry again, could almost feel her warm, stocky body against his, her strong arms dragging on his neck, pulling him close.

5.

At the Galway ranch Jerry was soundly sleeping when someone frantically shook her around midnight. Jerry came awake fighting, swung, hit something that yipped and fell. She blinked her eyes at her twin sprawled beside the bed. "What's the matter? Someone hurt? My filly, Mom, Dad?"

"I'm hurt! And you did it!" Pat said angrily. "Jerry, I need your help. Dad's gone crazy! Absolutely insane! He says he's going to run Uncle Joe out of town, kill him or something, and he won't listen to me."

Jerry sprang out of bed. "Why?"

"I told you. Dad's lost his mind. He has this dumb idea I'm in love with Uncle Joe. And that you are, too. Imagine! In love, the marrying kind of love, with an old man almost thirty-five! It's the Horse I love, I want to marry the Horse, you know him, that adorable fullback I told you about. So I was in my car with Uncle Joe asking him to help explain things to Daddy. Just sitting there, and I was hugging him and begging—"

"You stop hugging him!"

"You're as dumb as Daddy! I only wanted him to help me marry the Horse, because if I don't the Horse will leave the U, so if I marry the Horse that'll certainly prove I don't love Uncle Joe that way. But all of a sudden Daddy was going insane."

"Why would you want to marry that half-baked kid? No wonder—"

"Shut up and listen! Because this very minute your great big wonderful old man may be getting shot!"

Jerry was pulling off her pajamas, stepping into briefs, riding trousers, pulling a sweater over her head, scrambling under the bed for her boots. She strode to the door, hesitated, came back to pick up her heavy silver-handled quirt off her dressing table. "Dumb, dumb men, I swear horses have more sense!"

She stomped down the stairs, and outside ran to the garage. She scooted under the wheel of her English sports car, backed and turned into the long ranch lane to the highway, and drove north. On the way her father's big dark car zoomed past in the opposite direction. Neither driver noticed the other, each too busy thinking.

Up in Reno, Joe was parked on a secluded turnaround, giving his arm a rest from hanging onto the sagging car door. Watching, too, to see if Dion's car came up the hill. Finally muttered, "Best place for you, Joe, is home, no sense hanging around here waiting for more trouble, no telling what kind of nutty ideas will pop up in the dark." Started the car, drove off. Nearing his apartment building, he took an observant swing around its parking lot. No, no unusual shadows, no unusual parking. He cut his motor, listened. No hasty scuffling.

He left the car, used his key to enter the locked back entrance of the building, went upstairs to his corner apartment. Locked his door, fastened its extra chain lock, went to his bedroom.

Before undressing he checked the handgun kept loaded in his bedside table. Left the drawer slightly open, pulled off his clothes, slid naked into bed. He fell asleep fast, like an untroubled child.

The first ring of his bell from the front street entrance jerked him upright, wide awake. He swung his legs free of the covers, grabbed his pants, slid them on. Gun in hand, padded barefoot to the intercom located in his private entrance hallway. Into it he said cautiously, "Hello?"

The tube emitted a hoarse, choked whisper. "Uncle Joe—Joe? This is Jerry. I have to talk to you."

"It's late, baby. You better go on home. I have to tell you, your daddy's bad upset, cruising around, could be looking for you."

"I don't care, I can handle Dad. Please, Joe, I have to talk."

Joe pressed the buzzer, returned to the bedroom, hurriedly slipped on his undershirt. At the tap on his door, he opened it, a wide "Uncle" smile on his face. He drew Jerry inside. "Well now, baby girl, what's on your mind?"

Jerry's big dark eyes zeroed in on him. "Stop calling me that! And stop calling yourself my uncle! I'm no baby, I'm a woman and I love you. And I don't want you shot. Pat just told me Dad's threatening you and I won't have it!" The heavy quirt slapped against her twill trousers in angry emphasis. "Won't have it, hear? If there's shooting, they'll have to shoot me too. And if you leave town, I'll be with you. Just try to stop me!"

Joe choked back a delighted chuckle, tried to look solemn as he surveyed the defiant little figure before him, her legs spread in determined stance, quirt held menacingly, chin thrust forward, full rosy lips stubbornly set. *Man, I tell you, this sure is a woman.*

"Honey, you just about could be my daughter. I got around fifteen years over you."

"Damn fifteen years!"

It surprised him to realize that behind his resolutely aged pose his insides felt mighty young and nervous. Sweat started running down his back, his mouth was dry. Women never got to him much before, that was part of being Smiling Joe. But this was different. This little girl had hit her mark.

"Jerry, you got a lot of living ahead of you, schooling, fun, lots of things. Besides, you know how your daddy counts on you to be his boy, take over the ranch, maybe run his business someday, planned on it ever since you were a little tyke."

Jerry moved to him, reached around his neck, snuggled her head against his broad chest. The light pressure of the quirt she held trailed along his back. As she tugged his face close to hers, he wondered fleetingly if she was up to using the quirt on him if he held off. Not that he wanted to. And so, he didn't.

"Joe, I do love you," Jerry whispered. "Please, please marry me. It won't get in the way of Dad's plans. When we're married I can still run the ranch, and you can take care of the business part better than I could."

"Your daddy don't want me—" His answer broke off as a shuffle of sound came from the entrance hall. In that instant he remembered that he had left his gun in the bedroom and failed to relock the hall door after Jerry came in. Another rueful thought flashed through his mind—no apartment-house lock on a lobby door stops a professional with an urgent reason to enter. He swung Jerry behind him, backed toward the bedroom.

Too late. Two heavy-chinned, bulky young men, the one in front pointing a gun directly at him, stood in the living room doorway. "Hold it!" the front man ordered. Behind him the second man warned, "Go slow! That must be the Galway kid, her old man said the car was parked outside, and she better not be hurt."

"Kid, move away from the guy, nobody gonna hurt you," the front man ordered.

In a flash of movement, Jerry darted around Joe, quirt raised, slashing venomously back and forth. Silent, her face dark with fury. The front man lunged toward her and with a hiss like a rattlesnake the quirt bit into his right wrist. He yelped, the fingers of his right hand dangling helplessly as his gun bounced across the rug. The quirt was continuing in a hurricane of movement, slicing hands, faces of both men, never a hesitation. Joe grabbed the gun.

The man in back, arm guarding his bleeding face, made an oblique, slithering exit. Heavy steps pounded down the outer hallway. The second man crouched on the floor, arms wrapped around head and neck, blood streaming from slashes.

"Okay, honey, take a breather, you got it under control," Joe said. Then to the man on the floor, "Unwrap and stand up! Jerry, call the cops. I reckon this gun can handle things until you're back on the job. Phone's in the bedroom."

The intruder cautiously arose. "Hey, that gun ain't loaded, them bullets are blanks. Galway said no real shooting."

"Well now, guess I better keep the little lady and her whip in here till I check out these bullets. One of your legs oughta prove whether you're a truthful guy."

"Hey! They're for real! I just—"

"Go on, honey, call the cops."

Jerry turned toward the bedroom. Stopped as her father plunged into the living room, gun in hand. The bleeding man wiped his face, scooted behind Dion, vanished.

It was a standoff, two guns aimed dead center, ten feet apart.

Jerry darted between her father and Joe.

"Now, looky here, Dion, see what you've gone and done!" Joe chided. "Let a couple mob thugs loose in Reno, helped 'em get a foothold. They'll be like cockroaches, never get rid of 'em."

"Jerry, get out of the way!"

Jerry's legs planted themselves solidly and defiantly on the blood-splattered rug. "Don't be ridiculous, Daddy. I'm not moving until you're both rid of those guns. Besides, Joe didn't start this, this isn't even his gun, it belongs to those crazies you sent up here, aren't you ashamed!"

"Yeah, and I didn't even get to use their gun," Joe said regretfully. "Your little girl whipped 'em both with that pretty loaded leather whip. Fact, Dion, it don't pay to cross her. I tried, but she bested me."

"What's that mean?"

"It means I made Joe promise to marry me."

"I'll see him dead first!"

Jerry's jaw set. "Dad, listen to this. I'm giving you a rock-solid promise. If I don't marry Joe, I'll never marry anyone. You think I'm too young to mean that? Don't try me, I'll show you what can happen with your make-believe son. I'll turn into your old maid, sit-around-the-house daughter. Never ride another horse, sell all mine. Leave the ranch. Take up knitting, knit enough sweaters to warm everybody in Nevada. I don't marry Joe, you've lost me." Abruptly she held out her arms. "Oh, Daddy, let's be sensible. Be like we were, only with Joe and me married. I'll run the ranch just like you planned. You and Joe can run the business, I don't like the business anyway. Please, Daddy. Friends?"

She walked to her father, kissed his cheek, patted his hand, came away with his gun. Returned to Joe, took his gun. "I hate guns, they're too final."

Joe grinned. "Yeah, better stick to that little play-toy you just handled so nice." But the grin faded as he faced Dion. "By the way, you happen to warn the Old Man about these stranger thugs being here in town? Or maybe you called 'em in, local boys wouldn't do what you had in mind."

Dion ignored him. His gaze burned on his daughter. "He'll be no son-in-law of mine. Been around too much. Too old."

Jerry put a reflective eye on her father. "Daddy, I listen a lot to stable talk when the boys don't know I'm around. And what I hear tells me you've been around a lot. Now with that kind of history, how come you turned out so good to Mom, and your daughters? So if it worked out okay with you, why can't it work out for Joe?"

Father and daughter stared at each other, each trying to force down the other's gaze. A brief sad chill froze its way through Joe's middle. *Neither going to give in, guess it'll be me doing it at the end.*

Silent, motionless, the three seemed caught in amber. Then the fire in Dion's eyes banked as he looked into the black eyes that matched his. He moved toward the entrance hall. "I'm going home. Jerry, come with me, we can talk this out better at home, with your mother."

"I'll not change my mind."

"At least we can talk. Get a better feeling."

Joe broke in, "Go with your daddy, honey. We'll all do better with a little rest."

At the door, Jerry beside him, Dion turned toward Joe. "Too bad all this had to come up."

"Yeah. Feel the same."

Joe watched father and daughter walk away, down the long hallway to the front stairs. Jerry turned and waved. He waved back, went inside his hall, locked the door. He clicked off the living room lights and carefully parted the drapes that covered the angled corner windows. Below was the parking lot and street, the latter spotted with faint light from the distant street lamp. Soon he saw Jerry, her father beside her, get into her sports car. Dion kissed her, stepped back to watch the little car disappear. He walked then to his car which was parked near the street, bent forward to peer across the way into a dark empty lot.

Within a few minutes two large male figures, their outlines mottled by leafy shadows, moved into view on the opposite sidewalk. They hurried across the street, slid inside the car through the door Dion held open.

"Figured that," Joe muttered.

The car did a U-turn, headed for Reno's downtown center. "Calling them off?" Joe asked himself. He kept watching.

For nearly an hour he waited at the window. There was no movement or sound on the street below. "Yeah, called off the thugs," he finally decided. "For tonight anyway." Yawning, he returned to the bedroom, peeled off his clothes a second time. Tossed around the bed awhile, then fell into a deep, exhausted sleep.

6.

Joe didn't really wake up. His head was too full of fog. In that nightmare state he became scared of himself, terrified by his own gasps that sucked the air from his lungs, gagging at a throat grown too narrow to let the gasp emerge. Through no will from himself his legs dragged and stumbled over the floor, legs mere jelly slithering through space. Both arms, gripped by an unknown force, drew him through nothingness. No. Couldn't be nothingness. Because the stair banister rippled past him, seemed to change into a fat brown snake writhing toward escape.

He tried to call for help, tried to catch the snake, escape with it. But his tongue was too heavy, too fat, to free the sound. For an instant his mind steadied—*HOW—THE DOOR, CHAIN—MAYBE NOT—UH CLIPPERS?—UH?* The question and the answer gargled in his throat as a stifling something dropped on his face and he fell into darkness.

Light returned. Gray light, dawn light. He was in open space, large blurred shapes either side of him, dragging him over stones and brush. He tried to ask the shapes to let him stand up or lie down, he didn't care which, but the effort merely ended in a groan. His feet kept bumping, bumping over the rough ground.

Then once more he fell into dark, down, down through cold dark air, into a black pit that lasted forever.

7.

Reno's old-time residents used to talk a lot about the Galway family—well, used to means the old days, early thirties, into the forties—around bridge and poker tables, in bars, or wherever in late nights folks tend to ponder life's whimsies. But after old Dion Galway and his wife Inga passed on the talk dwindled. Especially after the only Galway left in Reno to remind folks about the story was that fat weird old-maid daughter, and all she did was stay home. Her twin sister, the pretty one, was long gone, married a hotshot football coach, was it San Francisco or Seattle where they settled?

Screwy about those twins, one normal, one freaky, didn't look a bit alike. One slim, elegant. The other, muscles like a boy, square-built, finally turned into a tub. Hard to believe that tub used to be a regular tomboy—or cowboy, more like it. Always running around with her dad's ranch hands. Her daddy's fault, she was his favorite, he spoiled her rotten. Remember when, years back, she cleaned out his stables, sold all those gorgeous Arabians and quarter horses, his along with hers, and all he did was say everything he owned was hers anyway, it was her right.

When she moved off the ranch and bought a house in town, he sold all the Galway property, club shares too, and bought a house beside hers. That was when his wife left him, moved to the coast to be with the pretty twin, stayed there, died there.

Dion Galway turned so crazy—guess his girl came by it naturally—that he holed up like she did, just stayed in his house, staring through the windows trying to get a glimpse of his pet. A few years of that and finally the girl gave in a little, let the old man move in with her. But what good did that do? Never spoke a word to him, that is, directly, their maids told around she spoke through them and not much of that. Shocked them, because every now and then that fat daughter would look up over her knitting needles and spit out, "Murderer!"

See what we mean? Crazy, real crazy. Especially after all her daddy did for her.

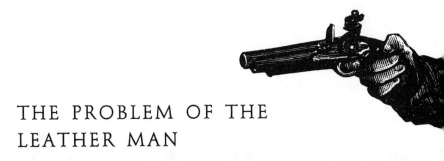

THE PROBLEM OF THE LEATHER MAN

Edward D. Hoch

The modern-day master of the short puzzle mystery, Edward D. Hoch makes use of historical settings in two of his longest running series. In choosing periods close to our own—for the Dr. Sam Hawthorne series, 1930s America—the author avoids having to lay an extensive historical groundwork of culture and values, but gains the advantage of plotting his crimes in a simpler era, when the intellectual faculties of the detective count foremost. Mr. Hoch is an expert researcher who has an eye for the bizarre in history that is exemplified nowhere more clearly than in this tale based on the real-life "Leather Man," a vagrant who for thirty years walked a 365-mile circuit of New England's roads clad in homemade leather garments. Mysterious in his refusal to reveal his identity, the Leather Man became a legend waiting for resurrection in Mr. Hoch's impossible-crime story.

Ever since I'd moved to southern New England in the early 1920s (Dr. Sam Hawthorne told his guest, lifting the glass for a sip of brandy), I'd heard occasional stories about the Leather Man. At first I thought it was a mere legend to frighten the children at night, but later I learned that there really was such a person—a laconic wanderer dressed in a homemade leather suit who toured Connecticut and eastern New York State for some thirty years until his death in 1889.

The summer of 1937 was when the Leather Man returned, and in Northmont we weren't ready for him.

It was Sheriff Lens who roused me with a phone call at three in the morning on the first day of August. "Hawthorne," I mumbled into the bedside phone.

"Doc, I got a bad accident out on Turk Hill Road, near Putnam. You were the closest one to call."

"I'll be there," I answered shortly and hung up. My head was back on the pillow when I jerked myself awake and clambered out of bed. I wiped my face with a wet washcloth, dressed quickly, and hurried out to my car. Except for an occasional patient in labor, it was rare for me to be called out at that hour. Although automobiles had become more numerous on the roads around Northmont, accidents were infrequent.

I reached the scene of this one within fifteen minutes of the sheriff's summons. A black Ford had run off the road and turned over in a ditch. Sheriff Lens's car was on the road about ten feet away and the sheriff himself was doing the best he could with the badly injured driver. A woman from a nearby farmhouse stood watching from a safe distance.

"How bad is it?" I asked the sheriff.

"Bleedin' from the head, Doc," he answered quietly, standing up to greet me in the glare of his car's headlights. "It's March Gilman."

I knew Gilman from the Rotary meetings, though he'd never been a patient or close friend. He was a man around forty with a successful feed grain business in town, and a reputation of chasing after the ladies.

"Bad wound," I said, dropping to my knees beside him. "Have you called the ambulance?"

"Right away, but they were having some engine trouble. That's when I phoned you."

I leaned closer to the bleeding man. "March! March, can you hear me?"

His eyes flickered open for just an instant. "What—?"

"You've had an accident, March."

"Leather . . . the Leather Man—"

"What's that?" I asked. I'd heard him clearly enough but I didn't understand the words.

"Leather Man . . . in the road. Tried to avoid him and . . . went into ditch."

"What Leather Man, March? Who was he?"

But that was all he said, and in the distance I could hear the clanging of the ambulance bell along the dark dirt road. I tried to stanch the flow of blood from his head until it arrived, but I knew the life was draining out of him.

As they were loading him into the ambulance, the woman who'd been watching moved closer. When she stepped into the light I recognized her as one of the teachers from the Northmont grammar school. "Miss Why-cliff—I didn't realize it was you."

"I still live here in the homestead," she replied, arms folded across her breasts as if to protect herself from the mild night air. She was an attractive but plain woman in her late thirties, unmarried and carrying on with life after the death of her parents. There were women like her in most rural communities.

"What happened here?" I asked as Sheriff Lens saw the ambulance on its way.

"I don't really know. He must have been driving fast. I heard the car go by the house and then skid and go into the ditch. I think it woke me up. I threw on some clothes and when I saw he was injured I phoned the sheriff at once."

"Did you see anyone else?" Sheriff Lens asked as he joined us. "This Leather Man he mentioned?"

"No one. But of course the road was dark." She hesitated. "There was a Leather Man in these parts long ago. I don't know much of the legend, but our local historian could tell you."

"I don't believe in ghosts," the sheriff told her. "The fella you're talkin' about's been dead nearly fifty years."

"Some people have seen him this summer," she replied. "I've heard talk that he's back."

"Rubbish!" Sheriff Lens told her. He was not one to believe in things he hadn't seen for himself.

Hannah Whycliff shrugged. "Will you send someone to tow this car out of my front yard?"

"First thing in the morning," he promised.

He drove to Pilgrim Memorial Hospital then, and I followed in my car. March Gilman was dead by the time we arrived.

Mary Best was busy with her office chores, getting out the August first billing, when I arrived a little before ten. "I just phoned you, Sam. I was worried when you weren't here at nine."

"I had a three A.M. emergency, so I decided to sleep an extra hour."

"The accident that killed March Gilman?"

I nodded. "I suppose the news is all over town."

"Pretty much. I gather he was someone important."

"Small-town important," I told her. Mary had taken over as my nurse after April married and moved to Maine. Sometimes I forgot she'd only been in Northmont two years and didn't yet know everyone. "What's my schedule for today?"

"It's pretty slow. Mrs. Ritter at ten-thirty and Douglas Greene at eleven, and then you're free for the day."

At noon I drove over to see Sheriff Lens. "Just looking at the hospital report on March Gilman," he said. "Died of massive head injuries. No surprise there. He had a bad bleeding wound and a lesser one that probably caused a mild concussion."

"I'm sorry I couldn't do anything to save him." I sat down by his desk. "But this business about the Leather Man still bothers me. Hannah Whycliff said the town historian would have information about the legend. Would that be Spencer Cobb?"

"Only one I know, and he's sorta unofficial."

Spencer Cobb had an office in our little library building on the far side of the town square. I found him on a short stepladder, checking an atlas of old New England maps in a leather-bound volume with a scuffed and disintegrating cover. "Hello, Sam," he greeted me. "What can I do for you?" He was white-haired, though barely fifty, and smoked a pipe almost constantly.

"I've got a historical question for you, Spencer. Ever hear of the Leather Man?"

"You're really going way back now. Come—sit down while I dig out some old references." He was actually the county surveyor, but since the job only occupied a small part of his time he'd taken on the additional duties of Northmont's historian.

Presently he laid an old photograph before me on the desk. It showed a scruffy man in his fifties seated on a wooden bench eating a piece of bread or a bun. He was clad entirely in a bulky, shiny garment with crude stitching plainly visible. The pants and coat seemed to be made of the same patchwork material—leather scraps held together by thongs. He wore a visored cap and boots that seemed to have wooden soles. Resting next to him was a leather bag perhaps two feet square.

"This was the Leather Man," Spencer Cobb said. "The photograph was taken not long before his death in 1889."

"Tell me about him."

Cobb struck a match and relit his pipe. "He first appeared in this area in the late 1850s, dressed as you see him here. For the next thirty years, summer and winter, he followed a particular route, walking along country roads from the Hudson River on the west to the Connecticut River on the east. It took him about thirty-four days to complete each circuit of three hundred sixty-five miles. He came as regularly as the full moon, though every thirty-four days instead of the moon's twenty-nine or thirty days. Once they established his route, some thought it had a mystic significance, with the three hundred sixty-five miles standing for the days of the year."

"Who was he? Did anyone know?"

"He rarely spoke—only a few words in broken English. Though he had his regular stops, if anyone questioned him too closely he would abandon that stop in the future. People were frightened of him at first, but they came to know him as a peaceful man who wanted no trouble. It was believed from his accent that he was French."

"What happened to him?"

"In December of 1888 someone noticed a sore on his lip that appeared to be cancerous. He was taken to a hospital in Hartford, but promptly ran away. The press identified him as a Frenchman named Jules Bourglay who'd fled his homeland following business losses and a tragic love affair. However, none of this was ever proven, and when the Leather Man died of cancer the following March, his meager belongings offered no clue to his identity."

"A fascinating story," I agreed. "But there have been recent reports—"

Spencer Cobb nodded. "I know. The Leather Man is back. I've been hearing stories all summer. Since I don't believe in ghosts I can only assume that someone is retracing the old route, for reasons of his own."

"I have a road map in the car. If I bring it in, could you outline the route for me?"

"Certainly. I have it in one of these old newspaper clippings. There's a great deal of material available because so many people at the time kept scrapbooks of his comings and goings."

I watched while he carefully copied the route of the Leather Man. If this new traveler was retracing the old route, I figured I should be able to locate him without too much difficulty. I'd become fascinated by the story, and curious about what he knew regarding the accident that killed March Gilman.

"Thanks, Spencer," I told him. "You've been a big help."

I went back to the office and plotted the distances on the map. "Why are you doing all this?" Mary Best asked. "What happens if you find him? Are you going to walk with him?"

"Maybe."

"That's the funniest thing I've heard!"

"Look, he's covering three hundred sixty-five miles every thirty-four days. That works out to better than ten and a half miles a day, every day. Why should anyone in his right mind do such a thing?"

"The original Leather Man did it. Maybe this is his grandson or something."

I could see she was laughing at me, but I wanted to find him. With the unfolded map beside me on the seat, I set off in my car along his route. Hannah Whycliff's house was as good a starting point as any, and I drove up there to begin my search. Her car was gone, and Gilman's wrecked vehicle had been towed away as promised. I parked in the drive and walked back to the road, looking for traces of the accident. The gravel in front of her house was unmarked, and only a broken piece of bumper remained in the ditch as evidence of the accident.

I tried to imagine where the Leather Man might have been crossing, then decided he'd have stuck to the road, especially at that hour of the night. But why had he been walking at all? Apparently he slept overnight with people, or in fields in good weather. What was he doing up at three in the morning?

I got back into my car and started driving.

After twenty miles of slow and careful searching over the next hour, I came to the conclusion that the Leather Man was nowhere to be found. Perhaps he'd given up his trek, if he'd ever begun it. Maybe the whole thing had been a myth. I stopped in a filling station that had a public telephone and called Mary back at the office.

"I can't find him," I told her. "I've covered the twenty miles between Northmont and Shinn Corners and he's nowhere on the road. Any emergencies back there?"

"All quiet."

"I guess I'll give up and head back in."

"Maybe you've been going the wrong way," she suggested.

"What?"

"You've been driving in a counterclockwise direction around his route. Maybe he walks in a clockwise direction."

"Damn!" I tried to think why I'd driven the way I did, and decided it was because March Gilman had been going in this direction when he went into the ditch and killed himself. Of course that proved nothing. If there had been a man in leather on the road last night he might have been walking in either direction. "Thanks, Mary. You could be right."

Next I phoned Spencer Cobb and asked him the crucial question. "You never told me which way the original Leather Man walked. Was it clockwise or counterclockwise?"

"Let's see—clockwise, I believe. It's not stated as such in the papers I have, but that seems to have been the case."

"Thanks, Spencer."

"Have you found him?"

"I'm on the trail."

I retraced my route and then kept on going past the Whycliff house, skirting Northmont and heading back east. I took it especially slow this time, and before I'd gone three miles I spotted a slim, brown-clad figure walking ahead of me in the road. He moved to one side as I drew up next to him, but I didn't drive past.

"Want a ride?" I called out the open window.

"No, mate. I'm walking."

He spoke with a strange accent, not quite British, and there was no arguing with his words. I made a quick decision and pulled up behind him, parking my car off the road. I hurried to catch up with him and asked, "Don't mind if I walk with you, do you?"

"Suit yourself, mate."

I fell into step beside him. Up close, I could see that he was indeed wearing a leather suit, not made of separate pieces held together by thongs like the original Leather Man, but one that fit him quite well and reminded me a bit of the buckskin garments one associated with Daniel Boone and other frontiersmen. He carried a knapsack of the same material, with a few possessions bundled into the bottom of it.

"Headed anywhere in particular?" I asked.

"I'm on a trek."

"That's a nice leather suit you're wearing. I hear people call you the Leather Man."

He turned his head in my direction and I got my first good view of his sandy hair and weathered face. He was probably in his forties, but I could have been off by ten years either way. His eyes were the palest blue I'd ever seen. He looked nothing like the picture of the old Leather Man that Spencer Cobb had shown me.

A car appeared over the hill ahead, traveling at a good speed, raising a small cloud of dust behind it. "Who calls me that?" the man asked.

"People who've seen you on your route."

The car slowed to pass us and I saw Hannah Whycliff behind the wheel, heading home. I waved and she waved back. "Haven't seen many people," he muttered. "Just when I stop occasionally for food or a night's rest."

"That woman who just passed us—you were in front of her house at three this morning."

"Might have been," he acknowledged. "When there's a moon I like to walk for part of the night and sleep through the morning. It's cooler that way."

"What's your name? Mine's Sam Hawthorne."

"Zach Taylor." He extended a bronzed hand and we shook.

"Zach as in Zachary?"

"That's right."

"We had a president by that name. Long ago."

"So they tell me."

We were setting a steady pace, a bit faster than I liked to walk. "You're not from around here. Are you British?"

"Australian, mate. Ever hear of a place called Alice Springs?"

"Vaguely. I might have seen it on a map once."

"It's real outback country there. Nothing but desert."

"What brought you to New England?"

"Just decided to see the world. Got this far and thought it was nice enough to stay a while. I spent the spring in New York and then came up here."

It was getting late in the day, almost dinnertime, but we kept walking. "Your trek is following the route of the original Leather Man, more than fifty years ago," I observed. "That's more than coincidence."

"Well, I was wearing this leather outfit and someone mentioned your Leather Man up in these parts. I looked up his route at the library and decided to follow it."

"You've been doing this all summer?"

"Yes."

"If you were out at three this morning you must have seen an automobile accident. A Ford tried to avoid you and went into a ditch."

Now he eyed me with open suspicion. "Is that what this is all about? Are you a policeman, Sam Hawthorne?"

"No, I'm a doctor."

We were approaching a railway crossing where I knew the crossing guard. He was an elderly squinty-eyed man named Seth Howlings, and as we approached he came out of his shed to lower the gate across the grade crossing. "Hello, Seth," I called out.

He turned toward me. "Dr. Sam! Haven't seen you in a long time. And on foot, too! What happened to your car?"

"I'm getting some exercise today. Is there a train coming?"

"Sure is! Can't you hear it?"

I could then. It sounded a distant whistle and in another moment it came into view. It was a twenty-car freight train, traveling at moderate speed. "You've got good ears to hear it coming that far away," I told Seth after the train had passed.

"Best there are," he said with a toothless grin as he raised the gate. "I could hear a cow mooing in the next county."

I chuckled and fell into step beside Zach Taylor. "How late you working tonight, Seth?"

"Till my wife picks me up. She keeps track of my hours."

"See you later."

We crossed the tracks and set off down the highway again. "You know a lot of people in this area?" Zach asked.

"Quite a few. I've been a doctor here for fifteen years."

"You hungry? I've got some sourdough bread in my sack here, and a little whiskey to wash it down."

"You're tempting me."

The whiskey burned going down, but the bread had a nice original taste. We paused only about ten minutes before we were off again. Another car passed us, but the driver was no one I knew. Traffic was sparse on this section of the road.

"I was asking you about that accident with the Ford," I reminded him after a time of walking in silence.

"Yes. You were, weren't you?"

"You saw it?"

"I never saw the car until it was on top of me. Don't know where he came from. I dove to one side and he ran off the road. I could see he was dazed but he didn't seem badly hurt, and I'm not one to get involved in those things."

"So you just kept going."

"Sure. I walked for another half-hour and then found a haystack to sleep in. How's the bloke in the car?"

"He's dead."

"God, I'm sorry to hear that."

"You should have stopped to help him, Zach."

He took out the whiskey again and downed another healthy shot, passing the bottle to me. "Last time I stopped to help someone at an accident, I spent a couple nights in jail. Damned cops thought I was a hobo."

"Aren't you, in a way?"

"Not a chance, mate! I've got money on me. Sometimes I even pay for my lodging and food, when I can't get it free."

"But you're wandering the back roads of New England."

"Man, I'm on walkabout!"

"What?"

"Walkabout. I don't suppose you know the word. It's an Australian custom—an Australian Aborigine custom, really—meaning an informal leave from work during which the person returns to native life and wanders the bush, sometimes visiting relatives."

"So this is your walkabout."

"Exactly."

"What is it you've left back home?"

"A wife and family, actually. I hope to return to them someday."

We walked on as night fell, and I realized that it must be after eight-thirty. Where had the day gone, and how far had I walked with this man? More important, how many shots of his whiskey had I drunk? "Won't you be stopping for the night?"

"Soon," he agreed. "Soon."

He told me more about his wife and children as we walked, and about life in Australia. He recounted exploits of the legendary bandit Ned Kelly, who wore a suit of homemade armor in his battles with police. After a time the whiskey bottle was empty and he hurled it into the brush along the road.

"I am too tired to go further," he finally admitted. Up ahead, a lighted sign announced a house that offered beds and breakfast for travelers. "I'll stay here for the night," he told me.

"Then I'll be leaving you and going back to my car." As soon as the words were out of my mouth I realized how foolish they were. We'd been walking for hours. It would take me half the night to return to my car.

"That's too far. Stay the night with me, mate."

I thought about phoning Sheriff Lens for a ride, but I'd drunk more whiskey than expected and I didn't want him to see me wavering a bit as I walked. Maybe it would be best to sleep for a few hours.

A fat, middle-aged woman greeted us at the door of the big house. "Welcome, travelers," she greeted us. "I'm Mrs. Pomroy. Looking for a place to spend the night?"

"That we are," Zach Taylor told her. "Can you accommodate us?"

"I've got two nice beds right at the top of the stairs. Ten dollars each and that includes a sturdy breakfast in the morning."

"We'll take them," I agreed, feeling sleepier by the minute.

"Glen!" she called out, and almost at once a small man with grey hair and a slight limp appeared. "This is my husband, Glen. He'll show you to your room. Glen—number two, top of the stairs."

He smiled at us halfheartedly. "Good to have you folks stop. Any bags?"

"No, mate," Zach told him. "Just us."

He led us up the stairs and his wife called out, "You can pay in the morning. I'll wake you at eight for breakfast if you're not up yet."

The room was large and cheerful, even by the uncertain light from a single floor lamp. There were two beds covered with flowery spreads, and a water pitcher and bowl. "Bathroom's down the hall," Pomroy told us. "We leave a little light on all night."

I shed my outer clothes and fell into bed, exhausted. The combination of all that walking and the shots of whiskey had proven to be too much for me. I had a glimpse of Zach climbing into the other bed, and then I was asleep.

It was daylight when at last I opened my eyes. I was aware that someone was knocking on my door and I looked at the pocket watch I'd left on the table next to the bed. It was five minutes after eight. Then I noticed that Zach's bed was empty, the spread pulled neatly into place. It looked undisturbed.

"Just a minute!" I called to the knocker, pulling on my pants.

I opened the door to find Mrs. Pomroy standing there. "Time for breakfast, if you want it."

"I'll be right down. Where's the other man?"

She looked blank. "What other man?"

"Zach Taylor, the fellow who was with me."

Mrs. Pomroy stared me straight in the eye. "You were alone, mister. There was no one with you."

Sheriff Lens arrived within a half-hour of my call. Mrs. Pomroy's place was across the county line, so he was officially outside his jurisdiction, but that didn't stop him from asking Mrs. Pomroy a few questions.

"Doc here says he came in last night with another man. You say he came alone."

She glared at me and then back at the sheriff. "Alone he was."

"Then why'd you give me a room with two beds?"

She shrugged. "It was empty. You were the only guest we had."

Sheriff Lens shifted uneasily. "I've known Doc a good many years, Mrs. Pomroy. If he says he came here with someone—"

"It was obvious he'd been drinking heavily, Sheriff. He couldn't even walk straight. Maybe he was with someone else, but not here."

The sheriff glanced at me inquiringly. "Is that true, Doc?"

"This fellow, the Leather Man, had a bottle of whiskey. We had a few shots while we walked."

The woman's husband came in from outside and she immediately lined up his support. "Tell them, Glen. Tell them this man was alone."

The short man glanced at me. "Sure was! I was glad to see he wasn't drivin', the shape he was in."

I sighed and started over again. "There was a man with me. He went to sleep in the other bed. His name is Zach Taylor and he's wearing a leather suit, almost like buckskin."

They both shook their heads, unwilling to budge from their story. Maybe they killed him for his few meager possessions, I thought, but then why wouldn't they have killed me too? "Come on, Doc," the sheriff said, his arm on my shoulder. "I'll give you a ride back to your car."

As I turned to leave, Mrs. Pomroy reminded me, "That'll be ten dollars for the room."

Back in his car, Sheriff Lens was silent until I spoke. "I found this so-called Leather Man, and when he wouldn't stop to talk with me, I parked my car and walked with him. He's Australian, on something called a walkabout. Trying to find himself, I guess. He saw the accident but didn't think Gilman was seriously hurt. He was afraid of getting involved so he kept on walking."

"What about the drinkin', Doc? Is that part true?"

"He had a bottle with him. After a while I took a couple of swigs from it. I'll admit it hit me harder than I'd expected, but I knew what was going on at all times. Zach Taylor was with me when we took the room at Mrs. Pomroy's place."

"Did you sign a register or anything?"

"No. She rents rooms and gives you breakfast, that's all. She's not operating a hotel."

"You think they killed him or something?"

"I don't know what to think. The last I saw of him, he was climbing into the bed next to mine."

"But the bed was made this morning."

"I slept so soundly Mrs. Pomroy could have brought a parade of elephants in there and I wouldn't have known it. She could easily have come in and made the bed."

"The door wasn't locked?"

I tried to remember. "I don't think so. I'm sure we had no key."

He stared hard at the highway ahead. "I don't know what to think, Doc."

"Well, I can at least prove he was with me. When we get to the railroad crossing back across the county line, stop the car."

We reached it in another ten minutes, and I saw old Seth Howlings coming out of the crossing guard's little shed. "Hello, Seth."

"It's Dr. Sam again! But in a car this time."

"Howdy, Seth," Sheriff Lens said, getting out to join me.

"Hello, Sheriff. Beautiful day, isn't it?"

"Sure is!"

I walked closer to him. "Remember when I came by yesterday afternoon, Seth?"

"Sure do! Just as the five thirty-five was passing through."

"Remember the man who was with me?"

He looked blank. "You was alone, Dr. Sam. Are you trying to trick me?"

"Alone?" the sheriff repeated. "Are you certain of that?"

"Certain as I can be. Dr. Sam walked up and we chatted some while the train passed. Then he crossed the tracks and went on his way."

"Alone?"

"Alone."

I was in the middle of a nightmare from which there was no awakening.

Sheriff Lens and I drove on. "I'm not crazy, Sheriff."

"I know that, Doc."

"And I wasn't drunk enough to have imagined the whole thing. In fact, I never would have had any whiskey at all if Zach Taylor hadn't given it to me."

"Still, that old coot would have no reason to lie. You can't think he's in some sort of conspiracy with the Pomroys! They probably don't even know each other."

"I don't know what to think at this point. But I'm damned if I'm going to let it rest! I have to prove I wasn't imagining this Leather Man."

Sheriff Lens thought about it. "Someone must have seen you on the road together."

"There were only a few cars, and no one I knew except—"

"What is it?"

"Hannah Whycliff. She passed us in her car and waved. I'd forgotten about her."

We drove on to the Whycliff house, where the image of the Leather Man had made its first appearance in March Gilman's headlights. Hannah Whycliff's car was in the driveway and she came to the door when the sheriff rang the bell. She greeted us both and then asked, "Is this more questions about the accident?"

"Not exactly, Miss Whycliff," the sheriff said. "Doc here has a problem. He was with this so-called Leather Man yesterday, but now the man has disappeared and two different people deny seeing him with Doc."

"I remember you passed and waved when I was walking with him. It was late yesterday afternoon."

She turned to look at me. "I remember seeing you, Dr. Sam. I wondered what had happened to your car, but I was in a hurry and couldn't stop."

"Then you saw the Leather Man?" Sheriff Lens prompted.

"No, Dr. Sam was alone. I saw no one else."

The thing was so fantastic I simply shook my head and gave a humorless chuckle. It defied the laws of logic. "Tell me, do you know Seth Howlings, the railroad crossing guard? He's just this side of the county line."

"I may have seen him but I'm sure I've never spoken to him. Why do you ask?"

"And how about a couple named Mr. and Mrs. Glen Pomroy, over in the next county? They rent out rooms in their house for overnight guests."

"I never heard of them. What are all these questions for?"

"We're tryin' to find witnesses who saw Doc with this Leather Man," the sheriff told her. "The man might have been responsible for that accident in front of your house."

"I never saw any Leather Man. The doctor was alone."

"Thank you, Miss Whycliff," the sheriff said. We walked back to the car.

I settled into the front seat and said, "She's lying."

"Sure, and so are the Pomroys and old Seth. But why, Doc? These people don't even know each other."

"I don't know," I admitted. "I only know they're lying."

"Do you think the Leather Man could have hypnotized them so they didn't remember seeing him?"

I snorted at that suggestion. "Hannah Whycliff drove past us in a car. The best hypnotist in the world couldn't have done it that fast."

"Then there's only one other explanation, Doc. Do you believe in ghosts?"

When I told Mary Best about it the next morning, she saw things a bit more clearly than I did. "We have to find the Leather Man, Sam. We have to locate this Zach Taylor and learn the truth."

"He's probably dead and buried somewhere out behind the Pomroy place."

"But maybe he isn't! Maybe he just went away!"

"Then why are they all lying about it? The sheriff even raised the possibility he was the ghost of the original Leather Man, but that one was French, not Australian."

"Can you get along without me today? I'm going out looking for him."

"You're wasting your time, Mary. Even if you find him, that won't explain why everyone lied."

"Everyone didn't lie. Only three people lied—four, if you count Mrs. Pomroy's husband. There has to be a reason."

I let her go. There were patients to be seen, but I handled them all without her. I spent most of the day thinking about Zach Taylor and my walk with him. He'd appeared there on the road, and then he'd disappeared. Maybe I'd never walked with him at all. Maybe I'd imagined the whole thing.

It was only later, toward the end of the day, that I realized what I'd done. March Gilman had been alive in that ditch after the car went off the road. After causing the accident, Zach Taylor had killed and robbed him. Deciding I might be suspicious of him, he bribed the Pomroys to deny his existence. Then he walked back and bribed old Seth and Hannah Whycliff too. That was the only answer.

And I'd let Mary Best go out alone in search of a murderer.

It took me less than a minute to realize that I was getting foolish in my middle age. If Zach had killed Gilman and thought I suspected him, he had more than enough opportunity during our walk to leave me dead in a ditch too. There'd be no need to try bribing four people who might later blackmail him.

I thought about it some more, and remembered something I'd read not too long before. I reached into the bookcase in my waiting room and selected a volume of essays, *While Rome Burns,* by Alexander Woollcott. One of them, "The Vanishing Lady," deals with the legend of a young Englishwoman and her frail mother, recently returned from India, who visit the Paris Exposition in 1889 on their way back to England. The mother vanishes, and the hotel staff denies she ever existed. Their room has different furnishings and wallpaper. All traces of the mother are gone. In the end, a young man from the British Embassy establishes that her mother died suddenly of the black plague, contracted in India. The conspiracy of silence was necessary to prevent panic from driving visitors out of Paris and ruining the Exposition. In a footnote at the end, Woollcott says that he traced the original story to a column in the *Detroit Free Press,* published during the 1889 Paris Exposition. But the author of the column could no longer remember whether he had invented the story or heard it somewhere.

All right, was there any possibility the Australian had suffered from some illness? Had he died during the night and his death been hushed up by the Pomroys, who'd then bribed the others?

But Zach Taylor hadn't appeared ill at all. He was the picture of health, in fact. And the Pomroys would have had no way of knowing that Seth Howlings and Hannah were the only persons who'd seen us. Old Seth hardly seemed the sort to be bribed, anyhow.

By late afternoon I'd had no word from Mary and I was beginning to worry about her. I went out to my car after the departure of my last patient, thinking I should begin searching for her. Just then I saw the familiar little roadster pull into the parking lot. The Leather Man was next to her in the front seat.

"I thought you were dead," I told him. "Where'd you find him, Mary?"

"On his route, just where he was supposed to be. If he wasn't dead, I knew he'd be there."

"Good to see you again, mate," Zach said as he got out of the car. "Your little girl here is certainly persuasive. Once she found me she insisted I had to come back with her. This disrupts my whole route."

"We'll drive you back to where she picked you up," I assured him. "Or anywhere else you want to go. Just tell me what happened at the Pomroys' place last night."

"You mean where we stayed? Nothing happened. I got up early and left. I wanted to be on the road, and you were still sound asleep. Sorry I didn't say goodbye."

"Did you talk to Mrs. Pomroy?"

"It was too early for breakfast so I just paid her and left."

A small, sharp idea was gnawing at my brain. "How much did you pay her?"

"Twenty dollars, mate. I paid for your bed too!"

I went back inside and called Sheriff Lens.

When we returned to the Pomroy house, Glen Pomroy was on the front porch, scrubbing the steps. He looked up expectantly as we approached, but his expression soured when he recognized me. "Is your wife around?" I asked.

"We don't want trouble."

"Neither do I. We just want to see Mrs. Pomroy."

She appeared at the screen door then, pushing it open slowly. "I'm here," she said.

"We found the Leather Man," I told her. "He paid you for both our beds."

"Yeah, I forgot that," she answered glumly. "Guess we owe you ten dollars." The denials had gone out of her.

"You figured I was too drunk to remember clearly, so you made up the bed after he left and lied about his ever being here. That way you got an extra ten dollars out of me. It may have seemed like a minor swindle to you, but it caused me a great deal of trouble."

"I'll be contacting your sheriff to keep an eye on you," Sheriff Lens told them. "If there are any more complaints from your guests you'll both be makin' your beds at the county jail."

When we were back in the car he turned to me and said, "That takes care of the Pomroys, but it doesn't explain the other two. They both claimed you were alone too."

"Seth Howlings is our next stop. When we get there, don't say anything at first. Let me do all the talking."

Seth was seated in the crossing guard's little shack, dozing, but he came awake instantly as I approached. "How are you, Seth?"

"Back again, Dr. Sam? I've seen more of you the past two days than I usually do in a month."

"I doubt that, Seth. I doubt if you've seen me at all. Who's this standing with me now?"

My question seemed to unnerve him, and he shifted his gaze from my face to a point just to the left of me where no one stood. Then he seemed to look in the other direction, but his eyes skipped quickly past Sheriff Lens.

"Seth," I said quietly, "you're blind, aren't you?"

His hands began to shake. "I don't need eyes for this job. I can hear them trains comin' from the next county! The sound travels along the rails, and their steam whistles can be heard for miles."

"How did it happen, Seth? Why didn't you go to a doctor?"

"I never had no pain, just halos around the lights, and my vision kept narrowing down till it was just like looking into a tunnel. After a while even that was gone. I figured at my age it didn't make no difference. My wife drove me to work here every day, and picked me up. So long as I could hear the trains comin' and lower and raise the gate, what difference did it make?" His face wore an expression of utter sadness. "Will they take my job away from me, Dr. Sam?"

I knew it was glaucoma, and there was nothing anyone could do for him. "Probably, Seth. I'm sure you're good at it, but you wouldn't want to cause an accident, would you? Suppose some little child wandered onto the tracks and you didn't hear him."

"I wouldn't want that," he agreed.

"This is Sheriff Lens with me. He'll see about getting a replacement for you right away."

The sheriff put a reassuring hand on Seth's shoulder. "I'll have someone out here within an hour, and we'll arrange with your wife to pick you up."

Back in the car, I shook my head in wonder. "To think we had a blind man guarding that railroad crossing—"

"How'd you know, Doc?"

"He answered people when they talked to him, but he never spoke first to someone. When I asked about the man who was with me, his immediate reaction was that I was trying to trick him. What did he mean by that? It was an odd choice of words if he had seen me alone at the crossing. And both times I saw him he mentioned my coming on foot or in a car, as if to convince me he could see. Then I remembered Zach never spoke while we were there. And Seth emphasized hearing the train, not seeing it. With his wife to pick him up, and relying on his ears, he could do the job."

"Blind people's hearing is supposed to be very sensitive," Sheriff Lens pointed out. "He must have heard the footsteps of two people if he knew you arrived on foot."

"We approached just as a train was coming, and that distracted him. Only I spoke, and after the train passed I remember falling into step with Zach Taylor. If he listened then, he'd have heard only one set of departing footsteps. When we questioned him, he feared I suspected something about his blindness so he stuck to the story he thought was true—that I was alone."

"So Seth Howlings and the Pomroys had their own entirely different reasons for denying the existence of the Leather Man. But what about Hannah Whycliff? Isn't it stretching coincidence a bit far to have a third person who didn't see him for some reason?"

"We'll call on Miss Whycliff next," I answered grimly.

It was almost evening when we turned into her driveway once more.

This time it took her awhile to answer the ring. "I hope we're not interrupting your dinner," I said.

"No, no. What is it this time?"

"I'm afraid it's still about the Leather Man. We've located him at last."

"How does that concern me?"

"You lied about not seeing him with me on the road yesterday. You see, the sheriff here started out his questioning by telling you that two other people had already denied seeing the Leather Man with me. That was a mistake. You quickly decided it was to your advantage to agree with them, to tell the same lie. You wanted the Leather Man to be gone, to never have existed."

"Why would I want that?" she asked.

"Because you were afraid he saw you murder March Gilman."

Her gaze shifted from me to the sheriff and back again. "Whatever gave you that idea?"

"Zach—the Leather Man—saw the accident and didn't think Gilman had been hurt badly at all. He hadn't seen the car coming until it was almost upon him. You told me you heard the car skid on the road as Gilman tried to apply the brakes, yet when I examined the road yesterday morning, just hours after the accident, the gravel was unmarked by any trace of skidding. Zach didn't see the car coming because it came out of your driveway, Miss Whycliff. It didn't skid. It wasn't going fast at all, but it went off the road to avoid the Leather Man. March Gilman was thrown clear and dazed. Before he became fully conscious you saw your chance. You came down to the road and hit him with something—perhaps a hammer. He was barely able to speak by the time I arrived, and he died soon after. There was evidence of two blows to the head."

"Why would I kill March Gilman?" she asked.

"I don't know. He had a reputation as a ladies' man. What went on between the two of you—"

"Get out of here, both of you! Get out this instant!"

I turned back toward the driveway, just as Mary pulled her car in behind the sheriff's. "We have a witness," I said softly.

Her eyes widened as she saw the Leather Man step out of the car and walk toward us. "No! No, keep him away from me!"

"He really exists, much as you wanted him not to. He's going to tell us what he saw."

"Keep him away!" she shouted. "I'll tell you! I killed March Gilman. And I'll tell you what he did to deserve it!"

"What's the matter with her, mate?" Zach asked as the sheriff led her away.

"She thought you were someone else," I told him. "She thought you were the avenging angel."

"No," he said with a grin. "I'm just a chap on walkabout."